THE LOVED,
THE LOST,
THE DREAMING

Michelle Browne

THE LOVED, THE LOST, THE DREAMING

More of the author's work can be found at
https://twitter.com/SciFiMagpie or
http://scifimagpie.blogspot.ca/ for more information.
Correspondence to the author can be sent to
shellebrowne@gmail.com.

For Andrey, who keeps the bad dreams at bay.

Acknowledgments

It takes a village to raise a child, and it takes dozens of people to help usher a novel into being. In the course of these short stories, the first of which were written while I was in high school, and the last of which were finished mere days before publication, I learned just how true this is.

First, I'd like to thank the biggest contributors. Andrey Taskaev spent many nights pouring tea, helping me understand arcane formatting issues, and listening to plot changes. Sarah Huntrods, Billea Alhgrim, Julia Rees, Travis Luedke, Jessica Curry, Ian Rideout, and Rachel Smith were extremely helpful in providing feedback and encouragement as I sweated over various details and editing changes. They are the godsparents of this book, and it would not be as good as it is without their sweat and care. Amanda and Jenna were kind enough to share their nightmares, too!

Kit Foster provided the lovely and unique art for the cover of this collection, giving the book the face it needed. I can't think of a better cover for this work.

My writing colleagues at ASMSG, who number in the hundreds, contributed with their shares, retweets, and lovely supportive words. Chris Shields, JC Eggleton, Travis Luedke, John Dolan, Richard Long, Jim Wright, Shannon McRoberts, Dianne Harman,

Martha Emms, Christy Foster, Ally Shields, and Vanessa Wu are the first names that leap to mind. These are the talented authors and the kind people who gave advice, provided interviews, and encouraged me when I was swearing about formatting in the wee hours of the morning. There are many, many wonderful people at ASMSG, and I would like to thank all of them for putting up with my frequent posts and being members of an awesome community.

I'd also like to thank my friends. Even the ones who didn't contribute directly provided a friendly ear, asked me about my work, and put up with missed parties and communication lapses as I worked feverishly. Your patience is definitely not going to be forgotten.

My parents deserve a special note once again, for their patience with an artistic daughter and my long hours of writing. Most importantly, they were there with a hug when the dark moved and the world was a scary place.

Finally, I'd like to thank you, the readers. By buying this book, you're sharing in one of the things I love most: telling a story. I hope the short stories within inspire and help you, wherever you're at in life. If you're afraid of the things hiding in the dark, may this book be a flashlight to help you get out of those shadowy places. Walk forward, into the light.

THE UNDERLIGHTERS

1—May 15, 0048 P.D.

The conversation went like this.

"You seem tired, kiddo. And—what happened to your shirt?"

"Uh...I killed a dragon on the way home from work."

"What? Very funny. Now, really."

"Look." I pulled the gory claw out of my pocket.

"This looks like a velociraptor claw. Where did you get it? Did you go Up to the museum?"

"No! I told you. I killed a dragon." He stared at me, trying to figure out which leg I was pulling the hardest. I turned up the light to its brightest without looking at the switch; he flinched.

"*Look*. There's blood on the end of this. And tissue. How would I get *that* from a museum sample?"

"Ooookay, where's the rest of the body?"

"I just sort of threw it in a hole and scuffed some dirt on it."

"*You mean it's still there?*"

"I'd assume so."

"Are you sure it's dead?"

"It's dead," I said confidently.

"Look. I'll go up with you and have a look at it if it's real. Sweetie, did you inhale Dust by accident?"

"No! I saw a dragon!"

"That looks like a dinosaur claw to me."

"*Dragon.* Not a dinosaur."

"Dinosaur. Dragons are imaginary. More likely, an extremely large iguana or a crocodile." He spoke slowly, like I was an imbecile. "Dragons aren't real."

In some part of his mind, I'd never really had to grow up. I was six years old and holding up a lizard for his examination. How could I really blame him for looking at that bloody claw and stubbornly seeing ketchup on a museum souvenir?

"Dad! It was a *dragon.*"

"And not a scratch on you when you were killing it?"

"Are you blind? Look at my shirt! You don't get this from fighting electrical wiring!" The fabric was dirty, and shredded over my stomach. It was really young, not even old enough to breathe fire properly, but it had still gotten in more than a few swipes. Light swipes, but still.

His eyes did the popping thing again.

"Janelle! Why didn't you tell someone about those? Do you want tetanus?"

"Relax. I was going to go after I told you about this."

"I don't want to hear excuses. You should've gone to the hospital and called me from there. I'll take you now."

" It's not as important as this, Dad! Are you listening to me at all? I. Killed. A. Dragon."

"Oh, for fuck's sake! After you're patched up!" A rare swearword. He was in panic mode. "Fuck. Just fuckin' great."

I sighed. "Okay, fine. A crocodile. Now, will you come look at the body?"

He inhaled slowly and exhaled. "All right. But later."

Dragons were the least thing to worry about, later. I can't help wondering what would've happened if he'd seen the body, whether it would've saved us a lot of trouble and frustration, or whether it would've mattered at all. But I've gotten ahead of myself. Having a journal is convenient, but it blurs the lines of hindsight more than a little.

Even I admit it was stupid to just walk around like that. I must have been in shock when I first came to Dad. I didn't faint or anything, but when we got to the hospital, it finally started to sink in, and then it started to hurt. Getting stitched up made me scream a little, even with freezing. It was all superficial, but nasty-looking, and I can still remember that it stung and throbbed like hell. I wondered how it was going to scar up, whether I'd be able to wear halters ever again.

Stupid, but that mattered more than the thought of my intestines spilling out over the floor, of the muscles being part of that monster's steak sandwich. I thought about tattoo designs for a while, and hoped the scars wouldn't be too ugly. Apparently going into shock makes me shallow.

My shirt and overalls had stopped the claws well, but they'd still been pretty shredded, lined canvas or no. I have to admit that I can see why Dad seemed to have figured it was a knife or bottle fight from that. He got to work on sewing my clothes with his pocket kit while waiting for me.

They made Dad stay outside to keep the room sanitary, but he kept looking around the corner worriedly, peeking through the glass door to see how I was doing. When I could, I tossed him 'calm the fuck down' glances and grins, and he relaxed. But not a lot. Soundproof glass or no, you can tell when someone's yelping in pain.

Obviously I didn't think talking about a dragon was going to land me anywhere other than in a Calm Box, so I told them I'd been skateboarding and the fall had scared an animal, some kind of big cat, into going for me. Cats wander into the drains and into the roads, sometimes, so it made enough sense. Coyotes, too, and dogs, but the big cats are the only things I could think of that would do that sort of damage to my shirt.

I told them the lie in the same was I was used to telling lies, full eye contact and flushed cheeks. Being embarrassed, but refusing to back down, is one of the best ways to make people do what you need them to.

They bandaged me up and used a lot of care making sure the stitches were fine, so it would all heal cleanly and with 'less cosmetic damage' as the nurse put it. I don't want to tell you how long it took—okay, I have no idea how long, *if* I could tell you. Probably at least an hour. Two. It felt like longer; you can believe it.

The best part is, I got a lot of dirty looks for their trouble from the scrubs and orderlies walking around. Yeah, stare down the scared and wounded girl, really judgemental, guys. I suppose they figured I was with one of the Rats and was therefore a waste of time. The look the doctor was giving me suggested he thought I was either a tart or tomboy muscle, but I was polite and friendly and ladylike (apart from screaming in pain) and after a bit he stopped giving me that look. Gangers aren't that nice, or grateful, when they go under the knife 'n' needle.

Afterward, Miranda, one of the nurses (according to her tag) pulled me aside under the pretense of changing the sheets I'd been sitting on.

"Don't mind Dr. Dhaliwal," she whispered. "We've had a few young people coming in with wounds like yours and he's concerned about some of the gang fights that have been going on."

I pricked my ears up at that, you can bet. "Same wounds?"

"Yeah. You wouldn't happen to know about a different kind of knife or sharpened foldie you kids might be using?"

I blinked. "What? I don't know. I'm not in a gang."

The nurse sighed, obviously convinced that I was still covering for myself. "I don't see soot on your face, but I understand if you washed it off to get treatment. Just, look, if you get the chance, tell them to use knives…bottles can have anything on them, but knives are cleaner cuts—sort of--and easier to patch up. If they're still alive afterward, you might as well make sure we can clean them up."

If they're still alive. I wondered if that was the only dragon around, and where its mother and father were. Obviously, I wasn't the first human it had run into, or tried to snack on.

"I'm…look, I'm learning to be an electrician. I don't know about gangs and I wish you'd stop treating me like a sugarplum." The nurse bit her lip and nodded. She still didn't believe me.

"Still, let them know. Oh, and put iodine or at least salt water on those cuts every day when you can. They should heal cleanly enough but whatever you were cut with, it was meant to shred flesh. Next time, you might not be lucky enough to walk away with some scrapes."

Dad kept looking at me funny as we went home. I knew that look and he'd given it to me around the time of explaining sex, and my period, and also when he explained about fizzes and shrooms. He was worried that I already understood what he was about to teach me.

He did the thing where he took a deep breath in and let it out slowly and took another one in, and rubbed his hands together. Every discussion is a solo bullfight, a duel for him with himself, even though I usually shut up and listen. He hates having to lecture me. He started going on about sugarplums and cuntgirls and tommies, and I interrupted.

"Dad, I promise, I'm not a Rat. I told you, I was attacked by a dragon." He gave me a look that said he couldn't decide whether to be relieved that I wasn't in a gang (he can kind of tell when I fib or tell whoppers) or worried about my sanity. So after a bit he just went into nodding thoughtfully, and I stopped talking, and

7

concentrated on counting the lamps along the tunnel walls.

It took a long while until we got to our own basement, but the walk made me feel better. Earth walls in the tunnels under the city made everything smell cool and safe, and lots of light made me feel better. Dad took the main routes, so there were no obstacle courses of awkwardly intersecting pipes to contend with. I wasn't in the mood for swiping dangling safeguard charms out of my face or dealing with shadows. Too jumpy. Too much like the Dark, Up above, where you can't see what's coming at you next. At least I had Dad to take me home, even if he didn't think the monster was real.

I was still pretty shaken up over the dragon thing and hurt and annoyed by Dad's lack of trust, so I went off to my room. He closed the door, moved the couch over to block it, and had a seat in front of his workdesk. He was working on one of his tiny balsawood planes. I shook my head and slipped off, my sock feet quiet on the carpet.

First, I wrote for a while—well, I wrote the stuff before, and have been working on everything else you're reading since then. Journaling lets most things that bother me out of my head. Usually. It isn't doing much of a job this time though.

THE LOVED, THE LOST, THE DREAMING

Apparently I'm fidgety tonight. Before I got back to writing this, I was playing with my circuits and dicking around with electronics, trying to fix things and get them running again. It's useful practice for work and it gets my mind off things. Not this time, though. All the time as I was trying to get the busted iPod to behave, I was considering the dragon.

As my soldering iron reheated, I pondered how something like the dragon could have ended up down here in the first place. Does it have something to do with all the toxic chemicals that were undoubtedly leaking out of all the old electronics and batteries? Sure, we've been doing some processing and salvaging. And there are heavy metals and all kinds of pollutants in everything, it's a reality of life. We work around it but you can only do so much.

But, as I clipped bits of copper and stripped plastic coating away, it occurred to me that I might be a dumbass to blame contaminants. Chemicals alone, even nuclear shit, don't cause those kinds of mutations. Missing legs or extra eyes or excessive growth, sure. But not fire-breathing fairy-tale monsters.

As I fixed the broken adaptor and covered the connection point with electrical tape, I thought about contacting the others, and thanked gods for underground cables and routers. Apart from being terrifying, the Dark also blocks out radio waves. Mind you, being underground dampens waves too. You can't win, but we try anyway.

So. I texted Chloe and Jaycenne to tell them to meet up by the sewage hub with Raheed and Kenny at about six, and to let the others know about the meet up, because I was busy.

'What about u? U ok?' Jay texted back. My heart hammered in my chest. She's good at picking up on things.

"No, I'm ok, just get everyone. See you soon!"

I clicked my phone shut, and my heart continued to hammer away.

"Dad, I'm going out, I'll be back soon."

I was putting my shoes on as I said this.

"Who are you meeting? Where?" "My girlfriend and the others, by the sewage hub. I shouldn't be more than a couple of hours." He scanned my face. The short, luxuriant salt-and-pepper beard that covers the lower half of his face is good for concealing his expression. And Dad is good at keeping a neutral face.

"Should you be going out with your stomach ripped up, young lady?"

"Dad, I'm fine. I'm full of adrenalin and painkillers and I'm going stir crazy in here. I let them know about being injured, but...you know. I just want to let them know I'm okay."

He harrumphed quietly. "I suppose that only makes sense. But don't be out late. I don't want you getting attacked again. Are you sure you wouldn't rather just have them over, and rest?"

"Nuh uh. I really need to move, Dad."

"Well, if you're sure. Just please, be careful, kiddo."

"I promise, I will. You don't have to tell me not to wander off twice."

"And I don't want you having a run in with those hooligans near the surface."

"Dad, it's okay. I just need to go make sure my friends know I'm all right and burn off a little nervous energy." I realised my voice was taut and sharp, and I softened it. "You have Chloe's number. If you call and you can't hear my voice, then worry about me being a sugarplum."

"I'm sure you'll be too busy to talk," he said, smiling. I could tell he was less tense; he could tell I was too confident to hide something. "Say hello to your girlfriend for me."

I grinned as I adjusted my shoes a final time. "I won't be too long and I promise I won't do anything too exciting. Love ya." I closed the door behind me.

The path to get to the sewage hub involved some flexibility, because it's a very low-ceilinged and narrow tunnel, but frequent use by teenagers made it smooth-going.

It didn't take me long to get to the Hub. It's a glorified title for a bit of tunnel that comes up underneath the road in front of an apartment building, not far from our house. The curves and tunnels stretch around each other for kilometres, crossing and criss-crossing, interrupted only by stairways down to other levels. Our tunnels often have to weave around the occasional tangle of wires before rejoining sewer and basement-to-basement paths, so sometimes they end up in awkward places. This one is only accessible because we need to get at the wires to keep our precious and intermittent electricity system running. The tangle of pipes provides a sheltering overhang, a kind of underground thicket of metal tubes. There's also plenty of clear space around and in front of it, but being crawly and tight, and not in the best state of maintenance, most adults walk past, or avoid it.

We weren't really supposed to be there, come to it. If anything went wrong, we could all be drowned in an overflow of sewage, or electrocuted, or both. Probably the worst way to die I can think of. Actually, being electrocuted in sewage is probably the worst possible death in the history of ever. Of course, the chances of that are very, very low, and accordingly, we don't care much. You run your chances of being electrocuted by cables or choking on your morning glass of chicoffee anyway. Or, I suppose, being eaten by a young and hungry mythological creature.

Chloe was there already, and greeted me with a showy hug and kiss on the mouth. Raheed gave me the evil eye and I pretended not to notice. We broke it off eons ago, but he still feels the need to give me deathly glares every time Chloe smooches me in public.

I gently disentangled myself from her and tried not to yelp in pain. "Where's Kenny and Jaycenne?"

"Here!"

They popped out from around a corner on the other side of the tunnel. I noticed Jaycenne was holding Kenny's hand and flashing him a smile. Raheed saw, too, and looked even more unhappy.

"Okay. So. Good. Um...so...I saw something strange in the upper tunnels. Why aren't Caleb and Aiden here?" I asked.

"Oops. Sorry," said Chloe, shrugging. "So, what's up?"

I managed not to roll my eyes. You'd think it would have occurred to them to invite the other people involved when I'd asked, but that's us teenagers for you, I suppose.

"Whatever. I think we should talk to them. Anyway...I saw...look, it looked like a dragon in the upper tunnels. I just wandered up after work because I wanted to go for a walk, and there was this thing..." I let out a very long breath.

"No way."

"The fuck?"

"Okay, come on—"

"Calm down, everyone," I said. "It...long story short, it went for me, but—I found a sports bat, guess a ganger left it there—and I sort of—well I got it upside the head, and it swiped at me, and it sort of...it breathed fire at me..." my face heated. I knew it sounded ridiculous, but they were rapt, even Raheed. "And I dodged and knocked a claw off, and hit it upside the head again—it sort of went down, but it swiped the bat with its tail, so I got my foldie, and then, well, I just..." I swallowed. I'm an okay talker, but I hate public speaking or anything like it. "I hit it until it stopped moving. There was a hole, you know, just a shallow kind of...so I threw it in and kicked some dirt over it with my foldie and went on my way."

I patted my foldie. Sometimes, the fact that I try to follow regs can be useful. Without the compact shovel, I'd have had to leave the body there. It was dented from hitting the dragon's head, but it had done the trick. A flaming longsword would have been better. I remembered the fine, light scales, the way they'd felt under my fingertips when I dared to touch the still-warm corpse. It wasn't quite what I'd been expecting from the fairy tales.

They all gave me looks that varied from semi-credulous suspicion to concern to disbelief that bordered on laughter. "Look at the dents on my foldie if you don't believe me!" I held it up. It was nothing an hour of hammering couldn't fix, but you didn't get that kind of damage from anything less than concrete or a fight.

Chloe examined a nail. "Babe, no offense, but..."

Kenny interrupted, but it was Chloe's doubting face that upset me. "Are you seriously saying I made it up? Because if you are, I can prove it."

"I have to see this," said Raheed.

"She's been through a lot," Jay shot back.

"No, no, it's fine." I lifted my shirt up. "This convince you?"

I had bandages wrapped around most of me and a bra covering my tits, so it wasn't really much of a flash. The dragon had gone for my belly, trying to use its sharp claws to disembowel me once its jaw was broken and useless. I pulled away bandages, swearing under my breath, to show them the gashes. They're shallow—I jumped away very, very quickly—but they are showy, and are definitely not as clean as a knife cut would be, not at all.

Even so, I rolled up my sleeves, showing off the rest of my battle scars. They weren't as bad as my stomach, but my arms were crisscrossed with thin red lines and scrapes in a really showy way. Raheed went pale and so did Chloe, but Jaycenne and Kenny were giving me the looks of respect I deserved.

"Oh, and if you're not convinced, I almost forgot that I had this." I reached into my pocket, took out the claw. Everyone flinched at the sight of the curved bone.

My stomach twisted as I looked at it, and I decided not to think too hard about the claws slicing towards my belly, the way my own blood had smelled. I stuffed it back in my pocket.

"So…anyone willing to help me haul the body back? If you don't believe me now, you will when you see that."

There was silence. Chloe's nose wrinkled. "A giant lizard covered in blood has got to smell…that's kind of nasty."

"It shouldn't smell too bad," I said.

"I'll help," said Raheed. I sighed inwardly. I knew that tone. Fight time.

"Me too," said Chloe. She shot me a smile that was supposed to be supportive.

Great, they were ready to compete. Time to put on my leadership face, the one I use to boss other electricians back to work when they start screwing around on the job.

I nodded sharply at them. "This way, then. If anyone else wants to stay, you're free to. Okay," I said, trying not to let my voice crack, "thisaway."

Jaycenne and Kenny scampered ahead of me like eager puppies, around the corner and down the way, crouching and crawling through the narrow section back to the under-roads.

There was a tunnel leading along the outside of the cement housing of the pipe. We were pretty low, but still close to the Heaven Tubes, almost dangerously so. Along this section of drained sewer, a breach in the wall allowed passage in, to the main road; there was also a narrow road along the outside of the cement leading back in the general direction of the school. It led down, and up, so there was scrabbling and crawling in some parts—like I said, the Heaven Tubes are messy, and close to older wiring systems from when people lived Up. It's a mess to get though at times.

It was in one of the low areas that I'd run into my dragon. It was a wider tunnel, because it led towards a short cut underneath the sewage block, and was used often enough that it had been worn into friendliness.

The part near the divide continued up, up, closer to the surface, and there it was, my battleground.

My heart tightened and my stomach lurched, and my wounds started to hurt, more than they had already. The ground was scuffed with movement and there were claw-marks. Even Chloe, starting to chatter at others, fell silent. You could tell something had gone down. I touched my belly.

"So, guys," I chirped, with more confidence than I felt, "where'd we stick the body again?"

Jay pointed to an obviously disturbed spot in the wall. We grabbed our foldies and got digging, expecting a clunk.

There wasn't one. We kept digging. There still wasn't, just an awkward silence.

"So, where's the body?" asked Raheed. Oh boy, I thought, this is going to be fun. He had that argument look on his face.

"Uhhh…"

Kenny sneezed. "I don't see the, um, body, but, um, there's, um…"

"Is this all you had to show us?" Raheed added, crouching next to him. He lifted something out of the ground, silvery grains. "Dust?" He shot me a patronizing look. "If I wanted to see Dust I'd go Up." He stood up and elaborately wiped his hands on his jeans.

I glared switchblades at him.

Kenny got up. "No need to be a dick. It could be that something weird happened or someone came and moved the body."

Raheed shared a glance with Chloe that I didn't like, but then Chloe stepped up. "Honey…are you sure you didn't get attacked by some Rat with hallies? This sounds more like a shroomy story than…"

How could she? I wondered. I felt my chin start to wobble. "Explain this," I squeaked, and yanked the claw out of my pocket again.

It was still intact as I threw it, but when she picked it up, it turned into dust as we watched. It was like watching an image pixellate in real life. Everyone went very quiet, then.

"Dust?" Chloe lost her condescending, 'I'm worried, sweetie' look. "It was…"

"Do you believe me now?" I muttered.

"I do," said Jay quietly, putting a hand behind me for support. I felt a sudden flare of gratitude; if anyone would be taken seriously, it would be steady, warm little Jay. Raheed still had that stupid-bastard eyebrow raised, and Chloe looked uncertain, but it was something.

"Either way, we should clear out this tunnel," said Jay, always health-conscious and practical. "You know what happens if you inhale too much of that crap." Of course we did. We'd been lectured on it in school more times than anyone could count. And, once or twice, we'd seen it. At present, I was praying that what had happened to me wasn't a result of inhaling a bunch of Dust without realizing it.

We tied our various bandannas and nose masks on (anybody with a brain has something on hand, and an extra or two) and got to work. If you mix Dust with normal dirt it helps a lot, so we dug a bunch of small holes and spread it into those, then covered them with dirt. The less Dust is swirling around, the less potent it is. Farther away from the surface, it sort of deactivates, I guess you'd say.

Anyway. You don't want to hear about the cleanup and boring stuff. Cleaning is cleaning, no matter what it involves, and cleaning sucks. We all finished that up, and then went down to the Rabbit Den for a bite to eat and some chicoffee.

Aiden and Caleb were both there, of course, at their own small table; naturally, we pushed our tables together so all seven of us could compare notes and theories. They still don't fully believe me, but at least no-one was calling me crazy by the end. It helped that Caleb had seen a strange-looking rat with a human face the week before and had been worried about mentioning it. Caleb is known for being pretty sane, over all.

THE LOVED, THE LOST, THE DREAMING

Aiden was all for jumping back into action and looking for more beasties, but I kyboshed that. He's awesome, but gods, he doesn't always think. Caleb, like Jay, was all about being responsible, and not wasting our unit's break-day on something we weren't qualified to handle. Kenny didn't know what to do. Raheed didn't say much, and Chloe was more interested in getting me home to rest.

Eventually, I agreed with Chloe, and left everyone else early. She walked me back to my place, said a few pleasantries to Dad, and kissed me goodnight. I spent some time just relaxing with Dad, but I didn't feel like discussing the rest of it. I did write all of this down, of course, because it's too weird not to record.

It's been a retardedly long day, so I'm going to sleep now.

2—May 16, 0048 P.D.

Surprise, surprise, I didn't exactly get a lot of rest last night. Bad sleep and then Pramjit was on my butt because I was jittery and it affected my soldering. I didn't do anything horrifyingly stupid—okay, I may have glued my fingers together with epoxy, but still. Nothing terrible. I got a lecture on keeping my mind on work even after I showed him my bandaged stomach, which was just jerky. He seemed tense too, though, and with a couple of newbies to train at the same time, I guess I shouldn't be surprised at his intolerance. Still mean and stupid though.

He was nicer after lunch and apologized, and let me go home early; the bending and moving around to fix the busted patch of wires around Hub 7 of the mall was really painful after a while. Somebody accidentally drove a Mole into the wall and shut out power for half the shops, and boy did I hate the dumb bastard for messing up so many systems. We had to go around and check everyone's wiring—easy, but tedious—and of course routes were disrupted, signals messed up...everything 'fun' you can think of. Assholes need to be more careful. There are more than two thousand people just in Sector A—my sector—and if you drive a Mole into the wrong wall, you could leave half of them in the dark. So, yeah. Stressful day.

THE LOVED, THE LOST, THE DREAMING

It also didn't help that Chloe kept texting me to see how I was doing and everyone else kept texting to share gossip and ask the same damn things. I kept having to plug my phone into the network and then unplug it, and with my queue getting all backed up, every time I'd update, I'd get about five bazillion texts. They all came AT THE SAME TIME, of course, because whenever people text you a lot, they're synchronized about it. We were all still talking about the dragon and my epic battle.

That soothed my ego, but people weren't making any bones about the fact that they thought Caleb and me were all a bit loony on some sort of hallie we had decided not to share with the group. As if. Dad would kill me. I remember how he reacted to the one time I came home with skunk on my breath, and I have nightmares enough without taking hallies. A little illicit vodka is plenty enough for me, thanks. Anything else and...it's not that I can't sleep. I usually would prefer it if I couldn't sleep, actually.

Enough about nightmares. I should sleep, and try to put today outta my head.

3—May 20, 0048 P.D.

I let Chloe talk me into a bite at the Den after work. In retrospect, I think it might have been a mistake. Anyway. The Den is a cheap but sort of nice place. First thing when you walk in is the chalked-up sign on the wall with the rate of exchange:

1 platinum = 4 gold
1 gold = 10 silver
1 silver = 10 coloured cards
1 coloured card = 5 white/multi

As if anyone would forget, but, like at the bank, they like to remind us so people don't try to bargain and cheat with the currency. Mostly the older people do that, but us younger ones get the brunt of it. Checkered table clothes, spotty chrome, and slightly-too-tasteful floral prints dominate the place. They do put flowers on the table, but crappy little grown ones, weeds usually, not the fancy plastic kind. Still, the effort is there. It's not a candle-lit dinner place, but it's a good lunch spot. Then too, they hide some incredible Old wines there in addition to the piss-juice you get from our underground grapes and mushrooms. Anyway, you get the idea: shabby around the edges, but respectable, and with good food.

THE LOVED, THE LOST, THE DREAMING

I was still pretty grubby because I'd just gotten off of work, and, stupid me, I didn't change even though she'd asked me out. She gave me a Look when I got there, and I held my hands up in surrender.

"At least I washed up. Come on. You said to meet you right away."

She pouted, and I had to admit she looked cute. "Fine, sweetie, but you know I like it better when you look pretty for me."

I made a noncommittal noise. Admins like her don't have to get their hands too dirty; the repair guys and IT techs handle all the computer stuff. At worst, she'd get correction fluid on a fingernail. Call me bitter.

It was one of those awkward lunches. I ordered sweet potato fries with coarse salt, and she, of course, went for the moss/dandelion salad with fried mushrooms. I saw her eye my tallow-fried deliciousness with affectionate contempt, but she wasn't above stealing a couple.

We shared a roasted catfish in vinegar for the meal, and a banana dusted with beet-sugar for dessert. It would've been romantic, and it was certainly a tidy little snack, but I had my mind on the cost. Math lessons in childhood came back to me. I wished that instead of telling me about four gold equaling a platinum and five pals equaling a colour, they'd told us the economics of having a significant other. Anyway, it wasn't the money, it was Chloe's favour that I was worried about, and whether this was a reproach for not having taken her out lately.

Our conversation was awkward. She kept forcing laughs and I would say things that were supposed to be funny, and Gillian, the server, kept looking at us weirdly, and a well-dressed chick at another table— off-duty cuntgirl from what I'd heard of gossip—was giving Chloe long looks, and I kept worrying about getting texts from Raheed, and…yeah. I was jittery and anxious, and could barely get things into my mouth.

Chloe had been making a few remarks about how Raheed was looking at me, at us, and that he was still the odd one out. I wasn't feeling especially warm about him—after all, he and I had been pretty turbulent as well as short-lived. But seeing him picked to pieces was another thing. I couldn't decide whether to defend or make fun of him. I was pretty relieved when our nothingish, scattered conversations about everything except the dragon and tunnels were interrupted by Gillian bringing the bill. It was well-timed, too; Chloe had just asked me something awkward about where I'd hoped my relationship with him would lead, way back when.

Before I could answer, Gill had her pad out, and Chloe handed her a gold card and got a fistful of change.

I raised an eyebrow; the meal had only been worth six coloured cards, not exactly fancy, and the nine silver and four coloured in change were a pretty hefty lump of money to be carrying around.

"Payday," Chloe explained. "My lucky Tuesday, I guess. Or maybe yours."

I kept my trap shut. I have enough change for a couple of platinum cards at home—almost—but I only carry colors and white-multicoloured cards on hand. Electrical work pays decently, but secretarial sometimes pays better. Knowing Chloe though, it's better to hide my cards. Just because even though she's getting a bigger paycheque, doesn't mean she wouldn't expect me to drop half -a-gold or more on her as often as possible.

I pulled out my purse and took a handful of cards out. "Do you mind lots of change?"

She waved a hand munificently. "Keep it. This is my treat." I knew trouble was coming just from that.

"So," I said.

"So." She gave me a coy look. "Shall we walk and talk?"

"Oooo-kay."

Well, as I said, when Chloe paid for dinner, I knew I was in trouble.

Sure enough, as we walked slowly out of the restaurant, hand in hand, she dropped it on me.

"Soooooooo, I've heard something delicious," she whispered, as we got up. "In fact, it's really juicy."

Oh, gods, she was in the mood to play it out. "Tell me more, don't make me wait."

"I dunno, babe, I think you should." She squeezed my waist playfully. "All right. Aiden and Caleb are....can you guess?"

I thought hard. The boys were pretty snuggly, so 'breaking up' probably wasn't the answer. Then, too, she wouldn't be gleeful if they were.

"Uh, tell me," I said, playing dumb. I may be a tomboy, but I'm still enough of a woman to see a social lead-on when I get slapped in the face with it.

"Engaaaaged!" she sang. "Can you believe it? Isn't it great?"

"Yeah, it is. Good for them." Funny, I hadn't seen any rings popping on either of their hands. I wondered what her source was. "I guess they'll have to adopt or get a surrogate, but that's great."

Chloe waved me off. "That's not important. The important thing is the wedding! Ahh, I can't wait—I hope it's soon!"

"Do you think they'll be able to get Old tuxes from Up, or make do with what people can scrounge?" I asked, interested in spite of myself.

"Of course they'll get real ones, I'm sure. Anyone who cares does. The clothing—oh! I bet they'll have a special search party *just* to get decorations. I can't wait to see what people bring! If only I had something to wear…"

Ah, here was the catch. A double whammy. Well-played, Chloe. Not only mentioning a new engagement—again—but…

"I'm sure we could squeeze in some time to go shopping soon," I said, like a sucker.

"Oh, would you?" With her eyes sparkling with excitement, I couldn't say no. I noticed, then, that she'd lured me out to a spot in the tunnel that was very out of the way. We were in an area that had a kind of grove of dangling charms overhead, a romantic little nook next to a sidealley.

"You make me feel so special, Janelle," said Chloe softly. "I love having a girlfriend who makes me feel like a woman."

I kissed Chloe, felt her tongue clumsy against mine, her breasts pressing against mine as she snuggled into my arms. At times like this, I can forget her occasional tantrums, her pettishness, and the other stuff that pisses me off from time to time. She's just my girl and she makes me feel beautiful and loved, at least for a few perfect moments. And even though she was really pissing me off this afternoon, I couldn't help losing myself in her kiss.

I opened my eyes so I could look at her face, see the intense focus that she has on every kiss. I was enjoying her soft lips and skin and stroking her stripey hair when I saw it.

It was farther off, sort of down the sidealley, which had more intermittent lighting. I didn't understand what I was seeing at first. My brain couldn't bear to wrap around it.

Thin legs, spider legs, long and bony and dry as old meat salted for too long. The flesh was tight to the body as well as the limbs, translucent and dry-looking, but heavily veined. There were about eight legs, but the body was not a spider's. Instead, it had a head—or skull, I should say—like a small dog's, or like a bat's. Large, empty dark blue eyes filled the sockets, and small pointed ears, no more than skin, stood up from the top of the skull.

The doglike, spidery thing turned, and lifted its head from the short neck. The nose twitched and the stumpy nodule of flesh that its neck and legs were attached to quivered. The dry, greasy skin revealed the veins pulsing. The skinny bones in its limbs twitched, and slowly, it moved.

THE LOVED, THE LOST, THE DREAMING

It scuttled slowly, stealthily along the edge of the tunnel, its movements echoed by the faint skittering of its steps. I almost wet myself.

"Chloe," I breathed, "let me go. Turn around slowly. Very slowly. Do. Not. Scream."

It hadn't really seen us yet, though it had been looking in our direction, or so it seemed. The ugly little terror had just been strolling along in the tunnel, looking for a snack. Tame rabbits, probably, based on the size, but a pack of them could easily take down something bigger, like us.

I rotated Chloe in my arms, centimeter by centimeter, slow as breath in sleep. She was as silent as I'd told her to be. Smarter than she pretends to be, my Chloe, or at least, she has good instincts.

Our slow movements were gradual enough that the little predator didn't see us. I was feeling pretty proud of myself when it once again looked right past us. Then, Chloe finally saw it. And she screamed, and jumped, and hit her head on some corn dolls dangling from a pipe.

The beast let out a harsh, clicking, strangled yelp, and fled back into the shadowy part of the tunnel shortcut. The part, the only unfrozen part of my brain remembered, that went closer to Up.

Chloe whimpered. "Jesus, Janelle, what the fuck was that thing? What the fuck?"

"Shhh, shhh," I hushed her. "Let's go back to the lit part of the halls." I was shuddering in spite of myself. I still am, a little. That thing was fucking creepy.

"Oh Gods," she moaned. For once, it was anything but sexy. She was scared as hell.

"Honey, are you okay?"

"I...Gods that was scary looking. I swear to Gods I've had nightmares about things that looked like that." My darling Chloe has always had a thing about spiders.

"I don't blame you. Come on, let's get back. We should probably warn the others to keep their eyes peeled." I tugged her towards the nearest link spot and plugged my phone into the common network.

"Guys, we just saw something else," I mass-texted.

"Lol what another dragon?"

"Sthu Raheed. No but a monster. Keep your eyes out and let me know if you see anything else. I want to make sure I'm not going crazy."

"Ha," texted Jay. "K we will."

"Thx guys."

I unplugged my phone. Messages would wait in the queue until the others got them, and if they texted me back, well, hell, I'd just deal with the queue avalanche later. At the moment, I had Chloe, and I didn't feel like dealing with anyone else, or thinking about the fact that I might be going crazy.

THE LOVED, THE LOST, THE DREAMING

Chloe, of course, wouldn't stop talking about the damn thing. I made some noncommittal noises while she talked at me; I needed to think about the crawler, and especially, if we saw one again, how to kill it. That is, assuming it wouldn't collapse into Dust, like the baby dragon.

My belly ached, and I remembered that I had to take a dose of antibiotics and re-wrap the damage. I cut Chloe off, mid-flow in a speech about how we needed to be careful and perhaps we were going crazy after all, and maybe we should get ourselves checked over for the Fever?

I was lifting a foot carefully over an errant pipe, but I turned around to shoot her a withering glare. "This mess on my stomach says we're perfectly sane. And you saw it too. I'd be happy to get myself checked up, but I am pretty damn sure they aren't just hallucinations. For once, I'm pretty sure Tunnel Fever ain't the culprit."

She reassured me that of course she wasn't saying I was crazy, after all, she'd seen the crawler beast too, and no-one was arguing with my stomach wound, but…

I let her protest and chugged on home, giving her the boot just outside the door. Instead of plugging my phone in first-thing, the way I usually would, I stomped into the kitchen to get cooking.

Dad wasn't home yet, but he always prefers having me get something started. He usually returns the favour, especially if I happen to be working or going out late. Today, the habit wasn't just politeness, it was a much-needed distraction.

I grabbed a couple handfuls of white button mushrooms and threw them on the frying pan. A sparing burst of water from the tap to boil the beans and hemp seeds, a little oil for the mushrooms, and some salt, and dinner was well underway. Dad and I both tend to eat simple foods and wholesome stuff.

The cooking relaxed me, and gave me the chance to think about nothing at all for a while. Then Dad came home, and I decided not to tell him about the crawler, because it hadn't hurt me and he already seems to think I'm crazy. I did tell him about some of the gossip, though.

"Where'd you hear about your friends' engagement from?" he asked.

I paused for a minute. "Chloe," I admitted.

"Well, from what I know, it sounds like she was dropping a hint." I nodded, not sure where he was going with that, but he didn't say anything else.

"It sure sounds like that, but then she mentioned wanting to go shopping for a new dress."

"So let me ask you, Janelle—do y'think you could foresee your relationship with her being—"

THE LOVED, THE LOST, THE DREAMING

"I'm really not sure yet, Dad," I said quickly. "It's a big decision, and I always figured I'd be more than an apprentice before I settled down with anyone." Then too, there was the problem of choosing—kids would be nice, but I wasn't sure I wanted to be the one to pop them out, and with a wife, the kid thing could be complicated...

He looked at me steadily. "That's probably a good choice." After that, I changed the topic to work, and how the hydroponic farm repairs were going. He took the hint, and spent about half an hour happily telling me about some old botany texts he'd found. He hadn't seen their like since university, he said. It reminded him of the old times.

That got us both thinking about the time before the Dark—which, to be fair, I don't really remember— and Mom, who I can't forget. The conversation sort of died off after that. I left the dishes to him, and went to play with circuits in my room, and to write this.

I guess I should mention what you've already figured out: the Dark has been in place for a very long time. We're mostly used to it, but not at all, having automatically timed electric lights and lanterns to regulate our days, earth-warmth instead of the warmth of sunlight. You can't override every old instinct.

Still, it's a different world. They even changed the dates when the Dust came. It's a warm, wet climate, Dad tells me, compared to the way the surface was. There are some bigger fields, way down below, where they're trying to get some other crops growing, but even with the ceiling painted blue, it's nothing like the real sky was. I've been Up a couple of times, one of them being a mandatory field trip, but I can't really remember things like a 'breeze', or 'wind', even though I've read about them a few times. I wish going Up wasn't so scary and so risky; I like the openness even if it is disorienting. Dust and the Dark wait Up there, but down here, it's safe. Or at least, the risks are known.

Sometimes I think about what it would be like to live Up there. We started in the basements of houses and moved downward, taking everything we could, salvaging and recycling and going deeper and deeper. Still, a lot of things got left behind. A lot.

He has a bag full of photo albums and whatever they could print and salvage from stuff that was kept online, but—still. The Dust has taken everything. My grandparents, a good chunk of my extended family...

Okay, I really don't want to think about that right now. It happened a long time ago, when Dad was a kid, it's true, but that doesn't mean I like thinking about it. I don't know why, but something about those almost-memories of living normally—whatever that was like—upsets me almost as much, sometimes more, than memories of Mom.

Though, Dad told me one time that our brains can actually make memories, if people tell us about the situations enough. You can remember something that didn't ever happen to you, at all. I didn't need another reason to doubt my sanity, but I think I just found one. Maybe it's all this underground living, and we're all going crazy, just very slowly. I like it down here, don't get me wrong; this is home, but apart from the littlest kids, I think we all know that it's unnatural.

I'm back. I know I need to keep writing this, to get my head clear, but I can't help wondering if someday it might be more important. If I have kids, I want them to know who I was right now, let them know what we didn't understand about the Dust. And maybe, just maybe, if the Dust goes away and we all get to live Up there again, someone should remember what it was like.

Gods I sound old. According to Dad, I would be graduating from high school this year, if people still scheduled things the same way. As it is, we're making do and I read text books and stuff and digital files in the evenings. Sometimes I try to find info about things like Dust, but it's been pretty freaking useless, the old information. It's like everything we know has been turned upside-down, though, or else we hadn't learned enough about the nature of the universe to make sense of it.

The Dust isn't easy to understand, to be fair. Maybe my expectations are too high. For example, the waters were fine—the Dust, not unlike pollen, is inert when submerged in water. Rain doesn't do much to it, either, but add a large, non-misty quantity of water to Dust and it dissolves. Cover it in dirt, too, and it settles down and won't pick up again, like it's been suffocated. Dust has the strangest properties.

Animals and plants—except for chimps, gorillas, and other apes, so I'd heard—mostly weren't too bothered by it. The higher your brain functions, the worse the effect of Dust, so any species able to dream, imagine, think creatively, was screwed. For humans, it obliterated everything, filled the air with darkness. You knew your city was next when you saw the clouds on the horizon, coming like a spring thunderstorm. It was a thunderstorm without lightning or rain, just a kind of fog.

It traveled in clouds towards cities, mostly inactive until it reached them. The country, apparently, was mostly fine, but the minute people started to gather en masse, Dust followed. Then the terrifying part would really begin.

THE LOVED, THE LOST, THE DREAMING

A little Dust here and there, you can handle, but the more of it you inhale, the more it clouds your vision, dark patches and mist thickening until you're blind even in broad daylight—blind, and a little mad. As it eats into your optic nerves and the occipital lobe of your brain, you stumble around, screaming about things other people can't see. It's worst in natural light: look towards the sun, and swirling blackness makes everything disappear. It seems to get worse when you have more in your system and more sunlight on your skin. Electric light doesn't have all the right wavelengths to activate it, so we're pretty safe down here.

At least, we have been pretty safe down here.

Dust. Inhale too much and sheeted ghosts and horrors gibber and shriek in the streets. Your mind slowly dulls, your hormones and emotions go wild, and you see endless terrifying images…until you don't see anything at all. The rich life-sparks of neuroelectrical activity are extinguished, gobbled by the Dust. Eventually, of course, you die, but not before you spend days, sometimes weeks, being chased by everything you find paralysingly scary.

Until now, though, Dust's horrors were only in people's heads. You could see them batting and clawing at invisible monsters, but nothing material. Having Dust take the shape of something, and convincing more than one of us…that scares me. Dust isn't conscious, that we know of. It doesn't travel in the tunnels or sculpt itself into shapes. Drive people crazy by eating their brains once they've inhaled enough of it, yes. But none of us have been Up enough to have that kind of exposure. And it got to all of us.

And that claw, the dragon's claw…it felt so real, Dad even saw it…he had to see something to not believe it was real. And, hell, having Dad painfully re-wrap me and have a look at the scabs and scratches reminded me—whatever else happened, it definitely left a mark on my skin. Dust doesn't attack people from the outside. Not like that.

I don't know. I'm confused and talking about Dust and what it does, scares me. I guess I can just be grateful for one thing, that it took the shape of one of the monsters under my bed from when I was a kid, rather than the stuff I dreamt about when I was a tween. Now, that would've been much, much worse.

That's all for tonight. Now I'm going to try and sleep. If I can.

THE LOVED, THE LOST, THE DREAMING

4—May 21, 0048 P.D.

I'm still jittery today. I just read over last night's scribbles and I am wondering if I'm going nuts. I mean, sure, teenagers have a reputation for being batshit crazy, but what was all that? Maybe the whole thing with the dragon was just a mass hysteria type thing.

Yeah right. I'm not the only one scared of the Dust and what it does. If I was, why would so many people tie charms and amulets to the byways and entrances to our homes to ward it off? And the crawler, with its spider legs...I don't know. Maybe I did hallucinate something, and Chloe played along. But she wouldn't stop talking about it. That wasn't my nightmare, though. She saw something, and she saw the same thing I did, and it scared the piss out of her. I couldn't have made that up, and—it wasn't one of my nightmares. It sounded like one of hers. At least what she's told me about them. The Dust...the Dust took the shape of one of her nightmares, then. And echoed at least one of mine.

The implications...I don't even know where to start. I wish I was a cuntgirl so I could just fuck my way to oblivion. No, I take that back. I shouldn't wish for things like that. But sometimes, just sometimes, I wish I were a little dumber and more easily contented.

I don't think I would have gotten into things like this if I just didn't care.

Anyway. Nightmares again. The ones from when I was a kid, about the old train car, and the man with the purple velvet suit, and the little girl. I'm getting the shudders and it's broad day-cycle, lights on full and everything. I wish Mom was here...I...I need a minute.

Okay, so. Work. And Drama, with a capital D.

It's true about Aiden and Caleb, which made me happy for them. They were extra snuggly and kissy. I admit I was a little jealous—am a little jealous—of both of them for finding a person that right so early in life. Some people's parents arrange their marriages, of course, but it's not that common. I really saw the way they were looking at each other, tonight, though, and felt Raheed's gaze drilling into the back of my neck. I decided to try not to think about what his body language was saying. I smiled at Chloe when she smiled back, but seeing our happy friends...I dunno.

We were hanging around Aiden's mom's place today. She's a soft-voiced woman with a big, generous heart, who doesn't mind having a pack of young people barnstorm her place. I took a look at her electronics while I was there—skill or small guest gifts being a mandatory courtesy—and fixed a couple of things, which she thanked me for profusely. I didn't mind doing it a bit, and the delicious goat cheese and mushroom melts she made were more than ample thanks. She's a very good goatherd—must be how she raised Aiden; after those stubborn beasts, Aiden would be easy to handle. Still, it was a small luxury, and I really treasured it.

Anyway. Enough about those cheese melts, my mouth is watering just thinking about them. I could have eaten the whole tray. Mmmmm. Right.

They were talking engagement details and where they would live. Generally you go with the family that's most poorly off, so you can help around. That is going to be Aiden's mom, Nora, because Caleb's parents have another daughter and they're a bit better off, what with their admin jobs and such. They're nice enough people, but I was glad Aiden's mom would have company. I can really tell she wishes Caleb wasn't an only child. Everyone talked about ceremony details, how they'd be arranging the rooms, and of course, whether they'd be splurging on plastic flowers and other fancy things from Up above. Aiden did a lot of smiling and stuttering—he's what you'd call a soft guy, more Between than masculine, per se—and Caleb was beaming and doing most of the answering for them.

43

I felt really lonely. Between Chloe being clingy the minute engagement details were mentioned, and her significant Looks all the time, I was feeling pretty suffocated. It was uncomfortable to say the least. I excused myself for a bit of air more than once.

The second time I came in, Raheed was having a pointed conversation in the corner with Caleb. My hackles went up instinctively, but I relaxed when I overheard the topic.

"…and that's why I'm worried," Caleb said quietly. "We're under quota in the sector for populations, but unless we can talk one of the girls into helping us out with a baby, the application could be that much harder."

Raheed nodded understandingly. He'd pushed me hard and fast on family questions, much harder and faster than I'd wanted, but I can't fault his genuine affection for kids. I might barely be able to stand him these days, but he is an excellent assistant teacher.

"I'm sure you could talk one of the girls into it. And even so, if you fostered one of the Extras…"

"It's worth a try. If we're lucky, they'll just let us marry anyway, even if we can't…you know." Caleb looked frightened and miserable for a moment. "I wish it wasn't this hard. I just want to be with Aiden and get our lives together really started…but we're going to have to show we can contribute to the population, and…"

Raheed nodded again, and patted his shoulder. "That's rough, man. To be honest, I was hoping I could talk Janelle into something like that, sooner rather than later…"

The fact that Caleb burst out laughing stung my pride. People treat me like I'm Between half the time, and there are times I'd prefer not to deal with the complications of being a woman, but I still have feelings.

Am I just ornery? I can't tell if Raheed's just more of an asshole than I thought he was or if I did something to piss everyone off. Maybe it's my period coming, or something.

Jay interrupted me at the door. "You look down," she said, her brown, almond-shaped eyes searching my face. She had her sleek black hair in a half-bun, showing off the characters on her neck. "Yep, they're new. It's a quote from a poem by Murakami," she said, following the direction of my eyes.

"They're nice."

"I've been learning to read Japanese," she said proudly.

I raised my eyebrows. She speaks Tagalog and Chinese at home, plus English, obviously. Adding a fourth language to that roster would impress anyone.

"That's damn cool—" I started to say, but her expression stopped me in the middle of the sentence. I guess she could tell I was trying to change the subject.

"What's up? It's not like you to duck out of something like this." Yup. Jay knows me too well.

"Oh, I was just, uh, thinking about wedding gifts for them, and I wanted to think out loud, so I came out here." Worst lie ever.

Someone laughed inside. I was guessing the vodka was finally being passed around.

"Well, I guess you can keep thinking, or you can come get tipsy with the rest of us," she said, grinning.

"Thanks, but I'm still on antibiotics. I really shouldn't, with these wounds."

She remembered and her face softened. She hugged me, very gently. "Well, I know a really good tattoo artist—Dad—so we can cover those right up when they scar over. You won't even see a difference. Well, except that you'll have some badass tattoos." She smiled.

"Jay…you think we were all just crazy, back in the tunnel?"

She shrugged. "Who knows? I'm not going to worry about it until I see another one. At worst, we are crazy and they'll put us on tranks for a month. Either way it isn't too bad."

"I kind of prefer the idea of being crazy. Would make things easier." I remembered something I'd heard the nurse say. "Has your dad been doing a lot of tattoos to cover scars lately?"

"Enough, I guess. The Rats and their girls are good for business, but he hasn't mentioned anything strange. Why?"

"The nurse said she'd seen a few injuries like this lately, when she was stitching me up."

Jay looked serious again. "I'll let you know if I hear anything."

"Thanks. I think I'll go in and sort of do my rounds before I hit the sack."

So, there I was, giving a few hugs and exchanging waves. Chloe offered to walk me home, and being jittery and tired, I took her up on it. Luckily she did most of the talking, repeated everything I hadn't heard and summarizing what I had with additional gossip.

Now, of course, I'm in bed. There will be more wiring to fix tomorrow, today was slack, and if not, I'll be on production or salvage duty. Joy. I love my work, but I need to sleep for it. That's all for tonight, reader. I hope there's someone reading this, anyway. Dad, please don't read this, if it's you. I hope you're my kids or something, reader. If I have kids. If I live long enough and don't go crazy. Okay, enough of that. Goodnight.

THE LOVED, THE LOST, THE DREAMING

5—May 25, 0048 P.D.

More nightmares. I swear, I'm this close to being absolutely bugshit. I keep dreaming about the man in the faded purple suit, and the little girl with the sharp teeth, and the witch, and…and Mom. I just…I see her coming to me, and wrapping her arms around me—I'm little, maybe five, no older than seven—and she holds me for a minute, and then, the darkness comes up around us, swirling, murky, and tangles around her…and then she falls backwards, slowly, her arms still open for me, naked fear on her face…

Oh gods, I'm crying. I don't need this right before work. Okay, I'm going to go clean up, and then I'll write more later. This has to be stress. Or maybe I inhaled more Dust than I thought. Or maybe it's worrying about Chloe's little hints; that's getting to me. It has to be stress dreams. What else could I be afraid of? Except, I feel hunted…it's like something is coming for me…as if the Dust is trying to follow me, or something in the Dust…

What is going on? Okay. Chicoffee and a mushroom roll and I'll be all sorted out. There's no such thing as monsters. Haven't read monster stories in years. Mostly, not since Mom read them to me…and then there's the one dream that keeps coming back. I had it just a few nights ago. Pinocchio was to blame for it, I think, or the idea of it, anyway.

It began in a train car. A dark, grimy, dingy place. There were other kids, I think, sitting on the floor, which had a discolored, dirty carpet. I remember a sooty look to the walls, as if the place hadn't been cleaned in several years, but I couldn't smell coal.

There was an announcement over the loudspeaker that we were going to be entertained by a puppet show to commence shortly. I recall people in white with dirty clothes walking in and out of the compartment— we were only in a small forward section, and stuck inconveniently near something important, perhaps the engine or a thing like that. I didn't like the way the workers slipped around or the way they looked at us, either.

Then the puppetmaster would appear, and I had the impression he was first standing in the middle of a street of people, then inside the compartment with us. The thing that usually caught my attention first was the red-and-yellow striped scarf wound flamboyantly around his narrow top-hat. His indigo-violet suit, with its wide lapels and flaring cut, attracted attention from a crowd easily. It was made of velvet, I think, crushed velvet, something flamboyant like that, and I think he had a large, dark-wood cane with a shiny sculpted metal carving on its head. He seemed dingy, yes, but too large for the small space of the train car.

THE LOVED, THE LOST, THE DREAMING

The story of the puppets, as it played out, was always less memorable than he was. It changed, too; I could never remember what the puppets did. It involved monsters though, and love, jealousy, revenge.

Then, halfway through the play, during the climax, the train would stop with a thump and shudder to a halt. The world outside was grimy and grey. I remember that the windows were covered with grit, whitish stuff, and the horizon was long and grey as well. I always noticed it around this point in the dream.

Then, one of the kids, a blond little girl, would run forward into the area where the puppet show was being presented—a sort of opening in the wall, not unlike a concession booth with the shutters that come down. The stage for the puppets was somehow inside the window, and there was a tiny little compartment behind it, full of dirty gears and pipes and mechanical stuff that served I-don't-know-what-purpose.

She would run up, and the puppet master would stand, and she'd go around the corner, then he would go down with a shout, though I only saw him actually fall down sometimes. The compartment was always emptied out after that—I have no idea where the other kids went, but they were gone, like ghosts, and I was all alone.

Then, every time, I would go around the corner of the door to see what was going on. My heart is pumping fast just remembering this part of the dream. I would see the puppetmaster on the ground and there would be blood on his suit, the uncoloured shirt underneath.

The little girl smiled at me. Too many teeth. Whiteless eyes, solid red, burning. I wondered, always, what the redness was on her shirt-front, and then I knew, and I screamed.

I always woke up just then, blood pounding in my veins at a mile-a-minute, creeped out and alarmed and wanting Mom to come hold me.

Coffee. Food. Normal things. I need to think about normal, real things. Work. Otherwise, this chronicle will just be a bunch of mad ramblings, not useful.

Scolding myself made me feel better. I'll try to write more soon.

THE LOVED, THE LOST, THE DREAMING

6—May 26, 0048 P.D.

And, I'm back. I've been feeling a little better. Had more sleep that didn't involve nightmares, have been avoiding small off-side tunnels and backalleys, and to be honest, I've been avoiding Chloe and Raheed when I can. It's really embarrassing to say that not being around my own girlfriend is making me feel better. The wounds are healing pretty well, though I hate peeking under the bandages. At least it's been hurting less when I move now. I still can't believe they made me work the next day after I was injured, but at least Pramjit has been easier on me.

I was going to write about this before, but I got distracted by all the engagement plans and whatnot. Aiden and Caleb are still getting that stuff underway, and when Chloe isn't dropping hints, I really enjoy hearing about it. It's nice to think about them getting their lives together; it looks like the application won't be as tight as they feared. Anyway…sanity. Work. Let's talk about something less stressful.

Things have been busier at work—we're doing system supports in preparation for the seasonal inspections of the power lines and power source connections. That means that a team of specialized people are going Up, to maintain the wind turbines and solar cells while the rest of us reinforce things and inspect them down here. The sun is still shining, apparently, and the wind is still blowing, but without maintenance, it won't do us any good.

I've been doing a lot more running around since I've been feeling semi-normal. It's good to lose myself in circuits and wire. The altruistic side of me really loves knowing that a few tweaks and inspections every week are enough to make sure that the tunnels have power. We've had to build so much from scratch, and have had to re-route and re-wire so many things. Even with--what is it--48 years of practice, the systems are sketchy and still a work-in-progress.

I hope to get to work in the Development sector eventually. Wiring up more farm caverns, helping to set up new basement homes for people...I have to admit, I'd really love to work on a moon room or to set up the sun in a farm cavern. Laying the ground work—or ceiling work, I suppose—for the drywallers and masons to cover, and for the artisans to paint, echoing the real sky, is something I can't wait to do. I love the idea of being able to help build the world.

Maybe someday I'll even get to see the real sun. I hear it's brighter than even the brightest lights, but having looked directly into them a few times, I find that hard to believe. How could anything be more blinding? I'll believe it when I see it.

THE LOVED, THE LOST, THE DREAMING

Dad's calling me for supper—he made potato pancakes, yum!—so I'll be back in a bit with more good news.

Ahhhh. That was tasty. Back to work and the positive side of things. Well, mostly positive. I didn't mention that Caleb is in computers, and he and I have been talking a lot about the wiring. He's one of the privileged few who really get to work with the internet and salvage servers. I get a little bit of internet access, but not a huge amount. It's pretty carefully controlled. We have a little contact with a couple of neighboring towns, and we're expanding closer to each other, but the Dust took out things really randomly. When I say 'neighbouring', I mean that they're a few hundred kilometers away from us. It's just an occasional lucky phone signal and a few stray blips on the internet that have let us know they're still around. The radios, too, were invaluable for that, even though signals outside of our town have been intermittent at best.

Anyway. Caleb. We were talking about the internet and how much we wish it was more complete. The sites we have found—everything from blogs, people's opinion pages, to the local newspaper—hints at all of this boundless knowledge as if it was completely commonplace. It's enough to drive you bonkers.

He and I went to the Catfish Bowl to get a drink, because we hadn't done that in a while. It's a bar that's pretty far from home, but they're easygoing, informal, and have amazing yam fries.

I chewed on a chicken leg—a splurge, I admit—and luxuriated in the simple, unpretentious stone décor. It's bar that was cobbled together from leftover bits and pieces of everything—and I do mean everything—and I love the way it looks. It's a bit rough around the edges for Chloe, but not for me.

"How's your vodka?" Caleb asked, as I sipped the clear, hard-tasting liquor.

"Delish. The strawberry syrup is a good addition. I like the way they mix things here."

"You gotta try the cave-honey dandelion sorbet."

"Sounds expensive, but my mouth is watering."

"Nah. It's not bad at all! You worry too much about money."

I laughed. "I'm trying to be frugal. Don't tell Chloe, but I do want a family some day, and kids are expensive."

He grinned, and then paused, the smile replaced by a thoughtful expression. "Hey—speaking of kids, can I ask you a favour?"

"Go ahead," I said. After three ounces of vodka, I was pretty relaxed.

"We'll probably try to give some Extra kids a home, but Aiden and I aren't that hardcore about tradition. And, to be honest, I kind of want a bio kid, if I can have one."

"Okay." I took another swig of vodka, much larger than my previous sips.

"Do you think…it would mean no drinking and other stuff, of course…" Caleb's handsome, peat brown face creased in anxiety. "I mean, we wouldn't have to have sex—I'm not into women, obviously—would you consider being our surrogate?"

He flinched barely in time as I sprayed him in the face with a mouthful of vodka.

"Shit, sorry! Just…uh…I, uh…"

"Uh…is that a no?"

I wiped my mouth. Considering that he'd been the one laughing about the thought of me as a mother at their engagement party, this was baffling. "It's not a firm no. I'm just really surprised, and I don't know if I'm ready to host something in my…womb, you know? I mean, I, ah…not that I don't want to help…uh…"

I noticed that the bastard was laughing at me. "Gotcha! That was worth being sprayed in the face for."

"You son of a bitch!" I yelped, laughing. "You're buying the next round for that prank."

"Why should I? You're the reason I'm wearing this round."

I laughed. He ran a hand over his short, frizzy cornrows and checked them for damage. "Damn, girl, you got vodka everywhere. Hope you don't do that when you swallow. I'm calling you 'the human fountain' from now on. "

"You do and you'll meet a swift and painful death." Caleb pursed his full, rich lips, and shook his head.

"I doubt it. You'd never kill me; my chicken roti is way too good."

"Yeah, okay, you win this round. I can't argue with that roti. Haven't eaten it since a feast day, but it was really good." I toasted him, and signaled the waitress for a glass of water.

"I'm surprised though," Caleb continued. "I thought you hated kids."

I shrugged. "I never said that. Not by a long shot. I'm not ready for them, either, but I certainly don't hate 'em. Who on earth told you that?"

The slight hesitation before he spoke was very telling. He picked his drink up instead, took a long swig. "Oh, you know. Just never heard you talk about it."

I tightened my mouth in a smile. "Well, appearances can be deceiving." I swigged the rest of my drink down and pulled three colours and a couple pals out of my wallet. "And on that note, I should probably turn in. I have a project I'm working on. Trying to mod one of those ancient Nokias to work on solar cells." I shook my head. "How did our grandparents use those things? The interface is just awful, not that beggars can be choosers."

"Stay a little longer," said Caleb solicitously. "You've been stressing yourself out. I can tell. And besides, nobody in the group has seen you for, like, a week an' a half."

"Oh, fine." Liquor makes me easygoing.

"Whatchu workin' on otherwise?"

"Meh. Line upgrades and maintenance. That Mole that slammed into the wall at the shopping complex screwed some things up, and old lady Parmi a few streets down reported someone tapping into her line because her electricity was wavering. Mostly I've been fixing tapped lines lately—people just steal power when theirs goes down. Fuckin' drives me crazy, man." I took a drink of water.

"Tell me about it. I keep having to try to get the info off these hard drives and thumb drives—half the time they're corrupted anyway. And cloud storage. What complete idiot thought it was a good idea to store things on the internet?" He shook his head in disgust and slugged back a quarter tumbler of sugar beet rum. He licked the orange wedge, biting off a bit of the zest to chew on.

"Yeah. I know. At least they left lots of stuff for us to salvage, Up there."

Caleb nodded. "I can barely imagine. I'd give a lot to have a steady internet connection, 24-7 access, and a private computer all to myself."

I laughed. "You're closer to having that than the rest of us." He sighed, pained.

"The worst part is, communication is so limited and poor because of the reception issues that it's hard to tell how much of the world has survived." He lowered his voice to a bare whisper. "That said, there have been a few blips from other places. It looks like Europe, Africa, and Asia still have people in them, anyway. The cables are in pretty piss-poor shape, or should be, but in the last few years, we've been hearing a bit more." My ears pricked at this. It wasn't exactly useful information, but it was hopeful, at least.

I was really feeling the liquor by then. The waitress had brought me another vodka when I wasn't looking, and I was drinking it absentmindedly again.

"S'good, but how will it help us get out of here?" I said.

"Research? I dunno. Maybe we can take the Dust down somehow."

I laughed a bit too loud. "Gods, I wish I'd lived in the time when people had all that stuff. Unlimited information, unlimited resources, new clothes and new tech and new everything, whenever they wanted."

"It's not all it's cracked up to be," Caleb said, slurring his words slightly. "Lots of stuff means lots of junk. You've gone on a salvage once or twice, right?"

"Yeah, sure. Rotating salvage. But I guess you're right. But still...I wish I knew more." I groaned.

He nodded. "I've cleaned, salvaged, refurbished old tech every day since I was old enough to ask for a phone. I get you, sister." The new glass of vodka was already half gone, and I took another sip, slapping it down hard for emphasis.

"Fuckin', but, computers are so wavery. I guess those stupid fuckers before never figured they'd ever have to function without the internet after it was invented. Fuck. If they had my job they'd have made real backups. Back up everything on those old..pinkie...finger...which finger is it?"

"Thumb drive. Also, baby, you are offish'ly cut off. You're wording your slurs. Slurring your words. Words."

I laughed. "What kind of slurs did you have in min'?"

He laughed at me. "Come on. You better get home and sober up."

"Look who's blushing! You...shit," I countered, giggling.

The waitress, looking amused and a little condescending, brought the bill discreetly.

Caleb patted me on the back and we left, a bit unsteadily. He was very warm, pleasant to lean on as we navigated our way through the far-flung tunnels. I laughed loudly when a bunch of dangling charms and dolls hit me in the face as we went through the hub, and even louder when he tripped over his own feet with no obstacles in sight.

As we neared home, the alcohol started to wear off. It was a good long walk, and I'd gulped down half a carafe of water just before we'd left. Caleb had the other half.

"I really need to piss," he complained, a few turn-offs before the tunnel towards mine and Dad's place.

"Go ahead. I think there's a collection closet around the corner."

Caleb excused himself, and I soon reckoned that he was gone for more than just a leak. The farmers would surely appreciate his contribution, though the poor bastard on neighbourhood privy duty probably wouldn't. We were close to one of the huge deposit pipes, where the shit-haulers had to take the neighbourhood's donations, and even through the ground, I could smell it a bit. I hoped there were some hemp fluff bundles in the cubicle for Caleb; getting there just before the late-night privy-emptying and restock really sucks.

I couldn't be sure, with alcohol fuzzing my vision slightly, but I thought I saw something move in the shadows.

Instantly, adrenaline surged through my body, sobering me up. I listened carefully, though my heart started to hammer in my chest. I've seen too many freaky things in the last few days.

Having a heavily tattooed cuntgirl step out of the shadows was still the last thing I expected. You know things are fuuuuucked up when that is actually almost more scary and more surprising than having a monster pop out at you.

"Yo," she said, lifting her head to me.

"Hey," I said. "How's your night?"

"Not bad." Lola smiled at me, the thick kohl on her eyes crinkling in a friendly way. "Haven't seen you around in a bit. You staying out of trouble, unlike me?"

"Heh. Trying. I got a bit tipsy tonight. Haven't seen you in a while."

"Yeah. I've been busy." She frowned, and the elaborate curling red and black tattoos on her left cheek seemed to move on their own. Perhaps it was just the tunnel light.

"When you say busy…"

"I'm not talking about being busy sucking cock and pussy. There's some shit going on in Heaven Tubes. And for once, it's not just a bunch of Tunnel Rats selling harder hallies than usual."

I shook the last of the liquor haze from my head. "Why are you guys all the way up in the Heavens?"

She shrugged sadly. "You know how it is. There've been some red fights lately, and add a few cases of people going on breaky salvages, and the authy geezeys flip their shit and assume we're all anarchs."

I nodded sympathetically. Nathu, the mayor's son, has been lobbying with a few alders to legalize a brothel for the girls, but a lot of the older people—the ones who still remembered the time when everyone lived Up there—are pretty uptight about it. As a result, even clean girls like Lola end up in the Heaven Tubes, dangerously close to the surface.

"So. Trouble," I prompted her.

"I heard you got in a red fight? That's not like you, babes," she said, concerned.

"Nah. It's…well…it was the weirdest thing…you know I don't take hallies or shrooms or smoke up…"

"With your dad, he'd kill you with disappointment," she agreed, laughing. "Yeah? Try me."

"I fought a baby dragon. It clawed up my stomach, but me and some friends actually killed it. I had a claw,

64

but when we all went back so I could prove to Chloe and Raheed that it was real, the body—and then the claw—had turned into Dust. Seriously, I'm not kidding about the wounds."

To my utter surprise, Lola just nodded, looking serious. "Can I see?"

I lifted the bottom of my shirt, showing off the bandages wrapped around my belly, and peeled them off painstakingly. The large scrapes are pretty well scabbed over now, but the pink, healing flesh and scraped skin are still unarguable reminders that I was attacked by something. She winced sympathetically, and I wrapped myself up again.

She pursed her dark red lips. "I woulda laughed at you a long time ago, but I seen some strange shit lately. When I was a kid, I had nightmares about flying snakes under my bed. Don't laugh. I thought they were real." Her rough, exaggerated street drawl softened. "Mom and Dad always told me it was just a bad dream. Well, guess what Marco killed in the tunnel the other day? I'll tell you what, it wasn't a rabbit. It definitely had wings."

A cold rush of panic surged through me. "You're serious?"

"Tunnel black and blood red, light true and hope dead," she answered. I shivered. Gangers might have a bad rep, for good reason, but when one uses the Oath, it means they aren't shitting around.

"The nurse said she'd seen you guys coming in with similar wounds when I went in. Have you heard anything from the others?"

"I thought it was shroomy, hallie stuff, same as you, but there hasn't been that many red fights. A few, but not this shit."

Finally, he came out, the water and hand sanitizer still dripping from his hands. Caleb is very careful about keeping himself clean, to the germ-phobe extent that the rest of us make fun of him for it. It didn't stop him from running up to Lola and giving her a hug.

"Hey, missy! It's been ages since I saw you around. You aren't in trouble, are you?"

Lola dropped her street drawl again. "As a matter of fact, I was earlier. It seems Janelle and I have run into similar troubles. She mentioned that you ran into a baby dragon of some sort recently?"

Caleb shook his head affirmatively, wide-eyed. "I was there. I thought it was just dust, and that Janelle had fallen on something—"

"I'm not clumsy!" I protested.

"...but this changes things. Lola, maybe you should come and talk to people some time..."

She shook her head as quickly as he said it. "I don't think so. Kenny and Chloe...that whole situation is still a mess. No, I'll stay where I am, thanks." She looked sad for a moment.

"I miss you around here," I said quietly. "You know, you can always pop by, we can actually catch up—"

Lola gave me a strained smile, and her accent and tone changed again. "Nah. Thanks, doll, but you're upright. Cuntgirls and sugarplums like me don't get to hang around Tartarus with the rest of you. Authy geezeys will tantrum, and your rep will get oxidized. You don't need it."

"But…" Caleb looked sad.

"I'd better go," Lola said quickly. "I'll be around though. Just whistle and the Rats will be around to help. Marco and Davey and Lung are negotiating a whiteflag with the Worms until we figure out what's jiving up there. The Heaven Tubes are ours, and we want them to stay that way."

I glanced at Caleb, taken aback by her support; he looked as surprised as I felt. She flashed a smile, showing off her still well-kept teeth, and disappeared into the shadows of the tunnels again.

Caleb let out a long breath. "Well, fuck me. I'm not drunk anymore. You?"

"I'm jittery. I wasn't expecting that. To tell the truth, though, I was making out with Chloe a while back and we saw this…spider crawly thing, lower down in the tunnels…"

Caleb had gone several shades lighter in fear, though his features were composed. I worked my jaw.

"I don't like the sounds of this," he muttered. "We should talk to someone. Maybe even an alderman."

"Who's going to believe two sub-adults and a sugarplum? They'll think we're covering for some sort of ganger activity," I whined.

Caleb shot me an annoyed look. "Well, then you think of something."

"I'll try." We were outside my place. I stepped up to give him a hug. "Take care, man."

"I will. I'm not having Aiden get hurt the way that dragon got you."

"Well, good night." I enjoyed his hug for a moment longer.

"Good night." He walked off, keeping to the well-lit set of main tunnels.

Cracking the door open, I tiptoed in quietly. Dad had waited up for me and had fallen asleep with the cheap hempie paper and a book next to him in the chair. I put the kettle on to boil as quietly as I could and gently shook his shoulder.

"Hey, Dad. Sorry I kept you up. Caleb invited me for a couple drinks, but I'm back."

"Zzzz.. What? Oh good, honey."

"Dad, don't fall asleep in the chair. It's bad for your back."

"Wah? Mmm. Sure." He yawned and headed off to bed. "Night, sweetie."

"Night, Dad." I shook my head and sat down, feeling exhausted. The alcohol had come back into my system, but more so, the exhaustion.

I made some herbal tea and pulled out my journal to write this. It's pretty freaking late now, but I wanted to remember everything. The day went really well, and I'm still glad I got to relax with Caleb, but I admit I'm worried.

Even in spite of all that, I have to say I'm really happy that Lola and Caleb have my back. For all the drama our group sometimes gets into, people really care about each other. I can't really picture how everyone lived so far apart and barely working together unless they needed something. It can be suffocating, when everyone knows everyone—but at least I know people would notice if I went missing.

That's all for tonight. I hope I don't have too many dreams. If I do, well, I hope I don't see 'em when I wake up.

7—May 29, 0048 P.D.

I can't believe it's only been a couple of weeks since the attack. I don't feel so great today. I will admit that, surprise surprise, I've been having nightmares again. I've hit the point where I'm starting to sleep deprive myself just because I'm so reluctant to be unconscious.

The crawling dog-bats have been a frequent feature. Picturing those thin, dry legs crawling over my skin, those snapping jaws nipping into my flesh as the hollow blue eyes stare back at me, the yipping and scratching of the beasts, the swarm approaching at the sound of a hunting cry—

It's vivid. Very vivid. I could handle that if it wasn't for the fact that Jay was complaining she'd had a dream about her pet rabbit suddenly sprouting big, segmented spider legs, and bursting out of its cage to attack her. The rabbit is fine, of course, but just hearing her say it got me spooked.

Fucking Chloe won't leave me alone, either. She's whining that I'm not paying enough attention to her and whining about being scared, never mind that I'm just as scared. She keeps trying to make me take her out as a distraction, but it's not making me feel any better.

Also, my fucking stomach hurts like fucking crazy. Gods, this shit takes so long to heal. It's mostly all hard scabs so any kind of stretching makes them crack open and boy does it hurt. I'm lucky it's flesh though, so I keep telling myself. I am really, really tempted to tattoo it over.

Dad wouldn't like that much, and he wasn't thrilled when I mentioned that I'd seen Lola around. He can be very uptight about certain things—I'm going to sigh and call it the generation gap. I know he has a point, that the Rats would love to add someone like me—I mean, my knowledge is useful, too—but I'm not interested in them. Getting attacked by that dragon was plenty enough experience. I'm already hideously scarred for life, thanks, I'm not going to go trying to acquire more scars, even if I'd make an excellent Tommie.

I'm starting to wonder what the hell is going on. Apparently city officials are, too, because an official warning about a possible escaped wildcat from Up was released. They figure it wandered far down and mentioned in discreet terms that it "had been linked to probable injuries". They also warned people to start hiding their children.

Probable injuries, my barely-alive ass. I'm living proof of real injuries. Okay, enough. I need to think about real things. Solid things. Things that I can control.

Well, sort of control. If you can't tell, I'm leading up to more friend drama. Joy of joys. I love these people, but I almost hate them sometimes.

I knew that talking to Lola would get around, since we hadn't been entirely alone in the tunnels. Caleb isn't the sort to spread secrets around, and the mess with Chloe and Kenny and Lola was well known, but I didn't want someone else letting Chloe know I'd been talking to Lola before I had. (At this point, of course, like me, you probably want a scoreboard to keep track of all this crap. I'll try to arrange for a diagram at some point.) I decided that I didn't feel like getting into a mess, and went straight for the head of the problem. I like to avoid things, it's a fault, but sometimes you have to just go in and handle something, straight up.

"So, heard you'd been talking to Lola," said Kenny, catching up to me after work. He's not much of a talker, even less so than Jay. I winced inwardly. "You okay?"

"Uh, yep, just stretched something too much." So much for the 'inward' part. "What's up?"

"Oh, uh..." he blushed and looked away, trying to play innocent. "Just was, you know, wondering how she was doing."

"You should ask her yourself," I said warily.

"It's not what you think. All of that was a long time ago. I just wanted...to you know, make sure she's safe. With the stuff in the tunnels. Um. You know."

"Shouldn't you be keeping an eye on Jay, too?" by this time he'd led me towards a side tunnel, towards the Hub, a bit of a loop-around from home.

"Oh! No, of course, but Jay and I are fine. She knows about Lola anyway. And she's, uh, cool with it, if you understand."

I cocked my head to the side. The poly couples aren't common, but there are a few around. Most people are shy about being open, even though I know one or two who have plural partners. Still, they sort of expect you not to do any of that early, to wait until you're established before you take on an extra partner.

"I didn't really realise you guys were poly," I said, feeling friendlier. He grinned sheepishly at me.

"You know how it is. We're not ready for the big label stuff and if people knew we were, well, you know. It means more taxes. And, you know, if you get someone else formally, it means they want you to take Extra kids on, if you can...not that we'd mind, like, eventually, but we want time to ourselves first...I mean, yeah. You know."

"Hey sweetie!" Chloe bounced over from the Hub's direction. Perfect timing.

"Hi...baby! Good to see you!"

73

She pecked me on the mouth, and in spite of my doubts, it was a delicious kiss. I didn't have to look at Kenny twice to signal that the topic of Lola needed to be dropped, stat.

"How was your day at work?" I let her guide me towards her place.

"It was good," she said. She lowered her voice to a whisper, and waited until we'd passed into an even less populated tunnel. "Interesting thing, though. You heard about the 'mountain lion' scare? Well, in the papers I was processing for sector management, I saw a couple of reports on injuries and missing persons in the last quarter. They've gone up a lot. And people have even been going missing. Not just gangers, though a lot more of them were injured, too."

"Missing people?" I'd heard about it, but it's not an easy life, down here, and I hadn't really paid attention. I wished I had, now.

"Yep. I'll let you know if I see any more info. It was pretty basic, just numbers and only a little bit of analysis...but I have to admit, it looked strange." She looked at Kenny and me expectantly.

"Want to come over for tea?"

"I should probably get home," I said, begging off. "I feel rotten today and I didn't sleep all that well."

She looked mildly disappointed. "Shopping another time?"

Shit! "Of course! I'm just beat today." I pecked her quickly on the lips. "You can walk home with me if you want?"

"Oh, I have a couple of errands. Need to run down to the farming level and grab a couple of things. See you soon!"

Kenny, being Kenny, didn't seem to notice that Chloe seemed a little off, and being me, I can barely figure out why she's annoyed with me. Oh well.

We walked home anyway, Chloe being too caught up in whatever it was to notice that Kenny hadn't followed her.

"So, um, Lola," he said again. "I guess Chloe's still..."

"I don't know," I said brusquely. "Chloe refuses to talk about it to me. It's not like I wouldn't like to see her around again, but..."

The look Kenny gave me was very sad and soft, and I felt like a horrible human being.

"I know you miss having her around."

"She's been one of my best friends since I was a kid," he said, staring at the ground. "I just don't understand why Chloe was so jealous about..."

"Chloe..." I felt torn. Do you badmouth your own beloved girl friend if it means telling the truth? Or do you stay loyal? "She..."

He finished the sentence for me. "She doesn't share her toys well." I cleared my throat uncomfortably and Kenny went on. "I wasn't trying to sleep with her. I just love her. She—she was such a good friend, you know?"

"Kenny...I miss her too. I...maybe you should just invite her back some time."

He gave me a sad smile, and I wondered if he was half as dumb—well, blithe and unaware is the phrase Dad would use—as he seems most of the time. "She seems to like the Heaven Tubes more than down here with us. And you don't get to choose whether or not you like the Heaven Tubes."

I sighed. "Look...I...I don't want to be rude, but I'm dying here. I didn't get any sleep last night. I'm gonna head home if it's cool with you."

"Yeah, I get you. Take it easy."

"Thanks."

I headed on home after that, trying not to glance over my shoulder guiltily. Dad could tell something was up, but the simmered potatoes and carrot stew were a good way to cover things. I tried to be non-committal, but he coaxed a few details out of me. He didn't have much advice, but he asked some good questions for me. Dad's a good listener.

THE LOVED, THE LOST, THE DREAMING

As you might guess, I wrote all this and it took a while, but I really am going to try to turn in early. As long as I don't dream of dragons, of mom being dragged into the darkness, and of whispering voices from places out of sight, I'll be just fine.

I really hope I'm not going insane.

8—June 7, 0048 P.D.

I can't even tell you how much insanity has ensued. It all went down on the 4th. After that it was a matter of picking up the pieces, and...well, you'll see. No-one will leave me alone, but I'm making them.

It all started when I took Chloe shopping (which, as it happened, ended up being the day after I last wrote). We walked around, went through the stores, and as Chloe hummed and hawed at a dozen different shades, I fiddled with my bundle of cards.

The shops are pretty far from where I live, so it's an expedition to get to them, and involves going down a level or two to boot. Dresses we make tend to be pretty simple—hemp and recycled materials, knitted and woven from whatever we can grow and scraps of the past. Leather, too, of course, and goats and wool, but it's rarely as luxurious and exotic as the fine synthetic materials you can find Up there.

We were looking around at the high-waisted dresses in fashion this year, admiring the swooping uneven hemlines. The almost triangular shape to the skirt that resulted accented the legs nicely, while playing down a flat chest—unfortunately for Chloe, whose assets are reversed.

THE LOVED, THE LOST, THE DREAMING

Me, I'm built—what was the phrase Kenny used when he was drunk that one time?—like a brick shithole, so they did nothing but make me look like one of those old skyscrapers. That is, tall, square, and out of place underground. I do have good, very muscular legs, though, so the skirt versions of the dresses showed those off nicely. The tunic tops and tight belts that are in right now were okay too, showing off my waist, though I don't like the fact that the belts are basically underbust corsets. It's damn hard to breathe in those.

Chloe, though, loved it, and I ended up putting down more cards than I want to think about for her choices: a russet tunic (matching some of her hair) with a violet angle skirt, and a tan-coloured kid-leather corset with beads and shiny grommets on it. Still, the little clusters of LEDs ornamenting the edges of the sleeves and at the edge of the skirt were very pretty; I liked their patterns. There was some jewelry involved, too, a necklace with fancy old glass beads and a very jangly bracelet. All in all, expensive stuff.

She gushed and gloated, and forced me to try a few things on. I settled for a dress belt, its small utility pouches nicely embellished with beads and flowers, the LEDs set into the middle of the flowers as stamens and pollen would be. I also snagged a close-fitting knitted shirt with short sleeves and a delicate but subtle design. She made me buy the outfit myself, though. She did splash out for a skinny ravelled scarf of leftover fibres in a million colours, and a cute little black pageboy cap, trimmed with white LEDs around the band part. The one I usually wear—hey, it's good for stashing things in, too!—is pretty worn out, so it was nice of her. I managed to talk her out of making me change my clogs, though. I like my heavy boots just fine, thanks very much. Ditching those would be like cutting my feet off.

My one indulgence was the hat, but I managed to talk her out of heading to another jewelry store. It's not that I hate the stuff, but it either catches on things and breaks, or I find myself wanting to melt anything metal down to use for more wire. You can't imagine how expensive some of it is, too. I figure, don't wear jewelry you can't afford to miss. I'll wear bone beads, stuff like chokers or pins, once in a while, but Chloe always huffs and says I look like a Tunnel Rat. Meh.

In any case, we headed to the centre of the very airy-tunneled district and settled down in the indoor courtyard for a carbonated drink. Those were Chloe's treat. Relaxing and enjoying the birds, high-density greenery, and increased artificial sunshine, I was happier than I expected to be.

I found myself slightly happier when Jay and Aiden popped by. Aiden, as I said, tends towards being

Between, and he happened to be wearing an absolutely gorgeous minidress with a subtle stripe. He's always clean-shaven, and with his mid-length, light hair, he had an androgynous beauty I couldn't help admiring. The standard tights we all wear hugged his legs nicely, and the knit scarf he'd thrown over his shoulders drew Chloe's envious eyes as well as mine. Evidently, we weren't the only ones with a cycled-day off, or half-day at least. Jay, dressed sensibly in blue denim shorts and plaid button-up over a black tube, greeted us with a wide grin.

"Hey!" Chloe stood to hug them first. "Fancy seeing you here! Janelle just took me shopping."

I swapped hugs with them in turn, and Aiden ordered a fresh round of peppermint tea for all of us.

"Engagement looks good on you," I said. "You're all glowy."

He smiled. "Thanks. I couldn't be happier. Though I admit, I'm going to miss my days of hellraising."

"Oh boy." Chloe pursued her lips.

"Well, you know how it is. You get married, they give you extra taxes, you have to show enough maturity to raise a child before they give you an Extra..." we all nodded along, Jay rolling her eyes at it. Her mother tends to nag her about this stuff daily anyway.

"I know where this is going," said Chloe warningly. "And your idea of 'fun' usually involves things like putting up 'sewage rerouted' signs so we can go explore 'restricted' hallways. Uh-uh. I just got a promotion, and I don't want to do anything that'll get me in trouble, thanks so much."

"Aw, come on, babe," I protested. Sometimes, she's a killjoy, and sometimes, she's the sensible voice of reason we need.

"I'm sure it won't be that bad," Jay added quietly. "Hear him out."

"Well," Aiden admitted slyly, "I have to show that I'm a responsible adult to get us child-rearing privileges, but that's after we've tied the knot. Until then, I can still goof off a bit, and I wouldn't mind getting in a few kicks first."

"Oh, gods," I said. "Sounds like fun. I don't know what it is, but I'm probably in."

"Well I'm not—not until I know what you're up to, Aiden!"

"I say we do something at least a little bit troublesome," said Aiden, grinning.

Chloe rolled her eyes. "I got that much."

"What did you have in mind?" asked Jay, cautious.

"Let's hit up the Sunnyside district and go wandering around in the houses."

Chloe looked like she was going to lose her shit. The city Up there was huge, and it seems like no matter how much we scavenge, there's always more. Still, Sunnyside is farther out—of course, people have picked over the close houses—and more to the point, Sunnyside is less...stable. Dust there isn't as hazard-thick as in some quarters, but it is damn thick.

Even I chimed in. "Go Up there? Are you insane?" After my recent encounters with Dust, I wasn't keen on going into a thick area.

"But it's where the witch is supposed to be!" That had come from Chloe. At that, we all gave her the 'are *you* insane?' look.

Aiden lifted his hands in protest. "Oh, come on. It's deserted. And there's supposed to be some Untouched houses."

The possibility of fresh copper made us all pause. If there were other precious things, untouched wire, even seed packets, that would make it worthwhile. Not to mention there would definitely be cards laying around—even more easy money.

"Okay, but we're going there armed." Chloe was firm.

"Duh, it's regulation," I said.

"To the teeth," she clarified, looking edgy.

"If you're scared, I can get A-ma to make some charms," offered Jay. Chloe gave her a nervous smile.

"If you think it'll help." She fingered her evil-eye bracelet, a blue glass bead bracelet that I'd gotten her on her last birthday. The little black-and-white eyes on the clear blue beads stared up at her peacefully, as though wondering what she was so nervous about.

Tell the truth, I was nervous too. Chloe might be playing with her bracelet and worrying about 'the witch', but seeing strange things in the tunnels had made me a little more lenient towards her superstitious streak. "So, how are we going to convince them that a bunch of barely-adults should be allowed to run amok on the surface?"

"We could get official permission to salvage," suggested Jay. She's good with plans and paperwork, which is lucky, because handling us is like herding cats. I admit I was slightly less happy about her efficiency that day.

Aiden shrugged. "That kinda takes the fun out of it though. Do we really have to? I was just thinking of an afternoon out."

"Whoa, whoa, whoa. This afternoon? No way we can get permission to go right up this afternoon," I protested. "Especially on salvage."

"Won't know unless we try, will we?" Aiden had his charming smile on. Having gone a few nights with only a slight sense of disquiet in my dreams, rather than raging nightmares, I couldn't help softening.

"Unless you don't want to make back the price of our shopping trip," murmured Chloe. I shot a look at her. Sure, I'm careful with money, maybe too careful, but guilting me about it wasn't nice.

"Okay, fine," I said. "I'm totally in, 'witch' or not. Sounds like fun."

Chloe looked twitchy when I mentioned the witch, but gave Aiden a sharp smile.

For the sake of a little cash, and boredom, we were going to wheedle our way into going Up. I want to pretend I said it was a bad idea, but lure of dangerous fun and extra money made me as gung-ho as everyone else.

"Okay, fine," I said. "Let's blow this joint and get planning on the way to the registration office."

Aiden led the charge as we headed back towards the registration office. Surrounded by their excited chattering and planning, I felt unease sliding in despite myself. You don't forget several weeks' worth of nightmares and weird shit that Dust was directly implicated in just because money might be involved. Against my better judgement, I followed along. I suppose I was hoping to convince myself that it had all been a dumb nightmare or a hallucination from inhaling too much Dust the one time. Until now, Dust hadn't really hurt people directly—as far as I knew, at least—and it certainly hadn't come down deep, closer to us, on its own.

I was lost in my own thoughts as I followed them, only catching fragments of the plan.

"Hey, Janelle, you still in there? Knock knock?" Aiden had noticed my disquiet.

"Yeah, just antsy after everything lately. Are you sure we can make this work? It's short notice."

"And it's a slack time," said Jay confidently. "We'll be fine."

Chloe passed me a mask as Jay started to plan out loud. Get her talking about strategies and paperwork and logistics, and it's the one thing Jay won't shut up about.

"When did we walk by your house?"

"Like, ten minutes ago? Wow, you really weren't paying any attention," she answered, half to herself. Chloe had decided the Plan Was Good, and even the threat of a witch and dog-spiders wasn't going to stop her.

I decided, stupidly, that complaining wasn't going to do me any good. Chloe had her family's spare masks for us to borrow, and they were good quality—everyone has at least one spare set.

"I can tell you're still worried, Janelle," said Jay, "but you won't be alone. We'll be with you. And besides, you'll have a tightsuit and a big fucking gun."

An impish grin spread across her face.

The gun made me feel safer, but I couldn't help protesting again, futilely. "Oh come on, we've spent most of our time around the training area and the Museum entrance! If shit goes down—"

"...there are always rescue squads at the ready. You know that. As long as someone's around to rescue you, what do you have to worry about?" Chloe frowned at me.

"And we'll never get permission to go to Sunnyside! It's for level 4-5s and we're mostly what, level 2s? Maybe two of us are level 3s?"

The expression on Aiden's face made me cut my own protests short. He had the sneaky look he gets when he's figured out a way around something. He exploits the hell out of it as an orderly at the Extra kids' temporary home, giving the really lonely or badly injured kids way more cookies than they're supposed to get. Even when it's for less altruistic reasons, Aiden's ability to dodge regulations via careful misunderstanding is legendary. "Well, we could tell them we were going to a level 2 area..."

There was a round of silence.

"Okay," I managed. "Let me swing by home and I'll get my inner seal suit." Everyone else was carrying theirs, and the amused looks at my utter failure to pay attention were pretty well-deserved. I couldn't help laughing at myself.

"We're already at your place, you goose. Go grab it," said Aiden, smiling.

"Oh, fine, for you," I said, and closed the door behind myself.

I dropped the shopping bag in my room, not feeling inclined to put things away, apart from the paltry remains of the three silver I'd dropped on our shopping. Even the thought of it made me wince, but I tucked my money under the bed and let it be. The money, at least, could wait until later, but my friends were expecting me to get in and out of here as soon as possible.

The suit was where it should be, tucked into the emergency closet by the door. I wiggled into the stretchy, rubbery fabric reluctantly. For all that, stupidly and in spite of myself, I was looking forward to going Up, the suits suck to wear. You boil in them, and they're not exactly well-aerated—I mean, as far as I understand it, the original suits were designed for going underwater. I can't imagine going to an ocean and swimming around in them! The originals are rare, though, and reserved for the Crows; a complex plant-resin rubber over a couple of layers of fabric usually does the trick almost as well, and it's what all the rest of us have to use.

THE LOVED, THE LOST, THE DREAMING

I re-emerged with the suit on under my clothes, and a bag tucked under my arm. "C'mon, let's go see what kind of trouble we can find," I said. My stitches have healed up almost completely, but I'm still glad Dad wasn't around to scold me out of it.

By the point that we'd finished the walking-around and preparing, and I was wearing my suit, going Up didn't seem nearly as scary. I hadn't been suited up when I'd run into Dust before, and with so much time away from it, the effects had diminished pretty well. Even if it's stubborn, Dust never lasts long away from the surface. Sometimes, too, you can even recover from its effects. Sometimes. Going out prepared, armed and ready for seven kinds of hell, and surrounded by friends—well, I'll admit it, I was almost feeling cocky.

Besides, going Up as often as we have—well, okay, several times in the last few years—is a mark of bravery.

It's not that people don't go Up, it's that most people don't want to. Going Up is for trained professionals, people brave (or dumb) enough to go on an official salvage with the Crows, or a last-measures resort for very special occasions. Sure, everyone has to go Up at least once, to get their Level 1s in case of emergency, but most people don't after that. It's dangerous, it's dark, and Dust isn't exactly something you want to spend time around, even if you're armed to the teeth and sealed tight to your asscrack in protection. So, of course, you go Up when you're at the end of your childhood—all of us had done that a few years ago. After that, though, you can technically start training to go Up more often. Just, it's depressing and freaky. But we liked it anyway.

As I've mentioned, I've enjoyed going Up. It's interesting and I like seeing the old technologies. If I close my eyes, I can feel the space around me. Sometimes I even take a minute and imagine the real wind, the trees—the sunshine—not for long though. Up is not the place to be for daydreams.

As we got to The Dock, it was as impressive and formidable as ever. The deep underground parking garage it was adapted from is one of the biggest open structures we have.

As always, the main entrance funneled us into the office outside, leaving room to glimpse the grand parkade through its windows and doors, but preventing easy access. I didn't even have to look at Jay to know she was staring hungrily at the firing range, linked by a bright orange door.

"So many toys," she groaned. "So little time."

"Not until we do our paperwork," Chloe reminded her. Jay, because she's Jay, perked up at that.

It was Aiden's turn to groan. "I'll never understand how you can enjoy going through a firewall of bureaucrats."

Jay shrugged and didn't answer, apart from grinning.

"C'mon," I said, eyeing up the first reception desk. I winced inwardly when I saw Tonya.

She didn't miss a beat; she may look sedentary, but Tonya's reaction time to people walking into the offices is athletic.

Her broad, bread-loaf face expressed placid boredom rather than ambient annoyance, so it looked as though we'd caught her on the right day.

To get her to soften up, Jay greeted her in Tagalog. The attractive rhythms of their fluid, relaxed speech soothed my ears for a few moments as they exchanged pleasantries. Jay shot us a wink, her rich brown eyes sparkling with mischief.

"...and I'm glad your mother is doing well," finished Tonya, in English. "So, what can I do for you?"

"Well, I'm not sure you know," said Aiden, letting himself gush for a change, "but Caleb and I are getting married!"

"Congratulations," said Tonya lazily. She knew where it was going already, but she wasn't getting the forms for us to sign just yet.

"So, we were hoping to take Aiden shopping for certain things this afternoon," Chloe chimed in, "but we *just* couldn't find that special something..."

"So, you want permission to go Up." Tonya's face was impassive.

"Just sort of quickly," I said. "For the afternoon. We wanted to scrummage but...yeah."

"In other words, you'd be doing this anyway, but you're asking my permission so you don't end up in Sols for punishment." She crossed her arms. Uh-oh. I decided to try honesty with a pinch of charm; Tonya's the sort of person who doesn't care about my innocent, wide-eyed lying face.

"...Not even gonna lie, I think you have the jist of it, Tonya," I said.

Chloe cleared her throat and didn't look at me. If we got in trouble for saucing her, it wasn't going to be Chloe who supplied the pepper.

"Well," started Jay soothingly, "there's also the matter of our required rotational hours in each trade and area, and we can always use a few extra..."

"I think we can arrange something, if you're that bored," said Tonya, with uncharacteristic abruptness. Jay looked put off, expecting to have to wheedle more and getting what she wanted before getting to use her diplomatic expertise. Aiden seemed as to be relieved as

I felt to be spared a bure-y onslaught of verbal paperwork.

Looking boredly at a few papers, Tonya made a note. "There's a squad going up for a rotation this afternoon. Una's on it and there's a couple other Rediscovery Experts coming as well."

Una. Nathu's wife. That was going to be a lot less fun than we'd expected. Our princeling's mate wasn't known to be an unobservant type. And Crows, to boot, with her. Crows are some of the scariest people in Underlighter City as far as most of us are concerned— they deal with the gangers, go Up for salvage missions more than anyone else...they're what you'd call 'different' people.

If Tonya was going to suck the fun out of the afternoon on purpose, she couldn't've done a better job. There was no chance we were wandering far from the level 2 area at this rate.

"Can you show me that you all have your gun use and proximity certifications up to date?"

"We all did our yearly update on guns last month," Jay said happily. If it was up to her, she'd spend all of her time at the training centres or on the firing range. She flipped out her tidy wallet and flashed the cardette, and the rest of us rummaged and fumbled to get the chips out. Tonya took each of them in term, looking bored, and scanned them. She made a few notes in her papers and shooed us off while she mumbled a few burey-coded bursts of speech on the phone. She shooed us away for the call and turned her back, but I did catch the phrase, 'annoying teenagers'.

We sat down to do the paperwork—there were only a few forms, but every time you go up, you have to sign a consent and take a brief and completely random quiz on the hazards. We helped each other out with a couple of particularly nasty multiple-choicers that only offered two equally bad options, but in no time, the annoying part was done. Jay bounced over to hand in the papers, and Tonya took them from her hand, faster than a striking snake.

"Let's see...Level 3..." (me) "...Level 2 with extra medical..." (Aiden) "level 3..." (Jay) "And level 2. Ms. De la Cruz, your permit is two days from expiry. Normally, we don't let people up when they're within the five day range of expiry." Chloe swallowed.

"Does that mean she can't come with us?" Aiden used his special soft tone of voice, and looked incredibly sad, as did Jay. I decided to do my best crestfallen face to match them. Cute isn't really my thing, but boy can I work disappointment.

Looking at the three of us, Tonya squinted for a moment, and finally, howled with laughter. It wasn't exactly the intended effect. Especially when she just kept on giggling and snickering.

"Oh, fine," she said, snickering and wiping a few tears of amusement from the corner of her eyes. "I haven't seen anyone in here to go Up in at least a day, and you all look so damn silly. I'll get May to check your equipment and get the outer-suits, and then you can go to the gun room."

Jay let out a burst of grateful Tagalog and Tonya shrugged, answering in English. "Just don't do anything stupid that'll make me wish I changed my mind, okay? Have a good afternoon." She looked down at her paperwork, dismissing us. At the green door of the inspection room, May was waving to us, and there was an unseemly rush as our quartet went for her.

The green door swung open. "Hey, kids! Let's get you checked out." She greeted us with a grin that crinkled her almond eyes. She said something in Chinese to Jay, who fumbled it in return, and May laughed.

"No need to be shy! You know the drill. Come in, come in!"

Once the door to the office was firmly shut, May relaxed. She doesn't so much walk as bounce from place to place on pure energy. Running her hands over our suits, she declared them perfectly sealed. The mask inspections came next. I hadn't changed my filter in a while, but otherwise, she declared us safe, and handed us the outer layers.

The slightly baggy outer layer of the suits locked in the heat, but the masks, fortunately, were coated in moisture-repellent stuff that kept them from fogging on the inside. Chloe and Aiden were the only ones with long hair; I keep mine short, and Jay is in a pixie cut phase right now. May tied bandannas over our heads before clamping the skull-caps on, and then, finally, let us put on the heavy masks, with their built-in comms.

The world was dark and we looked sinister, inhuman.

"You're beautiful! C'mon, kids, time to get your guns and get you Up there." She bounded out of the green door and towards the orange, and, like obedient Crow fledgelings, we followed her. Jay looked unreasonably happy, and I could understand just why, because I felt the same. All of us were excited, forgetting our fears and eager to go explore the old, mysterious world above us.

I won't lie, one of the parts I like best is getting a chance to carry my gun around. Generally it stays in a case in the lockers here, and she's nominally shared property, but really, I see that baby as mine. A sweet little Smith & Wesson M&P .38, with a 4 inch barrel: common as dirt, back in the day, and still common now, but dammit, she's a beauty. May had taken me out to shoot rabbits and rats for target practice in the tunnels. That alone had given me some serious respect for what my S&W could do—that is, kill—but I liked the feel of it, the weight of it at my hip. I'm far from helpless and I can throw a punch pretty well, but wildcats and really big stray dogs like a bit more convincing than a punch alone will offer. And I won't lie, I feel pretty cool carrying it.

My friends have their preferences, too. Jay is meticulous and devoted to her Glock .38, and Chloe has a dainty little S&W Model .64 with a pearly white handle. Aiden hates guns and can barely be convinced to shoulder a beat-down .22 shotgun.

"You should come back to the range some time soon," May urged us. "That back door doesn't get nearly enough use."

Jay laughed. "We're here every other week as it is!"

"Yes, but it's been a while," May wheedled. "And I know you're all going to get rusty and forget to exhale when you fire before you know it."

"We're not that bad," Chloe protested.

"No, but if you don't practice, you will be!"

"I'm sorry, May," I said, my voice sharper than intended. "I got attacked a while back and I wasn't exactly in fighting form. I wasn't trying to stay away."

The Crow in May, her professional side, cut to the surface, and she dropped her usual hyperbolic cuteness. "Are you sure you're in good enough shape for an expedition?"

"Yeah, I'm fine," I said, annoyed. "Look. Sorry, I've just..." Chloe tucked an arm around me, her attempt at comfort, but I felt possessed by her rather than soothed. Through the suits, it just felt weird, not reassuring.

May's face was covered by the mask, but I knew her almond eyes were watching and analysing my movements. After a long pause, she shook her head a little and looked towards the door from the gun room to the elevators. The blue door that would lead us to the firing range looked far more comforting, and I contemplated talking Aiden into shooting a few rather than going up. Still, the simple grey door that led through the training gym beckoned. May opened it, leading us away from the weights and esoteric bars and balances.

Our heavy footsteps echoed martially in the concrete palace. The grim, sharp lines of the old-fashioned concrete pillars and the angular silvery beams on the roof were a reminder of a different time. Back then, being underground had been the exception in life, not the rule. The distant white box-room of elevators awaited us.

The ride up is always nerve-wracking. I never get used to leaving my stomach behind when the elevator surges towards the surface. The hum of electronics I'm not allowed to look at, the twitchy feeling in my limbs, the terrifying feeling that I'm leaving my home behind...these are the things that scare me about going Up. And yet, they're the feelings I secretly crave, at times, because they always promise new and strange wonders. Or at least, they did promise those feelings.

I wish I had known what kind of wonders we were in for, this time. More soon...I need to take a break from this. As I told you at the beginning, it went down days ago, but I'm having to write it in parts. Should I have listened to my instincts, at first? Maybe. Maybe not. More soon, that'll help me think about it.

9—June 8, 0048 P.D.

So. Like I said, I'm back. Having to cram this in at lunch time—I never take my journal to work!—feels so awkward, but I need as much personal space as I can get, away from people. Back to my...adventures.

The elevator opened on the old apartment lobby. It was a tall building, and one of the first to be salvaged. I know the building well—it's one of the main training grounds—but it's still creepy as hell. Being able to sense that you're far above the ground—above! Not below!—without being able to see the distance, is terrifying. Some of the rooms are full of Dust, and very dark; others were pretty well-sealed, and it's mostly confined to the outside.

Chloe was already hanging back uneasily. The ambient level of Dust in here was low, but it was still there—dimming our senses, deepening shadows, fading colours. Ian, a brave soul, was sitting at a desk.

All of our masks were set to the open channel automatically, rather than being dialed down to 'local' or 'intimate' range.

"Welcome," Ian said, his voice friendly. "Ready for your expedition?" I don't think I've seen him more than once or twice without his suit; he's one of the most avid Crows, living close to the surface.

"You bet they are," said May. "I'm going to head back down. Kids, sign your names on the form and stay out of trouble. How long will you be?"

"No more than a couple of hours," I guessed. "Let's say three."

"With Una on rounds, you can bet someone will be coming to check on you if you're not back by then," Ian reminded us.

In spite of my standard-issue protective gloves, skin-tight and slightly nobbly on the fingertips, the pen slipped in my hand, left a shaking line in the middle of my name. The others followed me, signed their names on the lines. Our names on the paper seemed so tenuous and frail, considering what they represented. A line on a page in thick, gritty ink--the only thing tying me visibly to the world below, proving that this was the last place I'd been seen. I decided not to think about what would happen if I went missing, if the suit was ripped, if I ended up stumbling around Up here...

"Good luck!" said May, returning to the elevator.

Ian nodded us forward. There was nothing to do but go into the world, and see what we could find. Aiden moved ahead of me, leading the charge forward.

As we opened the apartment doors, we found ourselves in a grey world. The light was somewhat visible, here, in one of the thinnest areas. It wasn't entirely unlike the diffuse light during the evening cycle, but below, the light doesn't change like this. Patches of darkness swirled across the sky, across buildings. Even without Dust crawling in my system, the world was full of a moving, liquid blackness. Artificial light and the light of the sun could shimmer through, faintly, but barely enough to see by. I couldn't see their faces through the masks, but the way my friends straightened and slipped their hands to their holster belts told me everything I needed to know about their feelings.

The weird light and the interfering Dust were thinner in higher places, matching the air. As a level 1 zone, it was still relatively safe.

We dialed down to the 'local' frequency. The strangeness of the old world surrounded me. The big, angular box houses were all empty, sinister-looking, and many were covered in greenery. The wide streets covered in pavement—not walls, but streets and roads! It always amazes me—were broken and covered in plants and potholes. Thick grasses in front of the houses and the enormous trees dominated. A few of the clumsy, boxy cars they used to drive were still lining the streets, but they'd more or less rusted into place.

Half lost kingdom, half forest primeval. We followed the road. Its signs had rusted and been replaced by our own. All of us knew "Elton Street" reasonably well, but the marvel of the big, open world still hadn't worn off.

"Let's take Mercer to the Old Uptown though 18th, and then we can ease our way towards Sunnyside," said Jay, interrupting my musings. "I mean, 18th ave goes right into Sunnyside."

"Sure," I said. "You're the navigator."

We all walked close together, in a diamond-shaped formation. There were wild dog packs howling in the distance, and the forest-neighbourhood was alive with birdsong and insects. Their lives had continued uninterrupted—it was just ours that had been stopped.

There was no sense in picking through the houses around here—in spite of their rather decrepit condition, they'd been combed finely. Not even a stray marble remained, for the most part; even bones had been interred.

As we walked further down the grassy road, things changed. The darkness was lower, the Dust, thicker— there was less diffuse light, and our lanterns seemed to throw off less illumination. Down below, in our homes, the dark was never absolute—there's always a candle or a light burning somewhere, even if it's only in the paintings of windows. With a painted moon and LED studded stars to watch us, we could sleep easily. Here, even awake, it was a different matter. The darkness was alive.

It moved like water through the streets, thick strands and pools of near-opaque blackness swirling around us. Most of it was thick, greyish, foglike, but with a life of its own. Shapes blurred and shimmered in the distance and in shadowed-corners. There was still some sunlight in the sense that the world had a faint glow, but not much. Dad and old movies have given me an idea of 'dusk' and 'twilight', but this isn't like it—no stripey colours in the sky. Just murkiness, and shadows, and strange angles where the lingering light and Dust play on shapes.

Chloe was already shivering, and I didn't blame her. At this point, we were farther afield—out of the Level 2 area, which is partly but not fully explored, and heading towards the Level 3 zone. The murk was deepening, the houses and greenery even more shadowed and twisted by the imperfect light. The old people say our world above is one of endless night, but it's more than that. Night doesn't move on its own, and night doesn't follow you around.

"I guess we should probably start looking for things," said Aiden. His voice was a little wavery. This was supposed to be a Level 3 area, but the Dust levels were higher than expected—closer to 4. I widened the range of my 'Local' signal. Luckily, Jay stepped in.

"Keep your comms open, people. It's better to say something you regret than getting Lost up here. It looks like the Dust is thicker than we expected. I say we keep this trip tight, and revert to proper protocol, over."

"Agreed, over," I said. Next to me, Chloe was starting to cling, brushing my arm constantly. It was annoying.

"Can we just go look at a house and get it over with? Over."

"Remind me, what are we looking for exactly, Aiden? Over," I added. I tried to keep my tone light, but I could feel my palms tingling, beginning to sweat.

"Well, to be honest, I was hoping for fancy artificial flowers, but anything nice—vases, whatever, will do. Over."

"Okay, I guess we should hit them, over," I replied.

"Which one should we do first? Can we do the nice one with the door that's still standing? Over."

"Chloe, we have to check it for hazards first. Unless you want the roof for a hat, over," snapped Jay. It wasn't like her to be sharp, not at all. A stealthy trickle of fear down my spine made me pause. If Jay was already nervous, this didn't bode well.

Sunnyside had probably been well-named a long time ago, but now, with its decrepit streets and half-fallen-in houses, the name couldn't have been more ironic.

Chloe mumbled something too quickly to understand.

"Chloe, please speak clearly when you're on comm, over," I said.

"I said watch out for the witch, over," she said. A high-pitched note cracked in her voice.

"Um, sure. That house over there, the one Chloe picked out, over," I said. If Chloe was panicking, it was best to indulge her. I couldn't decide whether to worry or be annoyed. Feeling the reassuring, second-nature weight of my foldie on my back and the strap of the holster, I forced myself to calm down. I'd been out to these areas before, or close to them, anyway.

The house Chloe had chosen was more intact than the rest, with a big attached garage that had diamond-paned windows on top. It was older in style, according to what I remembered from school, but not ancient like some of the smaller places. Half of those, more than half, were in awful shape or had already been pillaged. That meant the walls would probably be in awful shape, but if the mold hadn't completely taken over and if its original owners hadn't returned to ransack it, it might be a gold mine. You could never tell until you took the door down. There were a few times in training for my Level 3 when we'd even found ancient bodies, still, preserved, and picked clean to the bone, lying peacefully in the houses.

Just then, Jay broke comm protocol. "Hey! Look!" I turned, and in the grime on the street, there was something glittering.

I knelt down and picked it up, examining it through the dark lenses of the mask. "Looks like a button. A nice one, too. Plastic. Not worth breaking protocol for, over." I handed it back to her. "That'd be nice for a sweater or a brooch, over."

Jay surveyed the ground closely as she took a step or two closer to the house. I wondered what had caught her attention this time.

"Sorry for breaking protocol, but I found another one! Over."

"Cool! Over." She held it up, a brassy thing this time, with a bit of plastic in its centre.

"Good start! How do you guys feel about the garage? Over." Aiden sounded hopeful, and I didn't blame him; it wasn't every day you found things lying in the street, in good condition.

I cleared my throat nervously and decided, hell with it, I'd be honest with them. "I won't lie, guys, I have a weird feeling that we should just head back. Over."

I'd intended to make this Aiden's show, since it was his shopping trip, but I will admit that being Up changes me. It's the one place I'm willing to lead. Normally I'll say my bit, but I won't disrupt the order of things. When I'm Up, I feel calm.

Usually, anyway. Today, we were all jittery. I couldn't help cranking my neck around, watching for hidden eyes.

"Neg, let's stick around for a bit, since we came all this way—over," said Aiden. It was a reasonable request, and I wondered if I was being silly.

"I know what you're saying, Aiden, but I don't like this either and I'm going to flip my lid if I have to stay out here much longer. Over," said Chloe.

"Widen frequency range to open, guys. We're pushing the boundaries and I don't want any accidents, over," I said decisively.

At this point, we'd been standing still, in our diamond shape, backs towards each other—there was a soft stirring in the grass, a faint breeze, but I thought I heard something rustling as well.

"We haven't got all day, guys. We've been walking around for at least forty five minutes, over," said Aiden.

Chloe stuffed her gun back in the holster and broke, running for the house.

"Chloe! What are you doing! Over!" She didn't answer, but her breathing sounded harsh and frightened.

I shook my head in frustration, and did something stupid and logical—I ran after her.

Chloe isn't the most athletic, but I had no idea she could manage the sprinting she did that day. She breezed past me and went for the house, throwing the door open. I heard a series of thumps as she raced down the stairs.

"Chloe, wait! Come back up these stairs right now, that's an order! Over!" The comms crackled with static. I heard whimpering and a shriek. There was no time to think. "Jay, stop all salvage activity and cover the entrance. Aiden, cover Jay and stay near the entrance of the house. Over."

"Copy that," spat Aiden. "What's going down? Where the hell is Chloe? Jay, where are you going? Over."

"Aiden, pursue Jay and try to bring her back here, copy that? Over."

"Copy. This is such a disaster. Over." Silently, I agreed.

The house was dusty, and Dusty, full of darkness and full of shadow. It was shockingly dry inside for all that; it looked as though the windows and doors had rotted far less than they should have. Our city, drier than many, had more than a few such time capsules, and they were always worth their weight in cards for the haul. I almost hesitated—the place was a wealth of technological trinkets and knick-knacks. There would definitely be some nice things for Aiden, and probably some excellent opportunities to pillage. Lace doilies on the bureaus and nice white table-cloths—people with disposable income and a sense of class had lived here...

I shook my head and frowned at myself. It was no time to be greedy. I couldn't smell anything besides the reek of my own sweat inside the suit—wasn't supposed to be able to. Why, then, did I smell blood?

"Chloe? Are you here? Copy? Over," I called. It's hard to hear anything from outside when you're in a suit, but I could feel the silence.

There was a long pause, and then, a crackle of static again. "—kkkhhhhfff—Janelle?—kkkkcccccfff—"

"Chloe? Do you copy? There's heavy static on your end. If you're in a Dust rich area—"

"—kkkkkfffff—I'm—h hhffff—help!"

I took a deep breath, feeling the panic boil in my blood. There was no time for that. Where the hell were Jay and Aiden? No time. One person at a time.

"Chloe, wherever you are, stay put, I'm coming for you. I'm going to work my way through the house. Over."

There was no harm, so I took a right and went through the living room and attached dining room, looking for clues to where she might be. This area was undisturbed—the pictures were still in place, the purple velvet couches looked immaculate and unused. The colour looked familiar; I looked away.

Then, around the corner, I saw the gleam of razor-pointed teeth in a mouth that was too wide. I had my gun in hands within a breath, and waited, listening. Only silence.

The child-sized shape was gone.

I shook my head. The place was full of dark, and Dust was starting to press on the windows. There was a small clock built into the corner of the mask, and I didn't like what I saw. Time was running strangely and far too fast. Shaking my head, I kept walking.

The comm crackled again and I glanced up the stairs. I could have sworn I'd seen something moving in the corner of my eye again. That was it, the gun wasn't going back in the holster. "Jay and Aiden? Are you there? Do you copy? There's still no sign of Chloe, but I heard her screaming. I'm currently searching for her, over."

Cold fear washed over me as my comm crackled. "Ffffff—kkkk—hhhh—emergency! Hhhrrr—kkkfff—"

Suddenly, the line cleared. "You should go home, little girl," said a faraway voice. It was soft as silk and raw as rusty steel beneath, a growl beneath a purr.

"Who are you?" I demanded. There was only silence, not even static. The house seemed empty.

The whole thing reminded me, suddenly, of the dream I'd had from time to time as a kid. I mentioned it before. It comes up when I get stressed out...it's not the only thing I've been afraid of, but it was a damn creepy dream. You know the one. The guy in the purple velvet suit...the little girl with blood on her teeth...this time, though, there was no grown-up to come rescue me, just me, my heart pounding, here, in this house, with my little gun and my girlfriend nowhere to be found. And worse of all, I was still awake.

The thumping and screaming were almost a relief. I was sure, this time; it was coming from the basement. Circling back around and ignoring the old blood stains on the floor, I finally found a set of stairs down, leading from the kitchen to a den on a lower level. What was with this house? It seemed not only to be bigger on the inside, I could have sworn I'd just gone in a circle.

Still, there was no time to think. My comm came to life.

"Janelle, help! Please! Oh gods, they're everywhere!"

Without another thought, I sprinted down the stairs.

THE LOVED, THE LOST, THE DREAMING

10—June 9, 0048 P.D.

I kept my back to the wall as I rounded the corner. It was dark, dark as only a place no one has seen in years can be. I crossed the door, leaning against it rather than just running down the steps. I needed to think, even with my blood pounding and my heart in my throat; I needed to overcome this panic. I took a few deep breaths.

The garage door was right across to me. So close. I took a deep breath and leaned to the door. It opened without my help, and I saw a small white child's hand, covered in blood. It reached for me.

I didn't have to think about it; I fired. There was a scream, and it wasn't very human. I was too busy tearing the door to the garage open and slamming it again to look at what, or who, was screaming. I knew one thing, though, it hadn't been Chloe.

There was a door leading outside in the left, east corner of the garage. The garage was empty, lucky for me, just two carcasses of vehicles. Well, not empty enough—something skittered across the floor, then several more somethings.

"Janelle, help!" that was definitely Chloe. No time to worry about whatever was in the garage.

I threw myself at the outer door, unlocked it, and tore it open. I could tell there was going to be a bruise on that shoulder, because I had taken the stairs down with too much momentum, but there was no time to worry about a little scuff mark now. Adrenalin ripped through my system.

It was a good thing, too, because when I opened the door, I was surrounded by a dozen chittering, eight-legged monstrosities that were much larger than anything I'd seen yet. Their yellow teeth were snapping and their dead blue eyes stared at me hungrily out of doggy skulls.

I kicked two out of the way, hard, and felt the bones snap rather than hearing them. The door to the garage was still open; I hadn't had time to shut it before rushing out. Based on the things moving in the shadows, and the darkness drawing closer around us, that was going to be a very bad mistake.

Worrying about any of that was impossible, though. Chloe was in the middle of the lawn and the spiders were worrying her, snapping at her limbs and trying to chew through the suit. And oh, she was screaming.

Kicking and picking the spiders up bodily, throwing them out of the way, I ran to her. Her suit integrity was breached, which was already bad, and there was blood on it, which was worse. That didn't stop me from yanking her up by the arm almost hard enough to dislocate it.

I had my comm on open frequency, but I cranked it up and flicked the emergency switch for maximum range. "Requesting support! We have an emergency! Repeat! We have an emergency! Hostile animals! If anyone can hear us, we are on 15th and 23rd in Sunnyside and require backup! Repeat, we're two blocks down from the old fire station, at 15th Ave and 23rd St in Sunnyside, over!"

Thankfully, the comm screamed good news into my ear. " Copy that, Janelle! We're coming! Over!"

"Copy, Aiden! Do you have Jay? Over!" I shot at a couple of the dog-spiders and got in front of Chloe, who was still screaming and panicking. I couldn't see her face, but I knew she was upset. Reaching over, I forcibly dialed down her range to 'local'.

"Yes! Long story! Is Chloe okay? I thought I heard screaming, and lots of it, over."

"Affirmative! We have a situation and there's no time to talk! Just get your asses to the front lawn of the house! Over!"

"Copy that!" Jay's voice. I breathed a sigh of relief.

The dog-spiders were advancing on us, and the dark shapes moving in the garage were breaking into pieces. More spiders, or worse? Turning and running was risky; they were moving in packs, and all it would take was a fumble to ensure that Chloe or I would go down and not get up again. Besides, she wasn't in condition to run. I grabbed her by the back of the suit and dragged her with me, slowly backing towards the street. The dogspiders were following and advancing.

"Kick them, stupid!" I screamed at her. "Kick at them! Over!" She was screaming and crying like a child, and I couldn't blame her.

Suddenly, a cool, brisk voice cut into my comm. "Crow unit 1 copies you. Una Biazotto here. We have your location, and we're coming in. Hold them off. Over."

The tiny fraction of my brain that could still think was trying to decide whether I should be more frightened of Una or of the spider-dogs. Since their sharp teeth were closest to my ankles, and trying to close on my hob-nailed leather boots, I decided to deal with them first. Una's teeth, I could handle later.

"We're here!" Aiden and Jay burst on from the side, guns at the ready. There were more spiders than ever and they were going for us, trying to crawl up my legs, onto Chloe.

I was glad, once again, for my little Smith &Wesson .38. I had at least 15-20 cartridges in the holster's pouch and four shots loaded. I popped off at least two with a full round of shots. Jay's Glock took care of a few more. Chloe was still too panicky to draw. I managed to knock off another, but my hands were starting to shake. Watching the way they moved, the unnatural shape of their limbs…it was hard to keep the others focused.

Chloe's shrieking through the com was unbearable. I lost my temper and whipped my head around to look at Aiden and Jay.

"Don't just stand there! Throw some fucking rocks at the fuckers! Shoot! Over!"

Funny how telling people what to do helps so much when they freeze. Aiden was the first one on it, fumbling for the nearest heavy object and chucking it to Chloe's left. It landed between two spiders, crushing the abdomen of one. The dog-spider let out a terrible clicking, stridulant yelp, a kind of rasping chitter of fear that I could hear clearly through the mask. Apparently, rocks scared them more than guns.

The comm snapped on. Men's voices this time, the first, even-toned and competent. "Chang Ho here. We're on our way. Confirm your position, over."

"We have a situation! Please send backup! We're two blocks down from the old fire station, at 15th Ave and 23rd St in Sunnyside, over!"

"Confirm 15th Ave and 23rd as current location, over?"

A different voice cut in. "Confirmed, over! Be prepared to shoot, over!"

It was a full ten blocks and our little chat had taken at least a minute. I prayed they'd be here soon, because the dog-spiders just kept coming. Dozens of tiny yellow fangs snapped at us and the air was full of evil, shrill chirps and yelps. Aiden was throwing things with good accuracy and Jay was picking them off carefully; I was doing my best to keep up with them. The way they were going for Chloe and then coming forward, dodging toward us, rather than skittering off, was eerie. Pack animals run when they've lost too many members, but the little horrors just kept coming. Darkness was all around us, the lanterns on our masks' foreheads only just cutting through it.

I noticed that I was out of bullets. Please, I thought. Just a few more shots.

And then, suddenly, I found just a few more. They must have rolled deeper into my pouch, or something. No time to think, only to reload and only to fire.

The ground was spattered with dark blood, crunching wetly underfoot. The armour on the dog-spiders and their dexterity made them hard to hit, but when bullets met their dry little skulls, the wet cracking sounds never failed to satisfying. The lamps were doing an okay job of giving us illumination, but if the Dust thickened any more, we would lose that very quickly. And shooting blind...I didn't have time to think about it. It was hard enough taking proximity statuses, yelling at Aiden and Jay to keep them from freezing, and trying to kick, stomp, and shoot my way to Chloe without getting a good suit breach to slow me down.

Then, the cavalry arrived. Their dark, sleek suits were lit with surface LEDs and their masks weren't the clumsy filter-and-centre-lamp designs the rest of us had—smaller, lighter, sleeker things I'd never seen before. Chang walked over and without a word, hefted Chloe in his arms. He set her down several feet away. I glanced over my shoulder and backed towards them, firing at a few and kicking as I walked, just for good measure. Una unslung an AK-47 from her back in a swift, fluid motion, and turned into Death herself.

Our crappy little pistols were nothing compared to hers for power. Hunter, the other person, covered her back while Chang provided support. Jay faced outwards to the street, keeping watch, while Aiden got to his knees. He was the one with the first aid kit, and based on the amount of blood on Chloe, it was a good thing we had him. Some of that was definitely hers.

I couldn't look at her while Una was firing. In minutes, the place was painted in blood and covered in crackling shells. The rest was silence. No wild dogs, no birds.

Una finally turned around, and her body language gave none of her feelings away.

"Permission to speak freely," she said. "Protocol released."

"Thanks," I managed to rasp.

"Let's get you back to the apartments," she said, her voice surprisingly gentle. "The Dust is coming, and you don't want it to get any darker. Are any of you others injured?"

"I won't know until I get my suit off," I answered. "Aiden? Jay?"

"I...let's just get back."

It was a long, grim walk. Chloe wouldn't let go of my hand the whole way back. Ian took one look at us as we were approaching the glass entrance and just flung open the elevator doors. We walked straight through and down, the dark and the Dust at our backs. Even when we were safe inside and had left the night behind, she shook until we got below the surface. The minute we were back in the elevator, she let out a big old sigh of relief, and then, the tears started again. I couldn't see Una's face through the mask, but her stiff body posture told me she didn't approve of Chloe's crying.

I'm going to say something that is going to make me sound like the most horrible person ever born. There were a couple of minutes, during her hysterics, in which I'd wished I'd left her out there. It wouldn't have been so bad except that she was still screaming and crying the whole way down the elevator. The rest of us were dead silent.

When we poured into the separate docking room, Una brusquely threw all of us in the direction of the showers, right next to the opening of the elevators. She and Chang and Hunter were completely untouched, but our suits were in bad shape. Not for long, though.

Hunter, a beautiful dark-skinned person who was so Between I couldn't tell xis gender, took care of Aiden and Jay, getting them out of their suits and masks faster than I thought possible. We all had underwear on underneath, of course, but if Hunter had been any less gentle, it would have been humiliating. Chang, a gentle and surprisingly young guy, handled Chloe. I wondered if I should feel jealous as I watched him remove her suit and peel her inner layer off, but there was nothing erotic about her. I could see that she'd pissed herself from the yellow patch on her white underwear, and felt a mix of sympathy and disgust.

Una handled me and that soon distracted me from everything. Her blue eyes were cold as they inspected me. I felt very naked as she took off my suit, her calloused hands sliding over my limbs. Those cornflower eyes met mine, and softened for a moment. I noticed that she was surprisingly young, with a soft mouth in her hard-boned face. She was tall, though, and solid, a real Valkyrie in the flesh. I let myself shudder, and it wasn't the fear and the cold. The guilty part of my mind screamed that this was the worst possible time to be looking around, that I should worry about the pink-tinted, bloody water running down the drain more than some woman's hands on my body. It was a bad time to react to someone's touch, and the sudden feeling of the water pounding into my skin killed the moment.

The water stopped, finally, when I wasn't ready for it, and left me cold and shivering. When they finally gave me a towel to wrap around my naked, shivering body, Una glanced at Hunter and Chang, and jerked her head towards the door. They looked at her and obeyed without having to ask a single question, picking up all the equipment and and escorting Chloe and Aiden out.

That meant Jay and myself were left behind. I glanced at Jay nervously.

"So," said Una, tucking her hands behind her back and straightening, "what exactly just happened up there?"

"Why don't you tell us?" I snapped, surprising myself. "You're the Crow. You spend way more time around Dust and Up there than we do."

Una looked back and I felt like I was swimming in ice. "I don't think you understand how this works, Ms.

Cohen. I'm not going to tell you about what I've seen on the surface, because this isn't a discussion."

"Oh yeah? Is it a friendly chat, then?"

"No, it's going to involve you ladies, possibly your pals there as well, getting a lot friendlier with me." She smiled and it was terrifying. "Especially since you, Janelle, were the one holding off those...creatures...for most of it."

Mercifully, she turned her searchlight, cutting eyes on Jay. "As for you, Ms. Kao, I would love to have a nice long chat about what happened when you went missing back there."

Jay swallowed, but looked back defiantly. She said something in Tagalog that I didn't catch.

Una laughed, and ruffled her hair, and said something in a different, strange language. Jay and I looked at each other, confused.

"You're not the only one who can swear in other languages, kid," she said, smirking at us. She couldn't have been more than twentysomething, really not much older than us at all.

"Look," I said. "I'm tired, Jay's tired, my buddy's tired, and my...girlfriend almost got mauled by her own nightmares. Can we leave this off for today?"

Una perked up at the mention of 'nightmares'. Her eyes nailed me to the wall, and gods help me, I liked the way it felt. "Nightmares?"

"Nightmares," I confirmed. Even Jay was looking at me, interest and fear naked on her face.

"I'll look forward to this conversation," she said, her voice soft and dangerous. Abruptly, softness came through, like light through the cracks. "I'm sorry for badgering you when you're all very upset and tired, but what you have to say could be very, very important."

I found myself nodding. "I...yeah. It's okay. Um. How will I find you?"

She smiled, and I felt my knees go weak, even though it was a very professional, thin smile. "No need to worry about that, I'll find you. We'll arrange something."

I nodded. She dipped her head to Jay, and rewarded her with a smile. Jay hesitantly smiled back. Through the glass, Una glanced at Hunter and Chang. Hunter was already on the way back, Chang nowhere to be seen.

"They were pretty scratched up," said Hunter, xis voice soft and raspy.

"Chang took them to the infirmaries? Good." Una gave xer a much warmer, more equal smile, and clapped xer on the back. She looked back at us, cooling noticeably.

"Who's she?" whispered Jay. "Or he?"

"Xe," I corrected. Jay blushed, embarrassed by her faux pas, but Hunter didn't seem to mind.

"Xe," Xe added, clarifying xis pronoun. "Don't worry about it."

Una looked even more annoyed at us for the accidental rudeness about Hunter's gender. "By the way, you're lucky your friend didn't end up worse off."

"Like me," said Hunter, chuckling. With xis helmet off, I could see a nasty bunch of scars lacing xis throat. That explained the voice. "You might as well run along, kids. We still need to decontaminate, and I'm sure Una's scared the bejeezus out of you already."

Una's small smile of amusement still sent shivers down my spine, and I remembered the smooth way she'd drawn her AK...

Jay shot me an annoyed look. "Hey, Nellie, we're dismissed."

That snapped me back. I winced. "You know I hate being called Nellie. Um. Can we have some, uh, clothes? It's just..."

Hunter laughed again, more kindly than Una. "The bag's by the door."

Jay and I went for it at the same time, and just as we were bending awkwardly to get our clothes out, she started to talk again.

"One more thing before you go," said Una. "Even before we have our conversations, I'd like to invite both of you to join the Rediscovery Experts."

At that, I turned around, and so did Jay. "Us?" said Jay hopefully. "Really?"

"Your friend Mr. MacAllister has some promise as well," admitted Una. "I like the calm-headed types. You're all lower level than you need to be for our purposes, but you're farther ahead than most. Furthermore," and at this, she was back in her remote, chilly mode, "it's going to make those conversations easier to have in private."

"What if we don't want to be Crows?" I shot back. I badly wanted to dislike her, since she was kind of being a bitch. It was her job, but still, sheesh.

Una just smiled at me, and my knees got weak again. She knew perfectly well that if we didn't want to be Crows, or at least to be Up there, we wouldn't be level 3s.

"See you around," I said, and turned my back to her. I walked stiffly towards the proper change rooms in the corner of the training room, Jay scampering ahead of me.

"So...what the fuuuuck was that, Janelle?" said Jay, as we wriggled into our civilian clothes at last.

"What? You mean Up there? You're the one who disappeared, I feel like I should be asking you that."

"Never mind Up there, I mean back there! I thought you were going to drop to your knees and go down on her at any moment!" Shocked, I realised that Jay was angry.

"Oh for pete's sake! I don't have a thing for her! I'm just tired and she is good at being scary."

"Well, it sure looked like you did."

"Jay," I said, feeling tears well in my chest, "drop it. Please?"

"Sorry," she said softly. "It's been a hell of a day. I mean, you know it's bad because I'm swearing."

"You never fuckin' swear," I said, grinning. There were tears of relief, shower water, and sweat running down my face. "But guess what? We could be Crows!"

"I can't believe it! Not gonna lie, I've been hoping for this day."

I thought about it. I wasn't sure that being a Crow was my chosen career path, but it was certainly a road to excitement—and, admittedly, money, even with the hazards. I slumped against the steel wall, stroking its chipped, vandalized paint absently. The cool metal against my forehead was sanity incarnate, real and solid. I needed real, solid things just then.

"So, what exactly happened up there? One minute you were excited about buttons, and the next...you went running off."

Jay froze. I could hear her breathing sharpen. "I don't know if I can talk about it. I...I saw something between the houses behind you and...I panicked. I had to get away from it, no matter what. At the same time, I had to follow it...something told me it was dangerous."

I let the silence hang for a moment, grateful for the cement walls between us and the rest of the training centre. Jay getting scared like that...that alone was frightening enough.

"I know what that's like. Can we talk about what you saw, later?"

"No need," she said quietly. "I saw...shapes like a short person, or people, in the corners between the houses, and they were watching me."

My first thought was still to get her in a Calm Box, but after what had happened up there, I wasn't inclined to argue. I was dazed.

"Let's talk later," I said, and left it at that. "I could use a bite to eat." She nodded, and left it at that.

The walk out to rejoin Aiden, who was shaken but proud, and to find Chloe in the infirmary, was a long and confusing one. All of us wanted to talk about things that had happened, and none of us wanted to, and the conversation went in aimless circle after aimless circle.

"I hope Chloe's okay," said Aiden, breaking another silence. "She looked pretty chewed on and banged up."

"Me too," I said. "Well, we're here, so I guess I can find out." I managed a smile at them, shaky and nervous as I was. I crossed my fingers, and hoped we wouldn't discover something terrible.

The emergency clinic near where Dad and I live is different from the proper infirmaries. There's usually a smallish clinic in every sub-sector, but the infirmaries are in the centre, towards the middle of the city.

We came in just as Chloe was being discharged. Sure enough, she looked pretty chewed up, with bandages all over the place, but she looked better already.

"Aiden! Jay!" She wrapped herself around them enthusiastically. "I've been texting everyone so we can all go out to supper." I groaned. Company was the last thing I wanted. I wanted to fuck off, go home, and let Dad tell me funny stories about his childhood or talk about airplanes or electronics, or the times when he was a kid. I wanted to write in my journal badly. Anything but going for supper.

"Hi, Janelle, sweetie," she finally said. There was a lot of strain in her smile.

I wrapped my arms around her, feeling awkward, and kissed her on the cheek. "I'm so glad you're safe!"

"Me too!" There was a long pause, and I could feel Jay and Aiden staring at us.

"You were so brave out there!" Chloe managed. "I can't believe you saved my life!"

"I'm just glad you're not seriously hurt," I said, feeling more genuine about it.

"Me too," said Chloe. After a half second, she added, "for you, too, of course! I mean I'm glad you're not seriously hurt."

"So, I guess we should, uh, get going for...supper," said Aiden. "The Rabbit Den?"

"Sure," gushed Chloe, back in her element.

I managed a weak smile, and decided to say what I meant for a change. "I am really tired, sweetie, and I'm sure you are too, more excitement isn't really what I..."

"We have to see everyone. I want them to know we're safe," she insisted, her eyes feverish.

I was too tired to argue, and nodded wearily.

"Fine," I said, "Let's go to the Rabbit Den." I really wish I'd known that I was inviting myself to a turning point. If I had, I might have refused that dinner after all. I had already been through fire, water, and brass pipes, and it was about to get more interesting.

We were barely ass-down in the chair before the interrogation started. The boys flooded us with questions. Caleb was all over Aiden, of course, and who could blame him? I was happy to see them happy. Kenny, bless his dumb, sweet heart, was wrapped around Jay, and Chloe had glommed onto me in a mass of bandages and stripey streaked hair and curvy girly flesh. Only Raheed stood alone. Our seventh wheel.

I managed to break away from Chloe so I could give him a hug. For once, he didn't bother making some snide comment, and returned the embrace warmly.

"I'm glad you're safe," he said simply. "Whatever else, I'd hate to see you get hurt."

There's no-one who'd call me an angel—I'm obedient, I guess, and I work hard—but no angel. The warm, plain way he looked at me cut right to my soul, and I gave him a weak smile back. And, damn me, for a minute I almost missed him, and for a few more I was just glad to still call him a friend.

Chloe glared at him, hurt, and snatched me away. I was tired, and elated, so I let her. It made the pain of feeling bad about Raheed go away for a few minutes.

So: dinner. There was endless chatter; booze and water flowed in rivers over the table. Seven people can make a lot of noise. In passing, I thought of Lola, and wished we were eight, but didn't mention it. There was no point in starting a fight when we were busy celebrating our survival.

Hors d'ouvres—appetizer thingies—went around and I scarfed what I could, snatching it. It was when I had my mouth full of battered yams that the shocking thing happened.

"...And they mentioned that we should join the Crows," said Jay to Kenny, very quietly. Of course, it was just as there was a pause in conversation.

"Great job!"

"Congrats!"

The guys whooped and congratulated us and ordered another round.

"We'll be able to pay for it, too," said Aiden. He was tipsy and flushed with happiness. "The money is awesome!"

I don't know if I've mentioned that the Crows get paid well, but in addition to the prestige, there is that matter of salvaging rights. The risk does have its share of payoffs. Jay and Aiden and I had managed to avoid talking about it all the way down, but now, Chloe finally heard about it.

I was expecting her to get upset about not being invited to join the club, so to speak—rightfully so; she'd been attacked, after all, even if she had been kind of useless through the whole thing. I could tell from her briefly crestfallen expression that they hadn't asked her. To my surprise, she was really sad about it, too. Maybe Chloe has a little adventurousness in her after all? I sorta felt bad for being angry at her, then.

Chloe melted into my side suddenly, and went for a deep-throating kiss. Drunk on success and tired, I let her. It was good to feel her relax, even if our friends were whooping and catcalling. I didn't even care about Raheed's feelings, I was so absorbed in her kiss.

"Get a room," a waitress growled as she swept past. "Sorry," I called.

"Don't be sorry, baby," said Chloe. Suddenly, she was sugar-sweet, impossibly happy. I smiled at her, and I can't tell you how foolish and light-headed I was. It was a perfect moment, for a second.

"We have an announcement to make, if I can get your attention, please," said Chloe suddenly. The restaurant—there were few people in it besides our table—went deadly silent. There was a dramatic pause. And then, glowing with pride, Chloe lifted my hand into the air. "Janelle and I are going to get married!"

I just about shit my pants. The pure, enervating shock of it must have shown on my face, because there was an awkward silence when I finally managed a smile. It must have been pretty sickly or unconvinced.

"Oh my gosh," yelped Kenny effeminately. "Congratulations! I can't believe it!" The few other patrons and the worn-out waitresses managed some scattered applause and cheers.

Raheed looked like he wanted to bash me upside the head for a second, but he took a look at Chloe and a very big grin spread over his face. He actually looked happy, but I couldn't put a finger on why.

He was the first to get out of his chair, come up and give me a big hug. "Congratulations, you two! How exciting!"

To be honest, Aiden and Caleb looked a little bit put out, and I couldn't blame them; they had been the first to get engaged, and here were we, coming along and stealing their thunder. I shot Caleb an apologetic glance as Aiden came up for a hug that was only a little forced. Still, the smile on his face said he planned to be a good sport about it.

"Congratulations, Janelle. Congrats, Chloe. We're very happy for you." His smile was strained.

I won't pretend otherwise; I was dizzy and not in a good way. The way Chloe had said it—without really asking me...I forced my discomfort aside and tried to bask in the happiness.

There was jabbering, questions about what had gone on above us from Caleb and Raheed and Kenny. I shoved a lot of food down my throat and mumbled replies. Jay said a few things non-commitally, staring into space. Jay started to explain and cut it off when she realised she sounded crazy, and Chloe yammered on about the future, and how heroic I'd been...

"And then she picked me up and scooped me off to the side and shot about five of the spiders with a single bullet!"

"Actually, I think Chang hauled you out of the way, and it was Una who tidied up the last of the spiders," I corrected her.

"And so modest!" Chloe gushed. Aiden cleared his throat quietly. "Oh—and Aiden helped patch me up, of course."

I was supposed to be basking in the attention, but really, I resented it. I threw down another shot of something hard and alcoholic. It burned on the way down.

"Yeah," I said, coughing. "it was great. A big, fucking fun adventure." The guys stared at me, and Chloe too. Aiden and Jay didn't meet my eyes.

"So, about your wedding, Caleb!" Chloe started.

I guess it was her idea of relaxing us, of relaxing me. The bill certainly didn't relax me, though Chloe picked up my portion. I'm sure she was doing her best. All that really happened, though, was a haze of exhaustion that only ended after dinner. Well—after-after dinner.

All of our friends dispersed, Chloe staying last with me as I finished a few listless bites of whatever the hell I was eating. I'm sure it was tasty, but I can't tell you what it was. The Den was closing, though, and the servers had given us the bill, taken some cards, and kicked us out. I still had food in my mouth when she came to kiss me. I barely managed to deflect her.

"Well, I guess it's goodnight," I said. "I'm pretty dead on my feet after everything."

"We should definitely go home. Let me walk with you, sweetie," gushed Chloe. "I'm so happy about all of this."

I managed a half-hearted smile. "Yeah, it's great. I, uh, thought we were going to wait a bit longer..."

She acted like she hadn't even heard me, and started throwing words at me in excitement. I caught about one in five and made grunting noises of agreement.

"Janelle, are you even listening to me?"

"Mmm."

" 'Mmm?' That's not really what I'm looking for from my new fiancée. Aren't you excited?"

"Chloe, I don't know where you're getting your energy from, but I've been shopping, I've been Up and running all over town, I've been attacked by monsters, I've been seeing things, and, I was grilled by the head of the Crows. I'm kind of running low on fucks, even for good things."

She gave me a hurt look, eyes welling with tears. I should have known better, really. She was feverish, and hysterical.

"Look, I'll talk to you tomorrow. I'm happy for us. For now, I think I'll see myself out." I turned around and walked off, leaving her standing in front of the restaurant. All the way home, as I stumbled and staggered, I wondered if I shouldn't have invited her back, or gone home with her, and felt relieved and awful for not doing so.

I came home late and exhausted and alone. Dad was awake, and reacted predictably. "Janelle! Where have you been for the last eight hours? You went shopping, but young lady, it's one o'clock in the morning...!"

"Dad, we went Up to go shopping, I left you a note, and then...look, things just...I'll tell you about it tomorrow!"

"Oh, no you don't, young lady."

"Fine! We went Up to look for stuff for Aiden, things went pear-shaped, and we impressed the fuck out of the Crows. Then, because I got Chloe out of a bad situation and because I was dumb enough to tell her that the Crows want me, we got engaged!"

There was a long moment of silence as he processed it.

"I think we should start at the beginning of this one..."

"Well, whatever else, a congratulations about Chloe would be nice," I grumbled. "She proposed to me..."

Dad had that look that said he was thinking long and hard about something but was not looking forward to sharing his thoughts on the topic.

"I'm very happy for you, sweetie," he said slowly, "but this does seem rather...sudden."

"Well, it's been coming for a while, I guess," I said defensively. "And I think Chloe was just really excited about me, you know, saving her and stuff..."

"I see. Now, put your thinking cap on, it's time to focus." Uh-oh. That phrasing meant he thought I was being stupid. "Why else would she be putting you in this situation, hmm?"

I mumbled something vague about Aiden and Caleb getting engaged.

"Riiiiight. So can you say, 'social pressure'?"

"She didn't ask me to marry her just out of social pressure!" I snarled at him.

"Now listen." He gave me a somewhat patronizing smile. "I realize you want this to be for the best, but sometimes, people have their own benefits in mind..."

I surprised us both by bursting into tears. Dad looked terrifically sorry.

"Shhh, it's okay, honey. I didn't mean to upset you, Janelle. Are you okay?"

I managed a nod, and wiped my nose hurriedly to keep it from running all over the place. "I....things were rough up there, Dad. I...I'm really overwhelmed right now, Dad. Can we please, please talk about this at some point later? As in, not right now?"

"I just want you to consider that there might be some alternative—"

"NOT! RIGHT! NOW!"

And then I stomped off to my room, and that's where I'm holed up right now. I've got no idea why I'm crying and why I've been here writing for the last gods-knows-how-long. All I know is that it's late, almost day-cycle, and my hand is numb and aching from writing so much.

No, I know why I'm crying. I think I'm going crazy, but other people saw what I did—some of it—and I'm still not convinced that I'm sane. And it's worse, because I just saved my...girlfriend's life, and I should be happy about it, but...I love Chloe, really I do, but a tiny part of me that I hate and don't want to listen to is really, really worried that he's right about this. Dad is, I mean...and...AAAAAUGH.

It's just, so...I don't feel ready. Gods, sometimes I wish I'd given Dad the okay for an arranged thing, because then I'd be prepared for it more, somehow. This...I dunno. I can't remember the last time I felt less like an adult.

I'm gonna try to sleep this off. And screw it, I'm calling in sick to work tomorrow.

It's been days, and I'm working, but I've been dodging Chloe and everyone else, and when I come home, I just collapse, barely even talking to Dad. I keep waiting for Una to contact me, but she's taking her time.

That's not totally true. I did get a note—from Nathu, of all people.

"We appreciate what you did and your courage. Please consider yourself and your three friends invited to a personal dinner with us, when you feel sufficiently recovered from your experiences. On behalf of ourselves and the Rediscovery Team, with gratitude—

Nathu Alatas."

The frigging mayor's son, his wife, and the Crows have incited—I mean invited—us to dinner 'at our convenience'. Gods help me. Now I really need to get back to sleep, and pretend I'm not excited and terrified to see Nathu and Una in the same room.

Sleep. Sleep would be good right now, but it doesn't want to settle over me, and I don't want to give in. It's like in that one play, Hamlet, I think, about the guy going crazy. "To sleep, perchance to dream, aye, there's the rub..."

11—June 10, 0048 P.D.

Surprise surprise, I had some unpleasant dreams, but that actually kind of worked for once. There was a blind woman weeping and long creeping limbs snaking out from shadows, and it all swirled into deep darkness and Dust when I tried to see what was going on. I heard a child crying somewhere in there, too.

Maybe I shouldn't have gone Up. Then again, I have always had bad nightmares.

Gods I miss Mom. It hits me like a wave sometimes. Dad is good at comforting me when I have nightmares—and just last night when I was in my room, he left some tea by my door—but it's so hard sometimes. Especially this whole thing with Chloe. Chloe's been on my ass every day, texting and trying to stop by, but with this big change, well, time to think would be good. He got that. I love Dad, and he has an uncanny way of understanding my feelings— sometimes, if he doesn't get stuck on principles—but I really wish Mom was around for all this crap too. Still, at least I've been able to talk to him about things. He's surprisingly understanding of his teenage daughter— I'm almost out of my teen years, I admit, but I do have my breakdowns.

Anyway. I have to stop writing this whiny shit because I need to get my ass in gear for work. Chat more later.

I guess it wasn't much of a coincidence that I was dreaming about missing kids. I finally saw Aiden today for the first time in a week, since the shopping and the party. Today's the 10th, and that was on the 4th, that all the insane shit went down...a whole week, it's been. I needed it, too, that rest. It figures that the minute I'd get back to things, shit would go down. The news I heard today shook me.

"A couple of our Extra kids have gone missing," he texted me.

The idea of orphans going missing from the one place they're supposed to be safest filled me with terror. I thought about my nightmares with the kids in them and almost lost it.

Aiden needed me though. He would be scared enough himself without a friend losing her shit—I had to talk to him, no question about it. "Want to talk about it after work?"

"Yeah. This is...this is too much weirdness. I have a nasty feeling about this."

Clicking my phone shut, I tried to set the sense of worry aside until after work. Aiden doesn't flip his lid easily, and the fact that he'd said he 'had a nasty feeling' already worried me. Aiden's gut is never wrong.

We met up at his place, after work; his mother, as I've said, is a sweetheart, and understands a need for privacy.

"Congratulations on getting engaged!" she said, the minute I walked through the door. I winced inwardly.

"Thanks, Ms. MacAllister!" I greeted her with a hug anyway. She gave me a warm smile.

"How's your father?"

"He's all right. He's, ah, happy for me." Well, she didn't need to hear the long version. She scrutinized my face. Her adorably oversized nose and the way she hovered reminded me of a sparrow watching for crumbs—in my case, clues. She could tell I wasn't happy.

"Now, I'm sure you have lots of exciting things to talk about—I'll make myself scarce. Do let me know if you need anything."

"We will, Mom," said Aiden, with a firm smile. He gestured to his room, just off the doorway, and shut the door behind us.

Aiden has very good taste, and he does a lot with very little money, though I know he'd love more. The woven hemp curtains over the faux window matched the delicate green of the bedspread, and some grasses and leaves in chipped but well-groomed planters along the side of the wall added life to the room. His furniture was wood, true, but his careful polish couldn't conceal the chips and scratches time had left. He smiled wanly at me.

"I won't lie, I'm glad Caleb and I will be able to afford nicer decorations once we're married," he said.

"Are you kidding? This place is great. You have such careful taste! My room is covered in electronic junk and circuit posters, but yours is so coordinated!"

He smiled wanly. "I'm still looking forward to being able to do more with that taste than wish I could afford to indulge it."

I shrugged my shoulders once and made an offering gesture. He paused, as though about to speak, and shook his head.

Aiden left the room for a few moments and returned with a tea pot. I accepted the herbal tea gratefully, wrapping my hands around the warm earthenware cup.

"So, you mentioned missing kids," I prompted him. He nodded warily, his light-coloured eyes looking troubled.

"Yeah. Two of the Extra kids—Louis and Noor— are just not there. We put them to bed one night, and the next morning..." Aiden seemed to shrink into himself. "They were just gone. Right out of their beds.

145

Nothing was missing, and none of the other kids knew what was going on."

I bit my lip and thought for a moment. "Just gone?"

"Just gone."

"No disturbed covers, nothing?"

"Nothing at all."

"Did the other kids say anything about it?"

"Nope. The dorm was quiet. The kids are usually so safe...I just don't understand it." I thought hard, turning over what it meant. I'm good at problem-solving, but I prefer doing it for circuits rather than people.

"So there was nothing weird? Nothing at all?"

"Not really. A couple of the kids said they'd had nightmares, but the nightmares didn't make any sense...Ryan, who sleeps next to Louis, said he'd had a dream about a big monster trying to eat him, and Karen said she'd had a dream about a woman with big claws and snake arms. They were both terrified, but the dreams didn't really match, so we may be able to rule out a kidnapper that they both saw. Possibly the kidnapper drugged them with something to make them hallucinate, but the kids didn't remember anything like that and there's no trace of ether. It's all very, very odd."

I nodded. It really didn't make any sense. "A ransom note?"

"Nothing."

"Some sicko who likes hurting kids?"

"Why take an Extra kid right out of the orphanage? There's a lot better places to get kids, like Sector D or from the single parents. The orphanage is dense!" He put his head in his hands.

I hugged him. "It's going to be all right," I said, knowing it was what you're supposed to say when someone is upset.

"I don't know that. It's not like they would just wander off."

"It does seem weird."

He sighed heavily. "The whole place has been in a complete fracas." To my surprise, there were tears in his eyes. "I just don't understand. I wasn't even on shift when it happened, but I feel so...responsible."

"It wasn't your fault."

"How do I know?"

"Well...be reasonable."

Aiden glared at the wall for a moment, and didn't look at me when he spoke again.

"The worst part is, no-one seems to care much, apart from us caretakers. We talked to the city wardens, but they pretty much shrugged and said they'd get back to us. It's like no-one else cares about the Extra kids."

"They're first for adoptions, though," I protested.

"After family members, and after the Extra kids who don't have any problems. The ones that are missing a limb or have something wrong with them? Good luck." He was surprisingly bitter.

"At least it's not like when our parents were kids, and the people who were Between or gay or not white or whatever would get picked on."

Aiden nodded. "I can't imagine that. What a weird society."

He pulled me back on the bed and we cuddled for a few minutes. It was perfectly innocent, which was very nice. The double-engagement thing was awkward, sure, but it hadn't made our friendship too weird. Just being around someone that things are never complicated with, and who never really has ulterior motives, really soothed my soul. I love Chloe, but sometimes I feel like spending time around her only ever leads to more and more complicated crap in my life.

Did I really just write that? Well, it's on the page, can't scratch it out now.

He was all warm and nice, but I didn't want to leave Dad waiting up for me again. Besides, he was making yam rolls for supper.

"I should probably go," I said, sitting up and stretching.

"Yeah. I think I might throw this one at Caleb, too. Even Raheed. He can be a dick, but he's certainly no dummy."

I decided to be graceful for once and not take the bait, much as I'd find it easy to insult Raheed. "Well, tell me if you think of anything. I'd like to think I use my brain at least sometimes."

He managed a smile at that, and gave me a hug. "Thanks, Janelle. You're a good friend."

"I try. Sleep tight, and don't worry all night, okay?"

He nodded. "See you soon."

I made some small talk with Nora as I rinsed my teacup in the sink, but it was all aimless, and I soon went home.

Dinner with Dad was good, though. I mentioned it to him and he didn't really have any ideas, so I'm stumped. I guess I'll leave off here for the night.

Man, what a mess. It seems like one thing after another keeps getting complicated, and I still haven't had that 'friendly' dinner with Una and Nathu. Ugh. Okay. Sleep. And hopefully, no children with sharp teeth or dragons or spider dogs tonight. Hopefully.

12—June 12, 0048 P.D.

Well, that was an...interesting dinner. Guess who requisitioned us all the way to the fanciest digs in town? I'll give you a hint—it wasn't Chloe's mom, though it was almost as arduous.

I came home from work to find that Dad had left me a note about working late on one of the hydroponic test chambers. Being stuck down in the farming caverns to tinker with finicky climate-control boxes until who knows when doesn't bother him. Not knowing when he'd be home for dinner, though, did bother me.

I'd made some of my famous biscuits in the morning. The herb and seed mix I use gives them a nice texture, and there were a couple dozen of them. Grab a couple, add an apple or a carrot and you have a perfect afternoon 'I'm hungry but I'm not allowed to make supper yet' snack. As I got some margarine from the fridge, there was a knock on the door.

"Hello?" The mail slot opened, and something fell on the floor. I got to the door within a couple of steps, but by the time I'd opened it, a very official-looking back was turned to me and proceeding briskly down the hall.

There was no point pursuing a messenger, so I picked up the paper. Well, there was no getting around the dinner issue this time. When you get an official summons, no matter how politely worded, you listen to it.

As if on cue, my phone rang. I jumped for it. "Hello?"

"Did you just get an invite to dinner from Princep Alatas?"

"Yep. Second one."

Jay sighed. "Well, I guess we ought to round up Chloe and Aiden. Let's meet at the Hub. Should I bring Kenny, do you think?"

I scanned the letter again. "Um. I don't really get the impression it's a social visit. Let's not, in case classified things get mentioned."

"Should we do host gifts?" She was frantic.

I glanced at the biscuits on the counter. "Well, I'm bringing a dozen of my ragamuffin biscuits."

"We have a big pot of egg drop soup," she said, after a pause. "A-ma! Call ya soon."

"See you at the Hub."

I turned my phone off, and thought hard about what to wear. The invite was for approximately an hour, and there was no point in pretending I hadn't gotten it. Time, then, to spruce up. I sifted through my closet, threw some things on the floor, put them on the bed, and finally went with my least hated fancy clothes, the black pantsuit and salvaged aubergine silk blouse.

Nice clothes alone would barely get me through the door, I admitted to myself, and I adjusted my fashion sense accordingly. I actually resorted to bobby pins and a hairband to keep my hair in place, and even added a touch of kohl and shadow to my eyes. Looking at myself in the mirror, I couldn't remember the last time I'd been so dressed up. I frowned, and threw on a bone pendant, an abstract woman-shaped bead on a simple ribbon. The woman's arms stretched over her head in a curve, which extended into an arching shape that looked a lot like wings—an angel spirit, I guess you'd call her, for lack of a better word. It looked nice, and it was a lot more 'me' than everything else I was wearing. If Chloe called it 'crude', she could suck an egg. Not having a utility belt on, even a decorated one—it would have messed up the jacket—made me feel naked enough.

No more delays. I scribbled a note for Dad, letting him know that the rest of the biscuits were in the blue clay cookie jar on the counter, tucked the paper box of biscuits into my arms, and set off.

Aiden, looking sleek in a fluttery pale grey suit, was already there to greet me. He'd put kohl on his eyes, too, and mascara, but had simply tied back his long sandy hair. A large box perched in his arms. From the delicious fatty smell of pork and potato, they contained his mother's stovies, cooked in true old-Scottish style.

"Hey, you look nice," he said, smiling. I smiled back, nervously. Jay popped her head in, the crockpot of soup balanced in her arms. Her rather lovely yellow and green striped sarong and a matching embroidery-edged blouse were still, miraculously, un-harmed by soup. Not a leak had marred their rich fabric. Jay's longer hair was restrained by a sequined butterfly clip, but she'd gone for only the lightest makeup. Her tattoos sort of did the job of makeup, anyway, with the way the characters emphasized the line of her neck.

"You guys look amazing," I said. "Just lovely. I feel a bit underdressed!"

"Yoohoo!" Chloe, dressed in the corset belt and angled skirt, and burdened down by a tonne of beaded jewelry, jangled her way in. I noticed she had a new blouse, too, a white one that was cut unsuitably high and covered her cleavage. She had an armload of cookies in a wooden box, probably her brother's, since he's the best cook in the family. "Well, aren't we nice looking," she said. "Better be on our way, hadn't we?"

I braced myself inwardly. She was obviously going to hide her anxiety by going into manic-social mode.

"You look nice," I said stiffly, and pecked her on the cheek. Too much perfume, and her corset belt was a couple of notches tighter than it should have been.

Given that she'd inexplicably covered her cleavage, the intended effect had been ruined.

"So, guess we better go," said Jay helpfully. "Might as well head off." Grateful for the distraction, I nodded at her.

"Lead the way."

We filed through the wide and well-kept tunnels that led towards the centre of the city with little to say. The seemingly endless tunnels widened and became more polished by the time we'd entered the busier parts of the core. The signs and decorations carved and painted into walls were more elaborate than the graffiti around our home, and there were more Moles and carts around. The wide stone tunnels hummed with activity, stalls and shacks set up in corners to sell a snack or interesting bits of crap to passerby. The air was humid and rich with human smells, spicy food, and activity.

A subtle current of wealth in the air became richer and more obvious as we headed towards the Honeycomb, the mayor's office and dwelling. The centre of the sectors, G, is the heart of the city, and the Honeycomb—named after its unusual wall carvings—is the heart of the sector.

"We're here," said Jay unnecessarily. She stepped down first, from the street into the antechamber. The antechamber with the casual court is, symbolically, always open, a huge round waiting room with desks for processing people. In its centre, like the stem on an apple, is another hallway, with doors off to each side that lead to the courtroom and a Special Requests office respectively. We headed to the central enormous doors at the end of the hall. The doors, made of real solid wood, had round bronze knockers with elaborate work on their curves. The metal panels set into the door were decorated with small gems, orange and blue and black, some of them striped and striated. It was, and still is, one of the most impressive things I've ever seen.

I lifted the knocker with my free hand and dropped it, feeling timid. All four of us jumped at the deep, surprisingly harsh *clang*. Even more startling was how quickly the door opened.

A footman in dark blue livery opened it immediately. The way he looked down his nose and magnificent ginger mustache at us made me suddenly aware of the fact that we were four oldish teenagers in fancy dress and clutching pots of food.

Aiden cleared his throat. "We have an invitation to dinner with Nathu Atalas. May we come in?"

"Invitations, please," said the guard, managing not to look condescending or amused.

Fortunately, we'd all been smart enough to bring our dinner invites. He took them one by one, had a look at the signatures, and finally, gave assent. "Come in."

The doors opened on the most luxurious place I'd ever seen. Most of us have stone furniture, of course, or salvaged stuff if we're lucky, but this was different. All real wood, a lot of it newer looking and obviously custom-made; embroidered and velvet cushions, lots of candles everywhere as well as electric lamps, and even a second level below us: from the railings to the paintings and carvings, it was a fine mixture of old and new, and elegantly eclectic in every way. I tried not to let my jaw drop.

The room was circular as well, with fine moldings along the edges of the walls and a slightly domed ceiling with a huge chandelier. The chandelier hung down into the centre of the balcony, over the open room below. A pair of cooks arrived from one of the many sets of mysterious doors, and graciously took our host gifts.

Below us, Nathu, Una, Chang, Hunter, and a whole bunch of other people I didn't recognize were seated at the round table. There was a set of staircases to our right coming down from our side and from the side opposite to descent below the sparkling chandelier. The room glowed with marble and pale wood and richness, and I couldn't believe we'd been invited into it.

The guard gestured to the stairs. Without further ado, Chloe hurried ahead, eager to make the first impression. We all walked in a slow, sedate manner down the stairs. I'm proud of myself for managing to not trip.

In addition to Nathu, Una, Hunter, and Chang, there were four other Crows. Nathu stood gracefully and my heart skipped a beat. He has a wonderful smile, and a very smooth medium complexion, golden brown. Add short dark hair, brown-black eyes, and a great frame, and you have the reason so many girls (and plenty of guys) had become very interested in politics when he came of age. His rich wine-coloured suit was made of something very fine, probably angora or a fibre blend.

"Welcome, friends," he said. "Thank you for your kind gifts, and please, be welcome at my table." He sounded relaxed, in spite of the formal greeting. Una also rose, a sincere but unreadable smile on her face.

"Welcome to our home," she said. In perfect symmetry, they greeted each of us, shaking our hands. When each of them had gotten around to all four of us, they reseated themselves. It was like watching a pair of dancers.

Nathu was seated in the chair opposite to the staircase, with Una next to him, and Hunter next to her. Chang was next to Nathu, on his left, and two each of the strange Crows sat on either side of Chang and Hunter. The remaining four spots, directly facing Chang, Nathu, Una, and Hunter, were left open for us. A pair of servants slipped over to pull the chairs out. Chloe manoeuvred herself to be next to me.

A woman with luxuriant red hair nodded to us. "Kelsey," she said. "A pleasure."

"Luke," said a plain-faced guy with brown hair. He gave us a warm smile.

"Oliver," the man next to Hunter said, his voice a low rumble. He was older than the others, his looks and origin best described as 'weathered' more than anything.

"Skye," said the final woman quietly. She was medium-dark skinned, with curly hair and sad dark eyes.

We introduced ourselves in turn, and finally sat down. I folded my hands in my lap and prepared for the worst.

Shockingly, it didn't really come. Una was a vision in a form-fitting navy blue dress that sparkled when she moved. She managed to be a perfect hostess to boot. All of her rough edges were tucked away; even her movements were more graceful. I caught myself gawping at her and she tossed me a wink.

I felt my face heat up and looked at Nathu, instead. I've only seen him from afar, but I've always liked him. It's not just that he's 'my type', whatever that is—he's intelligent and seems warm. Up close, that impression didn't change.

The other Crows, all of whom were dressed in black, chatted easily. I found myself starting to relax, listening to Kelsey talk about her hilarious close encounter with a rat. The Crows have an intimidating reputation, but they're still human enough. Of course, it wasn't all fun and games for long.

"...by the way, Janelle, we'd all heard about some rather impressive things on your last trip Up," prompted Kelsey.

I froze. Una glanced at me, her expression neutral. I'd had a hunch there'd be a test coming.

"Well, uh, we did have a bit of an adventure," I said. "We were trying to find some nice things for Aiden because he and his boyfriend just got engaged, and sort of wandered off the path by accident..." Oliver snorted into his cup of tea, and a few of the others traded knowing glances and small grins. Well, at least they weren't frowning at me, I thought.

"Anyway...we got Up and all of us could tell there was something strange in the air. We were still basically within our level, but it was much darker and

Dustier than it should have been. By a lot. We were looking around these houses and Chloe decided to check one out..."

"Well, she panicked," said Hunter pointedly. Una smirked for a moment but didn't interrupt.

"To be fair, we were seeing...strange things up there. Anyway, I went to go track her down, and heard noise around the garage. I ran for it, and when I got outside, well, I found her being attacked by a bunch of...um...*monsters*. Hunter and Chang can tell you more."

"Actually, we couldn't tell them much," said Chang. He spoke carefully, cautiously, as though he couldn't believe what he was about to say. "The dog-headed spider creature collapsed into Dust just after we got down."

I was drinking tea when he said it, and almost sprayed it out my nose in surprise. The same thing that had happened with my dragon had happened with the dog-spider. I hadn't seen them take it off, but then again, I'd been distracted with Chloe's hysterics and Una's hands.

"And then she rescued me," said Chloe smugly. "She killed about twenty of the little monsters all by herself."

Oliver and Kelsey didn't even bother hiding their feelings. "If I screamed every time I'd seen something scary, I'd be roadkill five times over," said Kelsey smugly. The other Crows were more polite, but I could tell they agreed.

Chloe assumed an expression of indignation and innocence. "It was terrifying!"

"All the better time to keep your head," growled Oliver. I noticed reddish streaks in his thick white beard for the first time, and wondered if he was related to Kelsey. He glanced at her, and continued. "Second time she went up, my daughter got attacked by a wild dog, 'cos we accidentally interrupted his dinner. She screamed, sure, but she got back up and shot that dog in the face."

Chloe blushed furiously, in the way that meant she was angry, and I jumped in to defend her. "Well, getting attacked by a swarm of monsters..."

"Don't matter," Oliver growled. His steely eyes, a blue that had faded to grey, cut into me. "I ain't heard of suchlike creatures before, but everything's got a spine you can break. Them creatures as don't have spines, you can usually step on. The key is not to panic."

Chloe was about to argue when Nathu cut in. "You made your point, Oliver," he said curtly.

"And where were you in all of this, Jay?" Chloe snapped. "I heard you ran off too."

Jay looked back at her calmly. "You could call it that. I saw something shiny on the ground, and got distracted, and then I saw something moving between the houses. I wanted to see what it was, because I thought I saw a very short, twisted person." I should've known she wasn't bolting out of fear. Jay is methodical and calm as long as she's not wildly curious about something. Then she saves the methodical side until she's caught whatever-it-is. Until then, she's like a hunting dog looking for a rat, all instinct.

Aiden cut in. "While you were handling the spiders, we were trying to track the stranger," he added. All of the Crows looked fascinated.

"We've been wondering if people had been living on the surface for a while," said Luke thoughtfully. "I'd heard a few rumours from old Crows, but nothing firm."

"Just legends," snapped Chloe. I glanced at her, surprised. She can be finicky, but this was a new level of brattiness. I supposed it was because she'd been made fun of. Guilt welled up, and I tamped it down, trying to pay attention to Luke.

Luke shrugged non-commitally. "Dust does strange things to people's minds, and of course we all know that people have gotten Lost up there. The idea that people could be eking out an existence up there, though...you have to admit, it's interesting."

Jay looked strained. "I just hope it was only a person I saw. It looked a lot less...normal than what I'm used to."

"Was it a little girl with a big mouth of sharp teeth?" I blurted out. "Blood on her face?"

Jay cocked her head to the side. "Well...in the beginning, yes. Then I thought it looked more like a...short person. It sounds crazy, but it reminded me of a thing from fairy tales...a...a goblin."

I glanced at the Crows, but none of them had cracked a smile. They were all deadly serious, and listening. I wasn't sure what was worse—the fact that I'd been expecting them to mention Calm Boxes, or the fact that they weren't. Every one of them, even Nathu, was rapt.

"From what I'm hearing, it sounds like Dust isn't just giving people visions," said Luke thoughtfully. "Seeing strange stuff is one thing, but having it attack you..."

Jay, Aiden, and I glanced at each other.

Nathu stared at his goat filet thoughtfully. Courses had been coming and going through the conversation. The air was so tense, I could barely savour the delicious baked sunchoke with rosemary, or the turnip-leek pancakes.

"Am I right in understanding that the three of you accepted an invitation to join the Rediscovery Experts formally?"

"Y-yes," I stammered. Aiden and Jay chimed in, affirming it. Chloe remained silent.

"I have a feeling it would be wise to investigate the matter further. If you're willing, I'd like to invite you three to go Up with a team and explore the area."

"I'm sure she'd be happy to go," said Chloe cheerfully. "She's the 'tough' one, if you take my meaning. I like to think of her as the man of house."

I whipped my head around and shot her a furious glare. The man of the house? The *man*? Never mind the fact that she'd just accepted before I could say anything. I felt insulted, *again.*

Nathu looked at Una sharply. They obviously didn't need to say something out loud to understand each other.

"Of course, it's your decision," said Una carefully. "Yours. This isn't going to be an easy task, and if it wasn't such a unique situation, we wouldn't even be taking Level 3s Up."

"Of course," I said, through gritted teeth. Looking away from Chloe made it easier to relax. I glanced at the large and beautiful mirror behind us, with its ornate frame, and made eye contact with myself. It helps me relax, weirdly enough. "I'd be happy to," I added, more sincerely this time.

Nathu looked relieved, and the other Crows all looked cautiously interested.

"We'll be glad to have you on our team," said Una, smiling with more warmth than I'd ever seen. She held my gaze for a long time, and I found myself grinning in a slightly goofy way.

Chloe cleared her throat. "Yeah, this is great!" There was a half-second pause, but it cranked the 'awkward' up to 11.

"We'll be needing other people as well," said Nathu, looking at Jay and Aiden. He pointedly did not glance at Chloe.

"I'm in," said Jay. She looked pale, but managed a smile. "After what I saw, believe me, I want to understand what the heck is going on up there."

"And me too," said Aiden. His voice was firm in a way I'd seldom heard. "If more kids go missing...I'm going to blame myself."

"Where the hell did they go, though?" Oliver muttered. "Some sicko takin' 'em would fit, but I ain't heard of anyone walking into an orphanage to hurt kids. Too easy to get caught like that."

"We're not sure," said Aiden. "There weren't any footprints, no real evidence that we found..."

"Had to have been planned," said Kelsey, through a mouthful of something meaty. "Someone sneaky."

There was an awkward silence. Everyone knows that Crows are amazing at sneaking.

"We'll have to badger the police who've investigated," said Luke. "I've got some friends."

"A few patrols outside the orphanages," suggested Kelsey. "And we'll have to keep looking for evidence. They'll have slipped up somewhere. Wasn't one of those monsters on its own, I don't think, or the other kids would've seen something."

The debate went back and forth. Aiden threw in a few words here and there, Oliver snapped things. I tossed a few conclusions out myself, but it didn't go anywhere.

While dinner cooled on the table, tempers heated. Even Skye, the quiet one, talked up, and she had a few choice words about missing children.

Finally, Una got tired of it. "Look. We're going to investigate everything, but we're not going to do it behind a dinner table. I suggest we hold off until the next meeting, before we're tempted to get our masks on and start the manhunt here and now. Any takers?"

There was a grudging silence. "She's right enough," allowed Oliver, letting go of the death grip he'd had on his fork.

"Excellent," said Nathu. The other Crows looked slightly relieved. "Now, after all of that tension, how about the next course?"

The rest of dinner was okay, I guess. Chloe made a couple more comments about me being 'the breadwinner' and having bought her dress, and etcetera. I guess she was trying to show off, but I was pissed. When we finally went to leave, exchanging hugs with the Crows and bearing the traditional guest gifts of some of the remaining food, she made sure that Una and Nathu didn't even hold my hand for more than a second. They noticed.

"Please, let us give you a ride home," said Nathu. "A cart will take half or a quarter of the time your walk will, and given how unsafe things had been."

"That's very kind of you," Chloe began, "but..." Jay and Aiden gave her sideways glances. Declining an offer, especially of a luxury, is just as rude as you get.

"...I'd appreciate it, actually," I said. "I'm pretty tuckered out."

Nathu smiled graciously. "Of course."

I didn't really expect him to drive us in his personal cart, but he did anyway. It looked nice, but I wasn't paying enough attention to tell you how it looked now. Brass fittings and leather seats and panelling, with the normal open top—that's about all I recall. The ride back was full of silence and tension; Chloe started to chatter, and stopped when the three of us gave her dirty looks. Nathu maintained impeccable neutrality, but judiciously dropped her off first.

I was the very last he dropped at home. As I got out, Nathu took a moment to press my hand, stalling me. I noticed that his eyes were a velvety shade of dark brown, and that they were full of concern for me.

"I hope you'll have a good evening," he said. "It's been quite a week for you, from the sounds of it."

I shrugged. "I'll manage."

He smiled warmly, in a way that made my heart flutter a bit. "I'm sure you will. It was a pleasure having you. I'm glad you've run into Una, as well. She's very interested in you."

More butterflies. "It's been great to meet both of you in person. Really, really great."

He smiled, and I noticed how deliciously full his lips were. "You're a very brave and special woman, Janelle. I hope to chat with you soon."

"I should go home," I stammered, grinning like an idiot.

"Have a lovely night," he said, and smiled. He drives well, and for more than a minute, I wished he hadn't driven off. Then I shook my head at myself, at the thoughts that were stirring in my head. Chloe is very, very jealous, and the things on my mind were not just improbable, they were—are—impossible. I felt unfairly annoyed at her.

THE LOVED, THE LOST, THE DREAMING

Dad opened the door before I could. "Welcome home, kiddo," he said, beaming. He was sweaty and smelled like dirt and happiness.

"Let me get out of this monkey suit and I'll give you a hug." I ran into my room and pulled the fancy clothes off as fast as I could, throwing my loose cotton pyjama pants and a drapey tunic top on instead.

"Dinner with the mayor's son! And here I was worried about you getting into trouble up there," said Dad, still smiling widely.

"Yeah, well, you know. You break a rock and find a geode. Good luck."

"You don't sound too happy about it."

"...I sorta had a fight with Chloe. She was really sharp. Kind of took the piss out of me."

He gave me a hug. "Well, I'm very proud of you, kiddo. Good job. Even if she did kick up her heels, you earned a big honour today."

I laughed bitterly. "I should tell you how I got it sometime soon!"

Dad looked serious. "That sounds like a good idea. You're sounding too old for your age lately."

I sighed. "You're telling me. Well, dinner was good—I brought some tasty things home for you, at least. Can I tell you about it tomorrow? I wanna turn in."

"Okay," he said. His brow furrowed, and he kissed me on the forehead. "Goodnight, sweetie."

"Goodnight, Dad. Love you. Sleep well."

"You too," he said. "Those shadows under your eyes are pretty prominent."

He was right to caution me. I tossed and turned for a while, thinking about Mom. Little kids getting Lost, wandering up to the surface...it was horrible, even as a thought. I mean, I worry about Lola sometimes, that she might wander up or just get Lost, but for kids it would be even worse.

Mom wasn't a proper Crow, but she went Up often enough. She was one of the ones who got Lost. Dad and I don't talk about that. As far as I knew for years, she had inhaled too much Dust through a faulty Mask, she wandered outside, and that was that. He lets things slip out once in a while. All I know is that she was trying to find my aunt—her sister—and she didn't come back from the rescue mission.

I was at school when she went. I remember her making me amazing pancakes that morning, and I remember complaining that I wished we had some strawberry jam left, and I remember kissing her cheek and saying "I love you" before heading off to class. That's it. And then I came home, and the waiting started, and never did end.

Usually it's so deep down that I don't have to think about it much, but the pain is still there. I refused to understand for months that she wasn't coming back. I would try to run away from home, bringing rope to the Heaven Tubes. When some Rats found me, they called the police and sent me home. Dad didn't let me out of his sight for months.

There's a rule about people being considered legally dead, or in limbo, if they've been gone more than six months. After that, you have to hold a Loss ceremony. It hurts to think about it even now. It's a dull ache that goes everywhere with me.

Speaking of dull aches, I've got things to handle tomorrow, including Chloe. And, I guess, Nathu and Una. I'd better stop writing, and crying, and go to sleep.

13—June 14, 0048 P.D.

"Oh, gods, I could be bound in a nutshell, and count myself a king of infinite space, were it not that I have bad dreams." Read that in school a long time ago—Shakespeare, I think, in *Hamlet*. I always liked that line, and it was true last night.

My mother's voice, once, called out something indistinct before fading abruptly. The angles of my dream world were strange, distorted by Dust, grey and oddly coloured. I woke up dizzy and panting, and shaking my head to try to clear it of the feeling. I kept dreaming about Nathu and Una. I chased them around corners of houses, Dust swirling around us and getting in the way, shadows dancing and snarling. Some of them looked like Chloe's hands, reaching for me. The little girl with the red eyes and sharp teeth darted through the wreckage, taunting me. She came close and nipped one of my fingers, and stole away, giggling. The basement was there again, the door, the white hand behind it beckoning and clawing at me. Sometimes my dreams are subtle, and sometimes, they really don't bother.

In this case, though, I wonder if it wasn't a warning. I did have a hell of a fight with Chloe today.

Work was fine, Pramjit complimented me on one of my fixes, and all was well. I would have had a lovely day if not for being bombarded with passive aggressive texts from Chloe. Every time I plugged my phone in, my queue had a couple of sharply-worded comments.

"Last night was interesting. Y did u ignore me?"

"So glad I have someone STRONG and MANLY like u to save me when I'm in danger."

"I wasn't ignoring you," I texted back.

"Y were u staring at Nathu? U were intense."

"Can we talk about this later?"

"Fine." The minute I saw the word 'fine', I braced myself.

Sure enough, Earthquake Chloe struck at about 5 pm, as soon as I was off work. She was there waiting for me at the office door, and she looked pissed.

"Hi," I said, taken aback.

"Hello, Janelle," she said. Uh-oh. My full name.

"You look nice," I said awkwardly. She had a low-cut shirt with an unfair amount of cleavage displayed. Amazing boobs always distract me, and it's hard to keep your eyes on an angry face when there's a great show going on just beneath.

"I'm sure I do, but that's not what your eyes were saying last night," she snapped. Her voice was loud enough that a few pairs of curious eyes were already directed our way.

I winced. "Um, babe, why don't we, uh, go for a bit of a walk."

"*Fine.*"

I managed to direct her off to one of the maintenance tunnel areas, a backalley that even rush hour couldn't fill. I glanced around guiltily, making sure that people weren't watching us closely. Chloe, of course, kept her lips pursed.

"So," I said, once I'd found a corner near a public privy, "you seem somewhat upset."

"Well, gee, I wonder why." She crossed her arms and tightened her lips.

"I'm sorry I didn't defend you more when people were ribbing you," I started. That much, I knew I'd done wrong.

"Oh, I'm angry about that, but that's not what you did wrong."

"Look, I don't want to play guessing games." I shifted my weight from one foot to another, and absently rubbed the surface curves of my foldie.

"Stop fidgeting, it's distracting. I think you know what you did."

"Chloe, come on. Please. Just tell me."

"Uh-uh. You're a big girl. Figure it out."

I lost it. "I'm not going to fucking 'figure it out' unless you tell me! You know I'm bad at this crap!"

"Gods, what is wrong with you, Janelle? If I wanted to deal with someone as stupid and dense as you, I would have dated a *hetero man.*"

Then I really lost it. "A man? What the fuck, Chloe?"

"You're insensitive, obtuse—"

"I don't like your fucking guessing games! And you won't even tell me what I did wrong so I can apologize! Also, stop calling me a fucking man! I'm a woman, and I like it that way!"

"You sure seem to like hanging out with Between people, so I don't think you are much of one. Besides, if you really were more of a woman, you'd understand how I felt last night!"

My blood was up, at this point, and the world was swimming before me. "I am a woman! And since when are you some fucking 20th century bigot? What's wrong with Between people?"

"It's not anyone else I have a problem with. It's you," she fumed. "And I don't see why you're so angry. You started this."

"You stand here and insult me, and call me a *man,* and you make all those fucking little comments about how I'm tough and insensitive and the breadwinner, and you wonder why I'm angry? Are you snorting Dust or taking hallies?"

"I'm not the one who hangs out with little sugarplums and flaps her cunt at every attractive woman who walks by!" she snapped.

"What the hell? I've never cheated on you!"

"You were hanging out with Lola! She tried to steal Kenny from Jay and she's trying to get back in so she can take you."

"What the hell? Lola and I were never into each other, first of all, and secondly, she never tried to 'steal' him! They were just friends!"

"People are never 'just friends'. You're living proof! You don't have any boundaries. You let that whore rub you down in the showers, and then you and her husband were practically eyefucking each other at dinner!"

"I was not eyefucking them!" I screamed. "And don't you fucking dare call Una a whore! She's a hell of a lot braver than your fat, cowardly ass!"

Chloe's eyes wavered and she burst into tears. "How dare you!" she screamed, through sobs. "How do you fucking dare? You insensitive bitch! You're supposed to be my fiancée and you can't even keep your loose pussy in your pants!"

At this point, I was so angry I was shaking. I hate fighting in public more than anything, and today, I didn't even care that people were glancing down our corridor and delicately walking around us.

"You're supposed to love me!" I screamed. "And all you do is rag on my ex—who, by the way, was kind of a dick, but you always start fights with him and make it worse—and accuse me of being a cuntgirl! I am so sick of this!"

"Well I'm sick of you!"

"I'm more sick of you! You didn't even ask me properly, you just announced we were engaged! How the fuck do you think that made me feel, Chloe? You just rushed it."

Her mouth opened in a round *o* of protest. "You're a horrible person!" she screamed.

I wanted to hit her, I did. Instead, I took several deep breaths and backed away, my hands in front of me. "Look. I can't even talk to you anymore," I whispered furiously. "I need time to cool off, and then we will talk. Later. Goodnight." With that, I turned on my heel and headed home.

Of course, because bad things like to travel in clusters, I literally ran into Raheed on my way home.

"Hey!" He looked surprisingly happy to see me.

"Please, I don't feel like fighting with you. I just had a huge blowup with Chloe."

"Sure looks like it. Your mascara is everywhere."

I wiped my hand and it came away black. "The one day I wear makeup to cover my puffy eyes..."

"Can I get you a cup of chicoffee?"

I stepped back. "Since when are you so nice?"

"Well, frankly, when you dumped me and broke my heart for that bitch, I've been waiting for you to get your comeuppance. Now that you have, I feel like being nice to you."

I pushed him away. "You're as bad as she is! Look, I don't want to see anyone I've been with right now. Not her, not you, not Todd, not Amy, and not even Kai from eighth grade!"

I guess the fact that I was really upset finally sunk into his stubborn skull. At least it wiped the smile off his face. "Now I know you're upset. Look, I'm sorry I said that. I've been wanting to talk to you for months. Can I take you somewhere to talk?"

Well, it couldn't be much worse than fighting with Chloe. "I'm out of fucks to give. Whatever you want." I put my hands up in surrender.

Raheed tucked an arm around me. "I want to be a nice human being instead of, what was it you said, 'a mean bastard'?"

"Okay. But no coffee, please. Life's been expensive lately and my savings are still wincing from that shopping trip." He laughed and guided me out of the tunnels.

We were near my place, so he took me up the set of stairs and into a tunnel that lead crosswise to the

Heaven Tubes. It's private, and it's one of the best makeout spots in my neighbourhood. Unlike the Hub, though, it's not somewhere I usually meet up with my friends.

In the privacy of the tunnel, I finally lost it. I sobbed all over his shirt and let the anger and pain rock me.

"Shhh," he said. "Shhh. It's okay."

"No, it's not," I snapped. "My fiancée hates me and I'm not all that sure about how I feel about her."

"It's normal to get angry at someone when tension is running high—"

"Since when are you a fount of wisdom? Besides, 'tension has been running high' for a very long time. I don't even know how I feel about her right now."

"Well, let's talk about us."

"Oh, gods. I really don't want to get back together with you, Raheed. Just because I'm not sure about things with Chloe doesn't mean I want to jump into your bed."

"Well, you only did one time." He paused. "Sorry. I know that sounded bitter. I didn't scare you off of dicks, did I?"

"No, I just like both guys and girls. Always have," I reassured him.

"I won't lie, I worried about it." He scuffed the dirt with his shoe.

"Another thing. I didn't ditch you for her, as long as we're digging up skeletons. I...I didn't like the way you always tried to control me. You still kind of do that, make me do things."

"You like it when people make you do things," he said defensively.

I opened my mouth to argue and thought about it for a minute. "Yeah, but you never gave me the chance to say no. I'd like that to stop. I want you to stop hating me. I left you because it wasn't working. I felt suffocated and I ignored you, and you closed off."

He looked like he was going to argue. I was drained and didn't care, but part of me was stunned by how...adult the whole thing was. It was upsetting to talk about, but with all the anger beaten out of me by Chloe's insults, it was easier to be reasonable with Raheed.

"You were my first serious boyfriend, the first one I did more than kiss with. I really cared about you, but we just...we make better friends."

He nodded. "And like I said...she's a bitch. I wanted to see you hurt, because you chose a worse person to be with after me. I guess it's immature, but I did." He hugged me again. "I'm not going to lie and say I'm totally sorry, but I admit that it's not nice to see you this upset."

He kissed me on the cheek, lingering. "I don't want to be more than friends again," I warned him, stepping back.

"Sorry. I didn't mean that like that. Just..."

"I'm going home," I said. "I'll talk to you later." He looked defeated.

"See you soon, Janelle."

"See you, Raheed." I only paused for a moment before I turned my back and resolutely walked home. I didn't even care if a monster came by, just then. I would have killed it bare-handed for something to do.

So, here I am now, having eaten as much as my tight stomach muscles will allow, which wasn't much. I gave up and talked to Dad about everything, and cried AGAIN, and he patted my head and made me tea and said I should write in my journal for a while. So, that's what I'm doing, and now, I'm going to try to sleep all of the bullshit off. I'd almost welcome nightmares at this point.

14—June 16, 0048 P.D.

My own drama just became a lot less important. I almost forgot about this, even though Aiden mentioned it to Nathu at the dinner the other night—the kids are still missing, and worse, another couple have disappeared. Once in a while, we do Lose people—they wander off or accidents happen. Sometimes people get lost in older parts of the tunnels and wander Up without meaning to. Kids, though, are a different matter. Without kids, there's no future, and having two more go missing means our future is being taken from us. People had gone looking for them after the police had done their investigations, but the trail just…died. It was like the kids had never existed in the first place.

The kids who went missing weren't Aiden's, this time. They came from a place across the city, and Nathu (gods bless him) wasted no time in circulating the news. I ran into Aiden and Caleb after work on their way to a presentation in our sector, and we talked about it.

"I can't believe it," he said, his head in his arms on the table. We were at the same bar Caleb and I had gone to just before we'd run into Lola. The pool table clicked and bounced in the background. The bar was full tonight, but the atmosphere was subdued.

Something sad was playing on the jukebox, something with a smoky saxophone and a lonely woman's voice. Believe me, I felt it.

"This definitely isn't a coincidence, though," said Caleb grimly. "Two kids going missing under weird circumstances, and now, two more? People don't just 'disappear', and they certainly don't do it in batches."

I sipped some vegetable liquor contemplatively. "Aiden, you said before that the other kids had had nightmares."

"Yes," he said, not lifting his face from the scuffed stone table.

"It's just...you remember going up...the way Jay got led away from the group...there's something I didn't tell you guys about what happened when I rescued Chloe."

Aiden sat up, looking alert, and Caleb leaned in. I lowered my voice, and forced my face to smooth itself. I don't like hiding my emotions, as I've said, but I knew I didn't want anyone in the bar to see how worried I was, just in case.

"When I rescued Chloe, well, do you remember how she bolted off? It was super strange."

"Yeah. Of course." He snorted. "Crazy...girl. I assumed she was just chickening out." Aiden rarely drinks, but when he does, he does it the way he handles a fight: deliberate, patient, and relentless. He already had four drinks in him, to my two and Caleb's one and a half.

"Well...thing is...I don't know if it was entirely her choice. I mean, she hates being above ground...anyway. When I went into the house, I...I saw things that reminded me of nightmares I've had. There was this little girl with lots of sharp teeth that I've had dreams about...I thought I saw her around the corner when I was looking for Chloe."

They stared at me, horror and incredulity in their eyes.

"Are you sure you haven't got too much Dust in your system?" asked Caleb.

I shook my head. "I've been wondering, but here's the thing. I saw a hand come for me out of the basement door when I was trying to walk past it, and I shot it, and it bled. Then I ran out to the garage—I was scared but I'd also heard Chloe screaming. Then the spiders came after her. And us." I took a deep breath. "Did she ever tell either of you about the pet dog she had when she was a teenager?"

Aiden thought for a moment. "Wait...the little tiny rat one, that she found in her closet? Didn't she find it had gotten stuck and there and starved to death?"

"And it was all dried up," I said, wincing in disgust. "Horrible. Thing is...she's also deadly afraid of spiders. She can't even look at them, let alone kill them."

"She's afraid of a lot of things," Aiden said to the table.

"Give it a rest, baby, they're still engaged," said Caleb.

"That's pretty mean," I added half-heartedly. "I'd be scared of dogs too. Anyway...thing is...first time I saw those dog-spiders, it was when Chloe was around. And I only saw them on the surface when I was around her."

Aiden gave me a blurred look. His fifth drink had disappeared. "So?"

Caleb, who was less drunk, tilted his head to the side. "Well, we know the dog-spiders are real," he said. "You all saw them up there."

"Exactly," I answered. "You see what I'm getting at?"

Aiden blinked fuzzily. "It's all a nightmare," he said. "And I am sick and angry because kids got snatched up. I wish I could just adopt them all. Protect them. Don't care if it's monsters or they're just wandering off. Wanna protect 'em."

Caleb drew an arm around his boyfriend's shoulders. "I wish we could adopt them all too. Don't you worry, babe, we'll have a huge family." He kissed Aiden, who smiled woozily.

"You're a good man, Caleb," he said, kissing him back.

I glanced away, feeling embarrassed. "I'm gonna head home before I drink myself stupid," I said clearly. At this point, they weren't exactly feeling chatty, so I decided to save my fuzzy ideas for later.

The walk home was lonely, though the tunnel streets and backalleys were full of passerby. I wasn't sure whether to smile and feel happy about my two friends—together for a long time, and very in love—or let the sad, jealous, angry feeling in the pit of my stomach take over.

Where was Chloe? She was supposed to be with me, kissing my face...or I was supposed to be with her, in her bed, my hands on her breasts and on her waist. We were supposed to be body to body and skin to skin, my tongue on her clit and hers on mine, twisted up and warm. I've slept with her a few times, but just then, the liquor and sadness in my system made the memories blurry and warm. When I compared it with the way things had been, I wanted to cry. Didn't, though.

I just stumbled home, drunk more on melancholy than alcohol, loving and hating her. Once or twice, I could have sworn I saw someone run past me, behind me, and heard them laughing. It was high-pitched, childish laughter. Shook the misery from me only a little, only replacing half of it with paranoia. Maybe I really am going mad. Sure looks that way. Except, shouldn't I be seeing darkness around my vision, and getting bad headaches? I don't know what to think anymore.

It was a blessed relief to walk in the door and find myself alone. There was a note on the counter and a nice big pot of egg noodles—Dad was out with some buddies, flying some planes and having a cup of coffee, and would be back in an hour. I was glad I'd done my drinking early; Dad's never been that much of a night owl, and coming home drunk and in tears would not have impressed him. He was worrying about me enough as it was.

There was a surprise waiting for me on the counter, though. In addition to a few cheap pulpy pages—junk mail from stores and a couple of bills in envelopes—there was an elegant antique paper envelope with my name on it, in a sharp, clear hand.

"Dear   Janelle,*

With the recent events, we are concerned about the safety of children in the city. There have been more disappearances, as the rumour mill has likely conveyed to you.

We need to know whether you and your friends are planning to join the Crows formally. If so, please mail back the sheet included in a sealed envelope. It must be addressed to me personally, with your name on the outside. Any mailbox will do, of course, but please don't hesitate for more than a day.

If you don't wish to join, there is no obligation and there will be no negative repercussions. However, I urge you to consider it, and to tell me of your discussion (whatever it may be). First, because the Crows need someone like you, and second, as a personal favour. The reasons are becoming more urgent, and cannot be detailed in a simple letter.

Please think it over. I admire how well you've handled unusual circumstances thus far, and would like to discuss them more privately with you in the very near future.

Yours,
Nathu Atalas."

My cheeks burned for reasons I didn't understand. Behind the paper was a page with a detailed waiver and contract. The pay was high, but so were the risks, warned the contract. Death, dismemberment, the Fever...there were benefits, of course, but salvage work isn't for the faint of heart. Monitoring surface conditions, a minimum of five patrols a month with more optional. Not bad, all things considered.

The one downside is, Chloe was already pissed at me for 'eyefucking' Nathu. She isn't going to be happy about this.

THE LOVED, THE LOST, THE DREAMING

I'm justifying it by telling myself that I'm doing it for the good of the city. The truth is, though, I'm doing it for a bunch of reasons. A) to prove to myself that I'm not crazy, because other people are seeing what I see. B) to save some people from being attacked by things from their own nightmares. C) to spend time with Una and Nathu. D) to burn Chloe's ass more than a catfish filet on a redhot frying pan. I won't say it's a noble reason, but I'm not gonna lie to myself. Also, I'm going to go make something with Dad, now he's home. Playing around with circuits and building stuff together is just what I need after another day like today.

15—June 22, 0048 P.D.

Oh gods. I don't know what to say about this...something happened up on the surface. Several 'somethings' have happened in the last week. For one thing, there have been more injuries. Here's the short version of the personal crap, anyway. I don't feel like writing out every single word, not when I'm this tense.

So. Not much happened in the three days between my arguments with Chloe and Raheed. Things were awkward at best with Raheed, and frankly, Chloe still hasn't apologized. We even met up once, tried to do the 'apologize without talking' thing, but even sympathy sex didn't do it. I really, really don't want to talk about that; it's a bruise on my soul right now.

Fine. We got as far as taking our clothes off and doing some making out. Then she saw my scars, wrinkled her face without thinking about it. She saw the look on my face and sort of put her clothes on and left, and that was the end of that conversation.

I cried myself to sleep that night.

Other than that, I worked, hung out with Jay and Kenny and Aiden and Caleb pretending nothing was wrong, watched for lurkers in the shadows, and quietly wrote the level 4 exam on the 19th.

THE LOVED, THE LOST, THE DREAMING

After what I'd been through the last time we were Up, the level 4 lesson—even the marksmanship test—was a breeze. Tonya got us—us being Jay and me—in with a lot more haste than usual—normally it has to be booked a week in advance—and she and May were very, very respectful. It was strange. I know word got around that we're going to be Crows, but I'm not sure I thought the signup through. I forgot that when people know you're a Crow, you get a very wide berth and a lot more respect. It hasn't started with our friends and neighbours yet, and I'm grateful for it. Between the dark things in the shadows, and the fact that I heard Mom and some children's voices calling for me in my dreams, the last thing I need is social rejection.

No attacks, though, and no dragons or dog-spiders down in the lower tunnels. Yet.

I'm going to start with the night before last, five days after my last entry, when I went on my first mission as a proper Crow. Let's start with the fact that it really, really was not what I expected.

Jay and I had gotten our letters of acceptance at the same time as we got our level 4 'pass' letters, the very next day. That was the 20th, if you're keeping track. I know we did well on our tests, but jeez, I've never seen the wheels of bureaucracy turn that fast in my life. Dad was very proud, and wanted to have a small party for me, but I told him not to, and reminded him about why. I really don't know why he puts up with so much from me. He did insist on taking me to dinner, though, which was really nice.

Dad told me a bit more of the story, speaking calming and distantly about what went down, all those years ago. People used to get Lost a lot more often, before the Levels were enforced. You don't have a city with thousands of people without a few of them wandering off or thinking they know better. Lilly, Mom's sister, was one of those people.

He mentioned that Mom would be really proud of me, and happy that I'm becoming a Crow, which she'd wanted to do—except for not wanting to put me at risk. I got very, very teary-eyed when he said that. Of course, he cautioned me and reminded me that she had gone missing by going Up, and I acknowledged that, but I also reminded him that I'm a) handy with self-defense, as my levels show, b) have now, officially, survived worse crap, and c) will be travelling with a team of professionals. The regulations have only come into place in the last ten years or so, and Mom went missing before that.

Still. I'm going to feel really, really bad if I leave Dad all alone in the world. I'd better not die any time soon, huh? Hopefully that won't jinx it. Then again, it looks like insanity is the thing I'm really at risk for.

Sort of a lateral move, I guess.

I'm going to skip over the days at work and the anxious times of fiddling with electronic gadgets and the staring at the ceiling, and tell you about being sworn in just before our first mission.

Nathu did that himself, and they gathered the rest of the Crows—there weren't too many of them, just Oliver, Luke, Hunter, Chang, Skye, Lindsay, and Una, of course. Jay and I faced them, the row of them, and we were sworn in. Both of us were wearing official kit, minus helmets.

"Please raise your right hand. Do you solemnly swear, before your fellow Rediscovery Experts, to uphold justice and the interests of the city?"

"I swear," I said.

"I swear," said Jay.

"To protect the weak, salvage worthy artifacts, and share knowledge about the time before Underlighter City?"

"I swear," I said. Interesting code of conduct.

"I swear," said Jay.

"Do you swear to convey any and all relevant information to the safety of the city to relevant bodies and persons, and not to withhold said information from relevant bodies for any reason, while keeping said information confidential if expressly commanded to do so?"

Jay and I confirmed it.

"And finally, do you swear to act as a neutral ambassador in the event that you encounter survivors Up above or members of another community during tunnel expansion?"

We confirmed it.

Do you swear all of this, by 'Tunnel black and blood red, light true and hope dead'?"

That took us both by surprise, but we repeated it after him.

"By tunnel black and blood red, light true and hope dead."

"Then I now pronounce you official Rediscovery Experts, commonly known as Crows, of rank Private, and welcome you to our team." Nathu's official voice—which carries more—softened, and he clapped our shoulders, grinning. "You're joining an elite group. There are a lot more Rediscovery Experts—you're keeping company with about seventy other common Crows—but you're among the upper echelon at the moment."

Jay, ever mindful of hierarchies and paperwork, looked intimidated. "Is there an official command structure? A title we should've been calling you by, all this time?"

Oliver glanced at Una and they burst into laughter, soon joined by the other Crows. "This ain't the police force, sweetheart," he managed to choke out, slapping a knee gleefully. "Command structure! That's a good one."

"Well, there is a degree of organization," said Una, her lips still twitching. "These six each lead a platoon of about nine to twelve people—two squads to a platoon. Four to six privates to a squad, one of them being a corporal, and two corporals report to sergeants. This lot of unruly customers would be your sergeants. I'm Commander, but that's as far as the structure goes. You'll find, though, that even though we try to use titles in the field, it's a lot more...flexible, shall we say, than in the police corps." Her face settled into the serious, harder lines I knew best. "If you can't think on your feet, and rely on your officer to tell you what to do, you're going to have a rough time."

"I oversee things in my role as City spokesperson and relations coordinator," said Nathu. "As you might have deduced from the oath, I also serve in a more private role for city security." He isn't just the heir apparent; he has an actual role. Though surprised, I managed not to show it.

Jay looked delighted by all the titles and pomp, something I won't ever understand about her, but the yapping was cut short pretty quickly.

195

"To business," said Una. "You might as well call in the corporals."

Chang spoke into a walkie-talkie, and a door I hadn't noticed before opened; twelve strangers, as eclectic in gender and looks as the sergeants, filed into the room quietly. I should have mentioned before that we were in the court room off the side of the antechamber in City Hall. They filled a quarter of the seats, but filled the whole room with their presence.

There were a bazillion introductions and they explained we'd be going on a special detail, and they talked about related events that had happened recently. Jay and I sat awkwardly in the front row together, with the sergeants leaning, easygoing-like, against the judge's and witness's benches.

A couple of the corporals raised their hands and basically confirmed that yes, they'd seen weird shit too—different than we'd seen, though. A serpent with wings and slavering jaws, an old man whose chest opened to let thousands of bugs escape, a slimy tentacled horror whose motions were strangely sideways, and utterly wrong. In every case, the people involved had held back on reporting the ideas and simply gotten themselves checked for the Fever at the nearest infirmary.

THE LOVED, THE LOST, THE DREAMING

When Una and Nathu heard that, they glanced at each other and frowned; and then, to my surprise, glanced at me.

"Can you describe, a second time, everything you've seen so far, Ms. Cohen?" I described my dragon, and peeled off the upper layer of my suit to show off the scars. That got some serious murmuring. I mentioned what I'd seen in the tunnels with Chloe, and the things lurking in the shadows. I touched on Caleb's experience, too, because it seemed like a wise thing to mention. Hesitating, I also mentioned my nightmares, but not in detail.

I was expecting them to laugh, or do something official, or kick me out, then and there.

"Under normal circumstances, I'd say you were all in the early to middle stages of the Fever," said Una. She paced back and forth, looking at all of us keenly. Suddenly, every corporal and even the other sergeants were sitting very straight in their seats. "As it is," she continued, "I'm going to suspend any conclusions until we hear further word. I've only lost a handful of people to the Fever, and all of them had serious suit breaches. As it is, I'd like you all to continue getting yourselves checked regularly, even the ones who passed the tests." She frowned. "I don't like the thought of a new form of the Fever, but if there's any chance that you're not seeing things—especially considering that Hunter,

Chang, and myself saw and attacked some of these monsters—we have a new threat on our hands."

There was silence. We all knew that most people were never attacked by Dust visions, and they definitely weren't injured by them.

A bit more talking, and the meeting was adjourned, after which we were all told not to yap about the monsters too much, but to make discreet enquiries of neighbours and friends about 'seeing unusual things, even crazy stuff' around the place.

When we came back from the break, they laid down a few more decisions. She laid out people's maps, and tacked Jay and myself onto one of Hunter's platoons, under Corporal Leah. Una also decided that she, Sergeant Hunter, Corporal Leah's team, and I would be doing a personal patrol of the Heaven Tubes.

(Una and the sergeants often go out on their own patrols, apparently, and as they said, the command structure is pretty loose. They like to mix up the combinations, even between squads, to optimize teams and make all of us flexible. It's weird, but it seems to work, if the way the other Crows act is anything to go by. And—I hate to think of it this way—it seems like a very good system to handle loss of troops.)

More squads will be patrolling around the Heaven Tunnels and Up entrances every day for the next week. They mentioned the lost kids, too, in passing, and the increased injury rates. Everyone was frowning and confused. Nathu started to look tired, something I've never seen before, and I couldn't help thinking about how much I wanted to give him a nice shoulder rub. Stupid, I know. When they started to talk about the little kids going missing, though, I was all business again. There were a lot of dark pauses, then. No-one could make head or tail of anything, and the meeting concluded on a very depressing note.

Jay and I went home in silence. I was busy absorbing everything I'd heard, trying to remember all the details about organization and flexible structures and blah blah blah. I hadn't really expected them to commandeer us for special ops work, but I suppose it makes sense. After all, who's more likely to run into strangers and boundaries than Crows? I thought they just did salvage work, but interfacing with more of the world makes sense, I guess.

I'm shocked by the fact that other people have been seeing weird things, but relieved, too. Nobody knows what the hell is going on. Dust is sort of responsive, sure, and it's sort of attracted to people and anything that emits electromagnetic waves. That, and travelling in clouds, is all the organization it's shown so far. How can a little clump of sparkly silvery crap be turning into monsters and attacking us? I just don't get it.

Is Dust fully sentient? Is it attacking us now? That doesn't make sense. We thought it was some sort of weird natural phenomenon, maybe from space or something.

I'm confused, I have a headache, and I need to sleep. I've got a patrol with Una tomorrow, and I couldn't be more nervous.

THE LOVED, THE LOST, THE DREAMING

16—June 23, 0048 P.D.

Well, I feel like a horrible, horrible human being right now. On one hand, I did get to run into Lola, which was nice—but on the other...well...you'll see.

Because of my new status, I got the day off work. It would have been nice, but there was a lump in my belly and I woke up with shaking hands. Half of it was from excitement, and half of it was pure fear.

First things first—I went to the clinic to get myself properly checked for the Fever, the way I should have, like, weeks ago. I put it off because I was scared of the results. Couldn't even write about it, but with the way things have been...I had to do it sooner or later.

Here's the scary part, and the first thing I was dreading—all of my results were in the clear. A tiny bit of dust exposure, according to the exhalation test, and normal levels in my bloodstream according to the 'we're going to jab you with sharp things' test; my mental faculties all passed, and my vision was absolutely fine, no dark occlusions. They booted me out with big smiles, after confirming my scars had healed nicely. For some reason, Dr. Dhaliwal's colleague was extra nice to me when he found out that I'm a new Crow. Go figure—these authority types only respect titles after all.

For some reason, knowing that I've come off in the clear scares me even more. What if it's some new type of Dust poisoning? It's not impossible. And, given everything that's happened, I'm still doubting my sanity—which is even worse than a clinical case of Fever.

I guess I should just get on with it. I'm getting sick of my own ramblings, and I have a guilty conscience to unburden.

It turns out that there are a few different meeting rooms that the Crows use. There are multiple elevators Up, the one near us just gets most of the (admittedly rare) traffic. I think there's about five total, but like I said, just because they're there, doesn't mean most people use them. Talking to the Crows, I understand now that people are, ahem, 'gently discouraged' from going Up, for the most part. We used to have a lot more losses, until they put the levels program in.

I can't help shaking my head. Who knows how long this stuff has really been going on for? It's taken a long time for things to get stable. Could kids have been going missing for years?

Too many thoughts. And talking about work won't get this confession out. Here goes...

THE LOVED, THE LOST, THE DREAMING

We were in the meeting room for recon just before heading out. Most patrols are only an hour long, and until now, it's only been maintenance, really. There wasn't much time for introductions, but our squad members are Wilhelm, a short stocky blondish guy, Vincent, a middle-aged and dark-complexioned guy with a good sense of humor, Ginni, a small dark girl with an easy smile and lots of henna tattoos everywhere, and Sammie, another girl leaning towards Between with curly brown hair. We pretty much had time to get each other's names and that was it. Socializing will have to wait for later.

Jay was paired with Vincent and Ginni, Sammie formed a team with Hunter, and blonde Leah paired up with Wilhelm. When I noticed them exchanging very warm looks, I shot a questioning look at Una, who smirked back.

"It's also not like the police force—fraternizing isn't a big deal, if you take my meaning. I stand by the policy that if you're thinking about someone and trying not to flirt with them, all you'll do is distract each other more." Her blue eyes transfixed me and I managed a weak smile.

She efficiently sent people out in various directions, taking the entrances to the Heaven Tubes in Sector A/B's overlap, and assigning Wilhelm and Leah to work from the overlap with Sector F. Hunter and

Sammie got the overlap of A and B from the other side, and Jay, Vincent, and Ginni got the overlap of sector C with B. As with our team, the idea was to work towards the middle of the sector's Heaven Tunnels, doing a cursory sweep from each end. When each team was done, we were to recon at the meeting room.

"Travel well in Darkness," said Una formally, as the other three teams prepared to depart.

"Travel well in Darkness," they all echoed back. Jay sounded less certain, as I did, but she seemed to be getting on just fine with her new teammates already. I watched her back disappear around the corner and wished, for a moment, that she'd stayed with us.

"Let's go," said Una to me. "We'll travel together, no getting separated." She put on the light mask and shrugged in the half-suit. I scratched my back discreetly.

"Man, I'm glad we're not wearing full surface gear, but this thing is itchy," I complained.

She laughed, and the merry sound of it surprised me. "You'll get used to it. Come on. We'll start from this entrance and work our way towards the middle. How are your boots, by the way?"

"Oh, they fit fine. I really like them, actually. Nice heavy boots. I like my boots heavy."

"Me too," she said. "I hate those damn pointy stiletto boots that've just come in. Can't walk in the godsdamn things without a blister." Through the clear goggles, her eyes sparkled. I smiled under my breather. We looked at each other for just a little too long. Finally, she cleared her throat.

"All right. Let's get walking."

She wasn't kidding when she said we'd get walking. The transition up to the Heaven Tubes means few stairs, apart from ancient maintenance access doors. It also means crumbled concrete, steel, and, the closer you get to the surface, possible breaches. We hadn't seen any of those yet, but I was glad for my light breather. The smell wasn't great either—with no-one to come clean it up, there was junk in the tunnel, and worse besides. Without me describing it in a lot of detail, let's just say that if you find yourself hunting for a nice, civilized privy closet, the kind that get reliably changed and cleaned once a day, you're going to be out of luck. A stinky hole with a half-full jug is the best you'll find, and don't expect a water jug and alcohol dispenser or hemp rag-cloth to clean with, either.

There were perks, though. There was lots of graffiti to look at and even crude signs from the various gangers, and all kinds of interesting things sticking out of the walls. For the most part, it was very quiet. Una drilled me on walking quietly in heavy boots rather than just clomping around, and on a couple of quick-draw techniques with a knife. I also learned a few things about ways to hit people with foldies that I didn't know were possible. Once in a while, one of the others radioed in, and I got to play with the walkie-talkies. "They didn't even use these when Dad was growing up," I mused, "and we're back to them."

"You must like technology," she said. "You've been staring every time we walk past a patch of exposed wiring." She was smiling again, very warmly.

"I really love it," I admitted. "I like dicking around with wires. Sometimes I make stuff, fix it. My day job, I'm a junior electrician."

"Really! I don't have the skills for that kind of thing, but I like hearing about it. I really admire people who can build things."

"Ahh, thanks. What do you do for, uh, for fun?"

"Well, I like guns, as you know...I like to read, too. I have to admit, I'm fascinated by the way things used to be." She swept a hand expressively. I'd never seen her so relaxed. "All that technology! The open space! The skyscrapers! Sometimes I just sit and try to imagine what it was like. One of my favorite things to do on a quiet afternoon is reading old newspapers and magazines."

I was about to answer, when the smile snapped off her face and she moved closer to the wall. She didn't have the big AK this time, just a tidy little Glock. I had my favorite pistol, of course, and as the sound of footsteps around the corner became louder, I slid a hand towards it. Una snapped a finger to her lips, glanced at me sharply. I shimmied close to the wall.

We were nestled in a dip in the wall, a sort of half-alcove where the pipe and the dirt were out of sync, and I was very aware of Una's warm body through the suit. I dragged my focus back to the tunnel. No time for distractions.

"Long time, no see," said Lola. I jumped a bit. She stepped back appraisingly. "Since when are you a Crow?"

"How'd you know it was me?"

She smirked. "Well, I admit I was trailing you. That helped." I shot a confused glance at Una, who had her poker face on.

"Why were you following me? It looks like you're working."

"I am, but this was worth losing a pop for. Whatcha doing with some authy type this far from Tartarus?"

"We're doing some investigations," said Una frankly. "By the way, how's Marco? I hear he got cut up pretty bad not long ago."

This time it was Lola's turn to be surprised. "How do you know Marco, stiff?"

Una laughed, but not as easily as she had when we were walking through the tunnels alone. "I'm not a stiff. I'm a Crow, not just a Mole."

Lola cocked her head to the side. "You're not a killjoy, I can see that, but what's with the blunder? I didn't think the city's pet scavengers were allowed to go looking for a rumble."

"We're not looking to rumble, and you're right, we're not cops. Just looking for monsters. Seen anything strange? There have been a lot of attacks lately."

Lola shot a glance at me. As usual, I suck at hiding shock, and she laughed. "It's awright. Marco said some of the Crows weren't too bad. He mentioned some big blonde babe might drop by one of these days, but I admit, I was expecting a sugarplum like me, not some big Tommie."

Una rolled her eyes. "Well, glad we got that cleared up. Just to clarify, I'm not city muscle. We're investigating."

Lola sidled around us, circling. I had never seen her like this, in 'working mode'—defensive, coy, and a little dangerous. Suddenly, all of her complaints that the normal work in the sectors was too boring made more sense. She might not be an anarch, but she's not good at the 'being tied down' thing. Well, she *is* good at being tied down, from stuff we've talked about, but uh, you know what I mean. I digress.

"Lola, chill out," I said, annoyed. "We're not here to razz you and I can promise you that's the last thing on Una's mind. You told me before that Marco killed something with wings a while back. We're looking for those, and we're looking for more—"

"—Monsters?" The nonsense and the aggression were gone. She looked scared. "Okay. No more fooling around. Follow me." She turned on her spiky heel, shiny skirt squeaking a bit as she walked.

Una gave me an eyebrow. "I figured you for the straight edge type."

I blushed under my mask and goggles. "I didn't meet her at work. We're old friends."

Una shrugged. "Even if you did meet her at work, that's your business. We're trying to set something up so it's safer for the sugarplums and they don't have to rely on scumbag meatheads to stay safe on the streets." There was a degree of anger and loathing in her voice that surprised me. Sounded very personal. I wondered what she'd done before becoming a Crow.

"Marco's all right," said Lola defensively, "but yeah, I know what you mean." She sounded sad, then. "Anyway. I'll keep my eyes peeled. Anything I should watch for?"

"We're not sure if it's linked to the monsters, but kids have been going missing. Only Extra kids so far, or kids from poor families."

"Well, we don't have 'em. You come to us, you do it after your first bleed or when you get hair on your face. Before that, we send 'em back home to their mamas."

Una nodded. "Okay. And another thing. There have been a lot of injury reports coming in, especially from gangers. When one of you gets injured, I don't care how, you walk down to the clinics, all right?"

Lola clutched her arms, defensive again. "Sometimes they turn us away. But I swear, the pissing contests up here in Heaven have been settled for a while. Not many red fights 'cause the Tunnel Rats found a route to get shroomies that goes around Snake and Slicer territory completely, which I'll ask you to conveniently forget, please. Other'n that, the boyos and the Tommies will scrap for fun, but...anyway, I told you all this before."

I shook my head. "Lola, girl, tell us something we don't know, then. We're not here on a purely social visit."

"I will when I have something to tell," she snapped. "Ain't nothing been happening." Una shot me an annoyed glance, and I receded, sheepish.

"Well...what hasn't been happening, then?" said Una.

Lola thought for a minute. "Hallies haven't been selling. Not shroomies neither. I heard a batch got contaminated 'cause people were having flashbacks in their dreams, but..."

"Flashbacks? What kind? Like nightmares?"

Lola eyed me warily. "Yeah. Nightmares. Why?"

I paused. "I've been having nightmares a lot lately."

Funny how things can be so timely. The Heaven Tunnels do have some lighting, but it's intermittent. That is usually fine enough, since anyone old enough to talk is used to dealing with darkness. You bring your light with you, built into your clothes or worn on a headband, the same way you carry a foldie everywhere: it's so much a part of life that it's not really worth mentioning. Just then, I was glad that these suits had plenty of lights built in, with the standard motion-driven recharge, because the few lights we had went out.

Lola's dress had red LEDs very unusual places— not just in her cleavage, but also around the cut-outs that showed her tattoos off. She looked very strange in the darkness.

Una crouched low, the lights in the top of her goggles shining eerily on her face. "Shhh," she hushed us. Her voice was barely a whisper, little more than a hissing breath. I leaned against the wall, and touched my gun.

There was a strange noise, a sort of high-pitched, squealing bark that was unlike any animal I'd ever heard. The tunnels made it echo.

"What the hell is that?" Lola whispered.

I thought for a moment. "Maybe a seal? Heard one in an old movie, once."

There was a long, strange hiss from the same direction.

"I don't think that was a seal," said Una, breathing her words.

The air in the tunnel grew colder, and the darkness seemed to thicken. From somewhere in her impossible outfit, Lola pulled out a tiny, crappy minifilter and snapped the elastic around the back of her head. She reached into another pocket in her boots and pulled out a nice long knife.

We all stayed stock still. There was a strange sliding sound, like something being dragged, but more rhythmic. No footsteps, though, the way you'd expect with something being dragged. The hair stood up on the back of my neck.

"What *is* that?" whispered Lola.

A wet sloughing sound and a foul smell answered the question. A great shining white thing, glowing with a sickly phosphorescence, oozed towards us.

THE LOVED, THE LOST, THE DREAMING

Lola screamed, and I couldn't blame her. Una clamped a hand over her mouth, but it was too late. The thing reared the narrow part of its body, and oozed over to investigate.

As it came closer, seemingly unafraid, I got a better look at it. It was covered in slime, and had a mouth that parted into three sections. Three sets of chitinous clawed arms extended from the upper parts of its body, Thick, sharp-looking hairs covered its upper body, and a mass of black, wet-looking eyes covered the upper part of its head. The smell was the worst, though—rot and corruption, deep and dirty.

Una's eyes were wide with fear, but she stood her ground. Her hands didn't shake as she slowly, slowly reached for her gun.

"Do we call for backup?" I mouthed to her.

She nodded slowly, and mouthed, "fuck yes", not the slightest sound escaping her lips. The grub twitched, the mandibles on the outside of its three-cornered mouth clacking eagerly.

Without warning, it sprayed a jet of something disgusting at us. Una, who was closest to the outside, was caught by the heavy blast and went down. She clamped her lips tight together and refused to cry out as she fell.

"Una!" I yelped. Thick, pale mucus covered her. She slipped and slid on the ground, trying to get up and unable to get the friction for it. She stretched a slime-covered arm towards me, looking terrified.

Lola started to back away, her foldie in hand. "Shit! Let's run! It's not fast, we can go down the hall—"

"No! I'm not leaving her here!" I snapped. I ducked into the alcove, using it as cover, and fired off a shot. The worm was concentrating on Una, but looked back in my direction, its mandibles and claws clicking irritably. She was shaking in fear, and her normally rosy skin was beyond pale. Still, she was trying to rise, experimenting with slower movements to get up.

Think ! I commanded myself. I didn't have a throwing knife, stupidly, but I did have my gun.

Experimentally, I fired behind the grub, aiming at the wall far from Una. It twitched again angrily, and clacked. This time, as its maw opened wider, I saw the rows of sharp teeth lining its gullet.

It lifted its head in the direction of the sound, and as it fumbled about myopically, I realised that it wasn't looking at the area so much as it was sensing the vibrations. That was the only way its movements made sense. And, unfortunately for us, all the vibrations were still on our side.

Una struggled and slipped about, trying to get a grip on the dry stone, but the slime was thick. She seemed to be making progress, but the thick slick spot of mucus followed her, stuck to her. Meanwhile, the grub was coming back, and its body language seemed—I don't know, eager. Hungry.

"Lola, shit, it's going to eat her, I think," I hissed. "We have to—"

Lola, her pickpocket skills coming instinctively, already had the comm in hand. I decided to go with it. "The big red button. Push that one. It'll turn the comm on."

"Fuck! The comm! It's not working!" Lola pressed the buttons frantically. I tore it out of her grasp and pried the back off with a smooth snap, and ducked behind her.

The light on the top of my goggles helped enough. The gloves I was wearing were thin and rubbery—I'd have to hope that would do the trick for insulation. Sure enough, parts had been shaken loose. The glue holding the circuit board in place had come off and the central speaker had been dislodged.

"Fucksticks," I growled. I could fix the speaker, but without glue and without my wire kit, it was hopeless. *If only I had my wire,* I thought. I could stick it back in place, fix the broken circuits...my wire or even just a damn soldering iron—hell, anything hot!

The light from my goggles shone on the wall as I looked up. The beast had drawn back onto the grublike part of its thorax, lifting its forepaws defensively. The claws were outspread and its bizarre maw was open. It was ready to strike.

Lola feinted at it and sliced at its flank, dodging back to its rear. The creature made its strange, barking cry again.

I shifted my weight onto the other foot, thinking. There was a soft *clunk*, and a sizzling smell of burning rubber from my boot. I moved it hastily.

A soldering iron was lying in the dirt, its head glowing orange. No time to think. I grabbed the cold end, blew the dirt off the hot end, and touched the iron against the loose connection point between the speaker and the circuit board. The connection melted back together. Lifting the board from the casing, I held the iron over the spots of dried glue to soften them, and quickly pressed the board back into the gummy areas. There.

Setting it down, the end towards me—no sense burning my boots again—I snapped the back on and hit the power button. It crackled to life.

"Crows in unit Leah, come in! We have an incident in the Heaven Tubes, Central Sector A! Aggressive hostiles! Over!"

"We read you!" Sammie. "What's your location? Over!"

"After the junction marked by a trout carving! Full of Tunnel Rat tags. Come fast! We have—"

"Closing on your location! Fifteen yards!"

What happened next was a blur. Sammie and Hunter got there faster than I thought possible, Sammie clutching the comm in one hand and a large trank in the other. They must have just been around the corner. How they hadn't heard the ruckus, I don't know. The tiger-grub screamed and opened its three-tiered jaw wide, aiming for the intruders and ready to blast them with mucus. Sammie hit it with a trank, Hunter drew and fired a shot faster than I'd ever seen anyone do it, and Una, still stuck to the floor, rolled to the side as it fell. The grub roared, its disgusting maw open next to her face, and inhaled shakily.

Before it could release a final jet of goo, Una slid out of its reach and drew her gun. In spite of her slippery fingers, she managed to cock and pull the trigger.

The tunnel shook with the explosion, dirt falling from the roof, and suddenly, the walls were covered with pieces of the grub's head and upper body. I made a face and was grateful for my mask. Without it, I'd be spitting out slimy insect chunks.

Una, covered in the stuff, tried to rise to her knees and slid down again. "A little help, please?" she said calmly. I crept over and offered her a hand. She slid around and managed to find some dry ground, using it as leverage. Finally, she was successful. She leaned on me and I felt the heaviness of her body, all that muscle, as she got to her feet. Disgustedly, she kicked the goop off of her boots, and set about pulling the rest off, slinging chunks of slime all over the tunnel.

Lola looked shamefaced. "I'm sorry I panicked," she said.

Una gave her a look I can't even describe—there was contempt, I guess? But maybe pity, and a little bit of compassion. "You're alive. That's what matters. And I think you understand what we're up against now, too."

Lola nodded, embarrassed. "I really do. Um. Sorry for that. If I can help in any way..."

"We'll be grateful for any help you can offer," said Hunter, stepping in. Xe has the best poker face I've ever seen in my life.

"I'd better go," said Lola awkwardly. "So. Um. I'll talk to Janelle if I see anything, okay with you?"

"It's fine," said Una, pulling slime from her hair with impatient fingers. "Just be careful, and let us know if you see anything else this strange."

"Will do," said Lola, giving her a sickly grin. With that, she fled from the tunnel, running in the opposite direction.

Sammie shot Hunter a glance, and Hunter shook xer head. "No need to follow her," Hunter added softly.

Una sighed, looking shaken and annoyed. "I think we found what we were looking for tonight." She clicked to the open frequency. "All units, come in. Any results? Over."

"Jay here, negative. Quiet patrol. Over." That was Jay. I exhaled, feeling a relief I hadn't expected. I'd been worried about her, in the back of my mind.

"Us too, until now," said Sammie.

"Leah and Wilhelm here. We saw something. Kids' footprints," said Wilhelm. "Tried to call someone, but…no luck. We tried to investigate, and…Leah saw something strange around the corner. High levels of Dust in our area; possible breach. We should come back to investigate when we have time. Over."

Una inhaled slowly again. "Right. Let's debrief in the meeting room and call it a night. We'll be returning to this tunnel, but I need a break, and I'm not risking further exploration with compromised judgement." She looked relatively calm, but no one contradicted her. I guess part of being good at anything is knowing your limits.

We all walked together down the tunnel and out of the Heaven Tubes, down towards civilization, towards home. Una hid it well, but a few times when she caught my eyes, I could see just how scared she'd been.

When did I get so good at seeing inside people's heads, reading their body language? I guess running scared and figuring out whose nightmares I'm having to deal with has taught me a few things. Yay? Not sure it's something to celebrate, though...

We had to march all the way back and deliver our report to the other Crows. Not fun. The slime Una was covered in—and me, too—started flaking into dry Dust. She got herself under the emergency showers before the briefing, to rinse off most of the Dust and slime. Seeing her dripping wet as she delivered her report was really distracting, but kind of sad as much as it was sexy. As far as I could tell, she was shivering cold. I wished I could warm her up, but kept my thoughts to myself.

One of the other sectors had shown a bit of activity, but apart from the footprints and something that looked 'slithery and sharp', there was really nothing. It was useful, but ultimately frustrating.

The meeting was dismissed not long after, but Una hung back, looking tired. I waited for her to finish chatting with Hunter and Leah, trying to look unobtrusive in a corner. According to my watch, we still had a surprising amount of day left to enjoy. I can't explain it, but looking at her, I was dying to make her feel better. She was hiding a sense of misery and I wanted her to be warm and safe. Actually, I guess that is an explanation. This is hard to write.

Everyone else had gone, and I did something I'm sometimes good at, being quiet until the right moment. Her back was to me, and I could see her shoulders slumping.

"Hey," I said, stepping out. She turned around, the guarded leader's look coming back to her face. To my surprise, it slid down. She rewarded me with a weary but genuine smile.

"Hey. Thanks for what you did out there. I guess we're even now, since you saved my ass this time."

"Well, Hunter did the shooting. I just got lucky."

"Lucky is quite the word. How on earth did you fix that comm? I saw Lola shaking it..."

"I don't really know. It was strange. There was...this will sound crazy..."

"...Janelle, trust me, it can't be as weird as what we just saw. Go for it."

"...There was a soldering iron. On the ground. It had a stand and everything. Just waiting for me."

She looked at me critically, the cool-headed and scientific interest gleaming in her blue eyes. "What happened to it after you fixed the comm?"

"I don't actually know," I admitted. "I just sort of put it down. And, well, I was more concerned about you."

She smiled. At the back of my mind, I thought about how much more she smiles around me than when we're with other people. "Thank you, Janelle. I have a feeling you have some mysteries of your own. Speaking of which, I've still got the jitters. I'd better get home and relax. An Atalas needs to be composed in public." She quirked her eyebrows at me.

I don't know how I got the courage to say it, and I had to stare at her boots while I said it, but I managed to get it out. "Do you want to come have a cup of tea at my place first? Just to relax?"

Una blinked, then gave me another of those warm smiles. "Oh, sure. After that, I could use one."

My heart fluttered in my chest. "This way, then. Dad won't be home for another hour or two at least, so we have some time to just relax."

"Thanks," she said. And with that, my fate was sealed. I led back to the familiar tunnels, and towards my home.

It was a very long walk. I can't remember the last time I've had nerves like that, with my palms sweating and the tight excitement making my muscles clench. Maybe when going Up, but it wasn't that kind of excitement—not as warm, as urgent, as this feeling.

"Sorry it's a mess," I said, as I unlocked it.

"Nice place you've got," she said.

"Well, you know, it's just Dad and me, but we do okay."

She pulled her boots off at the door and put her mask and goggles on the shelf. Our kitchenette was full of dirty dishes, to my embarrassment, and there was a laundry basket sitting out in the open, but it wasn't too dirty otherwise. I kicked off my boots and hurriedly chucked it in my room.

"Do you mind if I use your shower?" called Una. "Most of the mucus is gone, but I'm still slimy, and sweaty to boot."

"Go ahead! It's in the bathroom, just off the dining room. I'm going to use it after you, by the way."

"I assumed," she replied, laughing.

I washed my hands and stripped off my suit as I waited, putting it in the empty part of the sink. As I turned the water on and plunged the suit into it, I noticed that some of the mucus was already drying, flaking...into Dust. Very, very interesting. I made sure to fill the sink and submerge it, and rinsed the suit as thoroughly as I could. When I was sure that all the Dust and the remaining mucus had sloughed off, and that soap had destroyed what was left, I left it to soak. Then I went towards the bathroom to grab Una's suit.

I should mention that I wasn't totally naked—I had a camisole, bra, and underwear on. The idea was to go in and go out. I even knocked first. "Come in!" she called.

"I'm just grabbing your suit," I said. There was steam rising behind the white shower curtain, and my skin prickled in ways that had nothing to do with being cold and in my undies.

"Already washed it and decontaminated with soap. It's hanging to dry on your towel rack." And so it was—clean as a whistle.

"Oh. I'll let you finish your shower, then," I said awkwardly.

"Nah, come in," she replied.

"Pardon?" I wasn't sure if I'd heard her right.

"Well, you need to shower anyway."

I let the beat pause settle and thought frantically. Behind me there was the door, the living room and the tea and a thousand ways to avoid this. In front of me was someone, and something, I wanted badly. Something that hadn't happened, hadn't been given to me, in a very long time.

Una poked her head around the corner, light hair slicked to a dark brown helmet that cascaded down and stuck to her shoulders and upper back. "Well?" I met her gaze, dropped my clothes, and stepped in.

The water was warm and soothing, and I flinched at first from the heat. If I didn't know how insanely efficient recycling and heating methods are, I would feel bad about hot showers. Mind you, I had other things to feel bad about just then. Like the way she looked, sleek and wet. There were tattoos I hadn't expected, too. Lots of them.

"I wasn't always on the straight and narrow," said Una simply. "Then there was a very nice lady at one of the clinics...we had a good talk after she stitched that up." She patted a scar that stretched across her lower back, above her buttocks. "I got into the police force, met Nathu..." she blushed a little, not just from the heat of the shower. "He heard about my interest in salvage work, and, well, he invited me to join the Crows." Her breasts were full, and her figure was stockier than I'd expected—muscular and curvy. Delectable. The dark golden hair between her legs was slick with the water.

She caught me staring down, and smiled. "You should straighten up your posture more—you look great naked," she said.

I clutched my arms around myself, met her eyes. "Look. I...this isn't simple for me. And you're married."

She paused and tipped her head to the side. "Yes, but...we're not mono. Do you like Nathu, Janelle?"

"Yes," I rasped. "He's great. And attractive."

"I love him," she said. I was surprised by the feverent sound of her voice. "I love him deeply. And he loves me. But, both of us have a lot of love in our hearts." She reached out a hand. "There's enough love to share."

"I wish I loved my fiancée like that," I said, surprising myself. "But I never did, and I definitely don't now."

She gently set a hand on my shoulder, and I shivered. I let my hands drop to my sides.

"Are you sure about this?" she said. "You can walk away now. I...I had my suspicions, but..."

I shook my head. Savoured the way she looked, body slick with water. "I'm sure. I want this. I'll stay."

She drew me close, and I opened my arms. Came closer to her. The water flooded down on us, in the narrow shower, as I leaned over to kiss her.

Her mouth was hot, insistent, and I reached to the back of her neck to pull her close. Her tongue lashed against mine and I felt her breasts rub against mine. Our water-slick skin stuck together. And then, and then, oh, her fingers slipped down over my waist, down to my hips. Paused to trace lovingly over my scars, my hated scars, before settling slowly down between my thighs. I felt her part the curls above my lips, stroke my clit gently. I shuddered against her, enjoying the electric shock of her touch.

Pushing me back, she used her hand to keep my legs just far enough apart, and slipped her fingers over my delta, touching the edges of my inverted v. Her lips moved over my neck, to my mouth, covering me with kisses that were softer and more delicate than anything I'd ever felt until now. I moaned and stroked the back of her neck, ran my hands over her where I could. Her breasts were full, sweet, yielding softly to my mouth. Her motions between my legs were more insistent, her fingers teasing my labia apart. Then, she slipped her fingers inside.

Her thumb on my clitoris and her lips on my neck and oh gods on my nipples and oh gods, I was crying out, it felt so good...and then, when stars were flashing behind my eyes and I was gasping for breath, her sweet, sweet kiss. She was panting, I was wet and satisfied. I did what I needed, wanted, had to do. I pulled her back against the other wall and sank down, kneeling before her in the narrow tub. She leaned into the corner and savoured my touch. My hands roamed her breasts, teased her nipples, slid down over her hips and over her scars. I kissed the edge of her lips, worked my way in. She smelled clean and musky and good, rich and wholesome. Earthy. Closing my eyes, and settled in and touched her clitoris with the tip of my tongue. Circling it, skimming the folds and teasing her lips, I let the world slide away and pleasured her.

After the rush of pleasure settled into a warm glow, and after we'd gently taken turns washing each other's hair, we went to my room to lie together for a while. Her warm body was so sweet against mine, and touching her skin, damp and clean, was...how do you describe something that feels that good? It's not the first time tonight that talking about her, with her, is making me lose my words.

"Thanks again for earlier," said Una, pressing her lips against my shoulder.

"Well, I try. Did you like that tongue thing, when I..."

"No, no, I mean with the grub. I..." she sounded very sheepish. "I was scared. That doesn't happen to me a lot. I really, really hate maggots. Slime, too."

I squeezed her. "I hear you."

"S' ironic, though, since I enjoy swallowing..." she chuckled quietly, and let her breath out in a long, silky exhalation.

My alarm—the "oops, I had a midafternoon nap" one—went off.

"Dad'll be home in half an hour," I said sadly. "Technically I should kick you out."

"I know." She extricated herself from my arms regretfully. I watched her sleek form as she crossed the room and left. She returned, holding a bundle of clothes and her suit.

As she dressed, I watched, enjoying the sleekness of her shape.

"Was this a fluke?" I blurted out. "Or..."

"I'd like to see you again," said Una softly, "and not just in meetings, if that's what you're trying to ask."

I nodded. "I...look, after today...I should talk to Chloe..."

She looked nervous for a moment, worried, before hiding it under a neutral mask. "Did you want to stay with her and just enjoy sharing this with me anyway?"

My throat was suddenly full of a lump and my eyes welled. "I...I have an ugly conversation that needs to happen with her. I don't know when I can have it, but..."

She wrapped her arms around me, and kissed me. "I understand. Don't rush yourself. I'm not going anywhere, baby."

"It's complicated," I admitted. "She's supposed to be my fiancée."

I felt Una start to withdraw, but she paused, as if rethinking it. "Supposed to be?"

"The truth is, our two friends got engaged, and good for them...and because we've been together for a longish time, I guess, she assumed...anyway, I saved her from the spider-dogs, or helped, anyway...and she decided that it meant we were engaged. She just...up and said it, in front of everyone. Didn't even ask me, really." Now that I was talking about it, it started to hurt. Really hurt.

"Did she actually ask you?"

"Well...not really. No. And...I didn't say no, obviously, but...but I didn't...I didn't say yes..."

She bit her lip. "That's a bit complicated."

"Still want to be around me?"

"I wouldn't let you get away that easily," she said, nuzzling me. "So, I'll ask properly. Do you want to be around me, Janelle?"

"I really do, Una. I really do. Yes. Please." Her kiss, the scent of her musk, was rich as honey. She looked as good as she smelled and felt; Una's blonde hair, light and shining now, was a beautiful mess on her shoulders. "Thanks," I whispered. "This was great. This whole afternoon. Um, about Nathu..."

She smiled again, and this time, it was happier, more confident. "Oh, he'll be happy for me. Don't worry about Nathu."

"Well, see you soon," I said. "You...I can't believe how well you handled yourself up there. When Chloe had to deal with something she was that scared of..."

Una's eyes narrowed and the leader's face snapped into her expression again. "Oh, I know. Let's just say I don't believe hiding from what you're afraid of or screaming is the best way to handle it." She softened again. "See you soon, my dear. Rest well." Her sleek dark form slid through the door and out into the hall. I stayed in bed for a long time, just enjoying the way my skin smelled like hers.

Una Atalas. Blue eyes, blonde hair, tall and solidly muscled with a great rack and sharply defined hips. Likes guns, long walks through the Heaven Tubes, and reading about the time before, when everyone lived Up. Dislikes whiny and impulsive people.

Appears to like me. A lot. More than 'like' me. And I...I've never felt like this about anyone, not even about Raheed at the best of times. And, damn it, not about Chloe.

That's all for tonight. I need to chew this over, and decide how guilty I should feel. I am a horrible person for this—technically, cheating on Chloe—but I don't feel a damn bit of guilt. And that, I think, is the worst part. That I feel so godsdamn happy right now.

More later.

17—June 25, 0048 P.D.

There are more kids missing. Stupid, stupid, stupid! I feel like this is our—my—fault. We sent Crows up and work crews to patch the holes in the other sector as soon as possible, but it didn't matter. There have been more nightmares, the darkness has been heavier in the Heaven Tubes, and kids are going missing. Is the Dust attacking us? Calling the children? Are they leaving on purpose? Nobody understands it, and we're all angry as well and confused. The city has been restless. Seething anger, and heavy air, and darkness that's creeping from the world Up there down to ours. Thank gods we have a competent man who's basically in charge, and a competent woman behind the scenes. I don't know of anyone other than Nathu who could have put down that near-riot.

Our squad of Crows had just delivered an official report on everything that had gone down in the damn tunnels—well, the official, on duty parts, of course. Nathu was looking as upset as he could let himself, given that he was on the clock. Una and I didn't get the chance to talk yesterday, though she did send me a really, really nice message...anyway. I digress.

Nathu's personal office is on the second floor of the Honeycomb, which is a lot bigger than I'd thought it was. It's spare and efficient, the one luxury being the row of three lovely round windows, set into the wall and facing the street. They're like little alcoves. Just now, though, the otherwise picturesque view of the street was pretty much ruined by...a crowd of protestors. The thick glass is soundproof, but angry people waving signs and obviously shouting send a pretty clear message even without sound.

"Look!" yelped Sammie. I was glued to the glass, too fascinated even to shout.

"Shit," Nathu murmured. He stood and unconsciously brushed off his fashionable, subdued suit. "Well, I'd better get down there." Wilhelm, who had just finished describing the footprints, stepped back respectfully.

"I'll fetch the police," he said.

"Tell Brumi to have a squad on standby, but don't send them out yet. These are my people, after all." Nathu straightened his collar again, squared his shoulders, and seemed to brace himself. "Una, Janelle, Hunter, Sammie, and Leah—flank me, please. You all know what's going on in those tunnels. Ginni, Vincent, Jay—please wait here on standby."

He led us down the curving stone stairs. I fingered the stonework on the way down, counting the abstract flowers mindlessly. I slept really well after Una, but last night, not so much. My mind was full of dark figures and flashing teeth again. Then, too, this is the first protest we've had since...what? I was a kid? So, yeah, I was scared as hell.

We exited through the grand opening of the antechamber, Nathu leading us confidently, calmly. The closer we got, though, the louder it was. There had to be at least sixty people, standing and shouting and waving signs made of metal pipes and hemp cardstock angrily.

"Find our kids! Find our kids! Find our kids! Find our kids!"

"What do we want?"

"Safety!"

"When do we want it?"

"Now!"

You get the idea. Having sixty people shout at you all at once is a thing of its own, but when a couple of them are waving hoes and wrenches and other tools, and the others all have metal pipes...yeah. That's another thing altogether.

You're a Crow now, I reminded myself. *Put on your unreadable face.* So I did.

Sammie looked terrified, but Hunter and Una were looking over the crowd like they dealt with this crap every day of the week. Given Una's scars, she probably got used to worse when she did...whatever she used to do before.

"Watch Nathu," said Hunter quietly. "Sammie, hide your fear. Remember, they're angry but they aren't here for a fight. They're scared. Pick one at a time and concentrate on them; don't look at the whole crowd. Watch that man in the back of the crowd, the one with the crowbar and the mustache. He's angrier than the rest."

Una's eyes were cold with logic. "Janelle, be on guard. There's the man with the crowbar and there's a couple of very angry women behind the leader. I'm going in behind Nathu."

Nathu had already figured out who was leading the crowd and had walked right up to them. Una trailed at a pace or two behind, looking sleek and deadly. She was still beautiful, sure, but it was incidental. The way she was staying on the balls of her feet and discreetly feeling for her throwing knives said she was ready for trouble. The protestors seemed to get it, and as Nathu and she advanced, some of the shouting died down.

"Good to finally see you," barked the woman, before Nathu could introduce himself or greet her properly. "Where the hell have you been?"

"Where I always am," he said calmly.

"Well, wherever it was, you weren't there for us! Families all over the city have lost kids over the years. The signs and posters have been up, but where are the search parties? This is your job! You're supposed to take care of your people!"

"So, are you saying you think the missing children are connected? Do you know this for sure?"

"Why wouldn't they be?" the woman shot back.

"That's what we're trying to find out. Do you have any information? Even suspicions, at this point, would help." He looked earnest and determined.

The woman immediately softened. "I...two of our Extra kids have gone missing. I heard others had too."

"Others like mine," growled the guy with the mustache. He hefted his crowbar. The crowd had gone quiet. A few other people had that 'waiting for a chance to talk' face.

Nathu turned to him. "Yours?" Una was relaxing, even concealing a faint smile. He knew what he was doing.

"Years ago. Before your time, whelp. Fact, where's that father of yours? Seems to me he's mayor, he should be the one answering these questions. Not just some young pup like you."

"My father is coordinating efforts and wrangling forces so we can investigate this properly. When children were reported missing to the police, we started to do some discreet investigations..."

"Damn your discreet investigations! Them gangers are taking the kids!"

The crowd started to kick up again. Nathu silenced them with a look.

"Would you bet your life on that? What about your children's lives? What if you march up there and you find...nothing? The Heaven Tubes are getting more dangerous. People have been getting hurt up there..."

"None of them cover-ups!" snarled the older man. He had easily parted the crowd to come to the front, and even the first woman stepped back.

"Who did you lose?" said Nathu softly.

"My niece. Years ago. And they never found a damn thing. Was like she vanished outta her bed." The hard lines in his face were granite, weathered in place by eons. "I ain't standing for it happening again."

"What was her name?" said Nathu. He was holding the man's gaze, spine straight. The guy's anger didn't matter at all to him. He actually seemed to care about what was making the man angry, rather than being scared by the crowbar.

"Lilly," said the guy. "An' then we Lost her sister Miriam."

I tried to take a deep breath, but the world swam in front of me. Lilly had been the surprise baby for my grandparents, who were old but not that old...

Hunter, still standing on the steps with me, noticed that I was leaning on the column way too heavily.

"Go inside," xer said, not flinching. "Personal matter?"

What were the fucking odds? Mom's estranged uncle, an in-law who'd married into the family...Pete, or something. I don't even know. Hearing him say Lilly's name, and then Mom's...it came right back to me. I remembered him coming by when Mom was lost, barking at Dad like Dad could've done something, and then getting roaring drunk. He cried into his beer, collapsed on the couch, and slunk off the next morning, and I'd never seen him since.

I backed in, sat down, and listened.

"People of Underlighter City," said Una, speaking up for the first time. "You're all familiar with Loss—a loved one, a friend who contracted the Fever, people who wandered up in the days before we developed the levels...our world is a lot more dangerous than one we left Up there.

"We have been safe here, but that, it seems, is changing. I and the other Rediscovery Experts have begun to investigate these matters privately, and we have found some evidence. We won't rest until we've got them in our arms and on the way home." A tiny glance at Nathu cued him to pick up from where she left off. Una stepped back again.

"I know the names of every one of the missing children," said Nathu, smoothly taking over from her.

THE LOVED, THE LOST, THE DREAMING

"When a child cries, I lose sleep. This is my city, and you are my people. Nothing and no-one is going to get away with harming you from now on. This ends here."

Nathu looked good like this. A consummate politician, not that I mean it in a bad way: capable of leashing his emotions but letting them show just enough that his audience could tell they were there.

"Given the new information that has been uncovered, we'll be making more expeditions to the surface in weeks to come. And you can expect that this will be for purposes other than salvage and hunting for ancient luxuries." A hint of a snarl in his voice, something predatory. "If we are at risk, you can be assured that Una and I myself will be investigating things directly. A risk to some of us, especially those who are youngest and most unable to defend themselves, is a risk to everyone."

I saw a flash of something darker in his eyes, a hint of a certain thing I couldn't put a name to. I certainly hadn't seen it in any of the guys' faces—maybe Dad's, once or twice, when certain topics like people trying to hurt me came up. Something protective, burning and smouldering under the public face. He wasn't just blowing smoke up everyone's ass about this—he really was angry.

"Now, I know I can count on all of you to do your part in ensuring that no more children go missing. To those of you who are privileged to be parents, I ask you to keep an especially close eye on your children. These disappearances have been too frequent and we are doing our best to find out whether they are linked, and how. If you need to decrease time at work and spent on community duties, this can be accommodated for. In turn, I want to ask the rest of you to adjust for this."

A few people groaned, they couldn't help it. Nathu gave them a scorching gaze, as if to say, *how dare you.* "Those of you who are single or without children, I must ask a favor: for your friends and family, and for the sake of the children you may have some day, please, help us all by doing your part. Report anything you see and watch for suspicious activity. Even if you're worried that what you see is a symptom of the Fever, or another form of Dust poisoning, report it. We're taking anything we can get."

The crowd had gone from angry-protest mode to being on his side. Nathu's anger and emotion were well-leashed, but burned in him. He simmered with charisma. "Now, can I get those of you with children who've gone missing to step here, to the side. I think it's best if we take some information about it from you, anything you can remember."

At that point, Wilhelm appeared, bringing a squad of police with him. What had been a simmering mess turned into paperwork and bureaucracy. I have to admit, I was impressed. Having given my report, and with things defused nicely, it seemed like a good time to sneak off and investigate more. As people filed into the antechamber to give their statements, I tucked myself into a corner and started to edge away, using the shadows to cover the parts of me that weren't already covered by the official black suit. I'm good at lying, as I've mentioned before, not that I like using that skill much, but lately I've been learning to get better at sneaking.

Not good enough, though. The old guy with the mustache saw me walking away, back into the well-lit street—I should've mentioned how freaking dark the antechamber is, with those damn high ceilings.

He stared for a long time. I could see the wheels turning, and used the innocent, confused face. The old slowly-back-away trick didn't cut it, though. "Hey!" he called gruffly, marching after me.

"Shitfucks," I muttered to myself. "Can I help you, sir?"

He grabbed my shoulder by the hand that didn't have the crowbar. "Is that really little Nellie?" His dark hair was threaded with grey and white, and his puffy nose was crisscrossed with broken blood vessels. The shadows and bags under his eyes were prominent, layered. A strong smell of marijuana, but not, thankfully, of his BO, wafted into my nose.

"I'm sorry, I don't think I know you." I put my own hand over his and removed it, more gently than I wanted to.

"Janelle. Miriam's daughter. Your mother got Lost after Lilly went missing. You can't tell me forgot Lilly? Her kid sister? Your aunt?"

"I should go," I said firmly. I managed to do the calm-faced thing on the outside, but inside, I was panicking. Una and Nathu and the rest of the Crows were inside, dealing with the people, and there was a line up that went all the way out the door. I was stuck.

"You gotta listen to me!" He dropped the crowbar and grabbed my other shoulder. I'm not a small girl, and I can take a bruise or a punch, but this fucker was strong. "I'm your mom and aunt's uncle. Your great uncle, I guess. I haven't seen you in years. Joe. Don't you remember me?"

"After Mom went missing," I rasped unwillingly.

"I'd hate to see it happen t' more kids. Lilly...she was a good kid. Child of their old age. Would almost your age. 'Bout the same, actually." He peered at me. "Don't forget her, will ya? Looks like you already have, but..."

"I...uncle Joe..." He gave me a weary smile, and collapsed into Dust.

I reached into a pocket and slapped an emergency mask over my nose and mouth without thinking, pulling my goggles down. "Dust leak!" I hollered, backing away as fast as possible.

A concerned shopkeeper was soon on the scene, with a pitcher of water. I went for my foldie, and stopped, remembering that I was in the heart of the city, with cement rather than the cobblestones everywhere else. Hunter was on the scene even before Una, a look of concentration on xer face.

"What happened here?"

"Okay, so that guy who was talking to Nathu?" I babbled. "He claimed to be my great uncle Joe, and started talking to me, and *this* is all that's left of him!"

"Get more water," said Hunter. She walked over the vendor's stall again, got a second pitcher, and covered the huge pile of Dust. I crossed the street and went to a cafe, returning with another jug myself. The shopkeeper, a frightened, pale little guy, grabbed his dustpan and swept up the half-dissolved mess. At least the Dust was melting in the water. Anything normal was a balm.

A few more jugs, and the natural seeping of the water we'd already poured on, and it was soon cleaned up. Without another word, Hunter ushered me back over to Nathu and the other Crows and admins in the antechamber. The crowd was starting to disperse, but there were still lots of people. She flicked a hand at Una, who came running.

"Janelle? Are you all right?"

"I...I think so. Um. That guy who was yelling at Nathu, the one with mustache? He...he said he was my uncle Joe, and pulled me aside...we talked for a minute, and then he turned into a pile of Dust. Just collapsed."

Una looked me over, concern all over her face, and not just the professional kind. She ran through a basic Dust contamination exam, checking out my pupils and reaction time and a bunch of other stuff right there in public. She even had an aspirator gauge, and that read only barely above normal, well below the poisoning or even the Fever warning threshold.

"I think we'd better get a statement about this from you. Cohen, I want you on investigation duty in your own neighbourhood in the sector." Referring to me by my last name? And putting me on a cop's rounds, far from the Tubes? I opened my mouth slightly to protest. "It's nothing personal. We're sending a few Crows out to their own sectors to do some investigations on past missing persons cases and suspicious injuries." She shook her head. "I noticed a flicker here and there in the injury statistics, but they always listed perfectly normal causes..." Una cleared her throat. "Besides, I really, really don't want to see you get hurt, Janelle," she added softly. Then, in her previous tone of command, she added, "And this time, that's an order. I don't want to see you back here unless you've got information."

Time to be official. I couldn't be a crybaby on duty. These people were counting on me to look strong and competent. Una and Hunter knew it, and so did I. I nodded firmly. "Okay, I'd better go."

As I headed off, I glanced over my shoulder. What I saw stopped me cold. Nathu was sitting behind a desk, and in front of him, being interviewed, was my great uncle Joe. I turned on my heel and started to walk back in. I almost didn't notice the wide, respectful berth people gave me.

I went right up to the guy and put a hand on his shoulder. A mustache, yes, but his hair was the wrong colour, his eyes weren't bloodshot, and his nose wasn't broken. It wasn't Joe. Not even anyone I knew. Just a guy.

"I just wanted to reassure you that we'll do our best to find the missing children," I said. "Personally, as a Crow." Nathu shot me a glance loaded with confusion, and I smiled like nothing was wrong.

"Thanks. I know the kids would thank you," he said. "Got a little tense out there...but 'm feeling reassured about this city and its mayor."

"I'll let you get back to it," I said, nodded to Nathu. He gave me a terse smile, and returned to the questions at hand.

As I walked out the door, my blood was pounding. Had I misheard the guy when he said their names? Was it just an eerie coincidence, with two other kids named Miriam and Lilly who'd gone missing when Mom and her sister had? That wouldn't explain the Dust copy of Joe, though, and other people had interacted with the copy—or at least the Dust. I could still see the wet patch on the pavement.

Am I going crazy after all? Just when I started to think it wasn't my sanity going down the tubes, that everyone else was going through the same things...this. What the hell is wrong with me? Even writing about it now, I want a good stiff drink. And the nightmares keep coming.

The route home was just a blur. Intent on thoughts of the great-uncle Joe clone, and worrying about the fact that kids have been going missing everywhere, not just in our sector, I didn't notice the world around me at all. I was lost in thoughts of Dust and darkness, Up above and below.

"Oof! Hey! You look different in the Crow suit. What's your hurry, Janelle?"

"Aiden! Oh! That's convenient. Can we go to the Extra house where you work? I need to ask you and your coworkers some questions."

"Uh...sure." He looked very confused. "I just got off work, but I can go back. I mean, I'm off early anyway..."

"Thanks," I said crisply. "I hate to badger you, but this is really important."

"Yeah. Right around the corner. Man, it's strange not seeing you in grubby overalls and a t-shirt. The tight uniform looks good on you though. Very, uh, imposing."

I tossed him a grin, feeling more like myself for a moment. "Well, it's still me in here. Now, come on, I haven't got all day."

It wasn't much of a walk. I'd gone farther from downtown than I'd expected, and the orphanage is halfway between the sector's more residential area and the centre of the city, where all the offices and shops and stuff are. We took a couple of sharp corners from the main road, a sidealley shortcut, and we were there. A dingy but cheerful door with bright paint and lots of fingerprints on it, and above it, a much less cheerful sign saying, "Underlighter City Orphanage", with "Sector A" in slightly smaller print below it. The window onto the road was covered in layers of fingerprints and nose smudges, with more than the usual numbers of safety charms danging from its door.

Aiden pushed the door open and was immediately covered in children. Three little kids who'd been running around in the front room plastered themselves to his legs.

"Hi, guys," he said, laughing. "This is my friend, Janelle. She's here to help me with some things."

The biggest one—she was probably eight—detached herself and looked at me with big, serious blue eyes. I'm iffy on kids—I always worry that I'll break them, and damn, but they're loud!—but she melted my heart instantly. "I'm Jane. Are you a Crow?"

"Yes," I said. "I'm a Crow. I'm here to learn some things about the little guys who went missing. I'm here to help keep you safe." Tentatively, I reached out to pat her curly brown haired head.

"Will you make sure the nightmares don't come back?" I've mentioned before that when I need to be, I'm a damn good liar. This time, I didn't want to lie. Not to a kid.

"I'm gonna try, sweetie."

"Kay." She kept staring at me solemnly as I stood up. Aiden shrugged at the startled look on my face.

"Good afternoon," said the receptionist, a nice middle-aged lady with a ruddy complexion. "Can I help you?"

"Janelle Cohen. I'm here to investigate on the missing children's case." Her face fell immediately.

"We talked to the police weeks ago...what do Crows have to do with it?"

"There have been more cases. We're trying to find out whether they're linked." I gave her a reassuring smile, or my best attempt at one.

Somehow, it worked. Uncertainly, she smiled back. "Go right ahead. The night staff aren't here right now, but I'll let them know you were by. Will you be wanting to interview them later?"

"Yes. When will they be in?"

"Well, Kevin, who was on when they...you know...will be on at six in the night cycle, same as always. So, in a few hours. He'll be on tomorrow as well. The other is Janelle, and she'll be on at eight, but she's only here tomorrow."

"Thanks," I said. "I may be back tomorrow as well, then. Do you mind if we go have a look in their room?"

"I'd have to ask the ward head," said the woman nervously.

"I'll wait." She scurried off. I am really, really not used to people treating me like this. Even Pramjit's team would usually scoff at me when I yelled at them for slacking.

Aiden, who'd been chatting with the kids all this time, stood and brushed himself off. "Who are you?"

"Um...me? Janelle?"

"When did you get so...professional? And articulate?"

"Articulate—uh, thanks? Well...I have things to do. There isn't really room for screwing around anymore."

Aiden started to say something, and just nodded. "I guess I'd better take you to their rooms. Right now they'll be finishing dinner—these three troublemakers," he said, scowling at them in a way that made the kids giggle, "are going to come back to the playroom with us." Aiden popped out his key and opened the door separating the tiny waiting room and bin of toys from a hall, and the rest of the rooms.

"Are they allowed to run everywhere like this most of the time?" I whispered.

"Well, as long as someone's out here, if the kids feel like playing out in 'the window room', we usually say yes."

"Ah."

"Until now, this place has been safe," said Aiden tightly. "Letting them run around a bit was fine." The kids were chattering, but glanced distrustfully at us when he said that.

"Wait, so you're just bringing me back here? We don't have permission yet."

Aiden gave me a look of disbelief. "You're a Crow on an investigation. You don't need permission."

THE LOVED, THE LOST, THE DREAMING

I didn't say anything back. He'd obviously spent more time around them than I had, being a grunt electrician. I'm starting to realise how sheltered I've been until now, in my way.

The hallway was narrow and cramped but very cheerful, with lots of pictures on the walls. It smelled like disinfectant and warm food and, if this makes any sense, happiness. There were doors everywhere, and a lot more windows than usual. At every step, wide-eyed kids stared through the glass at us. There were very small classrooms, a dining hall—full of messy kids eating bowls of something that looked cheap but tasty—an infirmary, a playroom (where we unloaded our three tagalongs) and finally, the dorms. The dorm didn't have windows, just labelled doors.

"The boys sleep in here," said Aiden, staring at the first door for a moment. "Come on in." He pushed it open, only hesitating a bit, and I followed him.

It was basically a barracks, and at the moment, completely empty. Lots of cheerful paintings covered the walls. There was a tidy kind of chaos—busted, well-loved toys spilled out of boxes and shelves against the wall overflowed with colouring books and crayons. There were a few cheap e-readers covered in industrial-grade plastic, too, for books. About twenty bunk beds took up the rest of the space, ten on each side, with the room divided in quarters by partitions.

251

We had entered at one of the narrow ends, but there was also a door in the middle of each of the long walls, obviously connecting to other rooms. Over all, it was a cramped, cheerful place, like a police barrack, but friendly.

I stared up at the low ceiling, painted with a night sky that transitioned to a day sky on the end closest to us. The imitation windows on the wall were painted to show bright, cheerful vistas—a farm, a zoo, a pretty spring scene...nothing about the room suggested a place where bad things could possibly happen.

Aiden pointed to the closest corner, the bottom bed on our left. "That was Louis' bunk. He is...was...*is* blind, so of course we didn't want him on the ladder. Ryan sleeps above him."

I started to examine the bed. Sometimes you have to look at a motherboard really carefully to find that tiny thing out of the ordinary. I looked and looked, and there was nothing about the bed that was strange. The one above it was fine, too. I went through his stuff, which was in a drawer of the small round cabinet next to the bed. I found a toy rabbit and an antique book of Braille, but nothing else.

"You said the kids had nightmares, right?"

"Yeah. Ryan said he had a bad dream..." I turned over the pillows, even lifted up the futon mattress, and looked underneath the bed. Under the bed, near the edge, and in a corner of the mattress, I found a few tiny silver grains of Dust. Nothing in the top bunk, though, even though I rearranged that one too.

"There's a little Dust here on the bottom, by the way. Just a few grains, but it's there," I said. Aiden immediately ran for one of the rooms, which turned out to be a privy closet, and filled a glass of water from the sink. He brought it back and splashed it over the mattress. As the Dust melted and became no more than a greyish smudge, I looked around some more.

"Why don't you take me to the girls' room?"

"Sure. The kids should be done supper pretty soon, and then you can talk to Ryan and Karen, if you want."

I nodded. "Sure. I can't see anything else jumping out at me. Did the police dust for prints and all that?"

"Of course, but they didn't find anything. And there's carpet in here, of course, so there weren't any footprints." He looked upset again. Impulsively, I gave him a hug.

"Hey. I know I'm being all official, but...I'm here to help find the kids."

"Where were they weeks ago?" he said, lifting his hands bitterly. "Why weren't the police as concerned as you? I heard there was almost a riot downtown today because other kids went missing. How many more have to disappear before the damn city gives a shit?" I can't remember the last time I saw him so angry. Good reason, too.

"We've been investigating for a bit…the leads have just gone cold. It's been impossible. It's not as though nobody's on it. There's just no evidence left behind. You know that."

"True." He took a long breath and let it out very slowly. "I guess I should show you the girls' room." He opened the main door again and led me into the hall, to the next one over.

It was pretty much the same. Colourful, untidy, friendly, and ordinary as can be. Once again, the kid in a corner bed had been chosen, and her roommate had had nightmares, but everything else looked normal. There was a grain or two of Dust, though. The stuff sparkles in the light, which makes it stand out. We cleaned that up, and I sat on her bed to think.

"Any ideas yet?" asked Aiden. He looked at me hopefully. I wanted to snap at him that I wasn't a damn genius, but that wouldn't do any good. Besides, this was official duty. There's no room for snapping at a civilian when you're trying to help them out—and like it or not, Aiden was a civilian to me now, not just a friend. Things would change back after work—I hoped—but this wasn't the time to get all squishy and insecure on him.

I chewed the corner of my lip, thinking. "Was there anything connecting the kids? Anything special about them?"

"Well...they were both blind, but that was it. Nothing else. They didn't pay any extra attention to each other, they didn't pick on each other...nothing."

"They both got taken from beds close to the door, and at ground level, and both had trace amounts of Dust on their beds." I paced. "So...Dust could be consciously attacking people now, which is really weird. I mean, we saw it in the tunnels and I've now run into it multiple times...but how is it getting all the way down here?"

"Are you asking me?"

"Just thinking out loud."

"Okay."

I paced some more, and picked up a doll from Noor's bed. It had yarn for hair and worn clothes, and its eyes didn't match. A lot of love had gone into that doll. Somewhere, I hoped, a little blind girl was missing the way her doll felt. It was better than the thought of her lying in the dark: cold, still, alone. A small dead child in the Heaven Tubes or on the ground Up there...

I shook the images out of my head. "Okay. So. Dust might be—is—attacking people. And...it might be able to take human form. It's not impossible, since it can obviously take the shape of monsters. But so far, it's only attacked people. Could it have kidnapped the kids? Why would it do that? Hell, why is it attacking us? It's not like we've launched an offensive...Argh! This makes no godsdamn sense!"

"Well...you want to talk to the kids?"

"Sure. Did they talk to the police already?"

"Yeah, but...you know."

"I'll keep it short," I assured him. "Can you go get them? I'm out of ideas." Aiden nodded and didn't say anything else. He disappeared out the door, and I was left to stare at the pictures of flowers and the artificial stars.

I wasn't waiting long. He came back with two nervous, scared little kids. I stood up and greeted them with a smile. "You must be Ryan and Karen."

"Yes," said the boy. He scowled at me.

The little girl just nodded. Her dark eyes seemed to swallow the world, and I was shocked at how young she was. I mean, they were kids, obviously, but some children are younger than others even when they're the same age, if that makes any sense.

"So, I heard that you guys had nightmares when on the same night Louis and Noor went missing. Is it okay if I ask you questions first, Ryan?"

"Only if you don't tell me I just had a bad dream and yell at me," he snapped back. I shot Aiden a surprised look.

"Of course not," I said, managing a gentle tone. "I get bad dreams too."

"Kay. I was asleep, but I dreamed I saw a man in a black cloak come in and spread over Louis—I was asleep, so I could see though the bed—and then he picked Louis up and he was all swirly around the edges. And then I dreamed about a scary monster that wanted to eat me, and then I woke up and he was gone."

Ryan had rattled it all off very quickly, and his brown eyes cut into me accusingly. "That's a scary sounding dream. You're sure you were asleep?"

"I know the difference between awake and asleep," he snapped. "Apparently you grownups don't, though. I know I was asleep when he came in." He was sitting on the bed, too, and drew his arms and legs up close. "But they kept trying to tell me I was awake."

"Do you remember anything else?"

"No. Just the dream. And then everyone was upset the next day. Can I go now? I want to go play." He didn't want to talk, and I had a feeling he wouldn't want to help much. No point in trying to pressure a kid when they don't feel like it. They'll just hate you.

"Okay. Thanks for helping. Can you let me know if you remember anything later?"

He melted a little bit. "Okay. Thanks. Bye." With determination that only a kid can show, he walked off and closed the door—not quite slamming it.

Karen had been silent the whole time. "What about you, kiddo?" I asked.

"There was a witch," she said softly. "I wasn't dreaming, though. I woke up for a minute. Then I went back to sleep. But she thought I was asleep, so she didn't take me."

I watched her for a reaction. She stared back, with a hollowness and fear in her gaze that I recognised from the mirror.

"I understand that Noor was blind, right?"

"Yeah. She had dreams where she could see sometimes though. But she couldn't see how scary the witch looked."

"What did she look like?"

"She kept changing. She had long scary arms and she was dark and she had long nails. You know, a witch. She looked like witches look. She had a nice voice though. She reminded me of my mom."

"Your mom?"

"She was a ganger. Auntie said she was a nasty whore so they put me here." I bit my lip to hide the expression on my face. I was starting to understand why Aiden was so protective of these kids. "Don't look sad," said Karen. "I like it here. They're nice. Nicer than Auntie anyway." She smiled at Aiden, a ghost of a smile. Someday she'd be very pretty, I thought.

"We found some Dust under Noor's pillow," I said.

"The witch didn't say anything to Noor about Dust. She said she'd take her to a place where she could see, though. For real. Even without her eyes." Now that got my attention.

"See without her eyes?"

"I don't know what it means either," said Karen sadly. "And the grownups just said it sounded like I was dreaming, and other stuff." So much for being 'younger', the way I'd thought she was.

"Well, some grownups don't know how to listen."

"You did, though." She fixed me with her thousand-yard stare again. "Thanks. You're really nice for an important person."

There was a lump in my throat that had come out of nowhere. "Thanks. Is there anything else you can remember, Karen?"

She shook her head. "No. But I've had bad dreams. And they checked me for Dust Fever but they said my brain is okay. Noone understands."

"They usually don't," I said quietly. "Thanks. You can go play now, if you want."

The door opened, and the receptionist from the front walked in, followed by another woman who was obviously used to looking important.

"Well, I was going to welcome you to our establishment and say that you're free to ask anyone anything you need to know, but I see you've invited yourself in already," she said, looking annoyed. She had the look of a person who was annoyed a lot, but generally friendly. The mop of frizzy sandy-coloured hair piled on her head looked about as frayed as her nerves seemed to be.

I rose and extended a hand. "You'll have to pardon me. Janelle Cohen."

She didn't shake, and I revised my opinion towards the 'bitch' direction. "I thought Rediscovery Experts mostly stayed Up."

"It's complex. Normally, we do, as far as I understand, but this situation has some overlap. Would you mind if I speak to your night staff at some point?"

"Since you've already invited yourself in and spoken to the traumatized children without asking permission, I imagine you're welcome to talk to the staff whenever you like."

"I'm terribly sorry for giving you the wrong idea," I said, looking her in the eye. She had a couple inches on me, but I'm good with staring contests, if you haven't clued into that already.

"She wasn't bothering me," said Karen quietly. "She was nice."

That melted the woman immediately, though she kept the suspicious tone in her voice. "Well. I'm happy to hear that. Some of the police officers were...very impolite, and these kids have been through enough."

"I completely agree, Ma'am," I said. "I Lost my mother when I was eight."

"I see," she said, more softly. I revised my opinion a third time—she was just being protective of the kids. "Well. Have a good night, Ms. Cohen. Let us know if you need anything at all."

"Good night, Ma'am." She left with a little curtsey and went back to wherever. I'm sure it was important.

Aiden was just staring at me with his eyebrows as high as his hairline. Even Karen was grinning. "Aw, what?" I snapped.

"Um. That was Gladys. She's only in charge of everything and known as a fire-breathing dragon. That's why I was hiding in the corner just now."

"Did you forget already?" I said, grinning at him. "I killed a dragon once. Besides, she's just worried about the kids. Anyway. I should go."

"Okay. Want me to walk you home?"

"Well...I could use the time to think, but sure."

"Good night, Karen," said Aiden, smiling. He ruffled her hair.

"Good night," she said. "See you tomorrow? Night, Janelle."

He closed the door behind us and led me back down the hall, shaking his head the whole time.

Once we were out of hearing range, Aiden relaxed. Not much, though. "Well, that was intense," he said. "Since when are you so...professional?"

"I have a job to do," I said tightly. "People are being hurt. And I'm a Crow now, I can't just sit back and wait for someone else to handle things."

He gave me a weird look, full of respect and fear and—awe? I dunno what you'd call it. "Were you always like this and I just didn't notice? It's like you've turned into Batman, or something."

I rolled my eyes. "I'm not an ancient comic book character. Geez. This is serious." A smile tugged at his lips, but he didn't say anything for a while.

Finally, we were outside my place, back on the familiar, supposedly safe cobbled paths with their low clearances and sprawling little homes, and he broke the pleasant silence. "Don't lose yourself in there, Janelle. I like who you are, and what you're becoming, but you get obsessed with things."

"I don't get obsessed," I snapped. "I'm focussed."

He looked disappointed for a moment. "Relax. I'm not trying to hurt you. We're on the same damn side."

"I'm sorry. I know. I just...it's been a really long day and my sanity is frayed at best." He pulled me into a lovely warm hug.

"I know. Come over and cuddle some time. I'll invite Caleb and we'll have a cuddle pile."

"That would actually be totally amazing. Well, goodnight, Aiden. Sleep tight."

"You too. And don't work too hard, missy." He smiled more warmly and padded off, his easy strides carrying him down the hall and into the end of workday rush. I watched him go, then unlocked the door and went in.

Dad was already there. There was a nice potato soup waiting for me, too. "Hey, kiddo. Dinner's ready. How was your day, little miss professional Rediscovery Expert?" He was so proud.

"Um. Really crazy! Thanks for the soup. You're my favorite person right now, seriously." I gave him a quick hug. "Just let me get out of this suit. I'll be right back."

I ran into my room, carefully got out of my breathable but very close suit, rubbed on some deodorant powder, and hopped into the loosest cotton pyjamas I have.

"Ahhh. Okay, now I feel human. That thing breathes okay, but it's kind of tight."

I washed my hands quickly and splashed some water on my face, then sat down to attack my meal.

"You weren't kidding. Um, there's bread and refried beans, as well..."

"Thankf, Dab. Thif if delifuf." I swallowed. "Erg. Big bite. Sorry, I missed lunch. This is delicious."

"Eat up, there's a bit more on the stove."

We ate in companionable silence for a bit. Dad told me about the greenhouse, some new effects and crop techniques they were trying—basic, ordinary stuff. He's really excited to try another kind of tomato, and to see if he can get the greenhouses to produce more with some technical mods that I won't even pretend I understand.

Then we talked about his planes, and the model he's working on—he's not a big spender generally, but once in a while he'll hunt in rarity shops to find these models, and boy, will he spend to get them just right. That's another thing he's been experimenting with; different kinds of bamboo (rather than balsa) and grades of hemp paper and silk for the wings.

I enjoyed that, but I had to mention the thing that was chewing away at me somehow. When we were munching on apples with brown sugar for dessert, I brought it up.

"By the way, Dad, I thought I saw great uncle Joe today."

"Joe? Are you sure? It's been a long time..."

"Yeah, pretty positive. Uh...why are you looking at me like that?"

"Janelle...your uncle Joe killed himself not long after your mother...got Lost." Dad looked very, very worried.

"It, uh, must have been my mistake," I said hurriedly. "Same name. He looked familiar. Every guy with facial hair does, though."

Dad shook his head at me, and laughed. "Oh, ya think so? So you'd mistake me for someone else in a crowd, just because we both have beards?"

I mustered a smile. "That about covers it! Hey, just a sec, I'm going to put my slippers on." Making a beeline for my bedroom, I turned away so he wouldn't see the panic on my face.

And, of course, after dinner and after I pretended things were normal for Dad, I wrote until my hand hurt. I wanted to get all this down so I'd remember it, in case I need it for something official. It's not that I'm trying to be Una, but wearing that suit...it feels good to do something right, the right way. She texted me, by the way. Said "sleep well, my sweet Janelle." And Nathu texted saying, "You did well today."

Chloe hasn't said a word to me. Una's been warm in public a bit, but I don't think Chloe knows. I'll have to talk to her soon. Joy. Not to mention, what all of our friends will think when I tell them...when I tell them we're not getting married.

I feel like I've changed a lot. I write better...I feel different...if only I wasn't seeing things in public. Please, please let this night pass smoothly. Make these nightmares go away. That little girl was dreaming about a witch. Chloe—even writing her name hurts— Chloe was talking about a witch when we went up. I feel like there's an important link, that I'm onto something, but I'm too tired to figure out what.

Please, please let me sleep without seeing my mother or another ghost. Please. If there are gods, I'm begging. Guess I'll sleep with an amulet in hand tonight...maybe that bone angel. I've had it since forever. Well, here goes nothing. I'd do anything to avoid another night of nightmares...

THE LOVED, THE LOST, THE DREAMING

18—June 27, 0048 P.D.

We finally got some answers, and all that's left is more questions. Another kid went missing tonight...hell, I can't even begin to introduce all the fuckery that's been going on.

It all started, as a lot of things do, when some of the Crows were on patrol. I was still at work, too. Pramjit's been sending me to the weird, far-away tunnels lately, stuff where difficult work tends to be, and everyone else has been giving me a wide, respectful berth. Did I get a promotion when I wasn't looking? Become a Crow and suddenly all the Moles, the people who basically never go up, start giving you a very wide berth. How come I never noticed this before? Maybe I was too intimidated by Crows myself...anyway. Not important right now. Sorry, I'm still jittery and my mind is wandering.

Anyway, Pramjit got a call on the work phone at about two in the afternoon. I happened to have wandered back early, having finished the repairs to an auxiliary line faster than I'd expected.

He was clenching the phone so hard, his knuckles were white. "Uh huh," he mumbled. "Yep. Uh-huh." The tense look on his face and one-sided conversation told me everything I needed to know, even before he shouted for me.

I'd been yapping with Lucy, the secretary. Pramjit was in his office, around the corner. I heard the telephone *thunk* heavily into the receiver, and he waddled out faster than I'd ever seen him move. "Janelle! Official Crow business. You're dismissed for the day. You'll be paid for the three hours you got left."

"What's going on?"

"Fucked if I know, but get your ass into your suit and take the Tubes towards Sector C, and make sure you're armed."

"Yes, sir." I turned around on a heel, pushed the door, and let it slam behind me. I almost didn't see the shocked looks on their faces as they watched me go.

Getting home, changing into my light suit and mask, arming up, and walking all the way down to Sector C took longer than I wanted it to. I ended up with a small delay, too, to tuck that bone angel in under my suit for luck. Sleeping with it for the last two nights kept the nightmares away, and I can use all the help I can get. I even considered a prayer for a minute, before I went off, but decided against it. Everyone knows that the gods can't really hear you all the way down here.

I basically jogged up to the tunnel shortcuts. In spite of the work rush, people saw me coming and parted in front of me. I saw one or two other people in uniform, including Jay, and caught up with them. It turned out to be Sammie and Ginni.

"Sammie! Any idea what's up?"

"None," she panted. "I got hauled outta the kitchen of the Mouse Steak House by a phone call."

"Why would they be calling us from all the way across the city?" panted Ginni. "I know for a fact that Sue and Hitch and Abed are in C."

"Shut up and run," said Jay, taking charge. "We'll talk when we get there."

"This way," I said. "There's an extra cross-tunnel that we still use for maintenance and a stairwell and we can get into the Tubes from there." They followed my lead without question. We dodged dangling charms from overhead ventilation shafts, shredded past a few hubs of wires and pipes, and finally, ended up not far from where I'd killed my dragon. My belly ached with remembered pain as I thought about it.

All of us paused to catch our breath for a second, and to snap our masks and light breathers into place. "Okay," I said, my heart pounding, "I know this part of the Tubes but only back towards the centre of A. Can anyone lead us closer to C?"

"Let me," said Ginni. Her brown eyes looked sure and confident through the smudged goggles.

She took the lead and we jogged after her—more slowly this time, mindful of the trash and watching for risks in the corners.

The air seemed to thicken as we got closer to C, following where Ginni directed. A certain heaviness hung in the corridors, a sense of expectation and tension palpable even in the air. It felt too much like the air had on the night when Una and I had been attacked.

"On guard, everyone," I said. "Something doesn't feel right."

"What are we even looking for?" said Sammie, very quietly.

I moved to the side, and the four of us arranged ourselves in a rough diamond shape as we walked, a good defensive formation. Finally, our comms crackled to life.

"Come in! Come in!" Hunter's voice. "Do you read us? Over."

"Copy. We read you," said Sammie. "Can we get some details? Over."

"We need you to—kkkhhhhtttthhhffffft—repeat, watch tunnels. Any gangers or other suspicious figures—kffffthhhhhttt—missing child—"

"Hunter? Do you read us? Hunter? Do you copy?"

Sammie shook her head. "Comm's dead. I've seen this before. Shit." Her slim-lipped mouth pursed tight. "Okay. We're going blind."

"Damn," muttered Ginni. "This is going to be a weird night again, isn't it? I would kill for a plain salvage mission or a nice patrol walk in the Tubes. Even a ganger scrap." I opened my mouth, thought about telling her not to whine, but she flashed me a quick smile. "Oh well. Nothing like an adventure, right, girls?"

"Nothing like it," said Jay, grinning back at her, and flashing a smile at me. "But we'd better slow down. Don't want to miss something," she added, serious again. I couldn't help thinking that I liked this bunch even more by the day.

The tunnels over C are different than the ones over A, less narrow and twisty. Sammie suggested splitting into teams, but I rejected that idea. "Uh-uh. Last time that happened, Una and I couldn't hold our own." The girls glanced at each other. Shadows seemed to settle deeper around us, stifling even the bright glow of LEDs lining our suits.

"Watch the Dust levels," said Sammie tightly. "I don't like how dark in here it is."

"You'n me both," I said. "Okay. Lead the way, Ginni."

We banded together. It was colder, and our whispers and footsteps seemed to echo more than they should have. Mostly, though, all was silence. Too silent, in fact.

"Ginni, scout ahead," said Sammie, her lips barely moving. Ginni nodded and moved father forward, the bright lights trimming her shoulders and waist flickering in the gloom. Her long, thick dark hair blended in, and her dark skin seemed to melt into the shade. I'm not too bad at moving quietly, but Ginni put me to shame.

The comm remained ominously silent. Dust levels this high in the Tubes were unusual to say the least, especially without a visible breach. There weren't even any gangers around. Normally you'd see at least one on a long tunnel walk. We'd certainly been roaming for the better part of an hour. I hadn't checked my watch, though. It was hard to tell what time it was, in the soundless, deathly place.

There was a soft scratching sound, distant. A hiss of breath. That was all we needed. The three of us exchanged glances. Jay stealthily moved ahead, while Sammie fell back to guard our rear.

That left me as the monkey in the middle, with a hand on my gun and a keen awareness of exactly where every one of my throwing knives had been tucked. Sure, I had Jay ahead of me and Sammie behind, but that didn't mean I wanted to rely on them to act as meat shields.

Suddenly, Ginni yelped.

"On our way!" yelled Jay. Sammie picked up the pace and we tightened our formation, running ahead.

"Up here! I saw a guy—someone—in a cloak! Almost walked into him around the corner!" she called back. I felt a flicker of admiration for how quickly she'd gotten her fear under control. Really seems to be a thing with the Crows.

The darkness, though, was heavier. There were no lights here; all the torches were completely out. This section of C was obviously abandoned most of the time. Either that, or it was just the darkness, wrapping around us, sucking away our hope along with illumination...

I shook my head. No time for crazy thoughts and paranoia. The nightmares lurking in corners would have to wait. The bone angel was warm inside my suit, under my shirt.

We caught up with her just in time. She pointed into the dark, to a place where the light refused to go.

"There! In the tunnel!"

We could just barely see a figure hurrying away. Hunched over, its lines blurred.

"Hey! You! Halt!"

He whirled around, and from nowhere, a snarling tiger leapt for us, claws outstretched. We parted, and he overshot us.

I'd never seen one off of a screen, even though they're rumoured to roam freely Up there. It didn't matter, though. Instinct told me what to feel, overwhelmed my curiosity. The teeth, the animal's hot breath, the way it moved, spoke to something in my blood. We were all terrified, hearts pounding. Prey.

It growled, roared at us, and circled back. It was hunting. We were a herd of deer, of prey. It was going to enjoy this. Sammie let out a very small scream and backed away faster than the rest. It looked intrigued, and glanced in her direction. Prey, said its body. Delicious prey.

I could smell the fear in the air. We put a little more space between ourselves and the circling, prowling tiger.

"Where'd the guy go?" said Ginni suddenly. "There was a guy!"

I glanced ahead, forced myself to look past the orange and black beast taunting us. "Around the corner! He's getting away!"

"There's a fucking tiger! What are we supposed to do?"

"We're going to have to catch up with him," I snarled.

The tiger still watched, growling and baring its teeth. It prepared to leap—

Jay whipped out her pistol and aimed; as it rose, she caught it square in the nose. It yowled and roared, and turned just enough to the side. Ginni whipped out a throwing knife and paused to aim for its eye. There was another yowl as she hit home. The tiger circled and growled. I took a deep breath and readied myself for the stupidest thing I've ever done in my life.

Taking a running start, I jumped past the tiger, and screamed, "it's not real!" With every ounce of will I had, I tried to believe it. Didn't do much of a job.

"Did that thing just *shimmer?*" Ginni gasped. There was no time to look over my shoulder, but I could tell it wasn't following me yet. Unusual enough.

"It's not real," said Jay loudly. I heard their guns fire, and a roar of pain. It was weakening.

"Kill it, Jay," I muttered, and hoped she would. No time to turn around and watch, see if it dissolved into Dust. I had a monster to catch.

I ran on instinct, the darkness around me filling the world utterly. I was grateful for the mask and goggles. Their grip on my face, the feeling of the suit and the foldie and the weapons slung across my body reassured me. My heart pounded, the blood surging through my veins so loudly I was sure that every predator in a three kilometre radius could hear it. Even with the lights on my goggles and my suit, though, I had to face it. The dark was too deep, I'd gone too far ahead of my team, and, like an idiot, I'd gotten myself into danger.

Worse, I had the nasty feeling that I wasn't alone. In fact, I could swear that there was a soft hissing noise near me. I concentrated, focusing on my location and the soft echoes in the tunnel.

There was a hiss in the dark. "Who goes there? Do you sleep or do you dream?" He wasn't hissing like a snake—it's hard to describe—it was the sound of air wheezing out of his lungs as he spoke. Accumulated Dust? Asthma?

He moved to my left, breathing hard. "Speak! I can hear you breathing, you fool. Do you sleep, or do you dream?"

Some kind of code? Maybe like the Oath? Better not to answer, still. The ground was soft, shifty, here, as if I was in a room full of sand. There were some sandy areas, but I really hoped it wasn't all Dust. About the only way to heal extended Dust exposure is a stay in a Calm Box until your system finally manages to expel some of it. Even then, pass a tipping point and you're good as done. Might as well have burned yourself out on hallies.

My lungs were trying to contract, but my breath wasn't catching just yet, though. Maybe it wasn't too late. This might just be sand, not entirely Dust. Still a hell of a lot of Dust, though.

"Answer me, fool, or I'll assume you're a sleeper and act accordingly! You know I can't see you!" I was giving off a faint light, in spite of the yawning blackness. Why couldn't he see me?

THE LOVED, THE LOST, THE DREAMING

All at once, the darkness broke. A bright light at the end of the tunnel and shouting voices: Oliver's, Kelsey's, Hunter's, Leah's, Una's, and a different person's voice, a woman I didn't know. Behind me, I could hear Ginni leading Jay and Sammie in a charge.

"Hold fire!" Kelsey. "Don't any of you damn people shoot!"

I finally saw the figure near me, a hunched and cloaked figure. His face was covered, but he moved unnaturally as he took a step, first left and then right.

"It sounds as though I'm surrounded," he muttered to himself. For the first time, I heard real fear in his voice. I couldn't tell you why, but I felt a savage happiness, at that.

"We got him," I said, squinting in the light of the torch. "Jay! You guys okay?"

"The tiger dissolved," said Sammie, her voice full of confusion and wonder. "What the..."

The stranger hissed and jumped for her; but Leah stepped in the way and executed a beautiful takedown. He went flying, and let out a hiss of pain.

"Well, well. What do we have here?" said Una. I recognized the cold in her voice, and shivered. Even spending a night loving her and knowing how soft she is didn't make that tone of hers any less terrifying. She stepped forward, seeming to burn with a cold light that came from more than the LEDs.

"Nothing you could understand," the stranger whispered. "And I don't have your child. Whoever does is long gone. You slow, clumsy Moles would never catch one of us in time anyway."

All of us must have gotten the same look of revelation on our faces, but Oliver spoke up.

"I say we take him to Nathu," spat Oliver. "But only after we have a little fun first. This scum's been godsdamn stealing our children. I'd like to introduce him to reason and persuasion." He pulled a pair of long-barrelled shotguns from his back. "Reason is here on the left, and Persuasion's on the right. I think maybe a nice butt-end conversation'd do you a lot of good, sonny boy," he growled.

The man laughed. Oliver gave him a good kick in the ribs.

"Dad! Stop it!" snapped Kelsey. "Let's get the sonofabitch back to Nathu. Let him do the questioning. Then, if he's really our culprit, maybe we'll have some fun with him."

The stranger stepped forward, or rather, stumbled. She was barely wearing her goggles. "Where is my son?" she screamed. "Tell me, you bastard! Where did you take Ethan?"

The man just laughed.

"You're going back with us," said Una. "Tie him up, Oliver. No need to be gentle, but don't break anything."

Leah comforted the stranger softly. "It'll be all right, Marla."

"Not until I find your nephew, it won't. He has my damn son!"

"No, he doesn't. But he's going to take us to the people who do."

Wide-eyed, I looked at Jay and the girls. I've been feeling very adult lately, but just then, looking at her and Sammie and Ginni, I realised just how very young we were.

I need a break, and sleep, before I tell you what happened next. Oh, gods, I wish I had them with me tonight. Just remembering it is going to give me nightmares. I'll hold onto this bit of bone anyway. At this rate, it's not just dreams—I might start sleeping with a knife under my pillow. There really are things in the dark, and now, we have to hunt them.

19—June 28, 0048 P.D.

I try really hard to be reliable. Like I said, you, reader, might be one of my kids or you might be someone in the distant future. Either way, I want you to know exactly what happened. I'm not totally unbiased, but I hope it's clear enough. Believe me when I say, though, that what I learned yesterday made me very, very sick inside.

"Tie him up and gag him," said Una. She seethed with a carefully contained fury, and the general spirit seemed to agree with her. There was practically a fight to bind him up, until she made it clear that Oliver was the one she wanted for the job.

Oliver retrieved a coil of rope from a small backpack. He pulled back the man's hood to gag him, and the stranger didn't resist. Seeing his face properly for the first time, I winced. His features were pinched and pale, strangely twisted and disproportionate. Jerking towards the sound of Oliver's fingers, the stranger snapped at Oliver's hand like a dog, yellow and broken teeth glinting in our suits' light. Oliver slapped him, leaving a red handprint on the stranger's bloodless skin. The stranger's blindfold slipped, and Oliver tugged it back in place.

"Don't wanna see more of your fugly mug 'n I have to."

The man said nothing, but a repulsive smirk spread over his features. Grabbing a big, rough rag from the knapsack, Oliver pried the man's mouth open and shoved it in. It was more of a punch, really.

Part of me wondered if we shouldn't have made sure he was guilty of taking the kids before the boot-to-the-ribs treatment, but my instincts told me the question was pointless. His goblin-like features and his lack of surprise told me everything I really needed to know.

Most of the walk was a silent battle. Oliver flung him over a shoulder rather than letting him walk, and that kept Una busy. She had to keep him, Marla, and the others from surreptitiously punching and striking the stranger. I knew it was technically wrong, but I won't say I stopped them.

Suddenly, Jay rounded on Oliver. "Stop it," she snapped.

"What's that, li'l miss?"

"I said, stop it. We don't know he's guilty and putting the boots to him won't help."

Marla opened her mouth to speak, but Leah put a hand on her shoulder. "If you knew the pain of losing a child," Oliver snarled, "you wouldn't—"

Kelsey put a hand on her father's forearm. "Dad. She's right."

Una cast a chilling look over all of us, and a warmer one at Jay. She didn't need to say anything, but people laid off. Jay looked scared and proud of herself, and I felt like a scumbag for not saying anything when I knew better.

We walked all the way back to the lower levels in grim silence. It was broken only by Marla's quiet, angry sobbing. The darkness around us was softening, melting by the moment. I could only hope that was a sign that even the Dust was admitting defeat for now.

The comms started to work again, without the Dust to interfere with their reception. Una was still hanging back to glare Oliver into submission, so Leah called it in.

"We didn't get the kid, but we did get a suspect, Nathu. We're coming in. Over."

"Good. I'll handle this personally. Give me a few and come straight to the questioning room. I'll tell the other squads to keep searching. Over."

The questioning room turned out to be at the end of a long and complex route that led into D Sector, the slummiest part of the city. Our final location was a real hole in the wall, with its window boarded up and everything. Obviously, it was good for secrecy. Jay looked very unimpressed, but didn't repeat her outburst.

THE LOVED, THE LOST, THE DREAMING

Una unlocked the heavy door, and ushered us all inside. I'd never seen the inside of a jail before, and I'll tell you, I could have gone a lot longer without seeing it again. There was a table and a wall of very nasty looking things that I couldn't immediately identify. The pliers and pincers, though, I recognized, and a few guesses about what they were for made my stomach turn. A closer look, though, showed that they were all covered in dust—they hadn't been used in years. Good. Hopefully they wouldn't be needed today.

Nathu was inside the cell, sitting on one of two chairs. The furniture, I noticed, was bolted to the ground. I wasn't sure how to feel about that. It meant that at some point, someone had probably picked up the chairs or table and either thrown someone against them or swung them around.

It was weird to see Nathu on the wrong side of the bars, and he didn't look all that comfortable himself. A long spear was leaning in the corner of the cell; he walked over to it and picked it up, looking more reassured with its weight in his hand. He opened the door and Oliver threw the stranger in roughly. Una followed him, but closed the door after herself. The rest of us lined up to watch through the bars.

Una yanked the gag out of the stranger's mouth and seated him roughly on the chair.

"Nathu Atalas, Princeps of the city."

"Well, what a nice welcome. Are you going to pretend to ask me about the hard way and easy way first, or are you going to get started with the torture immediately?"

"Actually, I thought I'd start with an introduction. I don't see any need for that if you're willing to talk."

"I am, since it'll be useless to you anyway," answered the stranger. He almost seemed to be enjoying himself. 'Who's your blonde bitch there, by the way?"

"Una Atalas," she spat, pacing on the barred wall of the cell. She brushed against my corner of the bars and I brushed her hand surreptitiously. It made me a little happier to see how her shoulder relaxed, just for a moment.

"Aren't you going to tell me your name?" prompted Nathu. His voice was relatively friendly, but he was learning on the spear.

"We have no names. Not like yours. You may call me," he licked his lips with a slimy tongue, "Sandman."

I shivered.

"You don't look any less human to me," said Nathu. I couldn't tell whether he was trying to be noble or sarcastic.

The Sandman laughed. "I wouldn't expect a Mole like you to be smart enough to tell the difference. Tell me, blind man, are you really as much of an idiot as you sound to be?"

He turned his face to ours, and I saw that his blindfold had slipped. I drew my breath in sharply—his eyes were empty caverns, full of darkness and red raw stretched skin.

"With all due respect, you appear to be the blind one," said Nathu dryly.

The Sandman chuckled dryly. "That's what I mean. You see my eye sockets, and you think I'm helpless."

"I didn't say that," Nathu replied cautiously.

"But you assumed it! You didn't need to say it," the Sandman snarled back.

Nathu, to his credit, looked thoughtful and held his temper in check. "So, what do you mean by 'seeing' and being blind?"

"You don't understand the dreams. You're sleepers. Helpless. And when the time comes, we will destroy you with your own fears. I'm looking forward to it."

"Controlling dreams?" said Nathu, ignoring the threat. "What do you mean by that?"

"Are you so stupid and so blind, Mole, that you haven't noticed? Nightmares given flesh? Or perhaps you simply don't care about what happens to your citizens and their fears."

"You sound like you have Dust fever to me," said Nathu, managing to sound genuinely concerned.

"Pah! Dust fever. You primitives. Just talking to you is an insult to my intelligence. Inhaling Dust brings dreams." The white-fleshed man blinked, giving us a glimpse of his horrible, empty sockets. Something glimmered in their depths, dark and sparkling. "Doesn't hurt otherwise."

"We've found people with corroded holes in their brains," said Nathu doubtfully. "That sounds like it hurts to me."

"If you're too weak and you let it overwhelm you, of course it will. Stupid Moles. If you'd let your dreams guide you, you wouldn't die so badly."

Nathu's spear poked him in the stomach, drew blood as it scratched through papery skin. "I don't understand. What else does it do? No metaphors."

"Inhale and swallow enough," the Sandman sibilated, "and you get more than dreams. You can summon dreams too."

"Summon dreams?" Nathu's face was calm, but his corded muscles said he was scared.

"Summon. Instead of nightmares hunting you down, you can make them obedient. Or quiescent, at least." He chuckled in an ugly, dry, papery way.

The other Crows murmured at that, and I felt my palms start to sweat. This made more sense than I wanted it to.

"Are these controlled nightmares linked to the missing children?" asked Una.

"I'm not answering you, bitch. I don't like the way you smell."

Nathu shot a look at her and at his spear that suggested he'd like to use it on the Sandman, but Una shook her head.

"Answer me, then," said Nathu. "Are they?"

"In the way that children wandering into the forest would be taken by wolves and trolls and monsters. In the way that the creatures under the bed and in the closet are waiting to gobble little innocents down. We nightmares are always ready to take a stray child."

"I'm getting tired of you pretending to be clever," growled Nathu. "Now, I can tell you about old folklore and you can tell me your spin on it, or you can tell me something useful. Telling me something useful is going to make your time here a lot easier."

"Ahh, the threats. I knew we'd get there eventually. Fine. Yes, they are linked." I couldn't help gasping, and I wasn't the only one. Marla was clinging to the bars, eager for more, and Hunter and Leah were exchanging a few quiet, choice words. Jay and Ginni and Sammie whispered to each other and Kelsey. Oliver, like me, just stared into the cell, transfixed.

"Are you lying?"

"You'll kill me anyway, Mole. What use is it to lie? Besides, it won't stop us."

Marla moved forward, a vein throbbing in her forehead. She was pissed. Some of the Crows behind her looked ready to tear the Sandman to shreds. Nathu, however, kept his cool.

"What happened to your eyes?" I blurted out. Quick as a rat, he turned his sightless face towards me. I shuddered.

"So familiar, that voice. Too young though. But she said…"

"Who said," I demanded. "Who said what?"

He let out a dry chuckle.

Nathu gave me a sharp, hard look. I bit my lip in embarrassment, but the teenager in me said: he's looking at me! The shallow, stupid thought fled when I heard the Sandman chuckle.

"Now. Are you going to tell us where they took Ethan and the others, or are we going to stand here and slowly gut you for the rest of the night?" He poked the man with the spear again, and the Sandman flinched.

"Something can be arranged," he said. "Perhaps. But first, I want to know what your terms are. You can try to kill me, but you won't succeed. I'll flood your tunnels with Dust. If you're lucky, some of your people won't be so blind. If you're not, and you're too weak—

which you will be—everyone here will die more slowly and painfully than you can imagine."

Nathu crossed his arms. "I see we're in a pissing contest."

"Leave me be, Mole. I'd rather talk to someone else. I can tell there's plenty of you around."

"Oh? Who would you like to negotiate with? I don't think it's going to be any easier," he snapped.

The Sandman jerked his head at me. "What about you? I can hear you breathing. I know you're a woman, or a Between one."

"I'm not giving you my name," I spat. He stiffened at the sound of my voice, sat up.

"Pardon me, lady," he said. His voice was more respectful, almost cajoling. "I can already tell you're not as blind as they are."

I was intrigued, in spite of myself. Una and Kelsey shot warning glances at me as one. Oliver snarled, baring his teeth.

"All I see is scum we should have killed as soon as we saw 'em. We're not going to get anything out of the bastard. He'll just try to play us against each other," he warned. "Before, when we lived Up, I saw war. You think the men I had to fight didn't bargain? Same shit."

"I wasn't talking to you, you filthy old fool," said the Sandman. "I was talking to the lady here. The one who's been seeing strange things lately. Yes? Did I guess rightly?"

"We've all been seeing strange things," spat Una. "We're Crows. I've seen stranger things than you, and I've given them better deaths than you're going to get."

"Threaten away, Crow," said the Sandman. "It doesn't matter to me. There's a lovely young lady here who's been having very bad dreams. Very bad dreams indeed, I think. I'll bet you've been dreaming about dark things, haven't you, hm?"

I said nothing.

"Not dreaming about your mother being swallowed by darkness? Not dreaming about little girls with sharp teeth and blood on their faces? Hmm?"

I opened the door, I remember that, but after that it was a blur. I lost it. They had to pull me off of him. I remember the world swimming and I remember hearing his ribs break as I kicked him, and Hunter's arms around my shoulders, very roughly. Xe's shockingly strong.

Una hauled me out and to the far corner. I didn't struggle, and she wrapped her arms around me. "Snap the fuck out of it, Janelle," she said quietly. "You may have Lost your mother, but you're a Crow. Fucking act like it."

I panted, tears still streaming down my face. "Yes, ma'am."

She walked back to the cell, but left me outside of it before going in herself.

Oliver shook his head. "He's useless. Besides, he's pissing off the new recruit. I say we gut him like a fish. To hell with the consequences. We'll decontaminate what we have to, or burn him. Dust doesn't like fire, and I'll bet you don't either, asshole. "

The Sandman lay on the floor, quiet and calm. "If you kill me, you'll never get the children back," he said. "Never. In fact, I hope you kill me. They deserve better lives than to live with monsters like you."

"Monsters?" Hunter let xer voice waver.

"We're not the ones who let Lost people wander away into the dark. We're not the ones who leave children alone in barracks with only their nightmares when there are plenty of families to go around. We don't let people go hungry unless we can help it." The hatred in his voice was palpable, physical.

"...Are you saying that some of the Lost people have survived?" asked Kelsey. The hope on her face hurt to look at, especially since I could feel the same hope fluttering in my chest.

"I'm saying you left them to die, and not all of them did," the Sandman spat. "Luckily for those children, they're going to a better place."

"You're going to kill them?" asked Nathu stiffly.

"No, you savages. We're saving them. The rest of you will die, though. I'm looking forward to it." The Sandman bowed his head. Nathu poked him with the spear, but he didn't respond.

Hunter's comm unexpectedly crackled to life. "Tristan here. Negative on any finds. There's footsteps leading Up in one of the side tunnels, a child's and someone else's, but they switched to just the stranger's, and then...they vanish midstep. We lost the trail. Over." Even on comm, he sounded defeated.

"Send them to the meeting hall, over," said Nathu. The disappointment hung in the room like a pall of Dust on a heavy morning. "I think we should pack it in for now," he added. "It's either that, or torture some answers out of him." I could tell he wasn't offering it as a suggestion. He wanted someone to talk him out of it. No-one did.

Marla completely lost it. "Let me at him! Let me!"

To my shock, Nathu opened the door and let her in.

It wasn't pretty. She kicked and punched and scratched at the Sandman, who barely flinched under her assault. "How dare you?" she screamed. "How fucking dare you? I love my son, and if you don't help me get him back, I'm going to tear you to shreds with my bare fucking hands! You fucking monster!"

The Sandman rolled over slightly to smirk at her. The blood on his face didn't seem to bother him at all. I've never seen someone react like that, and I hope I never do again.

"You see him as helpless, don't you, Mole mother? You pretend to put on your little wings. You call yourselves Crows. You're nothing more than carrion hunters, and you're a dying race. We'll be better parents to your children, you'll see. You took all the useful things for yourselves, hoarded them below, and left us to starve up there. Your boy will be far more powerful with us than he ever would with you."

"He would have been fine with me! I love him! Powerful—he's already a smart little boy! What the fuck are you talking about?"

"You see a disability. We see an ability."

"He's blind in one eye!" Marla screamed. "He's four years old and blind in one eye! What the hell are you going to do with him?"

"It doesn't matter what they're going to try to do. We're going to get him back," said Una, flinty.

"That's what I meant," said the Sandman, disgusted. "You see what's wrong with them. We take a weakness and make it a strength, and when we're done, you won't even recognise them. Of course, you won't have long. All the people you kicked out and left to die will get their payback. And now, I think we're

293

finished. I'm quite done talking for the night."

Marla scratched him again, and screamed, but it didn't do a damn thing. Even a couple of very choice hits from Nathu's staff wasn't enough. Bloodied, but smirking and smug. Una gave him a kick of her own before leaving, disgusted. She ushered the rest of us out, except for Hunter. Nathu followed. He untied the Sandman, who didn't resist, but locked the jail cell door behind him.

"Hunter, can you keep an eye on this bastard? We'll send down a change of guard shortly, but I don't want him out of the sight of a senior Crow for the rest of the night."

"Will do," xe replied. "Luke might be a good choice. Chang, too. And consider one of the privates. They need to know what our opponents look like." I'd never heard such loathing in xer voice. Nathu didn't say anything, but the anger on his face made his feelings clear.

After that, he and Una called Marla over and spoke to her privately for a few; the rest of the Crows headed back to the meeting hall, and I followed with Jay and the others. We sort of chatted, but mostly it was quiet. The walk was long, and gave me time to think—or not think. Jay put an arm around me and didn't say too much. Ginni and Sammie made sure to do the same in turn, though.

THE LOVED, THE LOST, THE DREAMING

Whatever else, as much as thinking about Lost people like Mom hurt, it's good to have real friends.

The meeting was what you'd expect. Basically, every Crow was there, we all gave detailed reports, I mentioned some of the stuff I'd looked into with Aiden again but to everyone, and Nathu and Una described the questioning of the Sandman. Oh, and the incident with the maggot was brought up. Apparently I'm not the only one who's had weird run-ins, by the way.

As a tiny plus, I didn't make a total ass of myself when I had to talk in public. As a much more important plus, the other Crows were lining up to go on patrol duties. I felt some hope creep in when I saw how eager they were. I feel like we might just be able to stop these Sandmen if we all band together. The problem is, we have no idea when, how, or even if we're going to be attacked. The interview seemed to lead to more questions than answers.

I really, really wanted to relax and spend some time with Una afterwards, so I waited around for the place to clear out. Jay and the girls tried to lure me out, but I told them I needed to ask a couple of questions and talk about something involving Mom. Jay, being the incredibly sensitive and kind person she is, gave me space. I felt guilty for using that as an excuse, but I did need it. Just the way the Sandman dropped that into things...and then, the possibility that she might be alive...I can't stand thinking about it.

I made some excuses to stick around and helped her with paperwork and stuff until, finally, she and Nathu were free.

"Can I offer you guys a cup of tea or something stronger? My treat," I said. "You both....had a lot to handle today, and...yeah. You know." I stared at my boots as Nathu scribbled a few final notes about the proceedings.

"I'd love to," said Una, smiling wearily. "Please." She bent slightly to kiss me, full and sweetly.

I shot a startled glance at Nathu, who grinned. "Don't mind me. Can I invite myself for that cup of something warm? I'm going to be on call tonight, if I know anything, and a break would hit the spot."

"Oh! Of—yeah," I said, blushing. Una noticed my blush and her eyebrows shot up.

"So, about that tea..."

"I know a spot around the corner," said Nathu gratefully. "Come on."

It was only a hop, skip, and a jump away from the Honeycomb, which suited me fine. All of us were damned tired, and it wasn't the walking. A heavy conscience will weigh you down a lot more than a bag and a weapon. Believe me, Nathu was not happy about what had gone down in that cell. More in a sec.

Nathu's idea of a quiet spot was just the kind I like—not too pretentious, private, and not too pricey, either. I worried that he was trying to save my wallet, at first, since I'd offered to treat, but when the server grinned and greeted him like an old friend, I knew otherwise.

"What'll it be today?"he asked. The guy was a bit older, looked rough and ready. I'd bet cards he was the owner.

"Bowls of soup, a half loaf of potato bread, and the biggest pot of black tea you can make. Oh, and something harder on the side."

"Comin' right up. The soup today is leek with bacon an' onion." I groaned happily. "I'll take that as a yes. Won't be long." He hustled off efficiently.

I sat back and enjoyed the swaying hammock-style seat. Soft striped prints, lots of blue tiling on the walls, and little candles in paper shades everywhere, with a big old shelf of books and even a shared use computer: paradise. I'm not much of a reader, more of a movie person, but a nice quiet place to sit and talk is the only thing I like as much as a good noisy bar.

And talk we did. I was shocked to learn how much of a normal person Nathu is. His public face was a bit softer than usual. He cracked jokes, made a couple carefully worded complaints about Oliver's gung-ho ferocity, flirted with Una—and me!—and talked about, well, human things.

"I really like old movies," I admitted. "Like action movies, and some of the really ancient ones, like the black and white stuff."

His eyes lit up. "I love anything with a really good swordfight in it."

Una laughed and drank her tea. "You should see his collection some time. Anything with—what are they called—musketeers or knights. He's crazy about them."

Nathu grinned, his hair falling into his eyes for a moment. Una's got a couple years on me, but Nathu's got—I don't know, maybe a few months or a year on her, they're close in age. Just then, though, I could see a hint of the excitable little kid he must have been. He's so good at doing that public competency thing. I mean, sure, I've had a crush on him for eons, but I have a lot of respect for how he handles himself. Even his body language is elegant and orderly.

Between Una sitting next to me, relaxing and putting an arm around my chair, and sharing affection glances with Nathu while he and I chatted, I couldn't think of a better afternoon. We didn't even talk about much in particular, we just...enjoyed each other's company. It's been way too long since I got to do that with someone. Hell, I can't remember the last time I did it with Chloe, and Raheed was a mess all the way through. But with both of them, Nathu and Una I mean...I feel so much like myself. It made what happened after that even harder to handle.

Of course, all good things must come to an end. After a morning of being taunted about my mother and watching people hurt a very strange and frightening man, I had a really bad, weird encounter with Raheed. I've been keeping my tone light because I wanted to focus on the good stuff, but, well...this hurt. A lot.

We walked out of the tea shop arm in arm. My belly was full and my wallet wasn't too empty, owing to the pay raise that's come with being a Crow. I had two people I really like with me, and the possibility of things to come in the evening made my stomach tight with hope and anticipation.

We strolled about for a bit, walked down a nice private sidealley. It was really deserted, and flirting with them, both of them, was a delight. Unfortunately, it wasn't deserted enough.

"Fancy meeting you here."

I groaned. "Raheed...hi..."

It had been a while since I'd seen him. A long while, actually, since things have been so crazy, but last time we chatted he was in reconciliation mode. I pushed him away, but a little part of me was hoping we could finally move on with shit and be friends.

Nope.

"So, that was fast. New 'friends' already? Wow."

Raheed smirked and I felt the blood rush out of my head. Una wrapped a supporting arm around me.

"First, it's none of your damn business. Second, what the hell?"

"So, is it social climbing you're going for, now? I mean, becoming a Crow means you're too good for the rest of us mortals, right?"

"It's not like that! I'm just sick of what went on with her. Drop it, Raheed. Walk away." I stepped away from Una and Nathu, my fists clenched of their own accord.

"Chloe is going to be happy to hear about this," he said.

"You keep your dirty damn nose out of it," I snapped. "We've been arguing enough and she hasn't gone for a date with me in a month. It's not cheating if you've already broken up."

"Well, I hope she knows you've broken up with her," he said, leaning against the wall. "Or I could tell her if you want." He gave me a look that made me wonder why I'd spent even five minutes dating him.

"Funny," said Nathu, "I didn't think she asked you to help."

"Nathu, leave this to me. Please," I said. "Raheed, I told you things were bad. Chloe...Chloe and I aren't getting married anymore. We talked it over and it's been common knowledge for a while."

He shook his head. "Sure. Whatever you say. All I see is that you cheated on her, the same way you did with me."

"I didn't cheat on you, you son of a bitch! You were greedy in bed and we didn't understand each other. If you think I cheated on you—"

"—You know, I thought we understood each other, but much as she's a bitch, she doesn't deserve an ungrateful girlfriend like you," he spat. For a minute, it looked like his teeth were sharper in the light—had to be my imagination.

"I'm not fucking ungrateful! You prick! She was there to pick up the pieces every time you and I fought, and she talked me into being more than friends. There, happy?"

"I won't be happy until you stop kicking people's hearts around!"

"You weren't there!" I shouted at him. "You didn't save her from spiders and get yelled at! You didn't get called every time she was in trouble and you didn't get sucked up to every time she wanted something. You didn't love her and get used like I did. Fuck off."

"Whatever you did for her, you deserve what you're getting now!" he snarled back.

I punched him and man, did it feel good.

"Break it up," said Nathu, stepping between us. "Raheed. Take some time to cool off. When you're ready, come back and apologize to her, like a real man." He put an arm around my shoulder.

Raheed shook his head angrily, and spat on the ground. Then, thank gods, he walked off.

"I think I should head home," I said. My voice wavered.

"Do you want to talk about it first?" offered Nathu gently.

"Janelle...I know what you're thinking," Una cut in. "I know that look. We saw how Chloe was with you, and jealousy, well, I'm no stranger. What's your side of the story?"

"We...he was my first real boyfriend. It didn't last long and it didn't go well." I glanced around, but the place was still, mercifully, deserted. "He...we just didn't go together, you know? Well, you saw. He baits me and I take it. And...I suck at holding my temper. That was months ago. I had a bad time after him, and a friend who sort of was outside my main group got close to me when things were going real bad." I inhaled deeply, let out a shuddery sigh. "That was Chloe. She just sorta homed in on me right around the end, though we didn't get together until all was said and done with Raheed...and, um, he didn't take it too well. But the other day...I thought things were getting better..." I rubbed my eyes frantically.

Una didn't say much, but she did wrap me up in a hug. Pressed against her, inhaling her scent, I wished so badly that we were home in my bed. There's nothing like being next to someone you love, skin to skin, when the day's going to shit.

"I...I just don't get it. I haven't spent much time with my friends lately but...he was trying to be nice! He said he wanted to patch things up. We've...we've been really snappy with each other," I admitted. There were tears in my eyes and a lump was tightening my throat. "I fucked up a lot, but...I thought we were friends now."

Una kissed my eyelids. "Need me to punch him for you?"

"Don't tempt me," muttered Nathu. "At best, that was ungentlemanly. At worst..." he inhaled slowly.

"How the hell do you keep your temper all the time?" I burst out.

"I'm Princeps. I have to. And, sometimes it's more satisfying to make them writhe while you keep a cool head."

"Yeah, I suck at that. Um...look. I...I don't want to get you into trouble or make you look bad. I...I'm not really a hot mess, honestly. But...if you think I am, I understand. I..."

"No, no!" he said, concerned. "I do understand. When I was a teenager and...a lot younger, I had a few things to sort out myself. It's nothing that can't be..."

"Still. I should go."

Una looked really disappointed. Hurt, almost. "Are you sure you wouldn't like to relax with us? Go somewhere more private? I hate to leave you like this." She reached for my face, cupped my cheek.

That almost made me cry, just from pure overwhelm. "Thanks. Next time. See you on the next patrol."

I had to turn around so they wouldn't see the tears leaking out of my eyes. I managed to keep my breathing steady, but the little sigh of disappointment and longing Una let out as I walked away almost broke me.

And now, of course, I'm home. I skimmed over things with Dad, didn't eat much, and now I'm curled up in bed. What if they don't want me after this? I must look like such a damn mess. I feel like an awful human being for hurting Raheed like I did. Some of that shit was my fault, too. I know it was.

And now I'm whining at you. I didn't stop that Sandman from getting hurt, even though I knew better, I let him bait me...and I can't stop thinking about how he treated me. Must sound pathetic.

Okay. Pull yourself together, you dumb bitch. You've done some brave things too. Maybe that counts somewhere.

Just...it's so hard not to feel like I'm failing at everything right now. Time for sleep. Even nightmares would almost be a relief from wondering about how Chloe feels, and Raheed, and the ache that's bone deep. I keep dodging the words for these new feelings, but I know what they are. They're a richer thing than I've felt before, and now, I probably just scared off a woman I think I might...

Later. Sleep now, even with nightmares, is better than this agony.

19—June 29, 0048 P.D.

It's my day off and it's already shitty. It's been unofficially over with Chloe for a while, but things...things just got official. And, as it turns out, I don't need to feel that guilty about having gotten together with Una and Nathu before cutting it off. That stupid bitch...oh gods, I just don't understand it.

I should really, really start at the beginning of this. I don't know if I feel like it. The city's been on high alert, but after everything I've done lately, I got the day off from Crow patrols. Then I called in sick to Pramjit.

I don't understand why the fuck this hurts so much. It's a waking nightmare. I need to sleep.

Went back to sleep. Nightmares, of course. The witch was chasing me again. I was searching through the house that Chloe got lost in, and I saw little white children's hands coming out of every doorway. A little girl kept running just out of site, her teeth still covered in blood, a grin plastered on her face. The doorways and stairs seemed to move in strange directions—doors opened sideways, and when I turned the handle of one, spider-dogs poured out. I kept chasing after Chloe, and around every turn, she seemed to disappear. Meanwhile, Una and Nathu kept calling for me, worried. I didn't know who to look for, or where to go.

And then, Mom was there, right behind me. I shot her, and she turned into—into a thing, with long arms and claws and eyes full of darkness. She laughed at me, and I shot her again—

And then, of course, I woke up, and cried. Took a shower. Tried not to think about Una with me in the shower. Ended up thinking about her, and touching myself, wishing it was her or Nathu there with me. Right now, it's some ungodly hour in the afternoon, and I'm feeding myself chicoffee and porridge so I can try to feel human. Anything is better than this. I'm barely functioning.

Guess I should go back to why, instead of being a sad sack. Kenny called me. Luckily, I had the phone plugged in.

"Hey? This is Janelle. I'm on my way to work—"

"Janelle. I...hey, man, I gotta come by. Lola and me gotta talk to you. It's..." he sounded reluctant. I heard Lola prod him in the background. "It's important."

"Uh...oh...kay?"

"You might want to ask for the day off of work, she says. And, um, we're bringing an extra visitor."

"Uh...okay. See you soon?"

"Yeah. Bye."

He hung up quickly, and I had just enough time to tell Pramjit that I was too tired from official duties to be any good today. He let me off the hook without a single damn question. Guess there are extra perks to this line of work.

I had just enough time to make myself decent and throw on tea before the door rang. Dad, luckily, was working. I don't know how I've gotten so lucky with timing on the day's he works, but maybe there's some part of me that's really good at being sneaky. Hell, I know there is. I get away with a lot, of the few sins I do commit.

Man, I really don't even want to write about this. I opened the door to find Lola in shockingly conservative clothes, a sheepish Kenny, and behind them, a shy stranger. Lola greeted me with a warm hug. The fresh curlicues at the edges of her facial tattoo couldn't disguise her worried look.

"Hey, girl. Can we come in?"

"Uh, sure..." I stepped aside. "Welcome to the humble abode. It's been a while, eh? Sorry for the mess..."

Lola stepped in carefully. I'd never seen her so ladylike. She set a host gift of some cookies on the counter and settled politely on the couch, even crossing her legs at the ankles.

"Lola? Are you okay? Um...you're not acting like yourself..."

"I think you should sit down, Janelle. This might be a bit of a shock."

"I'll finish the tea," I stammered. Kenny scooted in awkwardly, putting some apples down next to the cookies.

The stranger came in last. She was pretty enough, with a tattoo of a flower on the back of her hand and heavily pierced ears. Her pretty brown eyes were full of nervousness, but even though she was scared, her shapely hips moved with natural confidence. The strut and her very high-heeled boots made her day job pretty clear. I wondered where this was heading. I have no real problem with cuntgirls and sugarplums, but it wasn't what I expected out of a meeting. Besides, she looked vaguely familiar, and that was weird enough.

She put a cluster of tea roses on the counter—beautiful little yellow blossoms. They smelled wonderful.

"Thanks," I said. She just smiled nervously. "Um, I'm Janelle."

"Luz. Nice to meet you." She shook my hand like she was afraid of touching me, and scooted to the couch to sit by Lola. What the hell?

I poured the tea, sliced up the apples, and put the cookies on a plate. Very civilized and nice. The tea roses went in a shallow bowl of water, and I put those in the middle of the table.

"So," I said, breaking the silence, "what's up?"

"Um." Lola glanced at Luz, and nudged her.

Luz cleared her throat and spoke. She had a tiny, feminine whisper of a voice, adorably delicate. "I was talking to Lola last week—talking shop, you understand. I'm a free girl, not a Rat, and since it looks like the brothel bill is going to pass after all, we're getting our groups together." Lola nudged her. "So. We were...talking shop...and I mentioned a customer of mine who'd been around a lot lately, especially in the last couple of months..."

Luz slouched, as if she couldn't take any more. I had a terrible, inevitable feeling.

"Chloe," said Lola dully. "Chloe has been seeing Luz for a long time. I wasn't sure if you knew."

"She, uh, told me first," said Kenny. "'Cause we've been friends for so long..." I wondered if they were more, but kept my mouth shut. There was something painful in my chest, catching when I tried to breathe in. "Anyway. I...she said it and I was like, I better tell her, since they were gonna get married..."

I put my head in my hands. "The engagement has been off for a while," I managed. "We've been fighting for the last couple weeks, she hasn't seen me..." I looked up at Luz, and realised my face was streaming with hot tears. "Was it the sex? I thought I was good at that, but...was there something I wasn't doing? She was always so quiet..."

"She said there was something missing, and she was...jealous," said Luz. "I would never talk about a customer, normally, but when someone gets hurt...that's different."

I mumbled my answer through my hands. Couldn't look any of them in the eye, so I just hid my face and talked to my palm. "I thought you guys had some kind of code thing. Besides, I'm just a partner. What difference does it make?"

"A sex trade worker sells their body. A whore sells their integrity. There's a difference, Janelle," snapped Lola, "and the cheapest cuntgirl working in Sector D to the fanciest sugarplums in the authy geezies' laps know the difference."

Kenny put a timid hand on my shoulder, reaching over. "I'm sorry, man. Like, I don't know if you believe us, because of, like everything that happened when Chloe tried to convince Jay I was cheating with Lola, but...yeah."

"I'm so sorry, Janelle," said Lola quietly.

I considered throwing the plate, the flowers, the teapot on the floor. A beautiful mess. It would be good to break something.

Instead, I broke. I sat there and sobbed. "I thought she loved me," I managed to squeak out. "I tried so hard to love her. I tried."

Kenny got up and edged towards the door.

"I'm sorry," said Luz softly. I realised she was the random girl who'd been staring at Chloe when we'd gone for dinner at the Den. That's where I saw her before. That was an eternity ago.

I looked up at her. I wanted to be angry with her, to blame her, but I couldn't. Yeah, she was—oh, how it hurt—prettier than me, certainly more delicate and more girly, but even the energy for jealousy was too much. A feeling of doom and of certainty that I'd had from the beginning finally seemed fulfilled.

"S'not your fault," I managed. "I'd like all of you to leave, please. Need time to..." I buried my head in my hands again, and sobbed. Lola got up, gave me a light hug, and headed for the door.

Luz paused, touched my shoulder softly, and walked past. I heard the door squeak. "Thank you," I mumbled. None of them said anything, but the door closed oh, so softly.

Then I went back to bed.

Had some drinks now. Feel better. Pen won't write straight. Not sure why.

Dad came home. Took the bottle away. Started to yell at me, like he does when he's scared. Slurred out an explanation. He sat with me for a long time and patted my head. Cleaned up the broken tea pot and the broken plate and the cookies and the glass on the floor too. Good thing he loves me. He even made me my favorite food, easy-over eggs on toast. Could barely eat half of it. Gods I hate myself right now.

Text from Una. What time is it? Slept for a while I guess. How is it 3:00 in the night cycle? Oh gods, did I text her while I was drunk?

I did. Shit. Said I loved her. Told her Chloe was cheating on me, too, and that I found out from a sugarplum.

No answer. Does that mean it's over? Am I losing everything? Back to sleep. This all has to be a nightmare.

21—June 30, 0048 P.D.

Things just got worse. I feel like this is my fucking fault, because I spent yesterday either drinking or lying in bed. Still. I know it's impossible, and it was actually my day off of everything, but...I feel so responsible. And it hurts. I really, really want her to be okay. My chest aches like someone's trying to cut my heart out, and I keep thinking that I have to find her.

Fuck Chloe. All the time I wasted yesterday being hurt and feeling hurt by her is time I should have spent on this. I've never loved someone properly before, and if we can't get to her in time, I'm not going to find out what it's like. If I'd only been on Crow duty—

Never mind that. I'll start with when I was called to headquarters, directly from my phone, first thing in the morning. Or rather, I'll start when the grim messenger who arrived at six in the morning cycle told us that the city was under high alert, and that all Crows and police were to report to the Honeycomb immediately.

Dad ran in and shook me awake. I ran for the bathroom, splashed water on my face, and stared into my own bleary eyes. Not too hungover, to my surprise. Oh well. I shook off the remaining sleepiness, changed into my suit, armed myself and tucked the bone charm in for luck.

"Are you fit for duty, Janelle?" he asked, seeing that I was dressed.

"Yes. And this is important. I gotta go, Dad."

"Be careful," he called after me.

"I'll try," I shouted back, but the door was closed. No time to dwell on it. Only time to run.

I jogged up to one of the levels between us and the Heaven Tubes for a shortcut, finding myself surrounded by Crows. Sammie and Jay were there already. Jay made eye-contact and I could tell by the look on her face that she knew. Well, she is Kenny's girlfriend.

"Not now," I said tersely, before she could ask how I was doing. A few other people, strangers mostly, chattered a bit about why we were being called in, but I ignored them. My heart hammered in my chest, and not because of the jog.

We couldn't get to the Honeycomb fast enough. There were police officers waiting for us, and stragglers were still coming in. No civilians, though. Serious shit, I knew already. All the activity in the square was more or less suspended, the stalls empty and the sellers huddling in doorways. I'd never seen the centre of the city so quiet, so still.

"This way," said Leah tersely, as the cops ushered us in. "To the main court."

"What's—" She silenced me with a glare.

As we all filed in, the room filled up fast. Add the police officers—all of them, not just Nero, the chief—and all of us Crows, and the aldermen too, and you have an idea of how cramped it was getting in there. And, of course, a couple of newssheet vultures had probably crept in, though my mind wasn't on journalistic integrity just then. A couple hundred people, all told. A hum, a buzz of chatter filled the room, vibrated through the pillars that divided the seats. Anticipation and fear filled it like a fog.

"Silence, please," said Nathu. He rose from the judicial benches and walked along the row in front of the prosecution and defense benches. It was a good place to be heard from. The deep hush that followed his words made it even easier to listen.

"Thank you. As many of you know, we have been experiencing extreme security issues lately. The rate of injury has risen in the last few months. More importantly, children have been going missing. This was unacceptable, and we have been conducting an investigation into the causes.

"A number of very strange things have also been seen lately, and they appear to be related to the attacks. By things, I mean...monsters. Previously, things we'd only heard of in descriptions of Dust Fever hallucinations, but these haven't been acting like hallucinations do.

"Recently, when another child went missing, we were able to intercept one of the kidnappers. Calling himself a Sandman, he alluded to people who had previously been Lost, and implied that they were linked to the kidnappings. As well, he implied that they had control over the Dust in some way, though our questioning couldn't draw out an answer about how that was happening.

"Last night, my wife Una got up to take a walk early in the morning, which she sometimes does to think. She didn't return."

Everybody lost it. There were shouted questions, people started talking and whispering—

"Silence!" In addition to good acoustics, Nathu's voice carried well. "As Una is the Commander of our Rediscovery Expert forces, this presents a challenge. Hunter Okonjo has stepped up to the task of acting as temporary Commander, but Una's safety, the information she knows, and,"—his public face faltered for a moment—"her personal importance all make her a valuable person. They know that losing her is a blow to our moral."

He was losing it. "A note was left on the wall towards the edge of the core, in the direction of A

Sector." Nathu cleared his throat. "If you want to see your wife again, come Up. We'll trade you your wife, alive, for our lives back. Come Up, and you'll get what you want." Somehow, I wasn't surprised that he had it memorized. The murmuring started up again, and he raised his hands.

"No interruptions, please. Please. The Sandman was also missing from his cell, and his guard, Wilhelm Verns, lay dead with his throat torn out. The other two guards outside, Julia Tan and Rachel Kern, were injured and are in the hospital, though I'm told they're stable and likely going to be fine."

Nathu bowed his head. There were several gasps and cries of shock and anger. I glanced at my fellow squad members and friends. All of them looked as sick as I felt. Ginni had tears in her eyes, but swallowed and held her head up. I admired her courage and wiped my own away. There was no time to cry right now.

"The note and Wilhelm's death suggest that someone means business, and the use of 'we' means we're up against an unknown enemy—it could be two people or it could be two hundred. I don't know what's happened to Una, but she's obviously going to be used as a bargaining chip to get something from us. I hope and pray that whatever's happened to her will not be what happened to Wilhelm." He inhaled deeply and started again, as if to block out thoughts of what might be happening to Una just now. I couldn't stop imagining it. Still, I knew Una would tell me to suck the tears up and stay strong. There was no time to let fear get the best of me.

"This could be a trap, and they've been very, very good at avoiding capture so far. We're dealing with a foe that's experienced and competent, and that has so far been...elusive. We need to change our tactics.

"I'm going need you Crows to set up patrols to start investigating the upper tunnels. We're going to need to send a couple of teams Up, as well. We'll be coordinating between the Crows and our police to ensure that...order is maintained here, and...if you'll excuse me, I'm going to start arranging investigations into Una's disappearance.

"I would like any of you with new information, no matter how...strange or even crazy it may sound, to come to your superiors. We are dealing with forces outside of those we've been accustomed to, and any information whatsoever, even if it's just...something observed from the corner of your eye, may be useful."

He swallowed and blinked rapidly, trying to recover his composure. "Thank you. I need to return to my office; I will ask a few of you to accompany me for further briefing. Crows, I'd appreciate it if you could wait here. Chief Nero, I'd like you to arrange for your superior officers to set up the patrols, and bring your advisors with you to my office. As of now, Underlighter City is under Martial Law. All citizens on the street must be escorted home for their own safety."

"Sir, what about the gangers?"

Nathu inhaled slowly. "I will be discussing that in private. Thank you. Send out the strongest signals you can so we can alert the nearby towns and try to keep them from running into the same problems. Now, if you'll excuse me, I need to prepare my city and alert emergency services."

There was, of course, a rush of questions, but he held out his hand and walked through them.

By the time he'd disappeared to his office, most of the police squads had been sent out. Fear washed around in the pit of my stomach. I worried about Dad, my friends...Una, over and over...but there was no time. I had to be a Crow.

A messenger, a young kid in the black uniform of the trade, tapped me on the shoulder. I was being summoned.

Going up the stairs was a nightmare. I had no idea what I'd find, whether something awful was going to be revealed.

Sure enough, it was an awful mess. There were papers pinned up everywhere, Nero and a couple of aldermen were arguing, the Crow sergeants were all there...and in the middle of it all, Nathu was sitting at his desk with one ear covered, snapping orders into the phone.

"I'm aware of the limits, but just do it! Bring people from resting shifts on so you can be prepared for an influx of casualties.

"No, I don't know how many we should expect. Just prepare yourselves for a large scale emergency and a lot of triage. There has to be someone there who dealt with the unrest in Sudomo's time!"

In addition to being Princeps, he was obviously being thrown into greater responsibility. I'd heard the rumours, like everyone, that Sudomo was too sick to really do the duties, but this proved it.

I stood awkwardly off the side, listening into conversations. The aldermen—one Between, one male—gave me disapproving looks and muttered at each other and me. Hunter and the other Crow sergeants made a ring around Nathu and started questioning him about Una's disappearance.

I had never seen Nathu so scared, so furious. "All I know is that she went for a walk, and then, she was gone. Una is not the sort of person who'd just disappear."

"We're going to find her," said Oliver grimly, grabbing Nathu's shoulder. "If the Sandmen aren't doin' this to scare us, I'll eat my damn hat."

Nathu crumpled, his head on his desk, in his arms. "My city is being hurt. My people are going missing. My *wife* has been kidnapped. I've doubled the patrols, I've been investigating things, but so many details have slipped through the cracks. I feel so...incompetent. She's gone, and it's my fault."

"You're not incompetent," said a rich, low voice. In the doorway, Sudomo Atalas was waiting.

"Father," said Nathu, sitting up straight. "I didn't expect you. You'll have to pardon me for..."

The Mayor doesn't go out much. Nathu has been taking over the reins for a long time, but really, they work in tandem to share power. He keeps his city running, the same way he has since I was a kid and he took over from his mother. Other than that, he is a doer, not a talker—leaves that to Nathu.

Seeing the man himself come out of the closet in his office made even the blasé Crows back up respectfully. The police, of course, were already saluting and standing at attention, but that's police for you.

With all that in mind, then you'll understand why what happened next left me, left all of us, flabbergasted.

"No pardons," said Sudomo. Shorter than his son and severe-faced, with a crisp and spotless dark suit, he had a grim, unyielding look.

"You're right. I'm sorry. I need to pull myself together to take care of the city." Nathu sat up, looking more alert, and discreetly wiped tears from the corners of his eyes.

"No, damn you," growled Sudomo. "This is your damned wife who's gone missing. Let yourself feel anger, let yourself feel sorrow. If you don't, they'll eat you up from the inside, and then you'll be no good to anyone." He embraced his son, patted his back.

Nathu accepted it. Sudomo looked around the room, meeting each person's gaze one by one. "That goes for the rest of you, too. I'm sure many of you have lost people in some way or another. Sickness, old age, bitter mistakes...some of them might even have gotten Lost." His eyes locked with mine as he said that, and I swallowed. "Losses and deaths happen. However, as long as I'm Mayor here, I'm not going to stand for an attack on my people."

He parted from Nathu, brushing the intensely personal feelings of a moment before aside like so much Dust. "Ten years ago, we had a rash of people who went missing. Something like this, but we hadn't organized the patrols as well. It happened before that, but because it was people in the outer edges of the sectors, and because some of them were low-lives, I didn't pay as much attention to them. My mother, in her days, was so busy trying to keep people alive that there was no time to worry about attrition." He stood, and glared at all of us. "I trust the welfare of the people in your quadrants to you. Now, if you'll all pardon me, there are certain preparations I'll need to make." He swept out magnificently. I've never seen someone barely five feet in height walk so tall.

Nathu stood, and watched his father go. He looked back at us with renewed determination in his face. Sometimes I forget how young he really is. He makes me feel like a kid, even though the age difference between us is a lot smaller than it seems. He has maybe a couple of years on me, tops. Just then, he looked a lot older.

"Nero!"

"Sir!" The police chief snapped to attention. A single dark curl had escaped from under his hat, I noticed. A hair out of place? Even he was scared.

"The Mayor is absolutely right. I'd like you to double your patrols. Pay special attention to the areas that connect to the Heaven Tubes."

"Understood, sir."

"Another thing. My Crows have been working with the gangers casually, and it's turned up results. If possible, I'd like you to recruit a few as temporary support. I touched on it earlier, but I need to be...specific. Make sure they know that drug use and trading at this time won't be permitted, of course, but offer other incentives."

"Sir?" Nero let his eyebrows rise.

"That was an order, not a suggestion. Recruit across gangs and let them know that their petty turf wars need to be set aside for now. It's time for them to choose their side. Try to get them to lead you around and assist in the search. If they refuse, lock them up. No brutality or harsh treatment. We don't have time to hurt our own people. I'd also like you to recruit from the civilian reserves, wherever possible. What will you need to handle the increase in manpower?"

The chief was at a loss for words, but he pulled himself together. "Yes, sir. We'll need seamstresses and, ah, smiths to make some temporary badges. I'm concerned about giving authority to civilians, sir, and about what will happen to those temporary badges after the fact..."

"We'll have to deal with that as it comes. Right now, we need more men out on those streets to keep an eye on things. Be on the alert for any unusual activity, strange creatures—I don't care how crazy it looks, I want you to watch for it. Reorganize your squads to compensate for the new people if you have to. I don't want one corner of this city unprotected."

"Yes sir." The chief stepped back.

"Please go relay my plans to my fa—the Mayor. I expect you to coordinate with other emergency services and information delivery systems. Please let him know that I want to send the mail service and the criers around with memorized messages. If they have to talk to every one of the 17,000 people in this city door to door, they'll need to do it. The Mayor will understand where I'm going with that idea. Dismissed."

The chief bowed, turned on his heel, and marched off slowly. That left only us Crows.

There was a bunch of chatter for a while, and I wondered why I was still standing there. It was over my level. I mean, sure, I've been working with the sergeants, but there's a big difference between working with people and actually being one. For all that they'd treated me with respect and listened to me, I wasn't one of the old guard, one of them. They worked with an efficiency and organization I'd never seen before.

Okay, I'll be honest. I was so freaked out that it mostly went over my head. I lost my ability to concentrate and be sensible. There was too much going on. When Nathu finally sent them off, he had to call me over twice before I realised the room was empty.

He took the phone off the hook, closed and locked the doors, and sat down at his desk again. I came behind it and gave him a hug around the handsome leather chair.

"It's going to be all right. They'll find her. We'll find her."

"I hope so," he said to the desk. "I called you up because...last night, when she went for a walk, she was going to see you."

"Oh."

"She...got a text and said it sounded important. She wanted me to come...but I was sleepy." He looked up, and I saw that he was crying again. "I should have come. If I had..."

"If you had, then everyone in the city would have been screwed," I said firmly. "Besides...this is my fault. Um. I guess I should tell you why I texted her...I was kind of drunk at the time."

His mouth twitched. "We figured that out, but go on."

"I...you already know that Una and I are...interested in each other. I...I really like you too. I had a girlfriend, yadda yadda, you remember...we broke up unofficially...well, I found out yesterday that she'd been cheating on me for a couple of months, and it just broke me." I stared at my feet, feeling ashamed.

"That makes sense."

"I also realised how much how much I care about Una. I'm going to help you get her back. I don't care what it takes."

He raised his eyebrows at me wearily. "It could take a lot."

"I have it. I'll get her back or I'll die trying."

"Maybe you should just try, skip the dying part."

"I wasn't going to try to die...nevermind." Somehow, we ended up laughing. Desperation does that.

"Una's an amazing woman," I said softly.

He smiled sadly. "That she is. I can't stop worrying about her." He turned a strained face to me. "What if we get her back in pieces?"

I shook my head. "Nah. They haven't hurt anyone they've taken. If you ask me, this is a hostage situation. The Sandman figured out that Una's been behind a lot of this and took her to scare us. Wait and see. They said they wanted to trade her, so they really want something from us."

"Interesting. How do you know?"

"Just guessing, but I think there's even more here than meets the eye. When he said that stuff about people getting Lost and being abandoned by us...I dunno. I feel like there's a big, big clue there."

He nodded. "I should get back to it. There's a lot to handle."

I wanted to make him feel better. I kissed him and threw my arms around him. He tasted of something spicy and sweet, like cloves. Nathu stroked my back gently, relaxed in my arms. Where Una was more muscly and more fleshy, he was on the spare side— about my height, a little shorter than her, and probably almost my weight.

Being close to him felt really, really good. Clean. Better than Raheed had felt, by far. I reached down without thinking about it and touched him through his slacks. He shuddered and sighed. His hand slipped up to my breast, squeezed gently through my suit. Then, his grip relaxed, and he moved just out of my reach.

"We...probably shouldn't get too distracted," he murmured reluctantly. "Save this for the victory celebrations."

"I'd be happy to do something quickly for you," I muttered. "Um. Just to help keep your mind on work."

He blushed and adjusted his collar. "I'd like that, believe me." He took my hand, looked into my eyes. "But I'd rather share that with Una when we get her back. Any other time...I'd enjoy that with you. But we're too short on time right now."

I straightened, feeling foolish. "Of course. No, I'm very sorry."

"No, no, Janelle, not like that." He got up, moved forward, and took me in his arms. "I really like you.

329

'Like' is too soft a word. I can't wait to get to know you better." His hand slipped down to my ass, very gently and smoothly. "Believe me. I just don't have the time I want to do it properly right now." Nathu kissed me, long and sweet. "Please forgive me."

"Nothing to forgive," I said, resting against him for a minute. "This is my fault. Like I said. And I'm gonna fix it." I stepped back, saluted him officially. "Tunnel black and blood red, light true and hope dead."

"Tunnel black and blood red, light true and hope dead," he echoed.

"I'd better report to Leah and Hunter."

"Yes." He hung up the phone. "Unlock the door? I should get back to work, and there are a lot of angry, scared people who need to talk to me."

"Talk to you soon, Nathu," I said. And without waiting for him to reply, I squared my shoulders and walked out the door.

It occurred to me, as I headed down the stairs, to be really, really glad the curtains were all drawn. Anyone seeing this might have gotten the wrong idea, or even the right one.

The streets were still shockingly empty. I took the main road and down a little ways, towards Sector A and home. I figured I might as well hang around the closest entrance to the Tunnels in preparation for going up to do a patrol.

Being me, I took the shortcut, even though it meant going through a few very narrow alleys. There was an access corridor that connected to the power grid for the street, something I remembered from my days as an electrician. Times like that, being forced to memorize the main power centres in the city was a pain in the ass. I never thought I'd be important enough to do the main repairs down here. Now, though, it was useful, and I knew it would be an empty route.

Not empty enough, though. As I made my way to the end and locked the door behind me, something moved in the corner of my vision. I heard a hiss of breath against my ear, and a hand wrapped itself around my mouth. Long, long fingernails. I tried to bite and jerked an elbow back to get my attacker in the gut, but something made of cold metal bounced against my temple gently.

"Don't turn around. We're going Up. There's someone who wants to speak to you."

"Raheed? What's going on?" I cried. His hand muffled my words. I struggled, but he held me firmly, pressing clawed fingers to my cheek. He moved his hand, keeping the gun trained on me.

"Not Raheed," said the monster before me, grinning. Too many teeth, and eyes missing, full of blackness. "Call me Strife. Akheilos. Come with me."

THE LOVED, THE LOST, THE DREAMING

22—June 31, 0048 P.D.

I've never been good at following instructions when I don't know the reasoning behind them. Even though the adrenaline was pumping through my veins, a rational, smart-assed part of me asked, "Akheilos? What kind of name is that?"

"Look it up," he snarled. His teeth were serrated, pointed. "Haven't read your fairy tales in a while, have you, Janelle?"

A punch in the heart. I hadn't read them since Mom had gotten Lost. Once in a while, I'd tried, but it brought back memories. Hurt too much. Myths, stories of old gods, monsters....I abandoned them a long time ago, and now, it seemed, they were coming back for me.

Cold black eyes looked into mine. Not Raheed's eyes, though the face was, heartbreakingly, still his. I reached for his hand. "Raheed, buddy. I know you're in there. Put the gun away—"

Rough skin, worse than sandpaper. Raheed had had dry skin, but never this rough and dry. He hissed at me, an inhumane, animal sound.

"I am the Lamia's son. I am Strife. I'm not your friend." He nudged me with the gun, stepped around to get behind me. "Come on. And keep your hands where I can see them."

"Just a sec, my butt is itchy."

"Excuse me?"

"Gimme a sec. I need to..." I turned around, facing him, and made a show of adjusting my suit. "That's better."

He lowered the gun slightly as I bent to scratch it. Before he could raise it from the relaxed position, I popped a throwing knife out of a sheath on my calf and stabbed him in the thigh.

He groaned and crumpled like a wet paper bag. As he clutched his right leg, he dropped the gun. I picked it up and trained it on him.

"Man, you really suck at this. You didn't even disarm me when you cornered me."

He hissed and, to my surprise, jumped to bite me. I managed to dodge, and kicked him in the stomach. "Don't move around too much on that leg."

"It doesn't matter. You and your kind will die, Mole."

"Mole?" I looked at him sideways. His sockets were empty, but the rest of his face was twisted in pure, deep hate. "Raheed, what's going on? Why are you talking like a Sandman?"

He hissed at me again and tried to bite. I kicked him in the stomach again. Part of me winced to see him curl up and exhale sharply, but the rest was full of a strange, cold kind of fury.

"Hiss all you want. Get up. We're going back inside and you're being held for questioning. I want to know why you're all freaky—looking and why your fucking eyes are gone."

"It doesn't matter if you take me in for questioning. They're coming. They took your whore and they're coming for you and everyone else down here. They'll kill your father and make you watch, and that stupid fucking princeling of yours who runs around telling people what to do. All of you are going to die and I'm going to enjoy watching it." He grinned at me, and I lost my temper.

I dealt him a boot in the stomach. "Threatening me is just going to get you a bullet somewhere that'll really hurt."

"Questioning me is just going to make you lose even more time."

"Lose time for what?"

"We're coming, I told you." He grinned up at me, looking alien and frightening. "We're going to take back what you've kept from us."

"Are you on hallies? And why the hell do you look like that? Talk faster, or I'm going to shoot you, and we won't get to wherever you want me to go to."

"Now, that's one thing we just can't have." He wouldn't stop grinning, those damned triangular teeth glinting at me. The wrongness of it was jarring. I couldn't stop staring. Looked weirdly familiar though. I remembered a video I'd seen once of a strange deep-water fish in the ocean. It was an ancient fish with cold eyes and teeth just like his—the name escaped me. It was something we'd seen in a school class and Raheed had been very scared of it. I remembered that much. Definitely not a coincidence.

"Are you going to stare all day, or was there something you wanted to know?" he hissed.

"Right. Um. Why are you talking and acting like a Sandman?"

His features softened and I heard his normal voice break through the throaty hiss he'd affected until now. "I was thinking about you and wishing we could be better friends. Walking in the tunnels where we used to go. Do you remember?"

I nodded, involuntarily. Seeing my former lover and my friend crumpled and bleeding, and knowing I'd done it, was starting to bother me. I forced myself to think of him as a threat, not just Raheed.

"Good. I'm glad. Right where we used to go to kiss, it was waiting for me. A creature of the Dust. It had sharp teeth and fins and it moved like a fish in water through the air of the tunnel. I didn't even have a chance when it swallowed me whole."

"Swallowed you?"

"It made me a part of itself." He grinned again, and Akheilos took over Raheed's face. "The Dust told me what was really going on. It led me down to Sector D where you were keeping the Sandman prisoner. I tore Wilhelm's throat out and knocked out the other two scavenger scum. The Sandman told me you were important and said I should take you Up. He left to tell the Lamia we would be coming."

"Who the hell is the Lamia?"

He wriggled strangely, and adjusted himself to sit. Tearing through part of his shirt casually, he started to dress his wound. It was still bleeding, but he wasn't bothered. The ragged him of his shirt revealed grey skin and—was that fin, like on a fish? What the hell had happened to Raheed? I flinched, disturbed by the utter wrongness of it.

"You might know her as the Witch." I yelped in surprise and fear, and instinctively looked up to see if any Dust-warding charms were hanging above my head. Damn. It figured that there wasn't one. Perhaps my bone amulet was helping, though. Superstition was a comfort, just then. "Pay attention. It was very late in the night cycle and I wasn't the only one thinking about you, so it seemed. Una was walking towards your neighbourhood."

"What did you do to her?" I snarled.

He smiled. "Oh, not much. Yet. I called the other Sandman back once I'd knocked her out and sent them Up to the Witch. Don't worry, your whore is fine—apart from being dumb enough to love you, you heartless bitch. A bruise, perhaps, but not a scratch on her pretty ass. I'm sure your little mayor's son wouldn't take damaged goods. Does he know you fucked his wife and that you've broken the hearts of half the sector, or are you going to tell him that yourself?"

Sparks of anger fizzled through me. I forced myself to think about nice, elegant circuit maps. Wire A goes to connection A...Wire B goes to connection B...

It was mostly under control when things got a hell of a lot worse. "Janelle!"

"Chloe?"

"What the hell are you doing here? And why the fuck are you pointing a gun at Raheed?" She looked at me, wide-eyed and shocked, and my blood boiled.

"Can it, missy. I met Luz."

"Whoa, Janelle." She raised her hands. "Let's talk about this. Um, I was on my way...I think you should put the gun down..."

Shit. I hadn't even realised I was pointing it at her. I trained it back on Raheed. He'd been starting to cross the space between us, and stopped.

"Chloe, you have to help me. She's gone completely insane! She thinks I'm a Sandman..." his eyes were closed tight and his face, fearful. He cowered, clutching his leg. "She threw a knife at me!"

Chloe looked at me with a shriveling kind of disgust in her gaze. Disgust, and fear. "Now, now, Raheed," she reassured him, inching closer. "Janelle...put the gun down. Put all of them down."

It wasn't like her to be so brave. "Chloe, I'm not crazy. We were holding a Sandman and I just ran into Raheed. The mayor's wife is missing and..."

"Janelle, I think you need to take a deeeeep breath." She used her childlike voice, and turned round, frightened eyes on me. "Deeeeeep breath. I don't know what you're talking about, but I'm pretty sure you've been...having a hard time with things lately. Maybe some things aren't...aren't real. Just put the gun down and we'll talk, and then we can get to someone who can help you make the scary things go away."

I admit it, I faltered. What she said echoed in me. Had I been dreaming about all of this? Raheed's eyes were shut and even his skin looked more normal now. A sick feeling of dread filled my stomach. Surely it couldn't all be fake.

All a dream, maybe. Lots of bad dreams. "Thaaaaat's it, easy does it," she cooed.

I lowered it slightly, but didn't let go. Her eyes flicked to it nervously. Raheed was still frozen between us, looking scared and miserable, with his eyes clenched shut.

"So, Luz," I said. "The girl in the Den. Lola told me about her. She said you'd been together for a few months."

"Lola lies," spat Chloe. She adjusted her bag of groceries on one hip. I noticed she was wearing the skirt I'd bought her and felt a twinge of sadness.

"Luz came with her. And Kenny too."

"You really trust them more than you trusted me?" The hurt face, and the voice wobble. She was doing the thing with her eyes that she'd always done when we fought.

"I have important things to get to. The whole city is in danger and Una's missing."

"First name basis now, huh?" Jealousy in her voice.

"Yes. And more than that. Look, you haven't talked to me and weeks, and...I don't have time for this right now!"

"Just figures. You go crazy and you manage to cheat on me."

"Enough with the guilting!" I snapped. "I'm not crazy, I don't have the Fever, and there's bunch of Crows who'll happily tell you..."

"Calm down. I just...put the gun down. I didn't say you were crazy, but...it doesn't look so good right now. I think you're confused, and..."

"Don't tell me how to feel! You cheated on me!"

"I did not! Those bitches and that asshole are lying! Besides, Kenny cheated with Lola on Jay!"

"No, he didn't," I said. "He told me they were friends and that you got it out of proportion. Look...if you really think all of this was a big mistake, the stuff with them, at least..." my voice broke and I swallowed. "Tell me you love me. Say it like you mean it, and I'll assume you're right and I'll even put down the gun."

She hesitated, opened her mouth. No sound came out. Chloe lowered her head.

Chloe can fib, but she can't lie. Hell, good a liar as I can be, even I can't really lie when it comes to shit like that. One look at her face and I knew the answer. I softened my tone and kept a grip on the gun. My voice trembled a little when I spoke. "Look, either way...if you wanted to...see other people...if I wasn't giving you what you needed..."

She looked guilty, and I knew what I'd said hit home. "Look," she said sharply, "this isn't the time. You hurt Raheed, and we need to get him to an infirmary." She knelt, put down her groceries, and leaned forward. "Raheed, uncurl and let me see...I'm really bad with blood, but..."

341

It was all the distraction he needed. As she set down the bag of fruit, he uncoiled and lunged for her. She screamed.

"Chloe!"

He got up, madness in his empty-eyed face, her blood on his teeth. She was still screaming, and her forearm gushed red, part of the muscle missing. Smiling at me with too many teeth, he chewed and swallowed. I felt sick to my stomach.

She screamed incoherently.

"Stupid Mole," he said, his voice a hiss. "If you were mad, you'd be lucky. The truth is a lot worse than a little insanity."

"Janelle, help me!" Chloe screamed. Her face was red and covered in tears.

I inhaled and squeezed the trigger. A bright red streak appeared on Raheed's left side, near his kidneys. I'd missed.

She was bleeding a lot. I knelt and ripped her skirt off. She wouldn't stop screaming, and even tried to kick at me. I was out of patience and I nailed her in the ribs with a good kick. "Shut it, you stupid bitch!" I wrapped the skirt around her arm one-handed, as tight as I could. "Get up and run to the infirmary. There's one around the corner." I was shocked that someone hadn't come out of one of the nearby buildings, but martial law was martial law. I grabbed her face for a minute. "Okay?"

"Okay," she whimpered. I pulled her to her feet.

"Go!"

Raheed—or Akheilos—lunged for me as I rose. He landed on both of us, snapping and biting. I hit him in the face with the gun, but nothing went *crunch*. Chloe rolled away, still screaming, and started to kick her heels. Her blouse had been white, but was now a mass of red.

His mouth was full of rows of the teeth, inner layers waiting to replace the damaged ones. As he lunged for me, I whipped the gun back and hit him in the face again, scratching my hand. Chloe wouldn't stop screaming. Finally, I pushed and kicked her out of the way and went for Raheed. He aimed for my shoulder with the next bite, snapping and snarling, jerking his neck in ways that should have broken it.

"Oh gods, what's wrong with his eyes?" Chloe screamed.

"Run the fuck away!" I roared at her.

Raheed aimed for one of my legs and his teeth met my suit. I prepared for the ripping sensation of flesh, but there was none. The one thing he hadn't expected was that my Crow uniform was specifically designed to repel the sharp teeth of undersea fish. Frustrated, he tried to bite again, but I dodged it.

"Stop! Stop fighting!" Chloe yowled. She jumped in the middle of us.

It was the worst thing she could have done. Stupid, stupid girl. Was she trying to be brave, or did she just want it all to stop? Not that it mattered. He leapt for her, jaws open wide, and bit her flank.

She screamed and screamed. I was sick of it. I kicked her away from him and put myself between them. Chloe rolled away and I kicked and punched Raheed, over and over. I heard his ribs *snap* and finally, he yelped a little.

"Enough! You're taking me Up there if I have to carry your sorry corpse. No more attacks and no more distractions. Get up."

He rose from a crouch, panting and glaring at me like an angry beast. His empty sockets burned with an inner light, something full of fury that burned hot and cold.

"What about her?" Chloe was in a bad state.

"We're dropping her in front of the infirmary and then we're out of here." I was shocked that we hadn't seen even one damn cop or Crow, but they could only be out in the districts, calming the rowdy and enforcing martial law. Stupid, stupid Chloe had broken it to get groceries. I wanted to cry, but I bit my tongue, hefted her up by the good arm. She screamed and recoiled, not that I blamed her.

"What are you doing? What's going on?"

"Just let me take you to the infirmary. There's one not far, and..."

"Get away!" She pushed me off.

"You're bleeding--!"

"Get away! You—you—monster!"

I snapped. "Fine. Akheilos, let's go."

The creature that was partly Raheed and partly Akheilos, the demon-man, looked confused. "I thought you said..."

"I know what I said!" I shot an angry look at Chloe, who was starting to look pale. The area around us was spattered with blood, and almost none of it was mine. "She can bleed out. I'm going to save the damn city, and the woman I love."

Deliberately, I turned my back on her, and pushed Akheilos forward, holding him by the collar of his shirt.

"Don't leave me!" she screeched. "Janelle! Don't leave me!"

It echoed behind us as I marched him away, and as I left her alone to die.

The place I was headed, of course, was the elevators Up. I couldn't think of a better, faster way to get Up than that, and there was no time to wander around the tunnels dealing with errant gangers or cops.

The centre had a few Crows around it, but—for once—none I knew by name. When they saw my suit and the injured guy I was dragging, there was an immediate rush for questions.

"Janelle Cohen," I snapped. "I'm taking him Up. This is a Sandman and I'm forcing him with me to get some answers."

"I'm going with you," said a familiar voice, greeting me from the side. Shit. May.

"May..." I inhaled and decided to do the dumb thing. So far, it's what I've done best at. "He told me..."

"The Lamia demands to see her. Come with her, and we will kill you," snarled Akheilos. May's eyes widened when she looked at him.

"Raheed! Your eyes! And...what's wrong with your face?" Even a hardened Crow like her could be shocked. He snapped at her hand, grinning madly. She dodged with ease, but gave me a look of wide-eyed terror.

"Her, and only her. Bring us Up," he rasped.

I gave her a long-suffering shrug. It was all a long nightmare, and I couldn't tell whether I was awake or trapped in sleep anymore. "Just do as he says. Please."

"Janelle, this isn't rational."

"Neither was leaving my ex to bleed out on the floor. By the way, she's back near A Sector and she's missing a chunk. If she's still alive, you should get to her." I laughed reflexively, and they recoiled. As Akheilos stared at me in fascination, something hopeful in his face, I finally heard myself. Horrified, I clapped a hand over my own mouth. Had that really been me, laughing like that?

The Crows looked confused and repulsed. May stared at me like a stranger, a ghost, and finally nodded. "Go in." Unspoken was a suggestion: *don't come back, though, if you're like this.* They thought it was the Fever, but it was something beyond that, something almost better but also far, far worse. Silently, I dragged Akheilos through the gym and training centre, and towards the elevators. Up.

I had my very light and efficient breather and goggles hanging around my neck, and I snapped them on before entering the elevator partition room, with its emergency showers. All the times I'd been here with my friends—well, the times I had—the last time we'd been here, when I'd dragged a trembling Chloe from her doom and felt Una's sweet hands on me in the shower...it was a jumbled century of dream, half real and half unreal.

Something inside me whispered, *hold on.* It wasn't my father's voice, or even my mother's; it wasn't Una's or Nathu's or Chloe's or even just Jay's. It was part of me and it wasn't, something clear and sweet and sane. *It will be over soon*, said the voice.

By the time we reached the top, I realised I'd been repeating it out loud, over and over. Akheilos, now more Raheed than monster, cowered in fear and—when the demon in him rose—leered and gibbered.

"You left her to die," he said. I heard Raheed's horror and Akheilos' glee in the same voice.

"It will be over soon," I said out loud, more clearly this time.

"It's only beginning. Nightmares don't end, Up here. The Lamia—"

The Lamia. I remembered, then, what her name meant. A child-eating demon. I smiled bitterly. "Does she eat children?"

"Saves them," spat Akheilos. "Saves them, but she's going to get her revenge on you. Then, you'll feel fear like nothing you've had before."

I looked at him steadily and thought about nothing, just something good and warm and clean. "I'm not afraid. I was born for this."

After that, he was quiet, and didn't say a damned thing.

THE LOVED, THE LOST, THE DREAMING

23—June 31, 0048 P.D.

When the doors finally opened on the empty apartment building, Akheilos had started to avoid my eyes. Maybe I was just so far gone that I had no fear left, and maybe a part of me was just too sane.

I wasn't surprised when he took off running in the direction of the scavenger walk from so long ago. The sky boiled with blackness, the darkness of Dust swirling angrily over us. It looked unusually concentrated. Even with the bright light of my LEDs, I could barely see a few feet in front of me.

Lights of eyes flashed and glimmered in the gloom. I saw hints of crawling things, creeping things, at the edge of my vision. Teeth gleamed and claws glittered, and furry, scaly shapes shifted in the shadows.

I ignored them, but my blood still chilled when something howled in the distance. Even if you're strong and sane, or trying to be, you can tell when you're being hunted.

The only thing to do, though, was focus on Akheilos, running strangely through the broken and deserted streets. There was no wind, of course, the Dust eats it, but there was something in the air, almost like a current. I've never been in a real electrical storm, but I have a feeling it would have been like the air was then.

There was little time to think, though. I ran after Akheilos and tried not to trip over anything, ignoring the shapes that interrupted and ran through the shadows. This had to be level 6 or 7 in difficulty, if I'd been trying to scale it. The only thing on my mind, though, was catching up with Akheilos.

He led me down rough, refuse-filled alleys, through half-collapsed shacks around the streets. I knew the area well enough—when there was more light to see by—but with the Dust swirling and the nightmares hovering around us, I almost got lost a few times. He taunted me, forced me to run until my lungs were burning, then swerved from a familiar road to a strange alley.

Still, I kept pace with him. When he led me to Sunnyside, the darkened sky full of gloom, I felt an old sense of terror seize me. We were, of course, right in front of the house of the witch.

I know I'm not talking like myself right now, or not writing like myself I guess, but I didn't feel like myself up there. I felt clean and good and cold and terrified all at once—there was something I had to do, something that couldn't be escaped, and finally doing it was a relief.

He stopped, then, grinning at me widely with those unnatural, horrible teeth. "Are you coming in?"

"Is Una in there?"

"Just come," he said.

The darkness was around and behind me and there wasn't even a little bit of light in the house, but I nodded anyway.

He opened the door politely for me, and I stepped in. Last time, we'd just run through. It was still a perfect time capsule---the purple velvet chairs, the narrow dark hallways, the expensive antique furniture with the doilies and trims. Delicate things.

"Are we waiting for someone?" I asked. Akheilos said nothing, but pointed his chin behind me.

The girl was there when I turned my head. White skin, unearthly white; dark hair neatly parted; an ancient dress, and a deep madness in her eyes. And all too familiar. Not just because I'd seen her before. Not because I recognized her from my nightmares, or from the last trip through the house. Her white hand had been the one on the door frame and she'd been the one Jay had chased around the house. No, I'd seen her in pictures.

My throat was dry as Dust. "You must be my aunt Lilly," I managed.

She treated me to a wide grin, full of sharp little teeth. "It's a pleasure to see you again. How have you been for the last decade?"

"Uh...growing up."

Something human flickered underneath her face. "Would have been nice to do that."

I felt sick. "So...when you got Lost..."

Her black eyes bored into me. "I was walking around a level or two closer to Up than I should have. I got lost and wandered Up. Have you ever been thirsty, Janelle?"

"Yes..."

"Did you know it takes three days to die from thirst? Less if you're already bleeding out, of course." She shook her head, blew a dark strand of hair out of her eyes. "Lucky the Sandmen found me when they did. I was almost dead. A little too close."

"But...but Mom..."

"She came after me," said Lilly. "Not soon enough, though. But it wasn't all bad, after the Sandmen found me."

I didn't like the way she smiled, and it wasn't just because of the glinting teeth. I imagined them sinking into my throat and a cold shiver ran through me. Lilly took a few steps around the coffee table, her feet not quite touching the floor. Suddenly, she broke apart, a dense cloud of Dust swirling where she'd been, and appeared a few steps away, towards the stairs going up.

"How..."

"A little talent, learning to control your nightmares, and patience," she said, grinning.

"Look, can you either kill me or just cut the crap? Unless you're this Lamia person...I want to talk about Una and the kids."

She laughed in my face. "Talk?"

"There has to be something you people want from us."

Her face contorted. She looked about eleven or twelve, but this was an old anger, borrowed and shared and treasured. I took a step back. It scared me more than her flesh-tearing teeth.

"You have no idea how much we want. None." Her eyes narrowed and she paced back towards me. "We live in a world of corpses and nightmares. The ones who still need to eat are always starving because the Dust won't let us farm. If you had to spend a minute up here, you'd learn about suffering..."

"I'm a Crow," I snarled back. "I've spent more than a minute up here. And believe me, I know a little bit about suffering. And whoever you are, I don't care if you think you are, I remember Lilly. Lilly would never have talked like you."

She sneered at me. "You know nothing."

"Enough chat. Take her to the Lamia," Akheilos hissed. Lilly returned a wide, toothy grin, and turned her burning red eyes on me.

"I'd almost forgotten. Come," she said, in her sweet birdlike voice. "Don't keep her waiting or she'll eat both of our livers."

"I wouldn't dream of it," I said.

Akheilos' face flickered for a moment, and I saw Raheed's beneath it. He looked frightened and fearful, and so sorry. Then, he was Akheilos again, sharp-toothed and cold-eyed.

"Come." He gestured up the stairs. Dreamlike, I followed.

The darkness deepened as we rose, and the angles between the walls and the ceilings shifted weirdly. Everything had a cast of wrongness over it, a subtle distortion of reality and space and area that hurt my eyes. I kept my spine straight and a hand on my guns. They hadn't disarmed me yet, but hadn't attacked me either.

There was a hall at the top of the stairs, leading off to the left and past several rooms. The doors were closed—maybe that was a mercy. I couldn't imagine what other horrors lurked behind them. No, worse, I could.

He opened the door at the end and I saw—nothing. It opened to blackness, swirling dust.

"Step out. There's stairs."

"No way. You first."

"Fine." He went out the door a little ways. Seemed to be standing on nothing. "Come. The Lamia is waiting below."

"Where are we—"

"Behind the house," he snapped. "You ask too many questions."

With nothing to do, I walked out the door. It was pitch black around and above me, where the sky was rumoured to be. Below, though, was a crowd, with a figure at its head.

Akheilos hurried ahead of me, leaving me exposed. As I descended, voices rose in an unearthly howl.

"Hail!"

"Hail!"

"Hail the witch!"

I could barely tell I was in the air, except for the fact that setting a foot too far to the left or right meant no resistance. The dust around us was so heavy, I could barely see the ground. That, and the howling, was terrifying me.

"I'm not—"

"Oh, but you are," said Akheilos, extending a hand to me. A few dozen cloaked figures hudded behind him and around us. A tall one stood in the middle of them, wearing a crown of bones and broken, twisted branches.

"Welcome," she said, still keeping her back to me. Her voice was oddly distorted, a choir speaking as one. "It's good to see you again."

"I don't understand."

She dropped the cloak. I saw the too-thin waist twist, the claw-ended fingers twitching as the figure turned.

"It's been a long time. So good to see you again, dear," she said. It was my mother.

My heart pounded and tears poured down my face. I couldn't help it. I blinked them away, feeling the way they stung and burned. She seemed to like it.

"Do I look familiar? Awww. How sweet. Don't feel too flattered." She shifted into another woman's body, then a man's, then another's, blurring their features into a nightmarish mix, before making herself look like my mother again. "It's not too special—just an ordinary body—but I admit this is quite a favorite. I've been holding onto it a bit longer than the others."

"What is going on? No-one will give me a damn answer and I'm sick of it. I know you have Una and you're pissed at Underlighter City and everyone in it, and I know you have the kids. That's where my knowledge ends."

She moved strangely, drifting sideways as she stepped in a way that suggested she wasn't very solid.

Lilly suddenly appeared, leaning against her skirt, and smirked at me.

"We do have the children, yes. We've already prepared some of them to live Up here, and to handle the Dust...but soon, that won't be necessary. We'll be able to live down there again."

"Okay...why aren't you living down there now? Why wander Up in the first place?"

"Accidents, being driven up here by gangers, desperation...the usual, for most people," she hissed. "The worst criminals were sent here to die. All of us are the ones you people abandoned."

I forced myself to choke down a denial, not to shriek that I hadn't abandoned my mother. The Lamia's face shifted to Mom's and then away again.

"I'm not planning to abandon anyone," I said instead. "Where's Una?"

"Oh, she's here." She snapped her fingers, the long claws clicking, and a cloth was whisked away. Inside a black iron cage, there was Una. I ran up to it and pressed my fingers against the square bars.

She still had her eyes, thank gods, but she looked more scared than I'd ever seen her. Her hands were tied behind her back, her legs, bound in a cross, and there was a gag wrapped across her mouth.

"Una! I'll get you out of there," I cried. My voice was already starting to break.

"Oh, you might. Then again, you might not. I was thinking she'd make a very nice trophy...I could make a necklace out of those nice white teeth, perhaps a cloak out of her skin...well, some of it, we might need a little more flesh for the proper effect..." she snapped her fingers again and they covered the cage. I watched as they pulled it out of my reach, away from me, but it was too well-hidden in the velvety dark.

"Stop it!"

"Then again, there's something I want even more than her. I want you."

"Me?"

"You. This body, the parts of me that are your mother's, miss you. What's more...I need a successor. Someone who can lead." She was close to me now. Her eyes were hollow, like the first Sandman's, but the rest was too, too close to my mother's face. It hurt.

"I can't be your successor. I won't. You have all these people."

"And I want it to be you. Besides, you can shape the Dust unusually well."

"What the hell? I've been checked! I don't have Dust poisoning--"

She frowned. "You're not a very good listener. My messenger told you that it was a matter of force of will. I'm surprised you haven't figured it out."

The bullets. The soldering iron. Hell, the baseball bat I'd found when the dragon came after me. It was insane, but everything around me was just as insane, and it made a certain kind of sense.

"I'm not up for trade."

"Very well. I suppose I'll have to kill her while you watch and then kill you. With all the things we can make from Dust, that'll be fun. Perhaps a pit of spikes...we might roast her over a fire...there's always having her torn apart or eaten by rats, I suppose..."

Una, out of sight, screamed through her gag. I couldn't hide the panic on my face, and the Lamia laughed when she saw it.

I turned back, forced myself to stop peering into the darkness to look for her, and faced the witch. "You wanted to talk. Cut the bullshit and the intimidation and let's talk terms."

"Keep in mind, while we debate the issue, most of my people will be raiding your greedy, heartless little city to take what they need from it," she hissed. "So don't drag things out. I want you to think about that while we talk. There are nightmares feeding on your family and friends right now."

"You're bluffing."

"On the contrary. We've been preparing this for years. Your interference just...sped things up a bit. Well, that and the drought Up here. Of course, once

your city is ours, we won't be going hungry again."
She smiled. Far too many teeth in that smile, at angles
and of a sharpness that no natural predator could
match.

"Can't we just give you food?"

"Oh, no, this is about more than basic survival.
This is revenge. For all of us."

"Good luck," I spat. "We've got patrols out. You're
going to have a hard fight."

"Perhaps...but we have the nightmares and the
Dust."

The cloaked figures—Sandmen, I knew now—had
formed a loose circle around us. Even with my
weapons, I didn't stand a chance of surviving if I ran.

"Why are you doing this? Why are you...working
with the Dust? Is it out to kill us?"

"Not exactly. It just...is. It came one day. Reality
gets quite thin, you know," she said airily. "And it
was...something precious." She looked serious. "The
first of me, of us, the first witch...found the Dust. The
stuff of pure dreams. She saved it and fed it and taught
it to grow. It feeds on wavelengths of energy—radios,
electricity. Even the human brain emits wavelengths.
It thrived here...and now..." she swept her hands about.

"Can it go back to where it came from?"

"I suppose, but why would it?"

"Good. You're going to make it do that," I said firmly.

"Or what?"

"Or more people are going to die! Look at this!" I drew one of my guns and waved it around. "Don't you see? If there's a way to get this Dust out of here, everything can go back to normal! We can help you. You don't have to be stuck Up here. Or better, people will come Up, and—"

"And go back to the way things were! You have no idea what the world was like when people were everywhere on the surface," she hissed. "No idea. It was horrible. If you knew how people suffered before—"

"They suffer now!"

"Not the way they did! I saved humanity and the Dust. There were far too many people alive before and they were destroying the world."

"This is not how you save things! Genocide isn't a solution—it's madness! You should have let the Dust die!"

"You aren't listening. Before the Dust, humans destroyed everything in their environment! The world ran on blood. If you'd been alive then, you'd understand. It's been doing good for you!"

"And what the people did then was wrong. But we're dying now, and—"

"And if you come back to the surface, it will happen all over again. Your people are safe and happy down there."

I inhaled and exhaled slowly. The fact that she sounded so much like my mother, and wasn't her, hurt deeply.

There was nothing to do but to keep arguing, if I could. "Then why is the Dust hurting us so much? You said yourself that it needs the wavelengths to reproduce—"

"The Dust hurts, too," murmured someone in the shadows. "It doesn't like your dreams. It wants to go home."

The Lamia turned around, snarling. "Who said that?"

Silence, of course. For good measure, she reached out a hand impossibly far, bones cracking and distorting. Her nails lengthened, curling and twisting like glass in a furnace.

She chose someone I didn't see—one of her own, based on the direction and the hissing gasp. There was a wet crunch and a meaty sound. My stomach roiled and my blood froze. As if in slow motion, I saw someone in the crowd fall. The Sandmen around the person moved aside, and where a person had been, there was a slab of twisted meat and bone. I retched, falling to my knees.

THE LOVED, THE LOST, THE DREAMING

I swallowed, wiping my mouth, willing the burning acid to leave my throat. "I bet you preferred me on my knees," I croaked.

The Lamia gave me a thin-lipped smile. My mother had never done that.

She's not your mother, I reminded myself. *She's not. She doesn't move the same way...your mother never disemboweled anyone...*

Whatever she was, it certainly wasn't human.

"My apologies," she continued, her voice echoing with shadows. "We won't be interrupted again."

"I think the Dust should speak for itself," I managed.

"If it could, it would. It can't, and I'm the closest thing it has. We have. The Dust is part of our life, and it will stay."

"And I don't think it wants to, no matter what you say. It's not from here, it was never meant to be here, and you need to let it go. It doesn't have to keep hurting us, or you."

I knew she wouldn't listen, really. She was half Dust herself, or more. And being partly made of my mother, she knew how stubborn I was.

"This is our home now. Crossing back into the other dimension—"

"No it's not! It's ours, and it's mine! And if you're so determined to live peacefully, give us back our children! And give me back..." my voice cracked. "Give me back the woman I love."

"You'll just hurt her again," purred the Lamia. She took on a suggestion of Chloe's shape, for a moment. "The same way you did the others."

That did hurt. She managed to imitate Chloe extremely well. I snarled at her like an animal.

"Save me the dramatics. I know we're not going to agree. So, how would you like to settle this?"

She gave me a cruel smile and shifted slightly. She was the strange, alien mixture of my mother and something else again. "I see we're at an impasse. What do you have to offer?"

"Combat," I spat. "It's been sneaking around and hiding with you people. I want a fair fight, just you and me."

She cocked her head to the side. "And you'll be representing your entire city? I hope they'll understand when you lose, then. But explaining it will be your problem, not mine. I accept."

"Good. When I win—" I wasn't having any of her little taunts—"you give back Una, you lay off our city, and you give us back our children. For starters."

"For starters? Oh, this is going to be fun. I'm sure your father would be impressed with your ruthlessness. Then again, he was the one who always advocated kindness, generosity, mercy...well, so much for the apple not falling far from the tree."

"Save the insults for the fight. What are your terms, bitch?"

"If you lose, every four months you bring us a tithe of children." The Lamia smiled and the smoky lights in her sockets flashed. "That's in addition to anything and anyone we take as spoils of war while you and I settle things here. You were saying, my dear?"

"And when I win, I get to keep my life, and you stop helping the Dust propagate, and let the rest of it move on. And the Sandmen can choose whether to stay or to go."

"In addition to Una's life and getting back the children we have added to our family? You ask a lot, little girl. I don't think I'm willing to bargain."

"Fine!" I was shaking in my boots, and my voice showed it. "You can have a tithe of our food as well as children, and…" I flinched. "And you can have me and any of the others who show extra Dust-shaping potential."

Sharp teeth, too large for her mouth, gleamed in the dark as she smiled. "That's a little better. You drive a hard bargain. I accept." She held out a hand. I hesitated, loath to touch her, and even more loath to be hurt by her.

"It's safe. For now." She smiled again. "No tricks until the contest starts."

Looking her in the eye, shuddering but holding her gaze steady, I took her hand. It was soft, and smooth, but the nails grazed my skin as she shook.

The Lamia stepped back. "I will declare the terms of the contest." I was about to protest, but she continued on in her smoky, oddly resonant growl.

"I declare a tripartite contest: shaping, combat, and a contest of wills," she said, raising her voice. There were squeaks, chatters, and growls from the audience. Eyes glowed in the swirling darkness around us.

The LEDs on my suit and the top of my goggles were the only illumination. I barely saw the dragon coming when it struck.

The enormous beast breathed a jet of fire at me. I rolled to the side. The Sandmen had backed off, giving us plenty of room to manouvre in, but a fucking dragon is still a fucking dragon.

"I don't have a weapon!" I shouted at her.

The Lamia's laughter echoed from the dragon's mouth. "It's a shaping contest. You beat a little dragon once before. This should be easy for you."

I inhaled deeply and forced away the panic. A baseball bat wasn't going to do the trick this time around.

An enormous glittering clawed foot descended into the ground next to me. The scales scintillated gunmetal-grey. I scrambled to my feet and drew one of the guns. Firing at the dragon's head, I wasn't surprised to hear it ricochet away. The giant reptile head swung down towards me. The evil yellow eyes glared at me. I stared, fascinated, at the creature--a magnificent blend of reptile and dinosaur and legend. Staring was a very stupid thing to do. She opened her jaws and I only avoided being eaten by tucking and rolling away.

"You can't run forever, Janelle! Attack! Run and you forfeit!"

She came for me again, her tail swinging towards my head. I got a terribly stupid idea, and jumped for it.

The meaty impact knocked the wind out of me, but I clung stubbornly to the double row of spines and plates. The bony protrusions were smooth enough to grip, though they were already leaving rips in my suit's outer layer I hoped they weren't ripping through my skin, too, but there was no time to worry about that. Feeling my progress up her back, the Lamia thrashed and shook. I clung to the spines for dear life. Her massive wings beat the air furiously, threatening to lift off.

I was in the middle of her back now. With sweating hands, I pulled one of the throwing knives out of my calf sheath. It was a long shot, and not long enough for stabbing, but it would have to do. I leaned to the side and took a swing at the membrane coming towards me. .

A gush of black blood over me and a roar of pain—success! The wing was barely nicked, though.

A shaping competition. Ordinary weapons weren't going to do the trick. The Lamia twisted her head backwards, snapping and flashing her teeth, but I'd found the sweet spot just out of her reach. I thought about a long spear, like Nathu's, with a barbed silver tip and a wicked bite. The smooth wood, the grip just right for my hand...

In my outstretched hand, it appeared. As the Lamia twisted her head to the other side, I wrapped my feet around a central spine and gripped the spear. Her jaw came towards my head. Clumsily, I stabbed upward, through her lower jaw.

Her screech of pain cut through the night. Dust swirled angrily around us as she shifted and howled in pain. She swung her mighty head away, jerking me off of her back. I clung to the spear's grip helplessly. Any moment now, my sweating hands would lose their grip—I'd fall at least fifteen feet to the ground, or twenty—enough for a broken leg—I lost my grip.

And stupidly, impossibly, found myself floating towards the ground in a giant bubble, watching the Lamia shake her head and claw furiously at the spear. One more good stab and I'd have her. A little upward motion, and it would enter her brain, and—

She shifted rapidly, clouds of dark Dust a furious storm around her, and took the eerie shape I'd seen before.

"I see this won't get us far," she sniped, rubbing her jaw. There was still a raw hole there. It closed as she stroked and pinched the skin together. My bubble popped as I reached the ground, and she spat at me. I expected it to be shaped into something, to burst into some monstrous creation, but instead she stared, and waited.

"Weapons...monsters...aren't you tired of always fighting, Janelle? You know, we can shape the Dust into nice things, too."

Maybe it was the injuries or the insanity, but I started to laugh and couldn't stop. Weakened, hysterical, I crouched and fell on my ass, still laughing.

"Nice things," I said, wiping a tear away. "You people have been trying to kill me. Show me something nice."

Instantly, the world around me changed. The air overhead smoothed from a frenetic, gritty mess to— blue. Blue like the colour we paint on the cavern roofs of the garden caves. The colour I'd seen in old movies.

"Don't you want to know what the sky looks like, Janelle?" said the Lamia softly. She came closer, her cloak replaced by a soft peach-coloured summer dress.

She wore a different face—Lilly's. If Lilly had grown up, that is. My heart hammered painfully.

"Look. Look at this." A meadow spilled ahead of us, behind us. From the top of a gentle hill, flowers of shades and varieties that I'd never even imagined spilled into infinity. There were even trees ahead, in the distance, and behind us—

"Horses?"

"We may not have much, but we do make beautiful things. We're not all bad." She looked so sad, for a moment. So human. "Did you really think we'd hurt the children? We take their eyes because most of you can't shape Dust with your sight to distract you. They learn to see in a different, better way. They're forgotten down there, with you, but with us, they have a chance to be even better off than people born to see. Are you so surprised that people will cut their own eyes out so they can see...this?" She stretched an arm out imploringly. "I can give you paradise."

"But...it's not real. It's all Dust. Without the Dust—we could bring this back. And—just because they're blind doesn't mean you should take them from their parents. They still have a good life with us."

"People look down on broken ones," said the Lamia, her features changing with anger.

"Maybe some do, but all sure as hell don't. The lady who owns the Rabbit Den is short a leg, and I

370

know lots of people who—"

"It's not always about the limbs or the body," said the Lamia tersely. "What about people who see things that aren't real? You throw them in a Calm Box and that's the end."

I didn't have an answer for that.

"Here, their fears may be more real...but we can fight them by giving them the weapons to defeat their demons."

"Yes, but it's all...fake. All of this is beautiful, but it's not real!"

"You know better than that. It's not that unreal, either. You are talented at shaping—one of the best I've seen. Shaping with your eyes open! I'm proud of you." My mother's voice dominated in the chorus. The Lamia seemed so, so human. I wondered if I'd been wrong all along.

"I...I...maybe, but it's still wrong..." my voice faltered.

"Come with us, Janelle," she cooed. Her face was softer again, my mother's. "I can make it all go away. Anything you want—you can shape it, here. You won't have to worry about your friends making you fall in love with them...the petty squabbling...being hurt by people you love..."

Raheed's face, before he'd become Akheilos, came to my mind. "Anything you want, you can get revenge for, or you can make it not even matter…anything at all, anything you want, is yours. That's the nature of working with the Dust and the dreams."

"I don't want anything you have," I snapped.

"You can start out again. All the people you've hurt will forget, or will forgive you…"

That finally called to me. I weakened for just a moment. The Lamia's eyes gleamed, held mine. She knew she'd found something.

"And you have hurt people, haven't you," she cooed. "I'm very disappointed in you, Janelle," she said. My mother's voice, sad and resigned. "I really raised you better than that. You've done some terrible things, little girl."

I saw them swirling around me, in the darkness—faint images of the past. They distorted and twisted in the air—images of Raheed and me arguing, the times I'd stomped off without talking to him…Raheed crying in his room…Chloe at home, getting drunk and crying in her room…little squabbles with my friends, in childhood, the kind that hurt…the time Chloe shouted at Lola for flirting with Kenny, while I looked on and stood back, letting her hurt my friend because I didn't want anyone to stop liking me…Chloe, crying to her mother about how she'd seen me kissing Una…me, kicking the Sandman so hard I'd broken his bones, just because he'd taunted me…

THE LOVED, THE LOST, THE DREAMING

There were a hundred thousand little sins, and they had eyes and sharp teeth. They solidified around me, full of crawling legs and slimy tentacles and nagging doubt, soft silky tongues that shaped the horrible things I thought about myself when I couldn't sleep at night. They told me I was going crazy, that I was a horrible person, that I was better off dead.

I fell to my knees and bent my head for a moment, trying to keep them out. It was too much. My eyes were blurred with tears and the sound of my own self-loathing echoed around me. I was the most insignificant thing in the world and the centre of everything awful in it. The malignant contradiction ate at me, whispered that a sweet, smooth death was the best way. Or, better, to let the Dust take me—reshape my fate into something less awful.

I'm not sure why, but I looked up then. It was mostly pain surging in me, the tightness in my lungs. Instinctively, I breathed in, and opened my eyes.

Behind the face of the Lamia I saw my mother's face. Sorrow and pain and deep horror in her features, horror at having to hurt her own daughter. Something was trying to hurt me, sure, but part of her, at least, knew what was going on.

Dad always told me the best way to handle your problems was like Alexander with the Gordian knot.

"He couldn't untangle it," he said, and went on to describe the math behind the knot, the thousands of tangles and possibilities. "In the end, he just cut through it with his sword."

Dad had been there when she wasn't. My friends had been there. My friends' mothers. I might be the worst person to cross the planet, but people loved me. And that, whatever it said about them, meant I had to be worthy of something. I couldn't shut out the voices of doubt, surging and whispering around me, and I couldn't cut off their razor fangs and unnatural limbs one by one.

I held my hands out the same way I'd held them when I was fighting the dragon. I had made myself a baseball bat from the Dust because it seemed reasonable. Now, I was through being reasonable.

What I needed was a real weapon, something to illuminate. No guns—this wasn't a time for something practical; the rules were suspended, for now. This called for the kind of weapon you only have in your mind. A sword of fire, full of light and fury. The heart of the sun and cold steel beneath it, with a gold hilt and gems in the pommel.

My eyes were closed and I was on my feet, legs in a fighter's stance. I felt the heat and the weight of the blade before I saw it. The weight of armour settled on my body. I didn't have to open my eyes to know it was bright gold and brass, reflecting and shattering the light of the blade.

"You work in dreams," I said. "And you took my nightmares, everything I was scared of. Everything we were scared of. Well, guess what. Sometimes, people have lucid dreams, and that's when nightmares break down." Then I stepped forward, breaking the circling doubts. Things crunched underfoot and I felt and heard hundreds of teeth and claws rattling against my armour. I knew I was bleeding beneath it, their earlier bites all over my skin, but it didn't matter.

"You know what I want most in the world, Lamia?"

She did. "You want your mother back," she said. Pitch perfect, achingly familiar, an exact copy of Mom the day she'd gone up on the salvage trip.

"And you can't possibly give her back to me, you bitch! This ends now! You're never hurting anyone the way you hurt me again!"

I swept my sword forward. Because it was a dream, I knew just how to strike. The blade moved sleekly, a force of nature, and I moved with it, one and the same.

The Lamia cried out, once, a horrible shriek that cut my soul to the core. Then, the world broke.

24—May 1, 0048 P.D.

I'd never seen a real Dust storm before this, and I hope I never do again. There was a furious sound, the roars and screams and screeches of a hundred nightmares breaking down at once. I crouched on the ground, covering my head and wrapping myself into a tight ball. I could feel Dust beating around me, battering me. It stung, even through the suit, and I could feel it sharply around me.

I wanted to call for Una, but I didn't dare open my mouth and inhale that much Dust. Even if it could be controlled, and even with my mask and filter, it was too dangerous.

When I felt it slow down, I finally uncurled myself. Stumbling to my feet, suddenly aware of just how scraped up I was—everywhere—I realised the world was *bright*.

It was very strange. There was a hole in the sky, and the Dust was moving towards it. The hole glowed, showing a night sky on the other side, but it was distinctly a hole. Meanwhile, around us, the air was starting to thin out. Or, I guess, the air as I knew it.

"Janelle! Are you all right?"

"Una!"

She came running for me, the ropes and the cage no more than Dust rattling off of her uniform. She swept me into her arms, kissed my mouth. Tears ran down her face.

"Oh, Janelle. I'm so glad you're okay."

The pain and the wrung-out feeling of my heart faded as she crushed her lips against mine, stroked my hair. Finally, when I gasped for air, she drew back and let me breathe.

"I thought I was going to lose you," she said, her voice breaking.

"Never," I said, grinning stupidly though tears. "Absolutely never."

I'm not good with saying "I love you" to people. At least, I wasn't. I said it then, and heard it echoed. It felt so good, it hurt. Only the way she felt, and the fact that she was solid while the Dust shivered up overhead, convinced me that she wasn't a dream of the Dust.

"Pardon us," said someone behind me. Una and I turned around.

One of the Sandmen came forward, eyes staring sightless into the distance. Xer hood was down, revealing dry, withered features as well as the expected empty sockets. Opening xis mouth, xe let out a chorus of sounds. I don't know if I can describe it. The closest thing I can think of is imaging silver bells speaking, bells that hummed and rang, a dozen angels speaking at once, and managing to shape the conflicting echoes into words.

"We (we, we) are the Dust (dust, dust, dust). We are dreams (dreams, dreams.) We are sorry it has gone as it did (did, did). We did not mean to harm you (you, you). All of the wavelengths here (ere), your technology, drove us mad (mad, mad, mad, mad)."

My throat tight, I nodded.

"We see you are full of feeling (eeling, ling, ling). We will not stay long (long, long, long). We will release the echoes (echoes, echoes) of your families' minds and be on our way (ay, ay)."

"Echoes?"

"We took on some of their thoughts as we resonated with them (em, em, em). We cannot undo the darkness that came on us in the confusion (fusion, fusion, fusion), but we are sorry (sorry, sorry, sorry). There is no reparation for your losses (losses, losses), but if you would speak with your dead (dead, dead, dead)…"

"Yes," I gasped. "Please."

The Sandman returned my nod, painfully and slowly. "Thank you, Janelle (elle, elle, elle). Your people and your dreams will be remembered (embered, embered)."

The Dust swirled apart. There was a faint humming, a resonance as if a thousand glases were being played at once, or a hundred bees were playing a strange symphony. I felt it in my bones. It rose up like rain moving backwards, towards the hole cut slantwise in the sky.

It was, in a way, beautiful. The darkness was slowly parting, and flickers of a strange light blueness were showing through the dark. Not much, yet, but I saw it, once or twice.

Something was happening on the ground, too. Where the Lamia had stood, the Dust was in motion again, but gentler, this time. The 'echoes', as the Lamia had called them, were taking shape. There was a moment when the Dust settled, there in the ground, into faintly human shapes—a dozen of them. Closest to me, a swirl of dust shaped itself into a woman with a cloak, a kind face—square but pretty, with clean lines on her features and an angular nose. A face that was very similar to mine.

She favoured me with a smile, a real one. "I love you, Janelle. I'm so proud of you."

"Mom?" I whispered. Tears trickled down my face again. I felt my lip trembling.

"Have a good life for me, sweetie. See you again someday."

Her spectre came forward, opened its vague arms, and wrapped them around me for a moment. I felt the warmth of her hug for just a moment. Mom. A lifetime of love and regret in her embrace. Regret that she'd never see me have a family, do things of my own, raise kids. She held me tight, reluctant to surrender me to the world. Still, inevitably but slow as could be, I felt her arms relax.

All at once, she was gone. Just more Dust swirling up, up, up to the rift. I fell to my knees and watched the Dust go.

Ache overwhelmed me, and my eyes stung. I closed my eyes against the blurring world, and felt Una come to me. Gently, crouching next to me, she kissed me, resting her forehead against mine. "Shhhh. I'm here, Janelle."

I cried into her arms, and let sorrow take over for a while.

"Shhhh." She rocked me gently. "It's going to be all right. I promise. You're not going to lose anyone else this time." She kissed my forehead.

"I…I just missed her so much," I sobbed. "And now I don't know if that was her soul, or reverberating thoughts, or the Dust being nice to me as an apology, or…" I didn't have any words left. My throat raw, I wept into Una's arms.

"At least you got to say goodbye," she said, her own voice harsh with tears. "And whatever it was, it doesn't matter, because she still loved you very, very much."

THE LOVED, THE LOST, THE DREAMING

I wanted to say something, but I was completely overcome. Exhausted, I fainted into her arms, letting my weariness take me to sleep then and there.

25—May 1, 0048 P.D.

The next thing I knew, I was lying in the fanciest and most comfortable bed I'd ever been in. I realised it was Nathu's room in the Honeycomb. Dad was sitting next to me, asleep in a chair. There was a warm spot in the bed next to me and the sheets were a mess. Some kind person had dressed me in a very nice robe, a soft ivory nightgown with the Underlighter City torch and circular black tunnel embroidered on it.

"What..." when I sat up, the blood rushed from my head. "How long was I out? How'd I get here?"

"You've been out for about sixteen hours," said a wonderfully familiar voice.

"Nathu!" He wrapped me in a hug and kissed my lips.

"Una got up a while ago. She carried you as far as the elevators when we found you."

"Wow. Hey—what happened to you?" There was a big bandage around his arm and a few cuts on his face. As he straightened and sat on the bed, he winced.

"A long story. Let's just say it involved twenty Sandmen, a standoff, Oliver, and no bullets."

"...Okay, I need to hear this."

He laughed and shook his head. "Soon. I have business to attend to."

"Pssss...Janelle? Are you awake?" Dad stirred.

Nathu kissed me again, very warmly. "I'll be back. Feel free to get up and go out and about. I wanted to check on you, but duty calls." He smiled and went for the door, leaving it half-closed after himself.

"I'm so glad to see you're okay, honey," said Dad. He looked tired and upset but incredibly relieved. I had a feeling he'd done some crying while I'd been asleep; now, though, he was smiling.

"Good to see you, Dad. Um. When I went up...I saw Mom." He went whiter than chalk. "It's complicated," I said hurriedly. "She did pass away a long time ago, after all. So...if you're feeling guilty..."

Old grief came to the surface. "I have. I always wondered if it would have been different if we'd gone looking for her even longer."

"I...some time I'll explain the whole thing if you want...but...well, no. It wouldn't. That's all." I hugged him.

"I'm so proud of you, Janelle. Una told us what went on. You did really well, kiddo."

"Thanks, Dad." I let the tears slip out for a while and just let him hold me like I was still a little kid. I laughed, then, even though I was choked up. "Do you believe in the dragons I saw yet?"

He chuckled, and I saw him wipe a tear away. "Yes, I sure do."

I rested a bit longer and we chatted—not about much. It was good to have something this normal after all the insanity Up there. In the warm, well-lit room, with a nice hot goat haunch and some roast potatoes for lunch, everything that had just happened seemed like a dream. The big, nasty scrapes on my legs, hands, and some badass bruises told the truth, though. "Take it easy, missy. They say you might have sprained a couple of things and gotten a bruised tailbone."

"That explains why everything is sore," I admitted. "But I've been asleep for eons, Dad." A cold feeling washed over me. "Are my friends okay?"

He hesitated, obviously debating a comfortable lie and the truth. "I wouldn't say okay, but they're all alive and should stay that way. Do you really want to go all the way to the hospital in that state?"

I slumped back on the bed, aware of a dozen aches and pains and stinging spots. "Last time I did that everything went to hell. Okay. Fine. I think I might take a nap again anyway. You got my journal though?"

"Yes, Janelle, I have it. Here you go. Here's your lucky charm, too." He handed me the bone carving. It was still in one piece, miraculously. "Haven't seen that in a while. Do you know your Mom got you that as a kid?"

It should have shocked me. Something that long ago, no wonder I'd forgotten it. And yet, that simple, cheap little symbol had carried me through—just because a superstitious part of me believed it would.

"Yeah, Dad. Glad I didn't lose it. Um." Tears prickled. "I think I'll write for a while. Sounds okay?"

As I settled into the sheets again, pen in hand, I heard him laugh quietly. "This time, I won't stop you. Write until you're tired, and then go back to sleep."

If there's one thing I've become after all this crap, it's a better listener. I did, and I did, and my sleep was sweet and easy.

When I woke up again, it was late afternoon and Dad had finally been called back to work. Una was there, alternately peppering me with kisses and shaking my shoulders.

"Janelle, wake up! There's a crapload of stuff you missed!"

"Wha? Oh, fine."

"I have a couple of hours of free time right now, so I thought I'd come and fill you in before I get back to the insanity." She looked exhausted but still impossibly bright.

"Well, I'd like to go to the infirmary in—probably Sector A. Is that where my friends are? Dad said they were all alive, anyway..."

"Do you want me to come with you to the hospital?" Una offered.

"Well...to be honest, I have a feeling there could be capital-D-Drama with Chloe, so, um...yes. Yes please. I should talk to her myself and all that...but I could use the support."

She kissed my forehead. "Absolutely. And it never hurts for the Princep's wife to be seen caring for people." She looked serious again. "I need to know what kind of shape the city is in. Don't be surprised if I spend most of the visit talking to the doctors and the patients. There's a lot Nathu will need to know, and not all of that info will filter up in reports."

"Did I miss any Crow business? What about the Sandmen? What happened after the Dust and all that? Is the city okay?"

"That's a lot of questions. Hold on."

Apparently, the answer to most of my questions was 'bureaucracy'. There had been a long and exhausting day of peace talks. Apparently while I was busy with the witch, the Sandmen raiding Underlighter City did some good damage. Punched some big holes. If not for the gangers' help, the fact that patrols were already out, and—well—beating the Lamia when I did, things would have been a lot worse. Apparently the Dust went surging back Up and took the most direct route possible. Not before the Sandman had done a hell of a lot of work, though.

"So, there's reconstruction going on everywhere—I hope you've been missing electrical work, because we're scaling back to barebones patrols for a while. Everyone with a day job is going to be back to ordinary work."

"I feel like I should be disappointed...and crazy as it is, I can't wait to go Up again—but it's going to be a nice break," I admitted. "I could do with some nice, normal things."

She gave me an unusually shy smile. "Me too. Come on."

"Why are we outside the Extra kids' place?"

"They had to make the orphanage into a temporary infirmary. There were a lot of injured people on both sides. A lot of...casualties." I winced at the implication and followed her in, hoping it would be better than it sounded.

I didn't get more than three feet in the door before my world was lost in pain.

"Fuck! Aiden, I'm hurt everywhere!"

He laughed and stepped back. "Sorry. I should know better. I'm so glad you're alive!"

"Me too! Oh, it's good to see you. Um. You already know Una..." I dragged her by the hand.

Aiden's eyes popped for a moment, but his smile looked like it would split his face. "I guess congratulations are in order!"

She pecked me on the cheek. "It's a pleasure to see you again, Aiden, but I have to talk to the people in charge to check on things. Can you..."

"Oh, sure, over there and second door down the hall. The kitchen is the clean-up room and the office." She darted off. Even out of Crow uniform and in black clothes instead, she moved like she meant business. I watched her butt and legs appreciatively before turning back to my friend.

Aiden grinned. "Aren't you glad I didn't join the Crows now? My extra medical levels have come more in handy than you imagined."

"I can imagine. What happened down here?"

Aiden walked swiftly towards the door. The secretary from before was nowhere to be seen, and the kids were everywhere. "Let's find Jay. I've been here since I got on shift a couple of days ago. All I know is that I've seen every kind of laceration and broken bone you can have, and that I've stitched up things that shouldn't have to have been stitched up. Come on in, let Jay explain things to you. I should run back to the front and keep an eye on the kids." He gave me a last quick hug and trotted off.

There was another round of squealing and hugging, but this hurt less—Jay had a leg in a cast and a pair of crappy crutches to scoot around on. "I had a toe bitten off by a thing that looked like a manticore," she said sadly. "Broke my leg, too."

"Damn your toe, I'm glad you're alive! How the hell did you only lose a toe?"

"I had my boots on." For some reason, both of us found that painfully hilarious.

"Whew," I sighed, wiping tears away. "It's good to see you. How is everyone?"

"Caleb is fine—he's helping with repairs on the other side of town—but Kenny got pretty banged up." She looked anxious. "I know he's not the sharpest, but I didn't know he was that brave. Do you know he fought three Sandmen out of District A and into the city centre on his own?"

"How many friggin' Sandmen got down here?"

"Well, half of them are still in the hospital and the other half are in peace talks. The minute the Dust settled, things started to calm down—sort of."

"Wait, when did all this happen? Oh, sorry."

Jay guided me towards the kitchen, out of the hall. Cramped as the place was, the people hurrying past us and the fact that every room was loaded made it worse. I couldn't have imagined this many people fitting into the place, but I guess that's necessity for you.

"It started in the afternoon a couple of days ago. Today and yesterday, since the Dust collapsed, have been fine. Did you not notice the city was a mess?"

"Now that you mention it, yes, but my mind was on you guys. How are our Crow friends?"

"Ginni and Sammie are over on the other side. They were on patrols, by the way." She bit her lip. "Sammie is fine, but Ginni got caught in crossfire and is hurt pretty bad. A few Crows went down. More than a few. Kelsey and Oliver are tough as nails, you know them, and Leah did all right, too. Hunter's all right, but Chang and Luke were..." That one hurt. "And Skye's in bad shape too. Plus a whole bunch of regular Crows. If it hadn't been for the gangers helping out, I don't know what would have happened."

We were both silent for a moment. The pain definitely hadn't set in yet. As I write this now, with the benefit of a couple of days of sleep and reflection, it hurts a hell of a lot more—but then, it was all so new there wasn't even room for it.

"Come on," said Jay. "I could use a minute to breathe and catch up with Kenny." She opened the door into what had been the boy's dorm.

It was a complete mess. There was blood everywhere and a stink of sanitizer and fear. In spite of that, the smell of flesh and medical salves everywhere. Every kind of person imaginable was sprawled in the beds—most were male, but a few were so wrapped in bandages it was impossible to tell. In spite of that, the ones who could sit were playing cards and board games.

"Janelle! Janelle! Hey, baby! You got a minute for a cripple?"

Jay's face lit up and she ran over. "Kenny! You shouldn't be walking!"

"I should too! I was told to, like..." Kenny came stumping towards me, with crutches and a big bandage over half of his head.

"Hey! How's it going? Did you have fun up there on the surface?" He grinned.

"Uh...well, I had help. Jeez, man, are you okay?"

"Well, I kind of took a claw to the face..lost an eye..." he looked sad. "But! Jay said she still loves me, so it's okay."

"What were you doing, dude?"

"I was kind of walking towards Aiden randomly when the Sandmen, like, started flooding down...they had all of these, like, monsters, first, and...it was bad, man. They were trying to go for the kids. So we built a barricade and stuff and got all the kids in, like, the way back part. Aiden heated oil on the stove and we threw it at them and the kids made water balloons that we threw at the Dust monsters...it was awesome! Well, except when they broke the window. That was scary." He looked crestfallen. "And they got me good in the face."

"You're just as handsome as you were before," said Jay, kissing his cheek.

"Or just as ugly," I countered.

"Hey!" he laughed. Then Kenny looked serious again. Oh boy. More fun. "Um. In the corner, you oughta...Raheed..."

"Janelle, do you want us to—"

"Nah. Tell your old man I'll need to talk to him about getting tattoos everywhere and I'm good. I, uh, I should go handle this myself." Jay started to walk after me, but Kenny put a hand on her shoulder. It's true. Some things, you can't handle by hiding behind someone.

There was a fair bit of space around Raheed's bed, and some blood on the childishly painted walls. It was all dry, now, but the stains were unmistakeable. He'd put up a good fight.

"Janelle?"

"Hi, Raheed," I said, my voice breaking. "Is that really you?"

"Yeah, it's me. Not Akheilos. I found out who that is, by the way. Someone read books to me in the hospital."

I touched his hand. "Hey..."

"Janelle...I'm so sorry. I was going for walks up there...a lot...thinking about us and trying to get over it, I guess...and I must have gotten Dust Fever. They said my levels were high—and then I ran into that Sandman..."

"Raheed..." my throat felt dry and cracked, and tears spilled down my face. "I was a bitch to you. If I hadn't been picking on you and pushing you away...if we'd just talked..."

Raheed turned his bandaged face towards mine, and sighed ruefully. "I'm sorry. I let hatred get the better of me, and I paid for it. You don't have to apologize."

I shook my head. "I hurt you too. I didn't talk to you, really, for a long time. And then...I should have..."

He drew me into a hug. "I just want you to know that I meant what I said, before...before things went bad...about us being friends. I care about you."

"How do I know you're not just going to try to do the same thing, where you flirt with me and hope I'll come back because you're such a nice friend?"

He turned his head down in shame. "You won't."

"I'm sorry, Raheed," I said, grief singing through me. "I didn't mean that. I thought I'd lost you, and I'm so glad I didn't. And...I'm really sorry I thought it was all you when I punched you, that one time."

He smirked in a sad way. "It wasn't all me, but it wasn't all Dust, either," he said. He blushed a bit, and smiled then, softer. "Besides...tell you the truth, Lola's been teaching me a thing or two about compassion."

I smiled. "She's a good nurse, huh?"

He instinctively looked over my shoulder, into the distance. "The best. Who knew she had it in her? She's working with the kids who had their eyes taken out, too. And...some of the grownups, like me. Blindness isn't nearly as bad as I thought it would be, is that strange? Anyway...she swears she'll go back to being a hooker eventually, but...she likes making people happy." Quietly, he added, "I sure didn't think she'd make me this happy."

I wondered if he was replacing me with her, in his heart, but it didn't sound exactly like that. He'd never talked about me so softly and respectfully. Faintly, my heart twinged with jealousy, but I didn't really mind.

"I'd better get going," I said. "Aiden asked me to come talk to some of the kids about what it's like Up there, so we can start getting the transitions ready."

"It's going to be a long time before all the Dust is totally gone, you know," he warned me. "Make sure you tell them that."

"I know. But the Dust promised not to hurt us, now that it knows better. That's going to help. As for the rest...it's worth the wait."

"Tell them that too."

"I'd rather you told them yourself, when you're feeling better. You were there when the Dust broke."

Raheed gave me a last sad smile. "When I'm better. I have a lot of healing to do. I need to sleep now, Janelle, but it was good talking to you. I hope you'll come again."

"I will," I said, tears thickening my throat. "Sleep well, friend."

He laid back, and had drifted off before I left the room. His breath was even, and I knew that there wouldn't be any nightmares chasing him tonight.

Kenny was back in bed to recover, but Jay waited for me in the hall. "Hey, pal. You okay?" I hugged her for a minute and didn't talk, too choked up for words.

We walked in silence back out to the front. The street really was a mess—not as much as the Extra housing, but almost. Scuff marks and broken stalls, Cafes with busted windows...it was a mess, and cleaning it would be a hell of a chore. "I should probably get going," I said. "I guess you're on guard duty here?"

"Such as it is. I'm not so much guarding as limping, but at least they let me keep an eye on Kenny." She shrugged and turned her unwavering gaze back to me. Steady Jay. My pal and my conscience. "Chloe...I heard she went into the hospital around the centre of the city, if you want to stop by."

"Actually, I...I think I'll head home for now. Tell Una where I'm going? I get the impression she's still busy as hell. With the kids and all that...I can't take her away from something that important, even if...even if it's hard for me."

"Okay. I...look, I heard you broke up and I'm glad," Jay burst out. "Okay? Please tell me it's true."

"It's true. But...if Raheed can forgive me, and I can forgive him, I should really get down there and say a couple words to her. Just to..."

Jay nodded. "Well, it's the right thing to do." She hugged me one last time. "I gotta get back. See you on Crow shift, I guess. Promise me you'll be all right?"

"Tunnel dark and blood red, light true and hope dead," I replied. "I promise I'll do the right thing."

"Okay. Well...good luck. And come by soon to my A-ma's for soup! She's been telling me to invite everyone who's not dead!"

I laughed. "Get in there. I will." I opened the door for her and she swung in gracefully. As I walked towards the centre of the city again, it was like my friends were walking with me. Nothing was perfect, and people had been lost. There was going to be a hell of a lot of crying to do. In spite of all of that, I was alive. One last debt to repay, and I could go back to the Honeycomb and sleep the pain off.

It took a long time to walk to the big hospital and it wasn't much fun. I got sore and really felt the effect of all that scrapping. My tailbone was killing me, as Dad had warned, and everything else seemed to be made of bruises. And then—

"Oh. I..." right in front of the hospital doors, there she was.

"Hi, Chloe. You look...well, you look awful but you're alive."

"Yeah. Fucking arm won't work as well after this. They said it will take months to grow back and probably years to use properly." It was heavily bandaged and in a sling. I tried not to think about Akheilos chewing what he'd bitten from her forearm, and shuddered. Back to what I'd been rehearsing for the last fifteen minutes, in a dozen different ways.

"Chloe...I'm...I can't give you your arm back, but I'm sorry. I'm sorry for the way things went down. I— I don't know what I wasn't giving you..."

"Janelle." She was drained, tired, all the fight out of her. I'd never seen her looking so old. I couldn't even hate her, even though standing in front of her hurt so much. "I don't have time for this anymore. Let's just let the past be. The whole thing was a mistake."

"The whole..." that stung to the core.

"I don't want to talk about it. You live your life and I'll live mine. If I see you in the street, smile and keep walking. Please. I like Luz and I'd rather find a girl like her than..."

"So we're leaving things like this?"

"Maybe some day we can talk. I don't feel like being an adult right now. I'm sorry." She swept past me, towards the edge of the city. I let her go, and felt one last thing break inside me.

The walk home took a long time. I went straight up to the room and crawled into bed without saying a word to anyone. Then, after I cried for a while, I wrote this.

We have a lot of work ahead of us. The Sandmen have been surprisingly willing to help, from what I hear. Someday, we may even be able to go Up properly again. The world we broke has been healing, and given enough time, we will too. I don't know if the age of man will ever be as epic and grand as it was back in the old days, but I do know one thing—sometimes, the only way to heal is to forget something for a while.

Tomorrow, I go back to work, helping Pramjit with wires and Una with the Crows and Nathu with forgetting about all the crap he has to deal with. We have a city to rebuild and plans for the future to make. Tonight, I'm going to spend one last evening as a teenager, and let myself cry over everything. Then, I can go back to the world.

26—May 4, 0048 P.D.

And this is my story so far. It's taken days to write, and I've cheated a bit with the format. I've cut out a few boring parts like being stuck in a hospital and having the Oath tattooed on me. I've cut out a few last nights of uneasy sleep, but the dreams about my mother being lost in the darkness have stopped. Now it's just real memories, and I can deal with those. I also cut out a little bit of the nice stuff—so I'll round things off by telling where all of us were just earlier tonight.

Nathu's room is a great place—I didn't mention the wood furniture or the soft sheets or the small stone fireplace before. I come here to think a lot, now, and to the library. There's been a lot of work to do, and my body's got a lot of healing ahead—some things were hurt that shouldn't have been damaged. I have my journal, though, to put things in, and I have Una and Nathu.

Una came up behind me as I was writing. "Get back to bed, you. Put that away for now."

"I can't say no to a beautiful naked woman. You win."

She guided me back to the huge canopy-covered rectangle of heaven and pulled me down. We kissed and touched each other's skin for a while—not making love, not saying much, just enjoying the sane quiet after a long, long day. Nathu read a book on the couch, smiling up at us from time to time.

"I've been meaning to ask," she said, rolling carefully on her side. "About the Lamia and your mother..."

"Yeah. You're wondering if I feel bad because...nah. I mean, I sort of...I had to kill what was holding her together and I don't feel bad about that. It freed the Sandmen anyway. Things might be tense now, but at least they can make their own decisions."

She stretched languidly, then propped her chin on her fist, thinking. "I hope the surface exploration missions will work. I know it's in the future, but...anyway. Your mother. Are you still feeling okay with it? You struck her down when the Lamia wore her face. That can't be easy." Her blue eyes were loving instead of coldly analytical, and it made thinking back to it easier.

"It...it wasn't exactly Mom. Part of her, yes, and I'll never know how long she managed to survive up there after she went Dust crazy, but it wasn't really all of her. I feel really bad for Lilly, too...it didn't really set in at the time, but now..."

"Your mother *is* dead, but as they say—it's tacky, but you know she'll never really be gone," Una said, stroking my cheek. "She—or her echo, her shade—is gone, though?" There was a question in her voice. I shook my head affirmatively.

"Yes, but I think it's better that way. I hoped, when I first saw her, that I'd be wrong, and she would have been alive all this time. But...at least I have Dad...and he's been there for me in all of this, too."

It hurt, saying it for sure, but it felt good in a way. Closure. Whether it had been the Dust or her echoes or—I don't want to talk about souls—it didn't matter. She'd loved me, and I knew she'd be proud of me for the way things had turned out.

"And now, you have us, too." Una smiled softly, stroking my cheek. I managed to nod again, but my throat was too thick to speak.

I nestled into the warmth of Una's arms. My love, smelling of corderite and creamy skin. Una jerked her head, and from the other side of the room, Nathu came over to wrap his arms around us both.

"I'm sorry, Janelle," he said, stroking my face. "I feel like this is my fault. I know it's not quite right, but I have a duty to my people...to my family..."

I shook my head, tears running down my face again, hot and leaving a stinging trail from my eyes.

My eyes. I still had them. It seemed so impossible.

"No, this was before your time, and...I always knew she was dead, really. Dad said so anyway. He might've bent the truth about why, but it's better than the alternative. I kept hoping, but....this is better. She's not a monster, this way."

Nathu stroked my hair while Una held me, and I felt a little better. I turned around to peck her on the lips, quickly.

Nathu gently turned me around, and Una let me go so he could take me in his arms. I luxuriated in the size of the divan, and the warmth of my lovers' bodies. "Your father can live in the great hall with us if you want," he offered. "I'm sure he'll want to watch his grandchildren growing up as closely as possible."

I smiled. Grandchildren. I can actually have kids. I am alive. Put like that, it all seemed so simple and so beautiful.

"This isn't going to be easy," said Una, reaching over to cup my breast. "We have a lot of work to do to get people Up, and settled. If they even want to go Up. Not to mention the reclamation—it's a mess up there. And—"

"Una, love, please stop trying to plan things when we're relaxing," groaned Nathu. "I have to lead this mess. I know what it entails. Believe me."

"Never. You wouldn't plan anything without me," she countered, grinning. She leaned over me to flick his ear, and he laughed.

"Fine, Una, we're at an impasse. Janelle, you settle this." Una rolled me off of Nathu and between them, and in a flash, had me pinned down, her breasts and hips pressed against mine. Then, Nathu was slipping a hand between us, and down, his fingers gliding over my hips and dancing to her skin. She groaned, and I felt her body respond, felt mine echo the response in turn. Pleasure sparked over my skin, and I let out a quiet cry.

"Well? We're waiting for an answer," she purred playfully.

"Don't look at me," I said, sliding my hand between his legs. "I just fix things."

THE LOVED, THE LOST, THE DREAMING

27—Date unrecorded, 0055 P.D.

"What's that, mom?" He pointed at the sky. "Pick me up! I wanna see!"

The young woman grinned, scooped her son up in her arms. The rest of the children were wreaking joyful havoc on the playground, watched by her wife and husband. As she glanced at them, both caught her eyes in turn, and answered with brief smiles. Nick would be back, someone else would be asking for her attention, or several someones would be asking for it, but for now, he could have a special moment with one of his mothers.

She kissed the top of his head, inhaled the sweet clean smell of him. She looked away again and towards the old man standing some distance away, on the turf.

He was wearing sandals, and despite his age, stood proud and tall, eyes fixed to the sky, the shining thing dancing above the playground and park. He was unaware of almost anything else, even the children, heart and soul focused on the little bright thing so high above them.

Nick craned his head back and looked around, loose dark curls flopping into his face. Automatically, half-smiling, she brushed them behind his ears. He stared at the shining thing turning sharp circles above him, and his small mouth fell open in wonder.

"That's just grandpa's plane, Nicky. It's very high up in the sky." As she spoke, she could see delicate red film flashing

in the sunlight, the plane gliding almost silently through the air as its wings caught thermals. It came closer, then darted away again, into the clouds.

THE GRAIN

I'm not sure exactly when it started, the dreams that I would get lost in. I do remember the first night, but I couldn't tell you how old I was, exactly. There was a sensation like going down a slide, feet up and head down. Sleep rushed over me, not settling like a warm bird but flying over me, faster than I could understand it.

I rose from a pool of mercury, which clung to my limbs and stuck to my skin as I lifted myself. I was wearing something white and flowing. To my faint surprise, there was no wetness, slickness, from the mercurial liquid. Only a faint, fresh chill in the air—a hidden breeze, perhaps, but the world around me was dark, and not with the darkness of sky. It seemed to be a sort of cavern. The light was grey, dim, cool and distant.

This is how I began to chase the dreams around, following them through caverns. Each night I'd take a different path from the pool, rushing headlong through a stalactite archway and into another world. I saw wonders and I saw terrors. Rabbits with the legs of spiders bursting through their sides, pets that transformed from sweet distractions to slavering, clicking monsters after a single touch. Flowers that were made of tiny dancing ladies, capering in silk and the remains of butterflies. Buildings that shifted and walked like men, pausing to converse with each other as they walked through cities on the road. A city in the desert where they traded dreams instead of money.

Deep in the desert, there are cities where men sell dreams and memories. Sell is not the right word, perhaps. Memories are the currency. A shared but ordinary memory, told well, is the price of a healthy cow; a brief anecdote, a chicken. For the knowledge and private things, skills are traded; items change hands, and market stalls empty.

Such memories have a fine face value, if told well, but if brief or ill-described, fetch small sums. There are women of fine repute whose descriptions beggared princes, and men whose fine plays set the nations at war and furnished their armies, as well.

Yet still more precious than the memories, say the sage's duty scrolls, are the dreams. The scrolls dictate the way of life, and so it is. The dreams are coin of a different sort. Where a man might go and work in a gold mine in exchange for a saucy tale, which he and his fellows could share in the city, dream currency is one that can be held, extracted. A memory flutters into the air and is used until it is shared, decreasing in value as it becomes more familiar. Dreams are a currency to be held.

A woman whose name was lost in time—only her sex remembered—was the first to hear the secret hum of the spheres and experiment with certain crystal alloy glasses. She taught her pupils, seeking the ones with moonstruck eyes and steady hands and ruthless souls, and they passed down their secret trade. To catch dreams and to make the equipment—the skills can be trained, but not taught. The precious clear headdresses and ornaments cupping the shaven skulls of every citizen collect only a few grains of dreams, and each night, nearly microscopic granules.

Months or years would pass before the silvery grains had accumulated enough to be seen by the naked eye, and to be large enough to sell. The powdery grains had a look and flow like liquid silver, and in the finest, secret corners of the markets, a few merchant-priests controlled the rituals concerning its trade.

Under the light of the bright moon, which lingered high and long in that cold-nighted place, lenses of dragonscale and amber could be used to magnify the worlds and wonders hidden in the grains. Up close, each apparently silvery grain was an uneven crystal, almost a tridecahedron, but its natural facets had been made by no jeweler. In their depths, each one threw off its own light in a dozen colors. At a fine enough magnification, horrors and wonders, lascivious and foolish things flickered. Each moment, a shifting mass of concentrated lovely chaos would appear and dissipate.

Marvels they were, but even with its powers, a single grain was never bought alone. Those who came to buy and sell their dreams would inhale the powder for sweet and stranger sleep, sell it for fantastic stories or gold to the alchemists, or sprinkle dreams of certain kinds in the shoes of lovers and enemies. As the merchant-priests sorted dreams into approximate categories, alchemists and magicians waited outside or in lines, hoping for just enough of the dust to make their potions. Mixed with fenny seed and the breath of a phoenix, it granted invisibility; with the tears of a sea-turtle and five bright emeralds from a gryphon's nest, finely powdered, it would cure any sickness, and—it was said—could bring back anyone even from the very brink of death. The necromancers used it with coals of the Pit for obscene things, to beguile demons for temporary service.

For a hundred hundred years, it was precious and respected as a thing to trade only in small quantities, delicately, with respect. A certain king came to power in the ten thousandth year of the cities' existence. In centuries to follow, his name was struck from temples, archives, and monuments, and replaced only with a glyph for unspeakable cruelty. It was he that decided the cold-blooded and long-lived dream masters would be best at practicing their art if they had steady supplies of dream powder.

A suddenly revived tourist trade and many kidnappings followed. Ten thousand chained slaves, sleeping in the finest beds in the empire, were drugged to sleep, and dreamed en masse. With their priceless dust and an army of magic users, the king set out to grow their trade and conquer the neighboring cities outside the desert. Under the flame-eyed sun and cool moon, his armies marched, silent as the sand dunes and invisible, thanks to certain obscene preparations.

I awoke in their dungeons, once or twice on my travels, chained to silk cushions and with slaves fanning me with ostrich plumes. I struggled and cried out, and the most delicate extract of belladonna and mandrake steeped in wine trickled down my throat, until I slept again. Dreaming again, dreaming within dreams, I awoke in my own life.

So it was, nightly, for some days or weeks—perhaps centuries. I cannot tell. Once again I awoke as a soldier, panting and sweating in the desert, but moving soundless in formation behind the shields and shifts wrought by sorcerers. I remember our swords in the necks of citizens, dragging the children back with us to be trained in the somnatorium, for refined sleep, producing the most dreams. I remember every moment of their screaming, their delicate skin chafing in the cuffs, the blood they left behind them on the sand. I remember the point of my sword on their delicate birdlike throats. I remember inhaling just a little dream dust, just a grain or two, to quiet the screams in my head for the night. I remember the madness.

I remember awakening in the palace far away the next night, in the cool south. Watching the vast spire-domed city from the highest minaret, where my dark-skinned and lovely people worked hard to create beautiful things, I wondered at the approaching army. There was no chance of a diplomatic marriage, but it would have failed anyway. War or sabotage were the only solutions, to keep my people from lying in their silk and twitching in sleep, dream-slaves to the conqueror. No magic was worth it, but his power was only swelling.

Awakening again, no longer a fine dark princess with glorious curling hair and spider silk and gold on my limbs, I found myself a sorcerer, working with the dust, a few grains at a time. To mix the stuff into the mad king's wine cup, swallowing it, a thing no-one was permitted to do—inhale a bit was powerful, a thousand times less, than to swallow even a grain...yet I slipped a little in my pocket before I mixed the rest for the king. When prepared, I brought it to the lady, whose body I had so recently borrowed. My silvery pools were far away, the dull daytime that night would pull me back from, as I watched her take the poison cup to the official envoy.

And oh, had I only been a servant, the lowliest, at the surrender dinner, to witness what came. I know only of what happened after from a dream night as a nomad, finding one of the fallen pillars lying in the sand. The story was in characters our people had nearly lost, and yet I pieced together hints of the narrative hints of the dust. A hidden scrap of parchment, stained with something brown like blood and burned by fire, gave further hints, but refused to yield the details of its secrets.

And so was the king's downfall, through methods that were struck from history after, and their consequences. The terrible price was worthy, but oh, even the few historians who had written of the king spoke not of the consequences of the princess' decision. Great and terrible things, waves of mercury and fire, armies of the dusty dead in their graves, horrors from beyond the stars coming to cut the world in two, were hinted at but not spoken of clearly. The world was fire and darkness, but it must have gone away, for people still survived. And yet, the shadow on the horizon hinted that things were still there, lingering in the desert...turning from the pillar, I pulled my long-trunked and strange-legged mount, and turned from history.

And now, awake and far away from my silver caves, my moonlit deserts, I have brought a relic with me somehow. Dream dust. I have a good gram of the stuff, sparkling bright in my palm. It came with me in my pocket, I suppose; somehow it was beneath my pillow. I wonder what just a grain on the tip of my tongue would do? Just one? Just one...just one...just...here on my tongue...just one...

FOOTPRINTS IN THE SNOW

Amy was cold. The dead of Saskatchewan winter was in her bones, a harsh dry cold that bit and scratched its way through countless layers. A down vest couldn't keep out the deep winter's teeth. She walked to school with blue lips and chattering teeth, rode the ramshackle bus into the city with icy limbs, and shook and shivered her way through class. At recess she avoided the deep snow drifts, the thick glittering crests rising white in the corners of the school yard. Instead of making snowmen or forts, she hovered by the doors, shaking and shuddering.

The school nurse had seen her every week since the snow started. Her mother had taken her to the doctor at least twice. No-one could explain why Amy was so cold. It had always been a hard season for her, but never had she suffered like this.

Paf, paf, paf, paf.

The slight squeak and owl-soft fall of her feet in the drifts was muted by the heavy air. She stood shivering at the stop, until the bright yellow beast pulled up groaning, to the curb. She realized she'd forgotten her homework again, distantly. Climbing in, she forgot about it, the ice-box chill numbing her her cares.

Finally at the school a little life came back to her. The frost-thin smile on her face worried Ms. Hewitt as Amy walked in, but her eyes, pale and grey-blue, were alight, livelier. It wasn't school that put a smile on the girl's face—it was the thought of freezing a little less.

She endured the day's lessons for the privilege of the warmth. Born on the solstice on a cold night in December, the cold had followed her since her birth. This year, though, with her birthday only a day or two away, it seemed more determined than ever to catch her.

The dreaded home-bell rang and it was time to wrap herself up again. Two toques over thin, colorless blonde hair; two scarves over a hollow-cheeked face with drawn features; three sets of gloves over tiny hands with fingers like willow twigs. A double layer of sweaters covered her emaciated frame, and the parka over it lent an illusion of fleshiness. Amy didn't notice her teacher's worried eyes, only concentrated on dragging her sickly frame out to the bus.

The walk home was always the worst. The sun would fall lower, shadows lengthen, and the hard grey sky grew steadily darker. Even the ghostly street lights spilling on the snow couldn't illuminate the world. The pavement was dusted with powder, a fine layer over slippery melt and packed ice. Amy's footsteps pattered softly, her rubber boots stiff and leeching heat out from the fake fur inside.

The snow was still falling, but things were waiting for her. A dead bush rustled and, there was a flash of movement.

Amy yelped, but whatever was in the bush settled down. *Stupid, stupid*, she told herself, *just the breeze. Or a cat. Or a rabbit.*

There were large, sharply defined paw prints on the neighbor's lawns. *Just dogs*, thought Amy. *Just a dog's prints.*

It couldn't have been a beast smaller than a husky, though. A German shepherd at the very least. Or even—Amy refused to think of wolves, their ghost breath steaming in night air, teeth flashing in snarls. Wolves had been more common in the last ten years, here. It might be wolves. The heady smell of meat and fur, the sound of dozens of paws crunching snow as the pack circled around her…

"There are no wolves here," she said out loud. Coyotes then? And still, it seemed to her that as a car passed her in the street, speeding, that its engine growled…

Frightened, her breath rasping harsh in frozen lungs, Amy lifted her feet. Her boots seemed to stick in the snow, heavy with crusted and frozen moisture. She whimpered, panicking, but her feet barely moved. The growl seemed to come again, behind her, its source close but not close enough to be seen.

She tried to walk faster, to jog, but slipped and fell hard in the snow.

The growling was much louder. She was sure she heard the sound of paws on snow, baying voices on the wind, a dozen beasts howling and hungry for her meager flesh....

Amy cried out again in fear, and pulled at her stuck boots. They were getting stuck wedged in the drifts, snagging on hidden objects and crusted layers of snow. The drift was a glittering prison, the hard shell unyielding. The scrabbling of paws and tough claws was louder, meters away.

She screamed loudly, cutting the winter air with her panicked child's voice. A growl—a bright light—

"Amy! Where have you been? You know you're not well, why didn't you come straight home? I was worried sick!"

The breath and heat inside the car steamed fro the windows her father stared at her. Shaking his head, he got out and picked her up. His breath smelled of beer, worrying but also reassuring. He shouldn't have been driving, but at least it wasn't Jack Daniels. Jack meant crying in a corner. Tonight, though, he was here for her.

"You got scared, didn't you?" It's okay. There have been coyotes around; you know they wander into town during winter. Be more careful!" Amy shook and made no reply, feeling ashamed of herself. "Come home sweetie. I'll get you hot chocolate from Tim Horton's."

Amy tried not to feel guilty for making him waste precious gas and money on a treat.

"Thanks, Daddy." She felt foolish, childish.

The car was on maximum heat. For anyone else it would have been sweltering, but for Amy, it was just barely warm enough. The chilled, frozen moisture trapped inside her clothes slowly began to melt, dampening her sweaters under the parka. Grateful to be warm, she unzipped her coat and basked in the heat. Her father was mostly quiet after he'd made his inquiries. Amy let her mind drift, but made sure to spare him a smile.

Her mother greeted their return with a shrill, panicky cry. Since her hours had been cut back, a cellphone was too expensive. Normally even the hot chocolate would have gotten a groan, but she was too worried to care tonight.

Carolyn had come out, cigarette in trembling fingers and a fearful look on her pinched face, braving the cold in a coat thrown over her house robe. "Dave! Why didn't you call home? I was worried sick about both of you and you shouldn't be driving—"

"Let me park, hon. She got stuck in a snow drift and panicked. Let the Monster be, she's scared as it is."

"I'm okay now, Daddy," Amy mumbled.

Carolyn pulled the door open and scooped her out. "Come inside, don't wait for him to park."

Carolyn seemed mad and worried, at Amy or at Dave for driving—Amy wasn't sure which, and was too tired and cold to care anymore.

Her parents argued quietly as Amy forced down a few mouthfuls of lukewarm macaroni with hot dogs. They stuck in her throat, and the food looked like someone's stomach contents. She soon excused herself to the den.

She did her homework dutifully but absently, skipping questions she didn't like in English, and doing the math and science first. As always, she saved the hard subjects for last. She tried to do the previous night's homework too. As long as she did okay, they would let her be, Carolyn and Dave. She could hear them in the tiny kitchen/living room, arguing in the way they thought she couldn't hear. At times like this, it was nice to be away from them. Hopefully it wasn't another argument about her. Being the strange one at school was bad enough, when she wasn't too cold to care. They loved her, Amy thought, and yet...

Amy put on the travel channel and snuggled under three of her grandmother's knitted blankets. There was a program about vacations she liked—usually about hot, tropical places. The host was a silly British man who looked friendly, like a favorite uncle. Turning up the volume to cover Carolyn's raised voice, she waited for the intro to end. Carolyn was screaming in frustration now, but it was nothing a closed door, volume control, and careful focus of her attention couldn't cover. Perhaps the warm place would be Israel or somewhere in Africa.

"Tonight, I'll be at an ice hotel in Finland!" The host began brightly. Amy changed the channel immediately.

She soon gave up on watching television. There seemed to be a winter storm warning on most of the basic channels, and the rest was a mixture of boring or scary grownup stuff or stupid childish cartoons. A claymation penguin cavorted on cheerful iceburgs—click—more cartoon people were visiting Santa at the North pole—click—Christmas music was playing, a pop star wailed her way through "Let it snow, let it snow"—click—

Amy dozed off, napping fitfully. She woke in her bed, in pajamas—her mother's work—and fell asleep just as quickly.

The night was dark, black as only a Canadian winter's eve could be. Snow drifted down, and under her worn-out blankets, Amy tossed fitfully.

Her dreams were shadowy. She thought she was walking in an open field under the moon. White as old bone and gleaming cold, it shone down from a black star-cut sky on the white ground. Amy strode in lazy dreamlike bounds over the snowy waste of the prairie, dead fields of wheat stalks dying below feet of snow, below her light-stepping boots.

Cautious as a fawn, she strayed closer to the only thing on her horizon. She was both farther and closer than she'd thought—a distance trick of dreams or the prairies, she wasn't sure which.

The thing she was approaching seemed to be a mere distorted grey rectangle at first, but it soon revealed itself as a barn, collapsing and weather-worn.

Her explorations had been cautious so far, but a sudden sound of feet or paws crunching on the snow behind her changed that. The sound was steady. She was being followed, and by something running fast. The wind rose, all at once, and snaky lines of fresh powder whirled over the ground at her feet. She ran for the barn a little faster, or tried to. The paws or footfalls behind her sped up, and a low growl cut the winter air. The beasts behind her howled, baying at the cold moon, telling it of their hunger for her flesh.

Amy screamed and ran through the snow, stumbling and lumping, fast as she could toward the open door.

THE LOVED, THE LOST, THE DREAMING

She reached it just as the breath of the hunters tickled the back of her neck. Hot and cold as frostbite, she felt a drop from the slavering jaws on her skin just as she rounded the door. She slammed it tight, and down went the heavy wooden latch on the shed door.

Panting, her chest aching and her frame shuddering, Amy collapsed on the cold straw and dust strewn floor. She knelt in a pile for several long moments before rising, trembling, to her feet.

The shed had been medium-sized at most, a barn only by pioneer standards. Now she found herself in an enormous structure, a dusty, complex maze far larger inside than it had seemed from without.

Half of it was falling down, dangerously, the multiple levels of lofts and ladders and pens overwhelmed her. Half-walls stretched on farther than they should have, and the destroyed part—the left half, closest to her entrance—twisted around on itself strangely. The corridors, lofts, and walls formed peculiar angles. Amy liked math, and at that moment, a cool and detached part of her child's mind fathered enough calmness to tell her there was something deeply wrong with the barn's geometry. Worst, strangest still, the seemingly endless corridors and maze-like structure were much, much larger than it should have been.

The howling and beating of paws and large bodies against the wooden door had long since ceased, the mournful cries fading into the distance. Snow blew through the broken window panes and under the door, through cracks in the walls. Amy rubbed her arms through her snowsuit and decided to walk further in to look for a blanket. It would be better to wait for the sudden snow to subside.

The howling had returned, but now it was the wind. The temperature seemed to be falling, and Amy, reluctant and fearful, walked deeper into the barn' darkness.

Cold moonlight filtered in through the windows as she searched. The corridors were empty, and half-walls and debris blocked her at every turn. Still, her body demanded warmth, the cold seeping in even through her parka. Its sharp fingernails tore through the down, raked along her bare skin.

Still she wandered, getting lost in the cold and twisted geometry. Her eyes felt wrong. Corners were subtly too wide or narrow, ladders started with two legs and ended in three, and stairs seemed to travel in the wrong direction. Amy's breath was sharp in her chest, rasping her lungs like a nail file. Worse was a sense that she was not alone.

As she climbed up a ladder, hoping for a horse blanket or even rags, she could have sworn she heard the floorboards behind her creaking. Without looking, she climbed faster, and found herself or the ground rather than in the loft.

A rasping sound, as if winter could breathe through its icy lungs. The air grew colder still and the wind battered the barn. Amy wondered if it was about to collapse on her. With unnatural swiftness, hoar frost was creeping around her feet. There was a rattling.

Terrified, Amy felt her bladder give way under the strain.

She turned around unwillingly, unable to stop her curiosity or flee. She saw two spots of blue looking back into her own eyes, a blue like the heart of a glacier, pure and cold as winter itself. Frost and snow swirled around the eyes, around her, and long claws of ice reached for her face. She screamed—

--And awoke, shuddering, to find her window open and her pajamas shamefully soaked. She whimpered and got out of bed, freezing to the bone, her teeth chattering. Snow had blown in. She saw that it was not only open, which it hadn't been when she went to bed, but that both the bug net and the glass layers were broken. The net looked as though something had punched a hole through it, or as if an animal had smashed it.

Her parents would be mad, but Amy was too cold and frightened to care. She changed into her other pajamas and put the soiled ones into the bathroom sink for her mother to rinse, then quietly woke her parents.

They changed the sheets with few complaints—nightmares were nightmares, her mother reminded her, and she couldn't be hurt by her imagination. The window, though, was a different story. Carolyn blamed Dave, Dave blamed a branch and Amy was too scared, upset, and miserable to admit the forces she blamed.

After soothing and tired scoldings, they sent her back to bed. Amy laid awake for an eternity, watching the cardboard-covered window for signs of the beast's return, and shivering in the chill of her room. Part of her was ashamed of being a burden. She wished the snow was warm, instead, so that she could surrender to the heat. Fearful, frozen, she didn't so much fall asleep as shudder into unconsciousness.

Amy resisted going to school, miserable and cold as she was, and tried to plead with her mother to let her stay home.

"I can't stay today, said Carolyn, her face as unreadable as a sheet of ice. "And I can't leave you alone."

Amy looked at Dave hopefully, but his face was downcast and directed at the floor, his feet, anything else. "I gotta look for a second job, pumpkin," he mumbled. Their ancient computer's blank screen stared accusingly from the living room's corner. Amy wanted to protest more, but abandoned it. The only thing to do was swallow her objections and wrap herself in layers of warmth, and pray that whatever had been howling for her blood in the night didn't follow her to school.

That morning, as her mother watched her trudge to the bus, she remembered the pale white sickly thing she'd given birth to almost twelve years ago. The lucid skin white and clear as river ice, veins and pitiful meat beneath the surface of her flesh clearly visible. A soundless little monster, too early and too small, that let out a whimper rather than a healthy scream. Carolyn had done some screaming, though. The blood had flowed, thick and heavy, dangerously so. Her body ripping itself in half to eject her child. At first Amy had only been a lump of flesh—shaped meat, a scrap of some butcher's table. Then her tiny bony limbs had flailed weakly and she'd let out a quiet cry. The squashed distorted thing was her child, then, a person, and Carolyn loved her.

Still, as thick flakes fluttered from the hospital-white sky, she couldn't erase the image, the soul-deep fear and disgust she'd felt as she looked on her daughter for the first time.

427

Amy was barely aware of her mother's conflict as she waved her off to school. Only the chill that cut through three knitted layers mattered. Mrs. Hewlett was so concerned she nearly sent Amy home, but the girl's quiet protests silenced her. She did send Amy to the nurses' office again.

Trudging down the long, cold halls of the school, Amy once again found herself being poked and prodded. Without a fever, coughing, or any other signs of sickness, save her skin's coolness to the touch, the nurse could only sigh and send her back to class.

Outside the school, winter was making itself known. The season always came earlier here than in most other places, but just a day before the solstice, it was snowing hard and fast.

A white Christmas, most likely, but a hard, cold, bitter end to the year, by ancient reckonings. The precious extra work hours for Carolyn meant nicer presents for Amy and less fighting with Dave, thought Amy, comforting herself over being forced to brave the cold on her way home.

Losing his job had made them argue more about Christmas, Amy considered. The hopes of a second-hand console for Christmas lifted her spirits a little as she got on the bus. For a moment, she could almost ignore the swirling storm around them. The chill in her bones seemed to awaken in the cold bus. Only halfway home, her thoughts and upper arms were sparkling with pins and needles. Her toes were so numb in her boots that she wondered if they were well and truly-frost-bitten. Her breath puffing in the air, she watched the snow blowing across the road.

It whipped the powder into snow-snakes, creeping ghostlike across the road. The bus driver cursed as he pulled to a stop sign, and she felt the vehicle skidding. For a moment, she wondered if the snow snakes were attacking the tires with icicle teeth.

She started like a rabbit caught outside its burrow when the driver barked her name. Seeing the girl's deathly white face and terrified eyes the like ice chips, he mumbled a gruff "Merry Christmas" at her as she departed. Only a few blocks, thought Amy, surveying the storm before her. Houses, the corner store, the lawns and bushes and cars in their driveways—all were covered in thick snow, and all were fading under the snowstorm around her. It was as if her world was being erased, eaten by a white monster.

She felt her airways resist as she inhaled. Her nose and mouth seemed to instantly coat with frost. Her ears were numb and tingling, aching in seconds.

Before her, behind her, the world was filled with white snow and screaming wind. Shuddering and ready to cry, Amy set out.

She had barely gone a block when the sound of footsteps in snow behind her filtered through. The bushes of the last house on the left writhed and wiggled in the storm., as if something was hiding in them.

It's just a storm, she told herself. Monsters are imaginary.

She thought of the warmest things she could—her mother's lungs, her father's hot chocolate, the TV room where she was covered in blankets and the furnace was on the highest setting. The lighter in her pocket, stolen from her mother's purse some time ago.

It didn't help much. The whirling whiteness blurred the world and layered her coat and pants in frost. The cold froze layers of moisture outside her scarf the cold crawled between the layers, under her skin. The wind howled, wolflike.

It was as if icy talons were tracing over her spine. The bushes were rattling again, and the sound of feet on snow behind her was growing. The padding of heavy feet on the crunching layers came inexorably. Frustrated and terrified, she turned around to look at her stalker.

Snow and frost and winter wind curled and flowed in a shape that was neither human nor lupine, a wrong-angled and disproportionate mix of both. Its body was loosely shaped, as much a dust-devil as a body. The long white claws, ice and hoarfrost shaped cold and cutting were a different story. Worse than the half-meter long nails were the eyes. Blue, implacable, inhuman, cold as the heart of a glacier…and full of primal hunger.

Amy screamed, but the air froze her throat and snow softened the rasp into silence. The creature's claws moved closer to her face, almost tenderly.

She broke into a run, going as fast as her weak, tired legs could manage. The world was blurred and cold, and full of a dozen howling voices.

The air was knife sharp, but she forced herself to run in spite of the pain. The houses and bushes were lost in the storm, and she sensed vaguely that she was running out of the neighborhood borders and towards the underdeveloped fields. The footing was treacherous, heavy, and her boots were sinking in the uneven ground. The dead grass, buried layers deep, would have given her more purchase, but it was long past the time when green things ruled. In summer, golden wheat swayed here, row after row of it, but in the depth of winter, all was pale and silent. Silver and black dirt that only crows would pause in.

She ran deeper, the howls rising, a sound like a wolf pack in snow crunching the hard ground behind her.

They were in farmer's fields now, farther than it should have been possible to run from the edge of suburbia. The beasts seemed to be vulnerable to the wind, being blown and whisked by air currents as their paws or feet struck ground. The icy breath at her back, full of rime frost and a chill beyond death, froze the back of her nylon hood into a hard shell.

Winter chased her and she let it guide her, not thinking, only fleeing the terrible paws desperately. Teeth that snapped and rasped with a sound like breaking icicles aimed at her heels, her legs, her neck.

There was a dark and twisted building ahead. A barn, falling down on one side, in an almost unnatural twisting shape. Perhaps it was pure bad luck or coincidence, but the rambling construction and weatherworn sides were all too familiar.

Her feet pounded against the frost-hardened ground. The solstice moon was rising behind the snowy cloud cover. She could feel it, the cold mistress of the long night watching her pitilessly behind the veils of weather.

Feeling small, her rational mind gibbering in terror as the demonic howling followed her, Amy focused on the barn and prayed its shelter would keep her safe, keep the ice claws from scraping her skin, from cutting through her white flesh…

Fighting the snow, the adrenalin racing through her blood, she ran hard. At any moment she feared the sharp crack and cold fire of a breaking ankle to have her legs twist and give way beneath her. And yet, there it was, the door, slightly open. Only meters away.

The baying of the hound-creatures, the swirling snow at her peripheral vision—she mustn't let it swallow her, she mustn't!

Pushing the door open, Amy leapt inside and slammed it shut after herself. There was a ferocious scraping and snarling against the door, but the heavy bar slid down, into place. The storm couldn't come in.

Strangely, the winds that had been howling outside a mere moment before failed to reach the inside of the vast building. One side was curving down, falling inwards to infinity around her. Her blood froze again as she recognized the impossible angles.

Her heart pounded frozen in her chest. Steady, she thought. It was just a dream. Still, as the howls of the wind and the snow wolves died down, she could have sworn she heard the word "Ithaqua", in a whispery scratch.

She crept deeper into the barn. The strange stairs and uneven levels were just as she'd dreamed them. Like an ancient sacrifice, she wandered in deeper.

Footsteps. Soft, but the creeping floorboards didn't lie. The cold in her bones was slowing her movements. The exhaustion she'd delayed was catching up to her. Fire, she thought. It would stave off the cold and make her safe. No time to look for a horse blanket. Just fire.

There was a little lighter her mother had, one of the cheap kinds that came in an extra small container. Sometimes she played with it when Carolyn wasn't looking. She had it in her coat today.

She took it out of her pocket and removed her gloves, fumbling. The little flint gave a sad spark, but yielded no tiny, pale yellow sprite. Light. Fire. Something she'd forgotten about in the abysmal depths of her nightmare.

The footsteps were closer and there was hoarfrost around the edges of the doorway. She crouched in the half-room of the stable, listening. Silence again.

There was a little hay at the bottom of the stall. She flicked the lighter and tried to make it brighter. She lit the hay and shivered.

A thin brown straw caught, flickering orange in the gloom, but soon darkened. The thin moonlight filtering through cracks in the roof only underlined the shadows. She tried gain. Flick, snap. A bit of orange ember, but no real flame.

THE LOVED, THE LOST, THE DREAMING

The footsteps and the sense of cold seemed to draw closer, to embrace her fear in the silence, make it a greater force somehow.

She flicked the lighter again, feeling it slip in her sweating, numb hands. There was no gas left.

A touch from something colder than metal brushed under her chin. She felt her face being tilted upwards. Impossibly, snow and frost swirled before her, inside the still air of the building. She looked deep into the glacier eyes.

Her soul froze, and she surrendered to the cold power. As her skin chilled and the winter slid under her flesh for the last time, she felt the heat, the burning fire that was at the heart of the cold. It was a strange kind of relief. Amy had a final mad thought of the moon laughing down at her behind its veils. Then she gave into the long, long night.

The next morning, her parents and the police searched the neighborhood they found a set of tracks leading from the edge of the neighborhood to the depths of the farmer's fields.

Farther out, as they grew more and more distant from each other, it seemed the child-sized owner had been running. Eventually, though, they simply faded out mid-step. Carolyn ran past the end of the tracks, crying out to the officers that something was glinting

Michelle Browne

in the snow. Dave, cold sober for once, beat the officers to it, but it was only a lighter, empty and almost buried in the fresh snow.

THE DOLLMAKER

My grandmother bounced up the steps of the shop with her usual false gaiety. Impatience to be shopping danced in her eyes, but she wanted to introduce the store, first. She loved introductions. "You'll love this little place," she said. This is what I did not say: *yes, I like antique shops too, but this place is very out of the way, and it had better be worth the hour-long detour.* I also did not say: *Grandpa looks like he needs to be shot.*

It was quite a peculiar place, but then, that describes more than fifty percent of Nova Scotia. It was a farm on the mainland, far enough from the ocean that it wasn't in sight, yet close enough to catch brine on the air. It was painted the same shade of blue as a cloudy day, and the windowsills had white trim. *Antique Shop,* said the signs outside. *Please come in.*

With an invitation like that, how could I resist? I followed, and quit my grumbling, because the little I could glimpse behind the windows looked exquisitely promising. The curtains were the prerequisite ivory lace, real Irish, from the looks of it. The door chime tinkled with a sound like the tines of a fork playing on a wooden xylophone. My grandmother chattered incessantly at my grandfather, who grunted occasionally, blinked in a thick, sleepy way behind his camera-thickness lenses. She bee-lined for the den, to inspect the display of pricey artifacts of her youth: the gold-leafed plates, the china, the relics of a time when washing machines were rare beasts and cars were tinny matchboxes.

I was frozen in the chandeliered entranceway. The ceilings in this house were low, and if I were just a few inches taller, I could have easily reached up and removed one of the crystals, tucked it in my pocket like a thief. But the golden chandelier didn't hold my attention for long. The next thing I saw was the dolls.

They were such dolls as I had never before seen in my life. These were not the dull, daft-eyed Victorian creations my mother and grandmother had a fondness for. No. Something much stranger, more suited to an art show than this elegant, dusty old home.

Perched there on the dark violet brocade, above the intricately carved, darkly shining wood, are dolls with a curious and eerie soulfulness. I stepped over to them, ignoring the lure of the other rooms full of knick-knacks for sale. There were half a dozen here. The bodies were soft, slender; their clothes thick, rich silks and velvets. They had lace at their wrists and necks, beautiful small charms stitched below their necks and on the trim of their clothes. All of the colours were dramatic, rich; no fading or cheap dyes were used here.

The clothes alone would have made them remarkable, but it was their faces and hands that intrigued me most, forced me to kneel and examine them minutely.

Their hands were smooth, more like mittens than the proper five-fingered models every other china doll displays. The faces too, were smooth and flowing, as if the features had been wrapped in a layer of misty gauze. Arching, smooth brows, pointed, vague noses, hollow eyes with expressive shadows. The mouths were lipless, the hair, painted in curling brushstrokes. They were blurred, formless, and yet oddly, frighteningly expressive, like the amputee Greek statues twisted in ecstasy. All were made of smooth white porcelain.

One was a jester; he laughed silently at a joke I didn't understand and had no wish to. His face was oddly brutal. Two were ladies, in flowing skirts with wistful expressions of unspeakable sadness. One was twisted, with doubled hands and two different faces. He frightened me. One was a gentleman. The last was Death.

Death held a dainty, elegant scythe, and smiled ambiguously. He wasn't cheerless, but his face revealed nothing, answered no questions. I stared at him for a long time before I drifted after my grandparents. I felt like a ghost.

There was a cheery tour guide there, who babbled on absently. I felt as though the sightless eyes of the dolls were following me. I wondered if the creaking of the wooden floor beneath my feet was merely the house conversing with them, if the soft sloughing of cloth brushing against itself was their whispered conversation. There was no relief among the delicately lettered price tags on the items in there, the stained bureaus and old books.

Instead, there were more dolls, one with the face of a lapdog, more jesters, more two-faced men, a king of spades. I wanted to laugh at some. Others made me shudder in fear. These were not the dolls children cuddle and slowly destroy with their brutal affection. These were something else, people and creatures photographed in clay in their unsuspecting moments. Elf craftsmen couldn't have created more exquisite clothing, rendered the insignificancies of buttons and lost earrings more intimate and expressive.

I left and circled through the rooms, seeing more of the dolls each time, and finally find my way to a staircase I hadn't noticed. It was slender, tucked right in against the wall, and the ceiling became lower and lower as I ascended. I followed it, and a bending, low hallway—painted white, now that I'd noticed; all the rooms had been egg-shell white—led me around a corner. There was a tiny set of steps, and more rooms than any house should be able to hold, all crammed against each other and unexpectedly spacious.

I peered through doorways—children's toys, more antiques, a washroom. Old rocking horses, well-loved, tiny houses, teddies, a baby's nightgown. Suddenly, a vague instinct grew stronger and directed me THAT WAY. And I followed it, and there it is. The room.

This was where nightmares were made and dreams were given the fearful dignity that was their due. There was a modern sewing machine on a disappointingly pedestrian desk, and on other tables around the room, bits of fabric, chests of buttons, of worthless jewels, of thread and gleaming silvery scissors and needles. And then I saw them, the dolls' heads.

The clay was shining, still moist above the newsprint, the paper marked darkly with wet spots. One head was there, perfect, smooth, perched on a stand. On the face was an expression of incredible agony and heartache. There were other heads there, rounded shadows beneath cloth. There was a leather book, thick, old, Victorian-looking. I have expected it. In chipped, peeling gold leaf on the cover, it says, simply, *Doll Making*. I heard footsteps and turned, too late, too late. There was a woman in the doorway.

She was not an incredible beauty, nor was she incredibly old, as enchantresses are. There was little incredible about her. She was entirely unexpected nonetheless. So that I didn't have to meet her gaze, my eyes traveled over her forehead first. Her hair was curly, and the fawn-coloured ringlets were looped with grey; her clothes were nondescript. Her eyes were keen, observational.

"I see you've wandered up to my workshop," said the dollmaker. I nodded. My words were gone.

"They're amazing," I said. She nodded.

It is an old art, doll making. Goes back to the first hex-figures, fertility gods, comfort objects. The fire in her pupils bespoke shaman around their smoky fires, holding up buffalo manikins, African witches, dressmakers' sightless dummies, mask makers' sightless, hollow-eyed wooden visages.

I was wordless. I could hear my grandmother clomping around below me, distantly, distantly, as if I were inside a glass ball. Inside a porcelain shell.

The dollmaker smiled, sat down at the chair before the Christ-head, began sculpting it. I was dismissed.

I ran downstairs, back to my grandmother's chattering and my grandfather's silence, and was peculiarly quiet on the drive home.

That night, it took me a very long time to get back to sleep. All I could see was the face of the dollmaker— the smooth, blurred flesh of a burn victim.

THE WRITER'S HANDS

She was too clever, they said, too dangerous, and women shouldn't ask the sort of questions she did. So they held the trial in Gasquette's backyard, the fireflies buzzing idyllically and the heavy bloom of peonies bending their stems forward like prisoners extending their heads to the guillotine. It was night, a clear evening in June. Whisky in a cut glass decanter gleamed richly, water of life for alcoholics—pretentious addicts, but addicts nonetheless.

The men nodded knowingly to one another as they spoke of her, knowing their wives were off in their fireplace corners like good little creatures (actually, the three were off in the arms of the butlers, trying to find what these financial marriages had denied them, and only partly succeeding).

The men agreed that she was a risk. Her prose was too good, too cutting, too honest, too true. Why couldn't she have the decency to write poetry or romance novels, for Heaven's sake? Something had to be done. So they strangled this nemesis of theirs, or rather, they hired someone to do it. She was attacked from behind, asphyxiated by a leather riding whip, and her hands were cut off. That was the *coup de grace*, the severing of the hands. Never again could those fingers jump certainly over the keys of the typewriter, nor could the typewriter get into the hands of another woman. They had had it chopped into three pieces and each of them had ostensibly buried their own third in the garden.

They thought she was finished. They were wrong.

The hands had been taken away, buried outside the horse stables. The hands didn't know this, and didn't care. Digging patiently through the heavy, fecund soil of the vegetable garden nearby, the night witnessed their rebirth above ground. They aided each other, the left and the right. Apart from a little dirt, they were in pristine condition: a lady's hands, white and thin, but determined and thickly callused about the fingertips. Apart from the lack of wrists or any other attachment, they were perfectly acceptable. The stumps where arms might have connected were smooth, fleshy lumps like an elbow. Though sundered, they were still twins, still connected, like siblings.

Together they scuttled along the ground, dodging the stems of the turnips, onions, and carrots lying corpselike below them. The moon hid her serene face behind a mantle of loose clouds, cirrus clouds thin and wispy as ravelled silk.

THE LOVED, THE LOST, THE DREAMING

Under a sky pregnant with foreboding, the hands plotted their course.

Gasquette was asleep beside his wife, unaware of his thorough cuckolding earlier that evening. His wife had known that Gasquette would sense her earlier sex and go through that wretched, boring ritual. Staring up at the ceiling, listening to his gobbling, nasal snores, she was wide-awake and quietly miserable.

There was a soft tapping coming from the window pane—a polite knock against the glass, but insistent, like a lady's rapping. *Tap, tap, please let me in, dear, if you'd be so kind,* said the knock. She thought it was a bird, a pigeon; there were enough of them in this bloody Gothic castle. She tried to remember why she'd consented to marrying him, to living in this stupid house, and failed. The knocking came again—persistent bird, this was.

She got up to shoo it off and saw a knuckle with a dainty gold ring resting behind it waiting patiently at the window. For some reason, she wasn't surprised. Opening the window politely, she ushered the hands in. Using the curtain cord to slide down to the rug, the hands paused before her. The left one made a gesture that the woman sensed was a curtsey. She nodded her head graciously in return. Scurrying across the thick Persian rug in a curiously respectable manner, the hands paused at the bed. It was much too high. The woman knelt, thinking it the right thing to do, and offered her own hands for the others to climb up on. The bodiless hands accepted, sitting docilely in hers like two birds.

They were warm, dry, and not unpleasant to hold; in a way she could not for the life of her articulate, they felt familiar, like a friend's. When she reached the level of the bed surface, the hands left hers urgently and crawled up to the sleeping form of her husband. Carefully, precisely, they closed around his throat.

Gasquette woke to find his neck clamped tightly by an unseen assailant; he gurgled out a plea for help. His wife watched calmly as his eyes rolled up and into his head, as he spluttered feebly, as he died.

She didn't know that this event was to repeat itself twice more that night. Nor did she know the horrifying surprise the house's new owners would find years later. The polished finger bones, smooth as ivory beads, would be all that was left. For tonight, though, still moving, the hands had more to do. They crept to the window glass and waited for her, tapping at it impatiently. She opened the window for them, thinking of pet birds she'd had as she watched them scuttle through impatiently. With a last gesture of farewell, the hands left her.

THE LOVED, THE LOST, THE DREAMING

She stood in the centre of the room for a few minutes and finally elected to go find her lover. She could call the neighbourhood physician in the morning. He would rule it a suicide, not a murder, she knew--not because he'd slept with her, but simply because he'd always despised Gasquette.

The next morning, however, she immediately sat down and began to write. Exactly what story revealed itself to her was never known—she burnt it in the fire place. An inkling of its contents can be determined by the fact that she was found by the window, rocking gently in place, smiling to herself and slowly twisting a piece of rope around her neck.

THE UNDINE

A long time ago, in the time of Crusades and of Christ and kings, there was a prince in France. The prince was an avid hunter and loved to fish next to the waters of the great river that divided his kingdom.

One night, as he sought the great prowling cats that came to fish there, at the cusp of the mountains, he strayed far from his fellow hunters. Silently and stealthily, watching for the great cats and other beasts of the night, he crept to the river. Where the water fell down across the old mossy rocks, a fine mist always rose up. He looked, sometimes, but on this night, with moonlight catching the water, he looked longer than ever. In the shape of the spray, a damsel bathed, perfectly naked.

Luxuriating in the water and tossing her hair, combing it, she was perfect. Skin silver as air on the water, blue eyes, and when she smiled, sharp sharp little teeth. The prince was infatuated.

Riding across the bridge and to the waterfall, he approached her without hesitation, without thought. On one knee, he begged her to marry him, and the undine, the water nymph, agreed. The undine, you see, wanted a soul, something she could get only by marrying a mortal, and bearing a child.

They returned the next morning to his kingdom, the prince bearing his beautiful bride to the castle in an exquisite chariot. Their wedding was celebrated with great pomp and circumstance, and all the kingdom rejoiced.

On the night of the wedding, as the new couple went to bed, the Undine took a moment to make her lover promise a few trifling conditions: first, never to look at her on Saturdays; second, to let her lock her chamber and be undisturbed on that day, and third, never to be unfaithful to her, as long as he drew a waking breath. Her husband, smitten, agreed that they were trifling conditions indeed.

And so, they lived together a very long while, and were happy. A year after the wedding, the Undine had a beautiful child, a well-formed princeling heir. But from that day, a shadow stole over her.

The undine, immortal and lovely, though soulless, had had a child, and that had taken away her immortality. Lovely as she was, and fey, she was now a mortal, and began to age. It was faint at first, but the prince—short of attention span and of temper, as princes so often are—began to notice. The fine, elegant lines, as delicate as finest spider-webs, and the silvering at her temples—no matter how graceful—

were signs of age. And a prince is many things, but in his own eyes, and in those days, in Gods's eyes, he was a little immortal.

And so it was that the prince's eye began to wander. A little, at first, and then a lot. The undine, though she often coveted the river, was dutiful.

Then, thoughtlessly, her maid glanced through the keyhole one Saturday as the still-lovely undine bathed.

To her shock, she saw not a woman, but half-a-woman, with a long, curling, elegant tail, covered in silver and green scales! The prince caught wind of the tale, which travelled through the castle like a monsoon storm. He had to see it for himself.

So there he was, one fine Saturday morning, peeping through the keyhole—and what did he see, but his wife with the tail of a serpent! Horrified, he burst in.

Angry and hurt, she cried out, "Oh, you have broken your first and second promise!" and vanished straightaway as he looked at her.

A few nights later, he heard her soft voice singing in the babe's room, and came in to find her cradling her son. Apologizing, weeping, and down on both knees, he pleaded with her to return.

"Yes," she said, "but remember the third condition. Break your word, and I won't be so forgiving next time."

And so it was that she returned, he quelled the rumors, and they lived happily. For a time. The silver at her temples showed more, and her skin softened. And still, she was beautiful, but she was growing older. Her chuckling infant had become a toddler, and then, a gold-haired boy. And the prince's attention wandered.

She took to walking about the castle at night, more and more. Generally she avoided the animals, which capered and danced away in fear when she came near. One night, however, she found herself near the stables. To her surprise, a familiar droning snore was cutting the air.

Could it be? Her heart hammered fearfully in her chest. She padded in, soft as dew in the morning, and found her husband, the prince, lying in the arms of a common trollop there in the hay. He woke in an instant, feeling as though someone had kicked him in the ribs, to find her pointing a finger at him.

Her eyes large with pain, she cried out, "You promised to be faithful with every waking breath!" He sat dumb, silent. She wept, as immortal nymphs cannot.

"Faithless man! Well, as long as you are awake, and have your breath, you can live. But as soon as you sleep, you shall die!"

And with that, she vanished again, a final time. The prince died a short time later, in his sleep, but his young son grew up fine and strong, and was wiser than his father in choosing a wife. He was scarcely a better man, but he married a human, knowing that if she grew angry, the only dangers were poison or cold steel.

The end.

LYRE

I still remember the first time I saw him. He crouched low over something small and brown and delicately furred—a rabbit, I realised, probably his supper, judging by the blood and meat lying on the snow.

Winter was close on us, as I remember; my hound snorted and growled impatiently, urging me to head homeward to the inn. Sick of looking for the mushrooms in the cold snow, I agreed with him.

Then I saw the stranger, and I forgot Stone's growled advice to turn homeward. Instead, I went to the figure, pulling my wool cloak close about me. Though a young man of my low station can rarely spare such time for curiosities, this boy—man, I now saw, for he was not tall—would likely be a subject of gossip. If not him, then the fine mount tied to the tree next to him. Gossip gets gold, we say, though more likely it's going to be a few pence than a doubloon.

He was watching me intently, wary but not frightened, a bow made of a pale wood I had never seen before clutched in his hand. It was an unusual thing, that bow, and it shone in the late autumn sun, the light of which was a pallid, watery yellow like new butter.

The light cast by the sun was feeble, but the fresh layer of whiteness on the ground took the light and refracted it powerfully, almost unnaturally.

"What are you doing here? This isn't Public Land," I said, once I'd regained my powers of speech.

"I was hungry," he said. His accent was rhythmic, slightly twanging, but elegant. His eyes regarded me darkly—they were blacker than onyx, darker than obsidian glass or anthracite; I could not read the tale that lay behind them.

"You'd best be on your way," I answered—why so breathy, I wondered?

He slipped me a sort of smile, and I was embarrassed in a way I couldn't define. "Lead me to a place I can get a proper meal, boy." I didn't mind him calling me boy, not with that age behind his eyes.

Fine weapon, and a cloak of good material, now that I was looking carefully: whoever he was, and however he came to be here, he hadn't been poorly off.

"Yes, my lord," I said. "There's an inn a kilometre or two away." The dog, Stone, pulled at his leash and strained away from us as I stepped closer to the stranger. A big, beefy, ugly thing—though good-natured—I'd scarcely seen him so unfriendly.

The stranger favoured me with a smile again. "Please." With a swift, silent movement below his cloak, he withdrew something. There was a soft sound of fingernail on metal and a piece of the sun fell into the snow before my feet.

I picked it up, felt the cold metal burn my fingers. I couldn't remember the last time I'd seen this much money in one place.

"To the inn," he said gently.

"Yes, my lord," I rasped. "Right away."

We travelled in silence. I walked next to his horse, a handsome beast with a shining chestnut coat, and long elegant legs. Its breeding could only have been the best, but this was no pretty nobleman's pet—it was a fine hunter, quiet and responsive, sleek and obedient. I'm no expert in horses, but this beast was immeasurably finer than any I had seen in my life.

Together we walked through the cold, the snow, leaving circles and footprints in the unspoiled white. The night was clear and crisp. Stone had settled down, having been given the rest of the rabbit. It was a strange man indeed who bore himself like that and had such a beast, and yet would skin a rabbit for a cold supper. No noble I knew went anywhere without at least two pages.

My companion was silent, and I kept my eyes down, befitting my station. I was careful not to touch his skin, which was the same shade as the longbow on his back. He didn't remark on how I avoided his contact, though he seemed startled by it. We walked in peace until the world interrupted.

The village, small and stinking, reluctant host of the few travellers in our parts, awaited us. The stranger pulled himself backwards, as though preparing for a disgusting task, and I led him to the inn.

My master, Eunid, snarled at my lateness even as he badgered the grimy stableboys to handle the magnificent beast the stranger had brought. He was nothing if not an efficient man, capable of bullying as many servants as he had fingers at the same time. With a motion, the stranger indicated that he would be handling the nameless horse himself. He presented a coin the same rich gold as the one he'd given me, and Eunid immediately stopped protesting and started fawning. Nauseated and embarrassed, I tried to slip back to the kitchens, to get back to the cook. I had a fair stock of the mushrooms, their delicate frost-touched flavour sure to appease the picky patrons, but it wouldn't guarantee that I could avoid a hiding.

I started to head back, as I said, when he grasped my shoulder painfully. "Where are you going?"

"I have to give Gertha these mushrooms," I mumbled.

"I'll get Sun to take these to her. You are going back out there to serve. That stranger's been eyeing your skimpy little ass since you walked in, and if you get any gold from it, you're going to take it. Do we understand?"

I winced and nodded. The last few times something like this had happened, it hadn't been pleasant.

"I don't care if he asks you to suck his cock or take it in the ass." His voice was friendlier. "Do it and I'll make sure you get whisky after if it hurts."

I hate the taste of whisky, but my thin frame was no match for his meaty hands. Hating myself, and feeling disgusting, I crept back out to serve.

"And put a smile on that face," he growled. "This ain't a funeral."

The night passed in a blur. Being told I would have to serve as a pillow had dampened any enjoyment I'd hoped to derive from it. Most men didn't look at me that way, and the ones I wanted to seldom did. I covered my shame with a smile, and hovered around the stranger.

Normally it would have been a worse chore, to flirt and toss him my stray smiles, to bend and flex alluringly, but the shame I felt vanished when his eyes met mine. I sent a few coy glances back, even daring to wink when I was across the room. I saw a servant girl or two trying the same thing, but the stranger's eyes kept settling on me.

It was almost palpable, the warmth, the heat of his eyes on my spine, my legs, my buttocks. I couldn't help stretching my shoulders as I felt him look at me.

Edda and Sun noticed. As Sun passed, she glared at me, whispered a nasty and relevant word under her breath at me. I hissed back a couple of choice phrases that only kitchen service could teach. She recoiled like an angry snake, and left me alone after that.

I didn't care. For once, I might have the chance to entertain a man I actually liked. Ever bone in my sixteen-winter body strained with anticipation.

The invitation, when it came, only arrived at the end of the night. He'd been covered in fellow drinkers and a few lush, plump whores for the night—they'd try to ease closer to his lap, and he'd politely push them away, but it didn't stop them. The musicians were the only ones he had eyes for, other than me. Round after round, their mediocre harping and fluting continued. He tossed them silver heedlessly, requesting ancient songs and strange melodies that they only half knew. In spite of their poor playing, he seemed entranced, tapping his feet and swaying his head in time.

I wondered if he was one of the *fair* ones, with their exotic shaded skin and delicate, fine forms. They wandered into town very seldom, only once every few decades, and spoke with difficulty. He seemed to fit, and any moment, might carry off maidens or start stealing children, but seemed to have little interest in any of that sort of activity. The way he'd showered us with wealth was telling, though, and the heavy bright gold...that certainly fit.

The night wore on, and I certainly wasn't any closer to the answer. The musicians tired and other patrons left, and at last, when the inn's tavern was nearly empty, the stranger glanced at me again.

I knew that look, that longing, but when he headed to the stairs without a word, I was surprised. Eunid was asleep and the other servers were too tired or in bed with patrons, so there wasn't anyone to admonish me.

I wouldn't have taken pleasure in it normally, but as I tiptoed up the stairs after him, excitement thrilled though my body.

Matching my steps to the stranger's, I was forced to halt when he came to his room. It was surprisingly simple, not the grand chamber I'd expected him to take. He turned around, not at all surprised to see me, but I shrank back when I saw the look on his face.

"If you're here because you were told to serve me—"

"I was," I managed, my voice uncertain, "but...that's not why I'm here." I didn't let myself wilt under his scathing gaze. I was used to harsh looks—most men, and boys, in the village made fun of the handful of us who were different. Having my delicacy mocked, being called a girl, even being reviled, when they weren't sneaking to the inn to see myself and the other youth—that, I was accustomed to. These scorching, almost inhumane eyes, judging me as I stood before him—all 5'4 of my skinny, darkskinned frame—that was another matter.

At last, he softened, reassured by something. "You can come in. I...I'd like you to."

Warmth, and skin. The excitement in my body, hard and needful. I had done this before, and it was so different this time, as if it were the first time. Our legs, his hands around me, coaxing and gentle. Slickness, over and over. His mouth on mine. His sleek skin, the woodlike scent of him. I didn't even know his name, and I loved him already.

Afterwards, we lay curled together. His warm limbs were smooth and elegant as polished carvings. The only thing that disrupted his handsome, almost fine-grained skin, was the line of red tattoos down his back, and the ugly mark on his shoulder. It looked to be another tattoo, but something about the wrongness of its angles bothered me...

"I wouldn't look at that for too long, sweet," he said gently. "It's not made for the eyes of non-mages."

"Are you a mage, then?" The question popped out before I could ask. His face froze, and his brown eyes met mine with sadness.

"No, I'm not."

"Where are you from? I've never met anyone like you, ever..."

"The *fair* ones made me," he said, his back to me. His smooth skin, smelling of oak and maple, was faintly patterned with markings almost like knots in wood.

"Made you?"

"I started life as part of a sapling, parts of two saplings. They sung me into the shapes they needed as the seasons passed. I grew, and eventually, they cut my limbs away and united me. My strings, they sang from starlight and the whiskers of cats and silver; my pegs were shaped from stones once castles, now lying on the riverbed. I was a lyre."

I should have recoiled, perhaps, but I didn't, spellbound.

"They loved me and I sang with others to make music, my soul quiet and my body warm under my master's fingers. Until..." he shifted, and it was as though a shadow fell across us. "Until...her."

"Her?"

"The strega."

I shuddered. When crops went bad in a fine season, or the cows had strange offspring, or the ghost-lights danced high in the trees, or when a child went missing, they blamed the strega. The ordinary women, the healers and midwives who knew forest secrets, used their power and knowledge to help. A strega was a different matter, and since she'd come, countless years ago, the village had slowly grown smaller and darker. Even the lights of the few large trade caravans brave enough to cut through the forest had been barely enough to sustain us.

"Why are you recoiling, my love?" he said gently.

"I know of the strega. What...continue. Please."

He was still for a moment longer, and let out another wind-like breath. "My master was the last in his family, an old man even by the standards of the *fair*. His mind lost in a new sibling for me, for us, he wandered close to her cave." There was a long pause, and I wondered if he was finished speaking.

"He was not at his strongest, and she killed him. I won't tell you how, lest I trouble your dreams further. She took me, and branded me as her own, and tried to sing spells with me. When I refused, she turned me out and cursed me with this shape, leaving me to wander the world."

I clung to him, wanting to soothe his pain. He clasped my hand and sighed. The warmth between our bodies seemed to fill the cold room.

"How did you survive on your own?"

"It wasn't easy. I had to learn to speak, to feed myself, to make a living. I stole from people and lived on the edges, and managed to hitch a ride into the city when a caravan came through. I worked as best I could until I found the people I needed: the sorcerer's guild."

I drew in a breath, sharply. I felt faint, and foolish for it, but sorcerers were nothing to banter about.

"What happened then?"

He sighed. "I was used to...various kinds of work, you might say, including less savory occupations. I told their counsel what had happened to me, they branded me with their mark of protection, and as it happened, their Highest had a certain quarrel with this strega. And now, provided I can fulfill the conditions to break her curse, I'm coming back to look for her."

The depths of his eyes, as he turned to look at me, were filled with something that made me shrink away.

"I won't harm you," he said kindly, "but I do need your help, my love. Will you aid me?"

"I'll do it," I said. I wondered if there was a reward, and suppressed it. "But—if we...if we do...handle her...will she die?"

"Yes. Most likely."

"And you? Will you die?"

He was silent. "I've lived more than my span of years in this shape, but that, I don't know."

The pentacle and the tattoos that marred his spine seemed to glow faintly in the light of the gibbous moon. I kissed the nape of his neck.

"I hope you won't," I said, not daring to say more.

He said nothing again, in the strangely answering way. I nudged him.

"Get some sleep, love," he said finally. "We have a long day tomorrow. The moon is almost full."

Eunid was reluctant to let me go. A handful of gold from the seemingly limitless bag silenced him nicely.

Lyre took me to one of the only pawn shops in town and outfitted me with secondhand boots, already broken in, and a couple of large rucksacks. Strangely, he insisted on buying several handfuls of iron horseshoe nails as well as more self-explanatory supplies. Once we'd stopped by a bakery to get some provisions, he proclaimed us set.

Handing me a small knife, he led me to the edge of the town, into the forest. As the village faded behind us, swallowed by the trees, I was grateful that it was still technically daytime.

"Should I ask where we're going?"

Ahead of me, veering from the road onto a side trail, Lyre took his time answering. "We're getting some cold running water and vervain."

"Isn't it out of season? This is winter."

"It can always be found when in need. And then, we're going deep into the forest."

His manner brooked no questions. I followed him in silence.

It was cold, and got colder as the day wore on. We started to walk towards the hills, fractionally closer to the mountains. I didn't complain, but hearing Lyre murmur strange words as he scooped icy running water from a stream sent shivers down my spine. They had nothing to do with the cold.

It was stranger still to find the small clearing with summer herbs and flowers growing freely, not a bit of snow in sight. Smiling to himself, Lyre spoke a few choice syllables in the echoing language before carefully culling some of the vervain blossoms. As we stood there, I just outside of the clearing and Lyre fully in it, I thought I saw a few shadows dance at the corners of my vision.

When we were far from the clearing, back through paths that twisted and turned in ways that were impossible to trace, Lyre finally spoke to me.

"Whatever happens," Lyre said, putting his hands on my shoulders, "promise me you'll take the rest of the gold and go to the city. I've no shortage of it left, and I want better things for you."

"You're coming with me, right?"

From the outside, Lyre wasn't much older than myself, but at that moment, the weight of ages seemed to rest in his eyes. "I want to. Let's focus on the task at hand."

"I don't really understand what we're doing."

His face hardened. "We're looking for the witch. We've got what we need to stop her from using her power on other people and on your village. That's all you need to know. Well, perhaps not." He pulled a small blade from his belt. "I hope you know how to use this."

I eyed his bow and nodded slowly. "Will you be using that?"

"No. Only innocent beasts deserve a quick death from the arrow. I'm a good shot. This strega won't be seeing a quick death."

Birds called in our silence.

"I can see you don't like it, but it has to be done," said Lyre. "If you want your village to be safe..."

I nodded, unwilling to voice my doubts. "We'd best keep moving," I said. He left it at that.

Hours seemed to pass. I could feel the sun slipping lower, the cold intensifying. The trees were firm and upright, pines and deciduous that mixed bare limbs with bristling bows. The birds still left in the season called and cackled a few times, but we saw no other beasts. There seemed to be more ravens around us, though, as the night came closer.

Lyre swore under his breath when he saw the ravens. "We might be too late. Still, we're near the caverns." He looked me earnestly in the eyes.

"Whatever happens, I love you. Know that. I need someone pure to break this curse for me. Then I'll finally be free."

I swallowed my embarrassment. "I'm not...I'm not pure..."

His intense brown eyes silenced me. "It's your soul that counts." He kissed my forehead gently, and embraced me. "I'm sorry for what's about to happen. I need you to listen to me precisely. I told you about the salt. You've got the gold in your pack, and the rest of the food. If you follow the footsteps we left and hold an iron nail in your left hand, you'll find your way back to town safe and sound. Do you trust me?"

"Y—yes."

He smiled grimly, sadly. "Then off to the cavern we go."

It was the longest walk of my life. Night grew thicker above us and the voices of ravens, louder and shriller. Larger and larger birds, thicker trees, surrounded us. There was no hint of the *fair* ones. Fickle they might be, and possessive, but even their grey nature was too light for this part of the forest.

The cavern was at the foot of the mountains, when we finally came to it. There was no mistaking it; an aura of raw power hung around its entrance. It looked unstable, built of stones heaped together, but Lyre looked satisfied.

"Her power is at its lowest on a full moon and she's not as strong as she was two hundred years ago. Good."

My eyes widened as I looked at him, and wondered how long he'd been waiting.

"The full moon is good because only white witches can use it," he said brusquely. "Come on. The strega awaits."

He walked into the cavern's darkness, and I could only follow him.

The cave was filthy and smelled of death. Bones lay in corners, and not all of them were from animals. I held back my fear, trusting Lyre. If anyone could get us out of this, it would be him. Still, I kept the light at the entrance well within sight. A few torches guided our way, but it was obviously not a place for visitors.

I don't know what I was expecting when I saw the strega. Pale, hairy limbs, large moonlit eyes, flowing, stringy white hair, and a mouth full of wolf teeth were not it. She opened her mouth to speak, and suddenly, Lyre was on her.

He tackled her before she could even move, pinning her slim body down with his determined weight. He clamped a leather-braced arm across her mouth as her skinny old limbs flailed, and put his weight on her. I heard a bone crack as he shifted, and through his arm, she screamed.

"Make a salt circle around us!" Lyre snapped. Without hesitation, I took the white rock salt he'd given me and made a good wide circle, unbroken, around the two of them. The strega's eyes followed me as I made my circle, and Lyre wrestled her. She screamed and he clamped his arm tighter over her mouth. He winced and I could tell she was biting.

"Don't stop!"

"There, there! It's done! Now what?"

"Put a nail through her feet!" He yelled at me.

I took a nail out with shaking hands. "How?"

"Grab a limb and stick it though! Like hot butter! You'll see!"

Never squeamish, I recoiled as I took one of her thrashing feet and pinned it down. Her skin was cold and slimy, like nothing human. I doubted I could get a grip with anything, let alone the nail. Finally, I managed to fight her leg down—she was shockingly strong for an old woman. Fumbling, I took out the nail and pressed it into her skin. Sure enough, as the iron brushed her skin, it sunk easily, smoothly. I felt it part flesh, muscle, bone, with no resistance. She screamed through his arm, but I pressed it into the ground, and it stayed put.

The next foot was easier, as the first wasn't thrashing, just stuck to the dirt floor of the cave. Her screaming, even though it was muffled, was horrible.

She clawed at Lyre, but his wild eyes were encouraging. He ignored the rasp of her nails, her fighting.

"First the left, then the right hand! Opposite order from the one you did the feet in!"

Taking her skinny old hand and driving the nail through, feeling it rip easily and surge through the slimy dry skin, was horrible. Her blood was black and smelled foul, and her screaming, unearthly, even through Lyre's restraints.

Finally, my stomach roiling and the stench of her blood and the grave heavy in the air, it was done. All four of her limbs were fastened to the floor.

"Take the vervain out of my bag," said Lyre, not taking his eyes from her. "And the water."

I took the glass bottle from the bag and set it to the side. The strega's eyes followed my motions frantically. I felt sick, but turned my eyes back to Lyre.

"Give me a handful of the vervain and be ready to pour the water on her."

He managed to free a hand and I saw that his arm was dripping something golden-orange. Not blood, but sap. Chills ran through me. He'd been telling the truth, that much was certain. Quick as the deuce, he took the vervain from me and used his other arm to prise her mouth open, just enough. Taking the handful of vervain, he stuffed it in her mouth and clamped her lips shut.

Putting all of his weight on one arm, he fumbled in his pocket, withdrawing a needle strung with something like spiderweb and sunlight and silver.

I had been steadfast, but I had to turn away as he sewed the witch's lips shut. Still, the sound of the needle piercing flesh, the drag of the stitches, seemed to echo in the cave. I could almost feel the needle through my own lips, piercing the soft flesh, drawing blood from the tender surfaces—

"Stop!" I cried.

He looked at me as though I was mad. "She'll kill us if she—"

"But it's horrible! Inhumane!"

He gritted his teeth. "We don't have time for a question of ethics. Give me the water." With a shaking hand, I offered the open bottle.

Beneath his breath, almost beneath the layers of the world, Lyre began to mumble syllables again. I couldn't make them out but I felt their vibration. He let up the weight on her face as he picked up the bottle, preparing to pour it over her face.

The momentary distraction was all she needed. Turning her head forcefully to the side, the strega spat out the vervain. Her black blood splattered the ground.

The witch, free, screamed a horrible syllable. I thought my ears would bleed as it cut the air. Hands clapped to my ears, it was a moment before I realised that there was a person less in the cavern.

Only a lyre sat where Lyre had been.

The strega looked at me and laughed. "Just when he was starting to like being human," she said, her voice bitter. "What did he know about loneliness?" She ripped a hand from the earth, leaving skin and blood behind. Whatever had been binding her was loosening by the moment.

"He knew a lot!" I shot back at her. "Oh, Lyre, tell me you're still there—"

"It's too late," she snapped, eyes glowing wolflike in the dark. "And now you're here, and I have a fresh heart to eat and bones to work with." Her black blood dripped dark from her lips. "He shouldn't have let his guard down. I'm near death, but with your heart to eat..."

I didn't listen to the rest. Her mocking laughter followed me as I left the circle, dragging Lyre through it with me. I did the only thing I could, and ran for the entrance.

Lyre was heavy, but the light was so close. Just a little farther. The witch screamed something, a last terrible, cutting word, and the world fell apart.

There was a horrible sound, as if the very earth were being sundered in two. There was a hideous screeching of rock, and the cave fell in. I could hear the twanging of catgut, metal, and wood breaking; I clutched Lyre in my arms as tightly as I could, curling around the wooden frame to hide from the falling stone.

There was a horrible silence, and the full moon glowed overhead—the cave had collapsed. A pale hand in the wreckage, wrinkled, bleeding black, and feminine, turned to dust as I watched.

But I had survived. I feared the worst when I rolled onto one bruised side, looking for Lyre. The wooden frame with a notch on one side was nowhere to be seen. Lying next to me, dazed but breathing well, was Lyre himself. It was night, but there he was, human. He kissed me, and I could taste the dust on his lips. Tears ran down my face, into my mouth. Then, he was gone. All I heard was a soft sound in the air, a hum of plucked chords in the still, cold night.

THE ROADHOUSE

She never told the story at any time other than Halloween. It was the only time people were drunk enough to believe it and when she was drunk enough to talk about it without getting the shivers. Not too much to drink, though, or she would start to taste blood in the back of her throat again. She'd clear it and begin, putting on the smile that always scared people.

"It started because of a boy," she'd say, "and it went downhill from there."

That night, Kenna was procrastinating homework, she was drunk, and she was bored.

"I'm bored," said Lindsay. "I say we ditch the Studio and hit The Roadhouse for some actual fun." *Screw The Roadhouse*, Kenna thought.

And still, the alternative, her current location, wasn't an improvement. She wrapped her fingers around the shot glass, steadying herself, and squeezed it hard enough to break. Lindsay was laughing, forcedly, and that meant after a few more drinks she'd loosen up and start laughing too much altogether. Then there would probably be a stupid story later involving body parts stuck in awkward places. That said, it was really the only thing to do in this town on a Thursday night, and likely to bear fruit on Facebook, so who was complaining?

She wondered for the hundredth time why she'd come there, to that hole in the wall. Studio was a decent bar if your idea of a good time involved people desperate to get laid rather than people who wanted to dance. Dancing there was a way to pass the time until someone asked you to come back to their place, or you struck out and went home, or you decided to drink yourself into a coma, for whatever reason. The music was too loud and it was ugly, and her ears hurt. The shadows cast by the garish lights were long and too sharp. The world twisted darkly in her drunken eyes. The only way to make it stop, before she got the creeps, was drink more or find something else to distract her.

She considered Garden. Cougar-city, lots of older women, she wouldn't fit in there. Besides, the coke dealers had started to hang out there. Since Silk had closed, there wasn't really a classy bar in town. Made sense, for a nowhere university town like this. All people needed was somewhere to drink, not a quality club. She missed Calgary for a moment.

"Kenna! Get over here!" Lindsay hollered.

For tonight's pub crawl to be successful, they would have to stop by Sal's, the location of choice for drunk girls looking to relax. The Roadhouse would only deepen the debauchery, and Kenna would get the creeps, and wake up with a hangover and vague memories of nightmares. Enough was enough. She dropped the shot glass and marched over to Lindsay.

"I don't want to go to the Roadhouse. Last time we went there my pant bottoms were soaked with red shit and I think it was blood."

"You're right," said Lindsay. "We should hit it, cab home and keep drinking there."

I don't want to, Kenna thought, *and that's the end and beginning of it. I would rather be at home reading a horror story or something. Get the shivers out of my system the easy way before they get to me.*

"Roadhouse it is, then," Lindsay said. "C'mon!"

"Wait, what? I thought we were going home!" But Lindsay was already at the door, and heading for one of the cabs parked outside; there was nothing to do but follow her.

The streetlights were blurry; it was a misty fall night, and students were out and about laughing too loud and drinking. Yet the streets were oddly silent, as they drove the short distance to the Roadhouse.

"Kinda cold tonight, huh?" Kenna said, too loudly. The cabbie didn't answer. His black hoodie offered no glimpse of his hair or face, so she couldn't even flirt, really. The weird sensation creeping along her spine lingered. Lindsay started telling a joke and forgot the punchline, mangling it; Kenna laughed anyway. It was hard to be in a bad mood on a night like this.

They stumbled out of the cab, shoving money at him, and he slipped off, his dark car disappearing in the night. Lindsay howled.

"Let's goooooooo!"

Inside, the usual crush of dirty old men and hot young things filled the bar, but there were plenty of university students too, looking to dance and have a trashy kind of good time. They weren't there for long before Lindsay's excellent dancing got them some attention—and free drinks. A childhood of ballet and jazz dance and a love for movement had gotten her into Kinesiology, and also into a lot more free nights at the bar than her parents had expected. Kenna kept up well enough, a pretty good partner even when tipsy, and they got their share of approving whistles as they staggered over to the bar.

A leggy waitress brought over a tray with two shot glasses of molten gold. "From the man in white," she said. She drifted off into the club, and Lindsay sighed with satisfaction.

"Well?" said Lindsay. "Are you going to stand and stare, or are you gonna make me drink on my own?"

Kenna nodded and took the glass, tongue still numb. She realized she hadn't said a word and hated herself a little more.

The world shifted a little as she tossed the burning ounce of gold down her throat. She had no idea what she'd just swallowed, other than that it was the same thing Kenna was gulping down.

It hit her head like sunlight suddenly shining on a mirror, bright and burning, and it felt good.

"What the hell is that?" Kenna gasped. "It's fuckin' strong."

Lindsay burst out laughing, and Kenna did, too. It seemed terribly funny, for some reason. "No idea," Lindsay said. "I got it from him, though."

Suddenly he was there, and he had always been there. A tall, handsome boy, twenty-four at most, with auburn hair, a golden tan, and tilted eyes that shifted between green and gold and blue in the club light. He wasn't wearing any jewelry, just a white suit jacket and pants, open over a white t-shirt. It should have been too much, but it wasn't; he looked fabulous, sharp and sexy. The perfect tailoring and cut of his clothes showed off a body that was getting its share of love from a gym. He was delicious, shining like the only clean thing in the club. Maybe it was the shot she'd just had, but Kenna would have sworn on a stack of bibles that he was glowing, just a little.

And, strangest of all, he was looking right at her.

"I'm Will," he said.

"Kenna," she managed to rasp.

"Are you going to dance with me, or do I have to walk up to you again?" he said. Kenna dumbly nodded, and he guided her from the bar to the dance floor.

He was a good dancer, Kenna had to admit. The best she'd ever met, probably. He moved effortlessly, and even when she'd started to sweat, he was still dry as a desert, looking around in dire boredom. Lindsay was shaking it with everything she had, and laughing, sweating, running off to the bar to get them all more drinks.

"I should show you where the real party is," he said. Lindsay came, laughing, and pushed shots into their hands.

Will tossed his shot back and waited for the girls to finish theirs. "There's no good clubs in this town, though," Kenna complained. "And I'm not going to someone's house. No way."

"You don't have to. It's right here," he said, grinning ferally, "in the Roadhouse."

"Yeah right," Lindsay giggled, "we're already here."

"Not yet," said Will. "Follow me. There's a lot more fun to be had."

He started to drift off, going at a brisk pace, and there was nothing to do but follow him.

"Where are we going?"

"We're going to see the Queen of the dance floor and her court." He grinned. "You'll have fun."

"Free drinks?" Lindsay asked.

"As many as you can swallow."

"All right!" Lindsay pumped a fist in the air.

"I just want water," Kenna admitted. Will made a shrug of distaste.

"There's better stuff to drink. The Queen hates water. But whatever, if you can think of it, we have it there." The dark smile was back, and enchanted, she followed him.

Kenna thought there was nothing past the dim exit signs, normally leading to the alley, but Will took her on a twisting, turning journey that left her hopelessly disoriented. Lindsay stumbled along after her, laughing and trying to ask Will more questions about whether he had any friends. He smiled but answered vaguely, when he answered at all.

She hadn't realized The Roadhouse had a secondary area, nor, that it had a backroom as large as this. She had a vague sense of having gone downstairs, except that there were no stairs, which made no sense at all. It had to be the extra shots she'd taken. Better not to trust something someone just handed you anyway, even if it had been Lindsay. *Stupid, stupid,* Kenna cursed herself. *Stupid shit. Now I might have a load of roofies on board or something worse, some other date rape shit.*

"I'll make sure you don't fall," Will said. And he did.

It took a long time, it seemed, to get to the place lit only by a red exit sign. A heavy, muscular man wearing black jeans and a t-shirt was waiting for them. The gleaming light showed many tattoos and a hard grin.

"Willy boy. Whatcha got for the Queen tonight? Or are they just tagalongs?"

"They're with me," said Will, poised on one foot. Kenna stared and admired the way the shadows slid over his trimly muscled form, the way he seemed to shine, to glow, in the darkness.

"I wouldn't presume otherwise," the bouncer said. Kenna hazily wondered at his lilting accent.

"'R'you Irish?" slurred Lindsay. The bouncer laughed, a dark, rich sound that rumbled out of a deep, whiskey-rich throat. His red tongue and sharp, lovely white teeth gleamed with reflected red neon from the EXIT sign above them.

"Everyone asks," he said. "Go ahead, Willy boy." Will grinned, radiant, and Kenna's knees went wobbly.

The world was tipping sideways already and his smile, directed with searchlight intensity at her, made it even more so.

"I'm not waiting up," Will said, and leapt past the bouncer. The crack in the door was narrow, but he must have been more agile still than he looked.

"Are you going to stare after his ass or go chase it in there?" the bouncer asked. Lindsay laughed, shrieking raucously, and Kenna's flushed face reddened even more.

"The private party," said the bouncer, grinning, "is this way. Come on." And he opened the door wide. Blackness yawned, welcoming her in, a lazy crocodile's mouth ready to swallow. Lindsay tried to push past him, but suddenly, he stepped in her way.

"Are you coming willingly?" he asked. A hot club beat simmered and pounded through the wall, but he was perfectly audible.

"Yes," slurred Lindsay. "Now lemme in!"

"There's rules. You have to come in of your own will," said the bouncer.

"Whatevs. Let us in!" Lindsay insisted. He shook his head. To Kenna, something darkened about him, as he gave Lindsay more than the usual bouncer's glare.

"Yeah, yeah, I'm willing and ready," said Lindsay, giggling and running a hand over his chest. "Will I see you in there?"

"And you?" the bouncer asked Kenna, fixing her with black-brown eyes. Lindsay coiled herself close to him.

"Yes," Kenna answered, her tongue leaden.

"Then go on in," he said, breaking into another smile. He reached down to cup Lindsay's ass, and squeezed; she shrieked with laughter again and kissed him. The bouncer pushed her through the door, grinning, and she tumbled away into the darkness.

"Better catch Will before he fades away on the dance floor," he said, Kenna nodded tipsily and threaded her way past him, trying to follow Lindsay.

She had a vague sense of going down stairs once again as she found herself on the floor. Just ahead of her was Lindsay, giggling still; as the door slammed shut behind them, Lindsay stopped giggling.

It was completely unlike anything Kenna had ever seen, and she wondered whether there wasn't something stronger in the drink. It was shiny and glossy and gorgeous, luxuriously bathed in strobing lights, cool white LEDs shining around tables in the dark. There was glass and steel and cool dark wood on the bar and on the dance floor, and around the edges of the room, booths and seats.

The dance floor itself was beyond the pale. People in every type of dress were shaking, slamming, and grooving to a strange and hungry beat, writhing in perfect tempo to both lights and music.

"I don't know who the DJ is," Lindsay screamed into her ear, "but I want to make sweet love to him for this beat."

Kenna had never seen anything like it, and in later years, even the nicest parties were pale imitations of what she saw that night. Will darted around from her peripheral vision.

"Welcome," he whispered, beautiful lips brushing her earlobe, "to The Court."

"Is this place always like this?" Kenna rasped. Will laughed.

"Yes, but we only take the space up here once in a while. You are a very lucky lady because you got here tonight."

"Yes, I am," Kenna murmured. People with long-limbed bodies, strangely and beautifully proportioned, tangled on the dance floor. Silk fluttered or clung to sweating, opalescent skin. She looked closer. She was sure she saw a few people with horns, some with tails, amongst the couples.

"Didn't know it was a costume night," she slurred into Will's ear, and he only laughed.

"Let's hit the floor, babe."

Dancing with Will was like dancing with fog, or a spotlight. Just as he slid away from her, he was all over her again, his hands hovering over her or smoothly outlining her curves, then caressing her again; he grooved and twisted around her to the beat. And, in spite of drinking so much, Kenna was dancing pretty well herself. She found Will's hands sliding under her shirt, under the halter and under her bra, but as soon as he'd lightly brushed a nipple, or slipped a hand down below the band of her skirt to brush a buttock, he was dancing away again, touching her waist gently to keep her the right distance away. Kenna moaned out loud with frustration and desire, and his laugh, a pretty-boy's ringing bell chime of laughter, answered her.

Lindsay, meanwhile, popping and flexing lithely beside her, slipped around Will's back and slowly shook her hips to the rhythm. The DJ had settled on something with a strange mix of flute, violin, and guitar as well as synth, but it was as perfect as it was strange. Lindsay and Kenna sandwiched Will between them, and he tilted his head back in pleasure.

"Mine," shouted Kenna.

Lindsay laughed. "I'm just helping you keep him from running too far off."

Will swept an arm around each of them, and they danced in a triad. The blood and liquor and music had gone to Kenna's head, and she danced as she never had, sweat trickling down her back, and Will encouraged her. His strange glow was even more brilliant here, bizarrely spiritual. He wasn't alone, though; other, beautiful young men and women with the same luminescence danced with others, as graceful and full of abandon as Will.

He signaled someone else in the crowd, which they'd drifted into the centre of, and a man slid out from nowhere. He had horns and a gorgeous silk shirt, open to the waist to reveal a washboard body covered in swirling tattoos. He seized Lindsay around the waist and began dancing with her, moving like a matador—darting, footwork as delicate as a tango, seeming to wrap himself around her like smoke around a light. Lindsay pulled him close and whispered something in his ear (sound was working strangely, Kenna thought; whispers could be easily heard even though the music was pounding in her chest) and they were gone. Suddenly, she had another partner, a handsome man with dark clothes and the lower part of his face covered by a scarf; and as he danced with her, Will disappeared in the crowd.

Kenna looked around. Everyone else was dancing with the same ferocious hunger and intensity. Strangely, she didn't feel outclassed; she intuited that these were people so far above distinctions that she could've walked in naked, or in rags, and it wouldn't have mattered. In fact, some people seemed to be naked, and others, in rags, but they were so beautiful it didn't matter. A few couples in booths or leaning against the wall made her stare, and whip her head around to stare some more.

In spite of the open, spicy air of the entertainments, a translucent screened area towards the back provided privacy. *And, oh,* Kenna thought, *if they'll do all that out here, I wonder what they're doing behind that screen.* The multiple panels were painted or silkscreened with a single large pattern: a black and white photograph of beautiful young men and women twisted in a concentric circle around a gorgeous woman. Like a dark Madonna, adoring lovers twined around her, bodies twisting together and their hands gently outlining, grasping her flesh. Kenna felt hunger course through her own body, looking at the woman, a shadow-skinned and succulent godsdess whose dark gaze seemed to meet hers.

From behind the translucent screen, she could see silhouettes tangling, the shape of a canopied couch. Kenna strained, and stared, her mouth open wide. Whatever was behind those screens, she wanted to see it, up close and personal.

"Hey," said Will, appearing from nowhere, "I see you have your eyes on the prize already. Want a drink?" He offered her something golden, not unlike the shot she'd had before, in the Roadhouse main building. Kenna shook her head.

"The prize?" Her horned, tattooed partner bowed silently and melted into the crowd again. Without noticing, she'd slumped into a booth with him, all scarlet velvet and rich leather cushions. "No, I'm still good. Maybe water."

He shrugged. "Suit yourself." With a single fluid motion, he tossed it down his throat. Impulsively she leaned across the table and licked his sweaty neck, and Will laughed.

"Thirsty after all? There's still one more for you."

"Nah, thanks."

He gulped the second down. He shuddered and tossed his mane; the ringlets were damp with sweat, and shone red and blue and green with the lights.

"So, what's the prize? I was staring at the screens. Nice pattern."

"You got it. The prize. Only the Queen's favorites are allowed to get behind The Screen." She could hear the strange capitals and Kenna felt a chill.

"I'll keep you safe, don't shiver," Will said.

"I wonder where Lindsay went," she whispered.

"Right here!" chimed Lindsay, another beautiful, glowing boy standing next to her. "Hakim says the Queen wants us." A couple next to Kenna and Will were sitting on the same side of their table, one booth over; from what Kenna could see, they were two wearing fairy wings and getting very tangled. They weren't wearing anything other than the wings, but Kenna didn't have time to stare.

Will did something that broke through Kenna's festive mood; he went pale and his face twisted in a snarl. "Very well," he said, after a moment. "Come on, girls."

"But I've only just sat down, and I'm really tired," Kenna protested. The other shining boy shook his head. Like Will, he was also clad completely in white.

"You don't turn down The Queen. C'mon." Kenna groaned to her feet, which were suddenly very, very sore.

They parted the frenetic richness of the crowd easily; like a red sea, the strange and lovely creatures cleared a path towards the screened area.

Will was suddenly silent and grim, but Hakim was blithe, joking with an enchanted Lindsay and sneaking caresses over her body. Then, they were there, in front of the screens. Hakim led them around the side, where a glorious red velvet curtain hung softly down, a part in the centre of the two rich falls of fabric.

A young woman, with long, slanted eyes—not Asian, not Nordic, but something in between—pulled the opening wide so the quartet could enter. Following a silent Will and a buoyant Hakim, Lindsay and Kenna crept in.

THE LOVED, THE LOST, THE DREAMING

The screen was apparently the outer wall of a small room. The ceiling, the carpet, and the walls were covered in the same glorious dark scarlet velvet, and rather than being tacky, the effect was luxuriant, royal. As Kenna said later, she wondered if Versailles looked like that inside the bedrooms.

All of the furniture—a small spindly table, a number of chairs, a gorgeous dressing table and mirror, and a small wet bar in the corner—was made of something glossy and white, the colour of ivory. The room was, once again, larger than it should have been, at least fifteen feet by twelve, far more than the conservative area covered by the admittedly expansive screen.

Standing around with white pitchers shaped like skulls, and holding things like jewelry boxes or chocolates, were a number of beautiful girls and boys. None were more than twenty-five and all were wearing more revealing versions of the white garments Will and Hakim had on. They were engaged in conversation or waiting to be told what to do; some were sitting on bohemian scarlet velvet and silk cushion piles in the corner of the room. One was behind the bar and serving others; they giggled coyly and curled around the elegant white barstools, drinking something golden from the skull pitchers.

On the piles of cushions—sofas set onto the floor, Kenna decided, from the shapes underneath the pillows—a couple and a triad or two were slowly, luxuriously, making love, putting on a show of it. Sometimes one of the attendants would set things down, and join in for a few moments. A participant would rise in their place; just who were the servants and who were the masters was very unclear. From the looks of it, they were all here to wait on someone else's pleasure.

The décor was carved and Gothic in its richness. A white-panelled fireplace in one corner kept the room warm, steaming hot, in fact. Kenna looked at the carvings on the panels and looked away again; most of them looked like engravings from the Kama Sutra, and the others were...darker in theme. She blinked and looked away. Lindsay, too drunk and giddy to stare, unselfconsciously began to trade caresses with Hakim once again. Kenna, beginning to sober up, was awestruck by the flagrant luxury of it, and let her eyes travel. Already dehydrated, the extra warmth was making her dizzy.

In the centre of the room was an enormous swing-couch, long and wide, in the same rich red and creamy white scheme as elsewhere. On the bed, alone, was the woman from the printing of the screen outside, a hundred times lovelier than in her portrait, and wearing red leather instead of being bare-skinned. Her black hair tumbled luxuriantly over the pillows and she rested in a half-seated position on top of the covers, a dome-covered white tray and elegant utensils next to her. She was Eve, she was desire incarnate, and fire and ice danced in the pupils of her dark eyes.

Hakim detached himself from Lindsay and drew them up in stately approach.

"Pardon me for interrupting the end of your dinner, Milady." She waved a long, pale, languid hand at him.

"Not at all, Hakim. What are these beautiful delicacies you've brought me?"

Lindsay giggled shrilly. Both girls were petite, with pale colouring and delicate bones, and not without delectable curves, but other than that, Kenna wouldn't have referred to herself or Lindsay as a 'beautiful delicacy'.

"The merry one is Lindsay," Hakim presented her, "and the quiet one is Kenna." Will, who through all of this was wearing a sour expression, stood behind Kenna.

The Queen looked at him and pouted. Even that made Kenna's heart ache. She would have done anything, just then, to see that adorable moue of displeasure melt into a smile. Lindsay was less restrained; she fell to her knees and began begging to do anything to make The Queen smile.

A faint, feline curve crept to The Queen's lips. "Very well. You may kiss my ankle, but just once." Lindsay, delirious with happiness, bent and delicately pressed her lips to the pale white curve, exquisite and shapely as a statue's. The white servants in the room paused in their entertainments to watch the foursome on the right side of the Queen's bed, and the Queen's reaction to the great privilege of the kiss. She shuddered faintly but turned abruptly towards the wet bar.

"Daniel, a drink for our guests." Unaffected, the handsome young bartender brought a skull pitcher and a tray full of delicate opaque white glasses and a goblet forward. He poured expertly and handed one to each of them, and last of all, a goblet of the golden stuff for The Queen.

Now that she could see the pitcher closer, it resembled a human skull, with carved lip and handle from the crown of the pate, and silver metal filling the eye sockets and other gaps. She held her cool, smooth shot glass, but didn't sip the liquid inside. Though golden in colour, and almost metallic, she noticed a faint smell of something coppery, and couldn't place it. Was it in the air, or in the drink, or both? Probably nothing, though.

"I hope you'll excuse me if I finish the last of my meal," the Queen said. Will stiffly nodded.

"Of course, My Lady." There was an unbecoming tang of sarcasm in his voice.

Kenna suddenly noticed how quiet it was inside the room. The throb of the club music still penetrated, but it was oddly civilized as much as insistent. Reduced and muffled—perhaps because of all the velvet and some sort of high-tech insulation in the walls—it had the same beat as a heart, with only a thin melody overlaying it. In the quiet, Will's attitude was a sharp and sour note.

The Queen frowned at him, and Kenna wanted to weep; Lindsay was, but Hakim held her upright. The Queen smiled and Lindsay calmed immediately.

"Don't mind me having a bite, my darling. I'm happy as long as I have my meat. There are certain hungers that can't be easily denied." The Queen smiled and moved the tray into her lap, setting the white dome upside-down on the cover beside her. There was a single bite of steak remaining on the white plate, which was paneled and carved like the rest of the room.

Kenna was entirely unsurprised, then, when the woman started to pick her teeth daintily with something that looked a lot like a sliver of bone, sharpened at one end and polished to show off the joint at the other end. It matched the décor.

"Do have a sip of your drinks," the Queen cooed. "I'll be terribly offended if you don't."

Will had moved around to Kenna's side, very smoothly, and positioned himself between her and Lindsay. The alcohol was still heavy in Kenna's head, but a bit of clarity was returning; enough that she could tell Will was tense, anyway, and very tense at that. An alarm in the far corner of her mind began to ring.

"I'd be happy to, but I need a glass of water, first," Kenna said. "To cleanse my palate."

The Queen frowned slightly. "Of course. Daniel?"

Quickly, silently, the bartender brought her a goblet of water. The Queen handed it to Kenna as quickly as possible, almost distastefully. She forced a smile back to her lips, and Kenna noticed her long eyeteeth, glittering white in the soft glow of the room. "Now, where were we?"

Lindsay giggled and leaned against Hakim. The Queen turned a charming smile on her. "Having a good time, my dears?"

"The best," Lindsay answered, between titters. "This is the best party I've been to, ever." With one arm around her waist, Hakim sipped from his white shotglass.

"Mmmmm. You haven't had fun until you've tried this," he said to Lindsay, and pressed the white cup against her lower lip. She wriggled in his grasp to kiss him, turning away from the cup. Will fidgeted. The Queen looked on, smiling, and let out a soft sigh of contentment as activity in the room began to resume.

"One of my favorite songs," she said to Kenna, stretching langorously. "I hope you like it." It was a command rather than the obligatory polite remark of a hostess, and Kenna, cowed, smiled and nodded. It was lovely—it had been nice when she'd walked into the room. And yet—Kenna could hear a strain in the music, something she hadn't caught before; it made her faintly sick. Dizzy and with stomach churning, she was more aware of things, and the steely plucking of the guitar in the Queen's room and sharp, hard pitch of the flute couldn't completely cover the throb of the dance beat outside the room. It had been almost impossible to hear before, in spite of the loudness of the music, but it was leaking back in through the walls. The two sounds clashed in an ugly way, the hair on the back of her neck rising with shivers.

"I wish this wouldn't end," Lindsay sighed, behind her. "Don't wanna go back to class tomorrow." The Queen patted the bed, and Lindsay tumbled onto the opposite end of it, giggling. "So sorry, m'Lady," she said, trying to fight off Hakim's hands. "S'his fault."

"Quite all right. I like to make sure my guests have a good time," the Queen said. Kenna sipped her water, feeling more sick and alert by the moment. The coppery, metallic smell was really very strong. Absently, she stroked the velvet coverlet and was surprised.

"Suede? Very nice," she commented. "It's really soft, your Highness."

The Queen smiled again, movie-starlet luscious. Her plump red lips formed a flirtatious moue of modesty. "I admit I have luxurious tastes. Suede and leather are the only things I like—pillows, coverlets, clothes, lingerie..." she winked at Kenna, unperturbed by the giggling and heavy petting on the other side of the couch. It rocked slightly, and Kenna noticed that the chains holding it in place were made of silver.

Silver. Suede. The smell of something metallic and bitter. It was all very strange, and suddenly, as darling as she was, the Queen was beginning to seem—disquieting. Strange in a way she couldn't name. "It really is an amazing private salon you have," Kenna said, and cleared her throat, "but I really should get Lindsay home, or she's going to be so sick tomorrow you wouldn't believe it."

"Oh, but I can make sure she's fine," the Queen said. With an elegant twist of her body, showcasing curves to make Botticelli weep, she leaned closer to

Lindsay. "You'll be all right, won't you, dear?" The pointed, lovely little canines seemed sharper than ever, as she spoke.

"If you don't mind, we really have to be going," Kenna said, more firmly. "But it's been an amazing night, and I've never seen a club like this. I'm sure we'll be back." There were faint murmurs of dismay in the room, and one of the musicians hesitated for half a moment. The music became a little louder, and yet, more soothing. Kenna felt some of her anxiety slip away. Surely there was nothing to worry about, it was just a long day getting to her, and worrying, stupidly, about Lindsay...

With a sinuous single movement, a strange unfolding, the Queen was on her feet. She clasped Kenna's waist, embracing her. The heavy perfume she wore mixed with her meaty breath, a repellent and strangely attractive combination. "If you like," she murmured, "I can make sure you don't have to worry about getting into my part of the club again. You don't have to leave now, not at all."

Kenna held her goblet of water carefully away as the Queen coiled around her, but stealthily brought it closer as the woman's hands tightened around her waist.

"I have papers to do, though," Kenna murmured. Her eyes were on the Queen, on the fire and ice dancing in her pupils. She didn't care about Lindsay, skirt raised, Hakim's head between her legs; she didn't care about the leisurely threesome or the dancing, just feet away from where she stood. She didn't care about Will, who was stealthily poking the middle of her back, annoyingly so. There was only the Queen.

"Would you really mind never having to write another paper?" she purred. "Never having to worry about a grade again? It's all so pointless, you know. You're not even studying something befitting your talents." She stroked Kenna's face. "I can always tell." Kenna nodded dumbly. The alarm in a corner of her mind was screeching furiously, but she barely noticed.

"Don't you wish," crooned the Queen, "that you didn't have to deal with any of it, ever again?"

Slowly, slowly, Kenna nodded.

The Queen glanced pointedly at the tray of golden liquid-filled cups. Someone had taken the precious glasses from Lindsay and Kenna's hands without their notice, setting them back on the serving tray so the drinks wouldn't spill.

"I wish," Lindsay was sighing, "you could do this forever, Hakim." She moaned, deep in her throat, and Kenna winced, suddenly aware that she was watching her friend get head without a scrap of privacy.

"I'm sure you wish for the same thing sometimes, Kenna," the Queen murmured. "Don't you, you poor, tired thing? A pretty girl like you shouldn't have to work so hard. You'll lose your looks if you keep up a stressful pace, like you do." Unwitting, Kenna touched her face. Zits were bad enough. How long would it be, really, before wrinkles? Her older sister had a few fine lines and she was twenty-five, for Gods's sakes. How long did she have?

"You should be forever young, and carefree," she was whispering. Her cheek brushed Kenna's as she drew her arms tighter around the girl. The cold silky skin on her face was perfect, not a blemish in sight.

"I should," Kenna rasped, entranced. She closed her eyes for a moment in bliss. Immediately there was a sharp, painful poke to her spine.

"I can do that for you, Kenna. I can make it all go away, and you and Lindsay can take it easy."

"Yeah, but for how long?" Kenna chuckled bitterly. "That's why we go out, but every night has to end."

The Queen's luminous eyes held her, drew her in again. "Not tonight. I can make it last forever."

"Forever?"

"Forever." Kenna half-closed her eyes in bliss, imagining it: dancing all night, as long as she wanted. The sex—no complications, here, just people playfully pairing up whenever they liked. A party that wouldn't end in just a few hours, that wouldn't leave her regretting it the next day as she returned to something boring.

"Forever. All I need is your body." The Queen's eyes fixed on her, and Kenna's lids snapped up. No more dreaming.

"I'm not really much for girls, but sure, I'll try anything once." Kenna glanced at Lindsay. "She might have to move, though."

The Queen laughed, piercingly. "No, no, darling. I need your body. I can make your spirit a shape, and your own gorgeous white evening gown, but I need your *flesh* to keep myself, and all of this" (she moved a long-nailed, slender hand around airily) "going."

It took her a moment to understand what the Queen meant by the word *flesh*, and even then, she still didn't. There was a long pause. "I like your velvet couch," said Kenna dumbly.

The Queen smiled. "Suede, actually. Girl-skin suede. It's softer."

Kenna pushed her away in shock. The steak. The bone-white knuckle toothpick. The white carvings and red suede and leather: bone furniture, skin dyed with blood. The flesh...

Defend yourself, her instincts screamed. *She can't bear anything but liquor,* Will said earlier. Childhood softball practice came back to her and she whipped her water-filled goblet at the Queen's face.

THE LOVED, THE LOST, THE DREAMING

The queen shrieked terribly, rending the air; Kenna's first instinct was to clutch her ears, plug them, scratch them off, anything to make the sound *stop*. She never had the chance. Will seized her by the hand, and, pushing Hakim away, grabbed Lindsay around the waist with his free arm. Will ran for the door before any of the others could stop him, and Lindsay stumbled after him. As they ran out from behind the scream, across the dance floor, the crowd parted like the Red Sea. Eyes followed them, and club lights glinted on reaching claws, sharp teeth, as they parted the crowd.

But Lindsay saw almost none of that, her eyes half-closed against the horrible shriek, loud enough to cut through the music, loud as it was. Next to her, Lindsay was wailing in drunken terror and dismay. No-one had stopped them before, but perhaps leaving would be more difficult. She could see something hungry in their eyes, and the strange clothes and looks of the dancers seemed threatening, demonic, rather than exotic or opulent.

They had come to the door back into the main part of The Roadhouse, at last, and were backed into a corner. "Open the door," growled Will, "or we won't get out." Even over the screaming of the Queen—oh, gods, when would it *stop!*—and the noise of the crowd and club, she heard him.

"You do it," Kenna moaned back.

"Open it. I can't get through iron," he howled.

Kenna nearly tore it off the hinges as she jerked it open and pushed them through. Then, all at once, the screaming stopped.

Kenna looked around. All she could see now—in addition to Lindsay clinging to her leg, whimpering—was the alley behind the Roadhouse. The same alleyway there had always been. No 'exta room' or hidden section. Only smoke or fog lying in the alleyway, in which she could just faintly see human shapes. And Will.

He was fainter, now, glowing with a slight silver light, but hazier around the edges.

"Thanks," he said. "Sorry about tempting you into all that."

"What's going on?" Kenna's teeth were chattering, and it was very, very cold.

"Nothing, anymore." He looked lighter. Relieved. Actually happy, instead of cheerful. "You killed her."

"I what? I only threw my cup at her. Is that why she was screaming? And what's all the smoke?" Lindsay was snuggling up against Kenna like a kid, but now, she looked around.

"Where's Hakim? Where's the party?"

Will shook his head, losing substance even as he did it. "She lured us in, one by one, and we traded our bodies for pleasure. Girls and boys from everywhere you can think of. Hakim," and he knelt in front of Lindsay, "was trapped and now he's gone. He can sleep."

"Whaaaa?"

"You had a bad dream," Will said, "because someone put something in your drink. But you're safe now..."

"Well, give Hakim my number," Lindsay mumbled, and passed out.

Will looked at Kenna. "I was the first of all. That's how I know."

Kenna bit back a second question. "Why water, though?"

Will smiled. "When was the last time you could loosen up at party that only served water?"

She let the question out. "Can I see you again?"

He looked at her. A hundred years of or a thousand of parties, endless nights of indulgence, of obedience to a queen of wasted time were written all over his face. His eyes were like long unlit subway tunnels. "You'll find what you're looking for someday. You won't be unloved, if that's what you're worried about." He looked across the alley, where soft smiles in fog were thinning out, the air, clearing again. "But I must sleep. It's been a long, long night."

He leaned forward to kiss her mouth, and shifted into smoke. Then there was only a faint smell of cigarettes and incense, and the reek of piss and beer in the alleyway.

DRAGONFLY GREEN

I

From above, it reminds me of a ring, a platinum strand—diamonds and emeralds fallen or thrown carelessly. It emerges from the sand just so, the green glass domes of the city shining, jewel-like, facets catching sun and blinding anyone overhead. Alongside it, the deep, dark scar of the Greater Chasm offers a glimpse of the underworld, winding alongside like a colour negative of the grape vines, like an antiriver. The city offers itself on a platter of metaphors, steeped in poetry.

I miss the forest in the depth of the chasm. I wish I hadn't left it. The wolves, the criminals they threw down for their pets to eat, they made the Chasm dangerous, but it was also beautiful. I miss the green darkness. Not this dry, hard, cold place. If I hadn't saved the girl in red from the wolves...well, that would be a different story. And still, I can't say I'm sorry for doing it.

I miss my time in the free air. Even a photographic memory doesn't make up for the difference. The sensations, though—the breeze on my skin, the humidity, the smell of the moranga trees in late fall—I remember them, but tenuously. With every recollection they slip away a little more. In that time, I never did appreciate the city, taking it for granted that they'd leave me alone, leave me to my dragonflies and my hut. I worried about the wolves on the ground, but it was the ones in the offices I should have taken an axe to.

And the wolves, their modified mockeries of the real thing—snapping jaws and eyes and claws, as close to a real wolf as a homunculus to a man. I used to hate them, fear them, but even one of those monsters would be a welcome sight after this. Now, in the cells, chilled by lack of sun and rendered pale as a grub by the constant semi-dark, I cannot even trust my own eyes.

This is no light for working under. Yet I can hear you scratching away at your pad, transcribing my stories. I know they've cut out your tongue, the better to deprive us of conversation, prevent secrets from leaving the cells, but the friendly sounds you make and the language you've been teaching me, the gesture language, provide some semblance of company. We, nameless and unloved, have made our mark.

Listen to me, then. You are so small. Is that why you're here, inferior height they couldn't correct? It would explain your limp, my friend. Though why I criticise when I cannot see you, blinded as I am, I don't know. I don't even know your sex. I can't imagine you're one of them, though; they don't put them with us, they're too rare. Murder one of us, they get off lightly, murder one of their own kind and they might be consigned to this place—though not until their ovaries had been harvested, of course.

It amazes me, this cruelty; I know we make up more than seventy percent of the population, but still, are we as disposable as that? If nothing else, their influence has made this city beautiful, hard as it is.

I remember wondering at it in my childhood, sweating in one of the terracotta classes. I was never from an aristocratic background, those who have written of me and my actions deserve that correction. It makes sense, though, that they might doubt the strength of a member of the middle class. It reminds me of the literature of Old France, remember? Vive la bourgeoisie, as they said.

Oh, my friend, this smile doesn't signify madness, though the deprivation would be enough; three nutrient pills, condensed, lukewarm water, and that is the sum of my daily meal. This isn't enough to drive me into madness, not yet, not yet, not when I can slip back into the hot school rooms, beneath the canopy of glass that encloses the city. Within the mind I am still free.

Why haven't they cut my tongue? That struck me as odd, though perhaps it was mercy. I'm glad I have someone to speak to, even you, my jailer, for otherwise I'd talk to myself, or try to recite the old conversations. In the face of deprivation, one's memory suddenly becomes much more acute.

Still, I remember when I first realised I was one of the different kinds, that I'd slipped through the filters. I was just a child, you know, but I knew enough not to mention it. They talk about it in the schools, of course. In a way, it saved me later; I didn't put up a fuss when I was deselected from the breeder's group. Perhaps you had the same problem, my friend, were you deselected? And did they throw you in the arenas, as they did with me?

Perhaps they didn't. You might have been lucky, I don't know. I can hear you move more slowly; my number is meaningless enough, but you might remember me from the gladiatorial days. That's possible enough. I was a good fighter, well known. The Queens sent their husbands, too, you know, even the third and fourth-class ones, to watch at the stadiums along with the masses, in their private boxes, I remember them. I could see, back then, of course. It seems as though I've been blind for years, you know that? It's only been a little while, and I can't remember how to move my eyes. They're gone now, of course, so I don't need to know, but it's a saddening thing, too.

THE LOVED, THE LOST, THE DREAMING

Little things keep slipping away, but I remember his face. He was in the commoner's stands, under direct light, suffering much more than the Queens and their husbands under the plush canopied cool of the private stands. As I recall, when he came to me, he said he was only a fifth-class husband, a third-class woman's property, not much more than a domestic slave, really. Well, he had fine glittering eyes and a lovely build, but there you are; privileged in looks and a hard luck story. I've always been sentimental, as you know, my friend.

I suppose it was that affection that undid me; I know perfectly well that it was. There *is* no supposition. He was a young creature, too, I might add, so when they hurt him, he can't be blamed for cracking so very easily. Well, I am of a forgiving nature. Not so the Justices. He was imprisoned, as I am now; I escaped, though, from the guards, with help. Perhaps if he'd known *her*, then, I would have been able to free him. I can only wish there had been time. Then again, if every wish were a grain of sand, it's no wonder the world was covered with deserts.

Oh, the girl—I can tell by your movements that I've confused you. There was a girl, years ago, who escaped. Now do you remember her, my friend? Her ancestress was the Cinder-girl, everyone knows the story, back in the green days, as they say, before the deserts and the Greater Chasm split the earth.

She wouldn't marry, you know, refused to wear green the way her class dictated—that was where her rebellion started. You remember her—she cut away all her hair, you know the Queens aren't allowed to, and then she joined the exiles and Chasm-chasers. She helped me get free, and you know they couldn't have done a thing to her, being of Queen heritage as she was.

She found me during one of the cell raids. I suppose she'd heard of me, and our circles of influence overlapped, so she knew about the resistance movement. I still remember her home in the Chasm—do you know there are places down there where it's still green, not just glass or in the sim-gardens? There's a river, and sometimes moisture catches, and it rains down there. She said she'd helped pioneer the artificial climate, that small patch of paradise caught between the lips of a thirsty desert.

Her house was carved right into the canyon walls, just like the others there—men and women alike were exiled, you know, and of course the Queen's press releases never mention what happens to exiles except that they're dropped in the canyon. Old laws, though, the sanctuary statutes, protect all the exiles and canyon residents, and with the girl there they can't do a thing to them anyway. The Queens are corrupt, you can't imagine it, but they would never harm their own.

There, in her green home with a small supper before us, in the still of the night, she told me a story. She'd found it in an urn buried in a sim-garden just outside the palace walls. She said it had been passed down from the Old Days. It was a pathetic thing, but I understood it, the meaning of the story. She told it in the first person, and I saw the light of her ancestress' face pass through hers as she relayed it, slipping into the old tongue to tell it properly. This is a translation, poor by necessity, but perhaps you will be able to understand it just as I did, my friend. And if you do, please, spread it. Even if it's false or futile, give them a little hope.

II

"Once upon a time there was a beautiful girl called Cinderella. Her mother died when she was very young, and her new stepmother and stepsisters were wicked and evil. They made her do housework and act as a scullery maid. One day there was a fantastic ball, and they wouldn't let her go. So her fairy godsmother waited until Cinderella's evil relatives were gone and made Cinderella a beautiful dress with glass slippers. She had a coach made from a pumpkin and four coachmen who had been rats. As long as she was back by midnight, the fairy godsmother's spells would hold.

"At the ball, Cinderella was not recognized by anyone. The handsome prince saw her and danced with her all night. At midnight, the clock struck and she had to go home, but she ran so quickly that she left her glass shoe behind. The prince took the shoe and tried to find out who the girl was that he had fallen in love with. He finally came to Cinderella's house, and because she was the only one who fit the shoe, the prince married her and they lived happily ever after."

They all knew the story—it was wrong, tinted by gossip, but everyone knows the outline. Looking at my aged, withered form, hands folded over each other, I know I looked peaceful enough, but beautiful? That this wizened form could once have allured any man, could have borne children, must have seemed impossible. Yet I am she, or one of her faces; the story of the cinder-girl is older than time; I—we—have thousands of faces.

Nonetheless, that is not how it happened. It is never that simple. I had no stepmother—I was an orphan, and I worked at the palace and at *their* manor. *They* were not unkind—ignored me, but no more or less courteous than I was to *them*. That's not all of it, either—nothing is as it seems. Did the people at my funeral know that the beautiful creature I married had known me long before the ball? He was beautiful, once, lovely but hollow. I worked as the scullery maid at the castle, as I said—I was scraping the coal from his personal fireplace when he came upon me. He picked me up, and without a word, dropped me onto his bed. I didn't fight or protest.

It wasn't just that fighting would have done nothing. I loved him. I had loved him ever since I'd first seen him, but he didn't particularly care for me. I wanted that so badly from him. When I found the shoes on the side of the road, glittering, gleaming, and a perfect fit, I knew what I had to do. On the night of the ball, I stole a dress and a mask from my employers. I didn't care. I was in love.

No-one recognized me, not even the prince. He held me closer than he'd ever done, guided me out to the garden. Then, as he lifted my mask to kiss me, he saw who I was. His eyes widened. I had to flee.

I turned to leave, but I tripped, and the shoe—the left one—broke. Glass dug into my feet, my blood spilling out over the snow. It was a winter ball, you know, white snow everywhere. He waited dumbly as I ran away. Distantly the clock struck twelve. It was midnight. I ran back to *their* house and wept in a closet. He could never love me. Everyone had seen us dance, thought I was to be his fiancé.

People think he was looking for the girl who would fit the slipper. Not so. He was looking for the girl with the lacerated, bleeding foot who had limped homeward, leaving a crimson mark of her passing in the snow. All he'd had to do the next day was follow my tracks.

So he came, holding the glittering pieces of my broken virtue in his hands, going down to the cellar to find me, lifting my skirt to see my feet. There it was, the left one, mangled and carved up, spider webs of blood on the cleaned, healing flesh. When he saw that the girl of the previous night was me—I cannot describe the look on his face.

Horror, fear, selfish smugness and complacency, but no happiness, no love. He didn't know I was pregnant, then, but it didn't matter; he would have to marry me anyway. I had hoped that there might be love. There was a brilliant white wedding, yes, and there were children—I, doing my duty by producing the royal heirs; I didn't even raise them myself. That was denied me; my children under the eye of governesses the moment wet nurses let them out of sight.

No fairy godsmother came to my aid. No-one knows that those wonderful, beautiful shoes crippled me. Tell me, do they know that my foot never did heal, that I walked with a limp for the rest of my life? That the glass wouldn't come out?

No, of course not.

Eventually, that is what happens to all of us: we fade into stories, the past tense. That is my fate, and I am content. To them, I'm just a story.

III

She waited, watching my face for an answer to the story, but I didn't say anything. I offered her what I could give; I liked her. I couldn't have loved her, but I was fond of her. She took it, spending the night with me—that was the old way of offering thanks, and that's all I could give. She didn't fall for me, for which I was grateful; as I said I couldn't have returned it. I had to go back—in those days I would have sooner swallowed sand than my idealism. I'm glad they didn't find her when they brought me in this time. My poor love. He couldn't have helped it, but I wish he hadn't been caught.

You told me a few weeks ago what had happened to him, the falling, as they do for our particular variety of crime. I know they'll do the same to me, soon, take me out into the desert, fly into the mesosphere—drop me through the hatch. I'm ready, my friend, I'm not frightened in the least. They don't know what we do. The emancipation is coming, my friend. The women will get a chance to have only one husband; our kind— my kind—won't have to hide. I know they'll drop me soon, but I have only one request: copy my tale down, and after my death, release it into circulation. They haven't stopped the movement yet. One day, they'll be free, or their children will be. I have forgiven them, Justices and Queens alike. There's enough hate in the world, and soon I'll likely be flying up, far from it all.

A last word of advice, then. Keep your axe sharp. Watch out for the wolves that walk upright. And last, if you have a chance to go to a green place, even in the depths of the Chasm, take it. The forest will rise up with you, and get its own back.

They're calling me. Hide your things, friend. I trust to your patience.

A QUESTION OF PERSPECTIVE

I can hear the radios piping in the news of your victory over me very clearly from my jail cell. It strikes me as being particularly funny that you're all so humanistic and you still haven't taken the time to reform the penitentiaries, as you'll be calling them. Solitary confinement will be the harshest punishment you deal out, or so you'd claim. You know nothing.

I was the greatest woman in the western hemisphere. I owned Europe. Then you came in, working away, chewing at the base of my power, and I found myself in this cool grey cell which measures six metres by four by two and a half. It is a large, empty cell, but it reminds me of my office, and of the ocean of mahogany, my desk, I would use to separate myself from the officers who brought in people like you. Next time I will be wiser.

I shouldn't have separated myself from you. That was the mistake. May the students reading this posthumous declaration of victory learn this from me, if nothing else: don't repress the artists. That is the worst thing to do. Like maggots, they will feed on anything, and the best thing to do is just gather them together for a state dinner, you know, to show there's no hard feelings, and put hemlock and opium in the wine sauce on the steaks. Or else you can always command them to turn their interests to the state. Kill them all or put them under your thumb. I should have known that it's better to turn freedom to structure than curb it all together.

Instead, with those fantastical stories spreading, the fanciful rumors were just what my opponents needed. Take a vocal majority and give them bright lights and a microphone, and you're hooped. I'm really not sure how I managed to miss that lesson, I won't lie. I had the work every dictator in history at my fingertips. I had manuals to learn from. I studied, I read, and still I failed. For now, at least. To be fair, I had an awful lot to work against. Keep an eye on that rumour mill, my darling pupils. It could just grind your bones for the paper's daily bread.

And, of course, there was the matter of my daughter. The coma, the seven researchers and their miraculous cure...the people loved the romance of it. Running against me was the best thing she could have done. And no, before you ask. That was one thing I didn't do, poison her apple cobbler at the state dinner. Someone else might have done it, given her political leanings, but it wasn't me. You always get that part of the story wrong. I expect you think she magically woke up because of a prince, too.

THE LOVED, THE LOST, THE DREAMING

While we're rounding off that list of misconceptions, let me clarify: I was not a cruel ruler. I wanted power, and I had it, and I wasn't going to lose it. Yes, I took your canvases and burnt them, and the books were walls of flame in the libraries of the burning piles, but these were the things you didn't need to live. Lord, but people whined. There was always enough food and meat to go around, no-one was out of work.

You will regret this, I say, but witness my smile, growing wider by the moment. You must think I'm mad. I'm not. Mildly annoyed, and missing my mirror collection, but I wouldn't say I'm especially angry. No, this is a good time for patience.

I am the metaphorical woman in the woods, that you came to in your time of need. You took me from my gingerbread cottage, and you wondered why I liked to fix things the sweet way. Sure, you were desperate for government, but if you didn't want my style of problem-solving, then tell me—why elect me? I rode in on your votes.

Do not think you have won. When your beautiful egalitarian system grows moth-eaten and the starving populace fills the streets, whom will they come to?

Your system will fail. I know it as surely as I know you will begin to wonder why my cell is so silent but for the scratching of a pen. And I will not allow you the satisfaction of finding a corpse here. I asked you to give me your newspapers. I savoured the propaganda I read, already spreading sweet, strong roots like milkweed, or a fungi living on the fertility of false truths. So I'll wait, and watch, and pretend I am remorseful, reforming and getting in touch with my inner child. Every dictator is a child playing with tin cars in a sandbox. I know only this: that I will be here when the starving multitudes cling to your hems like rats, and, finding your cupboards bare, they will turn to me.

Just wait and see. I have all the time in the world.

I can afford to be patient.

MY SHADOW SELF

I lost my virginity when I was sixteen. I had three children, I was divorced, and I took good care of my teeth. I died in a car crash.

I was a gardener. I had a heart attack in my backyard. I was happy.

I was a physician. I was not unloved. I was underneath the wrong building when a construction worker dropped the bar—literally.

I built violins and sold them. I worked in a music shop. I couldn't sing worth a damn. I liked coffee and I had a tattoo of a treble clef on my back. I choked to death.

I am still living. These are the stories the dead tell me, stories with gaps that relatives and governments fill in. You might call me a medium, but I'm just another coroner. I remember some better than others, and one most of all. It's her story that I'm writing now, now that the casenotes are filed in their sterile folders. The world isn't nearly as sterile as it looks.

A history, then. The descriptions I don't write in the official files.

The girl was switchblade thin and angular. Hers was a body and face that a hard life had imposed its harsh geometry upon. I thought I would cut my hands on her sharp face, all cutting edges and cheekbones. Tattoos ran the length of her forearms; her blonde hair was streaked with harsh black 'highlights'. She lay serenely, though I sensed she had never been nearly this quiet in life. Eighteen years old, found fresh in the gutter with a knife in her back. Identity checks and witnesses had come forward to reveal that she was a gang member. The usual turf wars over drugs and prostitution had occured, and she'd ended up lying silent on my table. Still, even with her tongue silent and her blood motionless, the story of her life wasn't done yet. She might be able to tell us something.

"You wanna make the first incision?" I asked my lab assistant, Jimmy.

Jimmy is a twitchy, nervous type. He talks a lot, but not when he's in the lab. He has very wide eyes and excellent night vision, but stiffs make him nervous. After a lifetime of working around them, I can handle anything.

(In school, I was that science-nerd chick who lobotomized the frog as my lab partner searched for a convenient place to vomit. Yeah, now you remember me.)

Jimmy picks up the scalpel. This is his fifth corpse, and he's still not used to them. His sterile, latex-gloved hand no longer shakes, though, as it did when he first began. He glances at me for reassurance. Then, a moment later, it's done. He smiles nervously. Tell us about your life, Lady Razor, I say silently. People say the dead tell no tales. I beg to differ.

I died young because of who I am and I'm not real sorry I did. It was a short life because I was only sixteen and doesn't that suck but don't start bawling your eyes out for me, I hate it when people do that. I died because I was in a gang—are you happy now? Maybe I should describe myself because then I can also tell you what my personality is kind of like. I have blond hair that's striped black like a tiger but my friends told me that was cooler than my natural blond, which makes me look too innocent. Mom said it made me look like an angel which is, according to my English teacher Charlene MacDougall, the most ironic thing she's ever heard, exactly like she put it with her pretentious fucking grammar that I don't get. None of my teachers like me, they say I have tons of potential but no drive and I also never hand in my homework. I'm not stupid or lazy but the stuff we learn in school is boring and for me, pretty much totally useless. I might also add that I'm white, and my face is like I should be pretty but somehow I'm not. That's what my last guy said when we broke up, and I broke him up for that, all right.

I guess I should explain that I was living in what they call a 'youth hostel' but that really means, in a real seedy area of the city with a bunch of kids who'd either left high school or got kicked out, not that I'd blame the teachers who would of done it. It's a safe place to go get high or crash or whatever, and lots of screwed-up runaway kids like me came there. Mom walked out on Dad for good reason and then I followed her a couple years later. Only I couldn't find her and I didn't know where she went, so there I was but away from my bastard father and therefore pretty godsdamn safe. Provided you slept with the guys there from time to time, you could do okay. Nobody called me an easy lay, even though I was, because I'm really good at giving people broken noses. I didn't have any sibs which is probably a good thing, because I would be one hell of a bad example for them. Still, I'd always wanted a couple of younger brothers or sisters, so the older kids who brought their sibs with 'em when they came got me to take care of them. Don't get the wrong idea, 'cause I don't have a good heart, I like to fight and I take care of myself. I don't want to rely on anyone 'cause that makes me real weak, wimpy, and plus I'd lose my safe status, and I wouldn't be able to get by sleeping around anymore. Gotta make it somehow, no pun intended.

THE LOVED, THE LOST, THE DREAMING

I guide Jimmy's hand vaguely, showing him the wound. The skin around it is discoloured by darkness and the seepage of blood into the surrounding tissues, no surprises there. "The upward angle of the wound indicates an underhanded stab," I explain. "That's highly unusual. Now, which hand did the murderer use to stab with?" Jimmy uses a steel rod sticking from the wound to calculate the angle, frowning slightly.

"The left," he says.

"Are you certain?" he falters.

"I think so..."

"Well, you're right." He smiles nervously, briefly. We work on in silence, and I think about the girl. She is everything I am not; blonde, underfed, tattooed, uneducated, emotive. This child thought with her heart and did what it took to survive. I had never been forced to do that. In a way, it was rather like looking at my shadow self there on the table. She was my reverse negative. I almost pitied her, but something in me sensed that she would have despised me for it.

And now I will tell you about the boy. I guess that's the closest thing I ever got to real love and then I totally blew it just like I always do. He worked at the tattoo place, drawing stuff on people's bodies before the other guy got out the needle machine to fill in the designs. I was in there getting a tattoo on my stomach and he was real shy which was weird to me.

I said, hey, and he said, hey, and then we started talking about tattoos and stuff and I said, let's get a drink sometime, you're cute. He said, I'm off work at eleven and I said perfect. I was surprised because he was obviously from whatever they used to call it, the word that means basically eighteenth-century white trash, anyway, same as me but real nice. And we actually kind of talked, or maybe screamed because the music at the bar was so loud. I said we could go back to the hostel but he looked kind of reluctant so I said, the alleyway and he said, let me get to know you first. Of course, I was so surprised that I dropped my drink glass and the bartender charged me extra. I said I wanted to see him again and he gave me his number and I gave him mine. Actually, it was so weird getting to know a guy before I slept with him that he caught me sideways.

I came back to the hostel and Mike went, hey, where the hell were you and I said, out. He said, you know we got a shipment of grass coming in and the Angels could of intercepted it. I said, yeah, but I met this guy and we talked. He wasn't with any gang or anything, and I could tell. Didja sleep with him? Mike asked. No, I said, isn't that trippy? Cool, he said, but getcher ass back here next time pronto, use the spare room and fuck him there if you have to. Yeah, okay, I said, sorry for not watching the kids. Mike said, it's okay, you know how to make it up to me.

When I think about it he was kind of an asshole and he never paid enough attention to his younger siblings, who really shouldn't have been there anyway, they were already getting eaten alive. And for Christ sakes, you'd think even a moron would realise that maybe it was a bad idea to be doing and dealing with kids around, that gets ugly. Anyway sometimes he was nice but even so it was wrong and even if their parents were F-ups, they could have figured something else out. Anyway, when he went down to handle the pot he got nailed because of some load of it about the Angels being underpaid.

I had to tell Gordon and Jaime that their big brother was dead. They were so used to people getting it like that that they just gave me big serious looks and nodded. I think they're too young to get it, and Jaime broke my heart when she asked me later, when is Mike coming back?

"Hello, Draculina," says Rob.

I give him the evil eye. He knows I hate vampire jokes but makes them anyway. Rob is a shlub, but it doesn't take that much to be a body porter. I like working nightshift; he hates it. Our differences don't stop there; the work ethic I have and that he doesn't is another thing that makes him one of my favorite people.

"What now?"

"Special delivery. New body." Speaking of bodies, there's one I wouldn't mind seeing on a slab.

"I'm almost done here," I answer coolly. "It can wait."

"It's kind of urgent," Rob whines.

"Okay. Jimmy, off you go."

"Me?" he protests.

"Yeah. See if you can find Dr. Jatira. He's on coffee break right now."

"Oh," says Jimmy, visibly relieved. He scampers off. New kids. You'd think he'd be an old hand after classes, but nope.

"And Rob?"

"Yes?" he says hopefully.

"Get lost. I have a cadaver to work on."

"I'm offended that you find a corpse more interesting than I am," he pouts.

"She certainly is. I have work to do, so go away." I shoo him out, ignoring the reproachful glance he gives me.

I pick up the scalpel and forceps and get back to work. She has almost finished revealing her secrets— drug addiction, as shown by an already blackened

brain and lungs and the dark trails of needle marks
that defiled her arms. I tried to push aside her
humanity, to not imagine how she might have looked
as a toddler, but I fail. Jimmy looks at her sadly.

"She's had a really hard life," he says. There is awe
in his voice, and sympathy.

"Yes," I say, after a moment. "Sex, drugs, you name
it and she's probably got it or had it." Just another
teenage girl who died in Michigan's slimy gutters.

Let me tell you how it ended. We met at the hostel
and had some fun—I finally had a chance to bed tattoo
guy, which was something, all right. I didn't even
shoot up first, which I usually do, it was really kind of
sweet, but I could tell he was very distracted, so we
got dressed after that and went for a walk in the
alleyway. He was fidgeting so much so I asked him,
what's up. He said, I want you to come with me and
maybe think about, I don't know, something long
term. I love you, he said. Please, think about it, but I
was thinking yes and my mouth said no. And then I
looked at him and I wanted to cry but I knew better
because girls like me can't cry and instead I screamed
at him, what do you want from me? These are the
streets, godsdamn it. And he was giving me this
wounded bullshit look and saying, it doesn't have to be
like this. I screamed back at him, Of course it does, it

always will be, and then I hit him and he went down so hard and I just felt numb and I sat there curled up on the cement next to him just hugging myself. Because I was following street rules and whether you follow them or you don't you get hurt and sometimes you hurt other people.

An hour later he got up and I still hadn't left and he had a huge shadow-blue black eye and he was asking me weakly, what the fuck happened. I said, I hit you, I'm sorry and he said, I know; why did you do that? I said, you weren't making any sense and I was just feeling totally crazy and I had to hit something and he said, that's okay but next time warn me when you get this pissed off. I laughed and said how can I do that when I didn't know I would get pissed off in the first place and he didn't really know. Then he walked away, still not quite walking straight and rode the bus to wherever it is that he actually lives, probably in some place next to a tattoo shop. And I looked at him and thought about that drawn-on body with so many stories on it and I did cry. It was the last time I saw him, not that that says much 'cause I did die the next day.

"Hey!" Oh great, another distraction. The girl is whispering to me, her dark eyes insistent and urgent. She wants this story off her chest, so she can slip off and relax. She won't settle down until I've heard it. This is the last time I'd like to get an interruption from another cop for.

"Hey, Robinson. What's up?"

Her smile falls off her face like someone slapped it off. "Not much. Just wanted to say hello. Sounds like you're busy."

I gesture to the girl on the table, spread and cut and more naked than anyone has a right to be. "I kind of am. I just sent Jimmy to handle something else. Can it wait a half hour?"

"Uh sure." She closes the door behind her.

I like Robinson, but the dead come first. The living, they're still experiencing their lives. The dead, they should have all the time in the world—but I don't, and that's why I hurry. That's why they rush me. The girl, looking off-put, clears her throat and gets back to her story.

I'll get to that—Marko came in and said, there's a fight coming, and I said, no shit, it's too early for this and I have a hell of a hangover. Then I sat up and tried not to puke before I reached the bathroom, which I didn't. It wasn't pretty and I didn't want to think about a fight so I took the day off and decided to scout, that is, walk around and basically try to think about what I'd do if everything hit the fan.

That for me is exactly what happened because something did hit the fan, I ran into a pocket of the Angel's girls and since I was wearing my bandannas, it was pretty clear where I was from. One of them told the others to clear off. She actually seemed nice about it. She smiled real sad at me and I smiled back 'cause it was the nice thing to do. And then I turned my back on her for a moment, which turned out to be a huge mistake, because there was this awful fiery feeling and I couldn't think. Doesn't it suck that the world always ends with a whimper?

I put away the tools; the sharp, dainty blades and precise forceps. We're done for the day. It feels good, even though this job is damn depressing sometimes. I think of Jimmy. He couldn't have known this girl in high school, he's too old. Nonetheless, I wonder if this isn't the kind of girl he'd have gotten a secret crush on—dangerous and way out of his league. I wouldn't be surprised. With one last glance at her, I leave to wash up. "See you in the coffee room, James," I say to my lab assistant. He barely nods, but I know he'll be there.

Twenty minutes later, Jimmy grins at me as he relates a practical joke one of his fellow assistants pulled. I tell him not to get any ideas. Now that we're in the open air of the coffee lounge, he has relaxed.

THE LOVED, THE LOST, THE DREAMING

I slide a cup of liquid tar (also known as 'cop lounge coffee') across the table at him. He grabs it, gulps it, and his face begins to contort as he tries to get it down. He starts to cough, his face reddening. I slap him on the back and he began to breath normally again.

As he recovers, I say dryly, "You might want to slow down, kid. Too much of this stuff will kill you."

"What kind of coffee is this?" he wheezed.

"You don't want to know. All you need to know is that it's good for two things: flushing out engines and staying up late to work on cases."

"Speaking of cases, that one with the blond was interesting, wasn't it?"

"Yeah," I answer after a minute. "It was."

He grins. "See you round, Heather."

"That's Doctor O'Connor to you," I correct him. He looks crestfallen. "See you tomorrow, Jimmy."

I watch as he heads towards the men's change room, around the corner and at the end of the other hall, and I shake my head. He has no idea. Finishing my tar coffee, I head back. There are more stories to cull before the day is over, and there will be more to write about. For now, though, I have the girl, and I hope that when I sleep, I won't hear her voice in the back of my mind, the quiet echo of a ghost. For times when they do, I keep this journal.

The dead have plenty of stories. This is just another one. Someday, there might be more. As I walk back down the hall to the cold, cold rooms, I smile to myself. I'm not great with the living, but at least with the dead, I'm never alone.

A SHOT OF VODKA

I

I was rifling through the box of letters beneath my bed today when I found it. Pyotr had taken Mark to a movie, and I was using the time to clean up. There's never time in the week, because I work, too. Still—on the occasions when I leaf through it, I prefer to be the only one in the house.

I don't open the box very often—I carry the contents with me everywhere. Moths, newspaper clippings, gutter-glass from street corners: the ordinary debris of a life as it passes along on its road.

That's a metaphorical view of the thing, I admit. As for the true contents of the box, most of them are Christmas cards and the like. Letters. There are photographs there, too, old photos I inherited and didn't mean to keep. These small things, lost things, all thirty-nine years of my life, are held in a Laura Secord Chocolates tin.

There was dust on the tin and the lid had to be pried off. I steadied myself, biting my tongue against emotion. I'm always startled when the tears don't come. Even though most of the troubles have been laid to rest, my soul still aches, from time to time. It twists within me, just a little, as I look down at the photographs. My mind cools and chills, hardens to icy precision as I examine them. It's easier that way.

A boy and a girl, not very old, one blondish and the other dark-haired, playing on the grass of a family's front lawn. The hairstyles and clothes are quaint, to modern eyes, as are the smiles on their faces. Surely, such a time could not have existed, when toddlers could play on the lawn, in full view of a neighbourhood, alone.

The same children, later, older, standing before a particularly thick tree at a forest reserve. The girl promises to be decent-looking thing, but the boy, more so: he'll be handsome. The girl's face is a little blurred, caught as she turns to look at him. The smile is clear, though, and the hair has only darkened a little since the last photograph.

The boy, now grown and with eyes that flash even in the photo, smiling broadly, an arm tucked around a woman. The woman is not the blond girl in the first two photographs.

A newspaper article with the boy's name in it. The photograph above it includes a picture of a car. The fenders are bent in half—almost curved—and the windshield has been broken. The car itself is on fire. It looks like a prop

THE LOVED, THE LOST, THE DREAMING

from a film, but it isn't, it isn't. I can never look at this picture for very long, even now. It stings like the kind of rain you get on certain storm days in March, little needles.

A letter is tucked under the photographs, worn and creased with age and numerous readings. Under the letter is a short story. My short story. That was published, and now, it's time to finish the tales. At least, that's what I said to myself when I sat down to do it.

I won't lie, I mused over a title for a long time. That's where everything begins, for me. I settled on this, "A Shot of Vodka", because when I'd distilled my life, that's what it tasted of. A shot of something bitter and pure and sharp. Like Winnipeg winter, it cuts straight to the bone.

You may not like this story. I don't like it much myself. It hurts, and it's not pretty. There are jokes where there shouldn't be, and the ending is awfully quiet; while it is a happy ending, it's bittersweet. This story is the truth.

You might even know me, in fact. You might be a family member with your fingertips poised on the edge of the page, politely surprised by the fact that I've made it into print. You might be thinking to yourself that if you didn't know I was a writer, you wouldn't have guessed—or other thoughts, nice or not so nice.

If you do know me well, though, you won't have to ask those questions. I'll be able to tell you that this story explains everything, the stuff I keep avoiding when you ask me what's wrong. I hope this is it. I hope writing it down cures it, somehow; I didn't want to admit to myself that it had been something I've been thinking about, but it is. And this is the only explanation I can ever offer for those occasional Saturdays when I find myself staring into space, hands clutched around a cup of strong, dark coffee— remembering.

II

Sometimes I wish my mother had been reading something other than *Crime and Punishment* while she was pregnant. If so, she would not have named my brother Rodion Raskolnikov, or me, Avdotya Pulcheria. Our surname is Kalinnikov—just from the sound, it's about as Russian as it gets—short of being named Ivan and Natasha. Names can be an embarrassment or a burden, but the biggest burden of ours has been unpronounceability and running out of space on paperwork.

My mother's parents brought her over during the Cold War; Dad's parents had been here for a couple of generations. By here, of course, I mean Winnipeg.

THE LOVED, THE LOST, THE DREAMING

Winnipeg: if a city is a state of mind, this must be manic-depressive: its moods include droughts, floods, mosquitoes, humid heat, and most of the other plagues of Egypt. It's also lively, music-rich, and beset with poverty—mostly, I admit, in the sections of town I didn't visit. Mind you, people here keep going, cheerfully, and that's more Slavic than anything— mock it, but endure it. You wouldn't think so, if your idea of Russian culture comes from, say, conservative America, but we're actually a hopeful bunch. Not naively hopeful, it's more practical, but yes, we're hopeful.

Then again, for a city with so much sunlight, optimism isn't that surprising...but before I continue the tale of this December day, I'll assault with a little more exposition. Seems to me that it's the thing a good Russian writer will always do.

Rod and I were close. I did love my brother, and rather a lot; it's a difficult thing to explain, and I suppose that's why I'm writing this. Though I looked on him only as a sister does, I did sometimes wish we weren't related—to look at us, one-to-one, you wouldn't have thought we were siblings. We looked nothing alike. Still, if he was not, you know, my brother, well...you know how it is.

People had remarked from the time he was very little, that he was handsome, and startlingly so. His name suited him. I suppose it's all genetic coincidence, his resemblance to the other Raskolnikov; nonetheless, there was that fine build and dark hair and inky, oil-black eyes, but he was only of medium height, not exceptionally tall, like his namesake.

I wished I looked more like him. I am the light-haired one in the family. Big brown eyes, slightly darker eyelashes and eyebrows, full-boned and sturdy, but not plump. Reasonably good-looking, I suppose, but in the ordinary way. To look at our parents it would be hard to see any trace of my looks in their faces. In the snow, though, we all hunch the same way.

It was very cold at the time. Our parents were out that weekend, visiting relatives in another town. We had decided not to go, and they left Rod and me to our own devices. The previous night had been a quiet one, as our evenings usually are; despite my brother's looks, he had no close female acquaintances that I currently knew of, even though there were plenty of girls who would have been more than happy to get in the sack with him.

So, Saturday morning did *not* begin with my return at one in the morning, already hung-over and crawling on my knees. Let it go on the record that, as I walked into the day, my soul was mostly unblemished and I was sober.

I was in a good mood, too. However, when breakfast was sitting on the table before us, glancing out the window was enough to displace my equilibrium. That certain kind of snow was falling, steadily, heavily. I groaned about it to Rod, and he shrugged his shoulders.

"Avya, Winnipeg. Winnipeg, Avya. Have you met before?"

"*Da*, darlink, but ees cold."

He groaned. "It is much too early in the morning for that accent." It was eight o'clock. No-one in the family slept in.

We crunched away at our cereal for a few moments. "Still have to do chores," I said.

"Ugh. It's time to handle some of the recycling, and it's snowing like a bitch."

"Wanna make a deal?"

"Yeah?"

"I'll handle the recycling if you do the dishes and the laundry."

Crunch, crunch, went his cornflakes. "Fine, what's the catch?"

"None. I'm going out with the girls to a movie. You'll probably get the house to yourself today."

"Not another horror movie?"

I shrugged. "Wasn't my first choice, but Parmi liked it and Nicole wanted to see it too. I'll probably be out all day."

"Suit yourself."

I put the bowl on the counter, next to the sink, and walked upstairs to change. Outside, the snow continued, stolidly, with a certain Communist courage. Snow brings equality, I thought. Doesn't matter whether it's a Ford POS or a Benz, if it's stuck in your driveway, you still need to borrow a shovel and possibly somebody's arms to heft it.

It was one of those mornings where a trite insight like this is followed by a string of meandering, stupid thoughts about shovels and which sweater to wear. Pulling off the plain blue pyjamas, I stared at the closet for a few minutes, glanced down at myself.

The door opened.

"Rod, go away. I'm in my underwear."

"Sorry. Whoops." His footsteps paused for a moment and then, resolutely, padded back towards the kitchen.

I had goose-bumps, at this point, and I was annoyed with him for barging in on me. I pulled out a grey sweater and thick cords, pulled on a pair of wool socks.

THE LOVED, THE LOST, THE DREAMING

My parka was in the nook by the door. I pulled it on and stuffed my feet into boots, hands into gloves. "See you!"

"Bye."

I opened the door to the garage, loaded up the car, and drove out into the cold.

Notes about the year 1985: the Berlin Wall was still up. Gorbachev and Reagan were in power. New Coke emerged and died within a three-month time span. Nelson Mandela was still in prison. My heart broke. The IRA was still bombing the shit out of the police department. Route 66 died. They found *Titantic*. Windows 1.0 was released. Things were bombed and a number of natural disasters occurred. It was a remarkable year, in the ordinary way.

Teenagers don't think about history, or not often. I handled the errands, and when that was done, went to a coffee shop to wait for the mall to open. That got me to ten o'clock—then I wandered around the mall for a while, and drank several cups of tea. Parmi and Nicole came at twelve, and the wandering changed to a plural tense. *Nightmare on Elm Street 2* was on at one, so we went to see that.

After the movie, we loitered in the food court. I do remember Nicole, cracking jokes about the film—and it was awful, after all. Normally, I would have laughed, but I didn't. I do remember, though, that I felt a peculiar sense of unease, something nagging at me—an emotional blister. I stared past their faces and thought about the snow. Parmi asked me whether the movie had given me a case of the jitters, and I started.

"No, no, vos byad movie, darlink," I said. "zat ees all." Parmi laughed.

"Yes, it was. So why are you scared?"

"I'm *not*," I said. "I'm just cold!"

"That's stupid. I'll get you a hot chocolate." Parmi bounced off with my two-dollar bill in hand.

Nicole patted my hand. "It's okay to be scared." I blinked at her.

"I'm fine, really. Just spacing out. I think I didn't get enough sleep or something."

"Yeah, yeah, whatever."

"Hot chocolate!" Parmi grinned at me, set the cup down on the table. I smiled and wrapped my hands around it, and tried to ignore the anxious look in her eyes.

"Thanks." I sipped it, but I couldn't process the taste.

I wondered what Rod would say about this. He would laugh, probably—put an arm around my shoulders, tell me not to get so panicky—and yes, he would have bought me a cup of something hot and sweet. And—

"Are you okay? You're really pale," Nicole said.

"Actually, I think the movie kinda shook me up. Uh…I hate to be a wet blanket, but would you guys mind if I went home and took a nap? I don't feel so hot."

"Yeah, okay." They looked disappointed, and I apologized, but, after all, being good friends, they didn't make an issue of it.

I wished, later, that I'd said more, because it was the last time I saw them for years.

By the time I got home, it was only four o'clock. It had stopped snowing, but it was still cold, and windy, too. Rod didn't expect me until eight, I suppose; normally, I'd have made a day of it.

As I let down the garage door and walked into the house, I realised that most of the lights were off.

It was so still. I called out again, and there was no answer. My pulse was speeding up, and my mouth was drying. I shouldn't have been scared, really, but I was. It was cold, over-cast, and I'd just seen a horror movie.

There was no logical reason for Rodya's silence. Then, it occurred to me that he might have decided to go to his room, instead of sitting on the couch in the den. That would have been a little more usual; he was a creature of habit. Still, to look for him meant I had to go downstairs, to the basement. I hate basements to this day.

As I opened the door and descended, the creaking of the stairs made me even jumpier than I already was. My feet seemed unnaturally loud, clattering loudly on the wood. I thought I could hear music—well, there was a percussion solo going on at the moment.

Sure enough, the music revealed itself as Soviet rock-and-roll—my pulse slowed. (To give you an idea of the sound, *Gogol Bordello* hadn't formed yet, but if they'd been around, that would have been the sort of music Rod would have listened to.)

Most of the lights down there were off, but a little light was seeping through the space between the door and the wall. I knocked on the door, and there was still no answer, so I opened it.

Does anyone ever expect such a thing? Rodya— and a girl, fucking.

For a moment, I couldn't tell what was going on. The mind couldn't grasp it. My heart? Not a chance. They both looked up at me, and there was something childlike. Just for a moment, an uncomprehending innocence.

Then the girl pushed him off, pulled the blankets over herself, and turned my way. I can't remember ever seeing such pure hatred in my life. Just for a moment. No fear, no shame.

"Dress," I rasped. "Out." I was the scared one, now. I couldn't feel anything, just helplessness, as she looked at me. The expression on her face was cold and very beautiful. I didn't look at her body, just her eyes—I can't remember the exact colour of her skin or her hair, just those brown eyes.

She picked up her clothes, never taking her gaze from mine, and put them on, quickly. She'd covered herself with the sheets, like I said, and managed to hold them under her chin. A minute later, she had a button-up white shirt and blue jeans on. She could have been anyone, dressed like that; no identifying features.

"My coat's in the hall closet," she said. Medium voice, steady. I blinked at her and nodded. "Snow," I said. "It's half a blizzard."

"I have a coat." She walked right past me, didn't even glance back. I barely heard her sock feet on the stairs. There was silence in the room, all this time—Rod had turned the music off. The front door opened quietly, and then snapped shut, and I knew she was gone.

The whole thing felt like a surrealist comedy of some kind, but somehow, I'd become the punch line.

Finally, I turned to look at Rod. He hadn't moved, but he was still half-covered. My feelings were starting to thaw. I didn't move—and neither did he. He wasn't quite cowering, but neither of us was talking, either.

All of a sudden, it was like I'd swallowed a shot of vodka. There was a surge of heat in my chest, my throat started to burn. I could feel my eyes watering and spilling right over. The feelings—are there words in English for them? In any language?

All I knew what that I hadn't been feeling anything, and now, I was suddenly feeling too much, too much to think through or process, or even to distinguish. I turned away from him, towards the door. I ran up the stairs—tripped—got up, and kept running until I made it to my own room.

If someone had asked me why I'd just thrown myself on the bed, why I was sobbing, there wouldn't have been a coherent answer. It was beyond understanding. There was nothing *to* understand, just feelings, and Gods knows how easy those are to piece together. Who knows how long I lay there for, just crying? It was a while, anyway, before that knock came.

"Avya, let me in," said Rod quietly.

"Fuck off."

"No." I didn't reply. "I'll sit here all night, if I have to." His voice was very soft, coaxing, but I think he meant it. "Don't make me do that?"

I got up, opened the door just enough to see his face, and slammed it shut.

"I'm still here."

"What part of 'fuck off' did you not get? Go away. Go find your girlfriend."

There was a long, long, pause. "My girlfriend doesn't mean as much to me as my sister does."

"If you think I'm going to forgive you just because you said that..."

He started pulling my door open, and I hung from the doorknob, trying to keep it closed. He won, came in, and tackled me. I started to laugh, and then I remembered what I'd just seen, and I pushed him away.

"Get the fuck off. What are you, five years old?"

He stood and sat on my bed, hands on his knees, perusing my face. If only he hadn't asked "Why are you crying?"—he said it so gently. As if he already knew.

I touched my face and wiped them, the tears, away, with the back of my hand. "Come on. It's okay," he said. "I—"

I knew it was wrong, you knew it, Rodya, and it happened anyway. I don't think 'wrong' occurred to us, at the time, in that instant. Nonetheless, the facts remain, count them as they stand against me. You aren't supposed to kiss your sister like that—on the lips—and she isn't supposed to find that her mouth has, somehow, slipped open. If she really is your sister, she shouldn't find herself responding. And even though you knew something I didn't, your hand should not have slipped under my shirt.

I was horrified, and Gods, the expression on your face—revulsion and fear and wanting and love and sorrow all at once, flashing across it, traffic lights reflecting on a wet road, shattered and blurring. Our parents still hadn't come in, you'll remember, and I think that's why you tried to explain the truth the way you did. When you said, "I'm not your brother", it was a truth my skin already knew.

And still you pushed me back, pinned me down, though gently. My nails were digging into the skin on your shoulders. No blood between us, but there was the bond, and that terrible, terrible confusion, the stain of that word with its sibilant consonants, two syllables hissed under the breath.

Still your sister.

And then I left. I couldn't look at you after that, and that's why I didn't leave a note. It killed our parents at the time, but believe me when I say it did the same thing to me. It was a choice between having to spend a year there, with you around, and running away. When you're a teenager, and barely thinking, you do things you regret. But, then, what would have happened if I'd stayed?

All I want you to know is that I have money and a place to live, and I'm not addicted to anything or on the street. I still have my adoption certificate, you know, they had photocopies of it there in the drawer. They didn't even lock that drawer in the desk—then again, why would I ever think I was adopted? I don't know how you found out, Rodya, how old you were; even on my birth certificate, it says that we're seven months apart in age. Mom always said I was premature, and left it at that.

You would have been too young to understand, so I don't think our parents would have told you. I think you were looking for something in that drawer, one day, when you found the file. I can understand why you'd want to look at it, but why didn't you tell me? What were you afraid of?

Know it's been years since I saw you last, years since I found the adoption certificates with my name on them in the locked filing cabinet. I broke in to do it, you know, I had to. You knew, and that's why you did it. I'm sorry, and if you remember, don't just remember everything that hurt. If you ever dare to read this, Raskolnikov, my Rodya, I wanted to tell you I'm sorry. For what else is there to say? Words fade into air after they've been spoken, and only the page can ever remember.

III: Interlude

I wish I didn't have to interrupt my own story to explain the factual things. Part of me wishes the tale could be left at that, and fast-forwarded to the better times, later. I would skip ahead to the good things, if I could.

To meeting Pyotr. To standing in St. Petersburg in February, wading through snow and dodging traffic. To the first time I sunk my hands into the dirt in the garden of the new house. To a rainstorm I spent sitting on a couch, drinking sweet black tea and lying in good, warm arms. There are things which need explaining: factual things. For this, I must travel through time once again, away from that evening, and into my life as it stood several years later. Forgive me for this, it doesn't reflect the usual, methodical approach taken by Russians to story-telling. But, then, I'm Russian-Canadian. That should give me leave to play with time as I see fit: hundreds of years of history on one side of the ocean, and on the other, so little.

Calgary calls my attention, now, and the year 1989.

IV

THE LOVED, THE LOST, THE DREAMING

I tap the end of my cigarette into an ashtray. It's herbal, no nicotine in it, but I have to smoke to keep up appearances. It's required in this profession, and besides, you need something to offer when the other journalists extract their lighters but no little white boxes. It's not worth it, being caught short, and I hate being left at loose ends. My life has enough of those already.

There are a lot of journalists around here, students from the university, too. It's that kind of bar. The journalists come here to pretend they're in New York, Los Angeles, an interesting city, with a bohemian scene. There are even a few strangers here, tonight, though; granted, it's Friday, but it's early. Then again, there have been more people in the bars, lately. The atmosphere is festive. Now that the Wall is down, everyone is celebrating. It's been an interesting year already, between Tiananmen and the death of a number of notorious murderers. I don't even have to mention all of the instability to the east, that explains itself.

It's already the end of November, heralding my least-favourite month of the year, i.e., December. The vibe is cheerful, but I'm not, and it's actually worsening my temper. I'm twenty-one, already out of university and employed. One job is useful, the other is journalism, but between the two, I make a decent living.

My work has more to do with facts than feelings, and that's the way I like it. Pure observations satisfy me, now; the attempt to distil something to its vital essence, to relay it as clearly as possible. My editors say that it's a skill and a weakness with me, this 'cold precision', but readers like it, so they still pay me. It's not much, but it's enough to afford places like this.

You know what it looks like. I don't even have to tell you: authentically scuffed bar, but sparkling clean glasses and Perrier on tap. I don't go for martinis, by the way, usually just a shot of vodka. But I'm cheap, as well as cautious. I usually try to nurse it—even though I don't drive. My aunt would worry, and I've had enough experience throwing the people I love into a panic as it is. She doesn't mind me drinking, but she doesn't want to see it become a real habit. Neither do I. I watch it.

I have a few more reasons, like the fact that, when I have gotten drunk—no more than a couple of times— every brunette looks like Rodya's old girlfriend and every dark-haired man becomes my brother. So, no, I can live without it, because whenever my vision blurs, I see ghosts.

It's bad enough now—I've only had one in me, correction, one and a half, and I can't help noticing there's a guy a couple tables away who does have a terribly familiar, very Russian look. He's alone. Maybe I should walk over and buy him a drink. He's cute. Still reminds me of my brother faintly. Then again, I see Rodya everywhere, even now.

No, wait, the nose and the eyebrows are wrong, and he's not wearing a sleek, easy grin. Definitely not Rod. Bad enough seeing ghosts when sober, I'm watching it tonight. If I have another one tonight, I will be seeing ghosts for sure. I can hold my liquor, don't get me wrong, but my eyes betray me.

Calm down, Avya, it's a bar. It's just a bar. Describe it. Writing exercise. You are in a boozed-up version of twelfth grade English, pretend you're describing it for an assignment.

Still, a bar is a bar, and this is the kind of place where people who wish they were questionable, but really aren't, come to relax. This escapist's paradise, with its dark décor and smoky rooms, offers itself up to us. There are plenty of writer-types hanging around, all of them wanting to write the next *War and Peace*, or, barring that, *Lolita*. Well—people actually want to read *Lolita*, so that's a better example.

Mmm, tragedy. Both of them are tragedies, in my opinion. And I should know, not just from reading all that stuff. (In both languages at my disposal, thanks very much, though my Russian isn't so good that I don't have to use a dictionary for books like those.)

I've had my taste of tragedy—in life as well as in art. I'm not wholly sated yet, though, by what I've seen and learned, and I suppose that's why I'm still here. Here: alive, in one piece, not addicted, sans tattoos and piercings, in decent physical shape, respectably employed, and a university graduate. Downside: some scars and more than a brush with depression. As I tally things up, it doesn't seem too bad. Now, if I could only relearn normal human love, I'd be perfect.

Boo-hoo, Avya. Get yourself relearning it, or something. I hate myself for bitching. And now I sound like an angry drunk, I know it. Then again, no-one's going to read this, so what do I care? Just a journal anyway. Oh, well. Scratch that. Ignore last lines.

Focus on ze attractive comrade in the corner. He's getting up, walking around, and he has a limp. And a great ass. Definitely an ex-pat, first generation—unlike me. Still, maybe we'd be able to empathise over the sense of displacement. Maybe we could talk and have a deep and soul-searching conversation. Maybe I could get laid and loosen up. Maybe I could be intimate and tender with him for a few hours or a night. Maybe he wouldn't notice the scars. Maybe I should get a life and keep writing about real things, like what happened to me.

THE LOVED, THE LOST, THE DREAMING

So. Stupid Decisions I've Made, the Greatest Hits edition. Running away like that was not the brightest, but it was better than being at home. I had a little money: all my savings, in fact; some clothes, and a couple of the sentimental crap-objects that make life just a little more bearable. Actually, I should be specific—I am actually still pretty proud of my resourcefulness. I had my jewellery with me, because if worst came to worst I could sell it, I had photographs, which I couldn't sell but made my happier, and clothes, as many as I could fold up into small compact bundles. And other stuff. I can't even remember now what else I had, but all the necessities were there.

Anyway. It came down, as these things so often do, to a coin toss. Heads it was Calgary, and Natasha; tails, it was Montreal. I got tails. I took the bus to Montreal, and lived there for two months. It was awful and impossible to afford. I'd always thought it sounded like a romantic city. Living in a slum, during the dead of winter, while eking out whatever I could on minimum wage soured me on the city, and it got to the point where prostitution seemed like a viable option. I wasn't feeling much anyway—not that I didn't try to make myself feel things. (Thank Gods I couldn't afford anything addictive. And pot just sucked, so it wasn't worth the money.)

And that considering prostitution actually seemed sane, that was enough to tell you how fucked up it all was. I actually got as far as standing on a streetcorner and getting into a guy's car. I choked up and couldn't go through with it, so my slightly disgruntled (but mostly sympathetic) customer settled for a handjob. It shook me up, all right, and it was a wakeup call.

There hadn't been enough time to really deplete my savings. I found myself with just enough money to pay for a bus ticket to Calgary, and a long shot. Natasha had visited our family perhaps twice, and otherwise left the communication up to birthday and Christmas cards, so she was definitely out of the loop. When I called her from the Greyhound station, more tired and frantic than any teenage girl should ever have to be, she drove over and picked me up.

I explained things as best as I could, before I had time to think about them, and forced her to promise she wouldn't call my parents. Natasha had chilly relations with Mom, but she was still a good sister. I had been reported missing, of course; that generally happens when you slip out in the middle of the night without explaining things. Apparently, I was pretty close to being presumed dead. It was a very thorough fuck-up on my part, granted, but I have no excuses for that. The point is, I was lucky: the stranger aunt took me in.

THE LOVED, THE LOST, THE DREAMING

Without Natasha I wouldn't have gotten by, and that goes more matters of the heart as well as physical survival. Natasha explained my adoption to me, too, the hows and whys, and I'll come to that story in its own time. I don't feel like writing about it tonight. I'm sobering up, kind of, or else my hand hurts from scribbling the rambles down.

Writing in a journal, at a bar. How teenage of me. I can't remember who said it, but it's become a cliché, now—bars are where our dreams go to die, or, failing that, to marinate. I don't know how I turned into a closet bohemian, but it's happened, sure enough. It's a lovely little sordid cliché, good enough to play the pity-me game with and use for substantial ammunition—so, of course, I play pity-me Solitare, when I play at all. I usually numb myself out with books whenever I can, they're better than booze, anyway, or codependency. The last thing I need is someone else to feel sorry for.

I live in the aureole around the Kensington area, the arts section of town. My apartment is shitty, even though I'm an adult and I should be established by now. Gods knows it's not because I have no reliable source of income. Call it a hair shirt, wilful punishment. Beats letting myself luxuriate in other vices, I guess—though I won't say I'm a saint. If I could, I'd let myself fuck around and get drunk, but

Natasha worries—and no sense breaking my heart any more than it already is. And no sense hunting for trouble, which comes with fucking and drinking uncautiously.

Speaking of broken hearts, you should also know that I tried to contact him a while back, sent him a letter about the short story I made of our lives. All based in fact, unfortunately, only with names changed ever so slightly. His answer was short.

I'm sorry about your feelings, but not what happened. Why did you run away? You abandoned me, when we could have done something about this. I will never forgive you for that, Avya.

Sincerely,
Your brother,

Raskolnikov.

I was only eighteen when I got that letter. It left my heart looking, feeling, the way an orange does just after it's been thrown against a concrete wall. Still, I pulled through, thanks to Natasha: my sardonic, loving guardian angel. And someday soon I'll get back in contact with my parents—just not tonight. Tonight, I'm going to think about the Wall, and drink tonic water. It's bitter, but it'll sober me up. A little sobriety, a little perspective. That's all I want right now. And maybe I'll even go over and talk to the cute guy. Or maybe I'll just sit here and sober up.

Flip another coin. Heads, I talk to him. Tails, I get myself a tonic and take the train home to tea and biscuits. Now, what does the quarter say?

Tails. Okay, okay, home it is.

V: Interlude

I pulled that from the diary entry made that night, and from what I recall of the mood. It wasn't written in a drunken scrawl, I wasn't in the habit of drinking enough for that—drunkenness meant loosening the lines I'd drawn around myself, the ink separating my life's article from the others in the newspaper. I preferred control, then.

Time, love, and becoming a mother, have softened me, thank Gods. I'm glad for the last two in ways I can't even describe.

Back to the past, however, to 1989, before I explain too much of what was to come.

VI

1989: Tiananmen Square Massacres. The holding of free elections in the USSR. The destruction of the Berlin Wall. The last Golden Toad was seen. I returned from the dead. Ayatollah Khomeini died. The

Soviets left Afghanistan. It was a year of beginnings and endings, indefinite, ominously circular.

That month drew on, and the curious hunger gnawing at my soul only bit harder. Two days after Christmas, I finally gave in to four years of pleading and called my parents. The space between each ring felt like a century. There was a Scene, and crying, and an agreement to get on the next flight out. Natasha agreed to lie for me (again) and say that I had only gotten into contact with her recently—the truth was out of the question.

December 26th, 1989: the day the prodigal daughter and aunt returned. When I saw them again, I had to tell them that I knew about the adoption. They were too happy to see me not to forgive everything. They asked no questions. The sudden resurrection of a child leaves no room for useless questions. Natasha and Mom made up their coldness. Mom couldn't have understood why I cried when I saw them forgive each other, not fully, but it wasn't a time to ask questions about tears.

Returning, however, meant seeing Rodya again.

He'd moved over to the university of Regina, by then. He'd been out and about in the day, visiting friends, and was about to get home for dinner, as Dad said. I remember looking at his face when he mentioned that, noticing the way his eyes were still red around the rims from crying. The only thing to do was let myself freeze again, just a little. "That's wonderful," I said, smiling broadly. "I can't wait to see him!"

What was I supposed to do, tell the truth and break their hearts all over again? I remember being catapulted back to myself, to emotions I hadn't unearthed in years, and, just as quickly, shoving them under the bed. By that time, I was very good at making sure that things like that didn't show on my face.

So, there I am, with my happily weeping parents and aunt, waiting for my brother to come and complete the lovely familial tableau. I couldn't, and wouldn't, break that, but there was a way to get back at Rod, just a little, without fracturing people's hearts. "Can we let me be a surprise?" I asked. "Don't tell him I'm here…"

And, of course, they agreed. In the forty-five minutes I had before his arrival, I wept a little more, laughed, and helped Mom and Natasha with supper. I lived in the moments, letting myself thaw for the time being. It seemed better to rally myself for the night, to think about pierogy and the borsh on the stove, than to let myself brood. It was a war: and in war, you can't think about the fighting to come until you've fed the infantry.

Too soon, the doorbell rang. I picked myself up and strode over to answer it. My heart was beating like volleys of cannon fire. Hands sweating, skin blanched, I opened the door.

I thought he would fall over. It's one thing to hear the expression, 'looking like you've seen a ghost', it's another thing altogether to *be* the ghost.

"Avdotya?" Black eyes; dark, soft, lashes. "Really?"

His voice was cracking, he looked like he was going to faint. And, for all that I'd been maintaining the protective layer of ice, just looking at him was like walking into a furnace.

Stay there, I told myself, don't let him know what you're thinking. Don't crack, don't melt. Just *don't*.

Then Rodya threw his arms around me. His chest, those hands, settling into the curve of my lower back; his chin on my shoulder—it should have been fraternal, sexless comfort. Why, then, did he have to pull back just a little, to kiss me, and why did I stand there, accepting it—and then, kissing him back—and why did my nipples have to tighten? I was physiology, I couldn't control it, and yet...

All at once, my—*his*—parents left the living room, Natasha in tow, and came to us. All at once, we were chaste as could be, willingly herded towards the table for supper. It was a long night. It might even have been sweet—after all, I'd missed my parents. I'd cried over them, as any other child would. Reconciling Natasha and my mother—that was even finer, nearly enough to lighten my guilt. With Rodya there, though, smiling—yes, even laughing, when my father made jokes—the food turned to ashes in my mouth.

Still, I made it through dinner in one piece, and survived another lengthy familial conversation afterwards. I even tried to enjoy myself—I could thaw a little if I kept my eyes away from Rodya. I looked to Natasha for guidance, but her face was tilted towards my mother's; they were lost in conversation. I couldn't blame them, but, selfishly, wished Natasha would reassure me, or, perhaps, pull my parents aside and tell them why I'd run away.

Nicholas and Maria Ksenia Kalinnkov: I should call them by name. For all that they aren't my biological parents, it doesn't matter—they might as well be. They love me enough. And, that first night, when I stared at the living room ceiling (I couldn't face my old room, though the bed was better), I wouldn't have been so torn, if not for that. Love for them, and for Natasha. Honesty versus harmony, their pain or mine.

As I thought about it, listened to the clock in the dining room ticking, I heard Rodya's feet on the stairs. I still knew that step; there was his shadow on the wall.

I lay still. He looked at me.

I stared, resolutely, at the ceiling. Feeling something would undo me.

He was barefoot, in a button-down shirt, flannel pants. The shirt was pale blue, or white, and so were the flannels—pale, clean colours. His eyes were unreadable; his hair reflected no light. Ghostlike, he drifted towards me, moving with a somnolent grace.

"Can't sleep?" I whispered.

He stopped, shook his head. We looked at each other for a long time.

The need for him, and then, on its heels, anguish: I hadn't moved, but now, Rodya had broken the stalemate, was coming over to me. He pulled the covers back, slowly. I was wearing a long t-shirt, and my underwear beneath that, but as he stood there, looking at me, I might as well have been wearing nothing at all.

It wasn't just a matter of being mentally undressed. I couldn't move, not at all; his gaze was a pin and I was the butterfly. It wasn't that his expression was predatory; merely resigned, even melancholy, but unrelenting in direction. He hadn't touched me, nor had he spoken, but now, his hand moved forward—as if of its own will—and slipped under my shirt.

In that moment, everything changed. Passivity hadn't lessened his hunger. Any other boy—no, man, now; we weren't children anymore—any other man would have asked, or stopped. Yes, I had responded to him in the hall, earlier; now, I didn't. My hunger died; my nipples were flat. I wanted him to ask me for this.

I lay still. His fingers fluttered over my skin tenderly, sought the clasp of my bra. Unbuckled it. I flinched, visibly. He kept going, slid his other hand underneath the cheap, worn-out cotton, moved the straps downward, off my shoulders.

"Stop," I whispered. "Please."

Unblinking, he shook his head. "I can't."

"Please."

"I'm sorry." He leaned down, kissed my mouth. "I need this."

"And I don't." My voice rose to something near a normal volume. He covered my lips with his hand.

"Please. I don't want to hurt you. Keep your voice down." His fingernails dug into my cheeks. I didn't say anything, and he loosened his grip, just enough that could speak again.

"What's the matter? Don't you think they want to know why I ran away?" I whispered it, but it didn't help. "I don't want to hurt you." His voice trembled for the first time. I nodded—tried to—and closed my eyes. I could still feel his grip, uncertain, on my neck. I could scream, but what if he squeezed? His fingers had found the right place, the tender little hollow at the base of my throat, the right place to clutch if you wanted to strangle someone.

Then I thought: my pain, or theirs? Mine. I relaxed.

"Thank you." He kissed me again, very gently. His hand moved out of the way. He knew I wouldn't struggle, after that. I couldn't feel much, only pressure a sense of warmth. He moved my arms upward; I didn't help. My body was limp and cold. Hairs rose when the t-shirt was pulled away; there was a sense of pressure as he got up onto the couch, resting himself on my hips. He kissed my neck, my breasts, slid off the bra; I was aware of it, distantly, but my head lolled back on the armrest of the couch and my gaze found the ceiling.

He kissed as much of my flesh as he could reach; I knew he was doing it, in the way you know someone is tapping on a window—it doesn't mean you can touch, through the glass, or feel the warmth of skin through it. After a time, he rose a little, to pull down my underwear, and slid in.

I realised, distantly, that he was wearing a condom. As he began to move, inside, I thought, at least I won't have a baby. Then I slipped out of my body. He could have what he wanted, from that, but he couldn't have *me*.

When he was done, he rested on my body for a little while. His fingers were in my hair, his mouth was on mine; then, he pressed it to my ear.

"I'm sorry, I'm sorry, I'm so sorry," he whispered, over and over. "I'm so sorry, Avya. I love you so much. I'm so sorry. I can't help it." Then, moisture on my cheek, his body shaking. He sobbed silently, kissed my mouth over and over. "I'm so sorry."

The next day, Nicholas and Maria woke me late, made a huge breakfast. After that, we went out to the museum, to the mall; we drove around, the five of us. We laughed, we talked, we lived in the active and present tense. We looked like the families you dream of living in, the kind in which nothing seems to be wrong, the kind that might have come from a CBC commercial. It all looked so peaceful.

That night, Rodion came again. When I resisted, he placed his hands around my neck and tightened until I saw scintillating lights and black spots. Then he came to my body again, trying, pitifully, to make love. And, again, he cried afterwards.

The day after that was just the same. That night, though, I didn't resist. It was easier just to curl up inside myself, in a hollow space in my chest, or slip out of my flesh entirely. It wasn't *me* he was fucking, it was a doll; soft, limp, vacant.

VII

On the fourth day, we left for the airport. I hugged my parents tightly. It wasn't their fault I had been raped every night, not really, but I wouldn't have put up with it if not for them. And I still loved them, but I hated them, too. Surely they'd noticed that I wasn't myself? Why hadn't they said anything?

I looked at my mother, as she kissed my forehead, and I felt as though I was seeing her for the first time: a nice woman, a good woman, but not quite settled into the world. She seemed so fragile, just then, holding me, that I wanted to break. My father: A face like Rodya's, but a gentler look, and not without intelligence. And yet—he could only see what he wanted to.

When you look at your parents for the first time in years, with old wounds recently reopened, you can't help but see things more clearly than you could ever expect. At least, that's what happened to me, and as Natasha took my place, I wept a little. Not much—just a few tears—I didn't even realise I was crying until we reached the taxi, and noticed that my cheeks were wet.

I'd hugged Rod last, not allowing myself to feel his arms, and he was the last one on the step as we drove away. I stared after him for a long time, until the cab had rounded the corner and the house was out of sight.

Then I stared straight forward. Natasha didn't look at me, only stared out the window—uncharacteristically silent and lost in thought.

We made it to the airport on time, sure enough, and wandered around for a while before the flight. I wandered around the shops a little, and so did she; we both needed time apart, to not-think and look around at the lovely, cheap distractions on offer.

She and I arranged a meeting place and time, but Natasha caught me alone in a bathroom long before it. I ran into her at the sink; lost enough in myself that I didn't even notice her until she turned to look at me.

He expression in those deep chocolate irises, those shining, bright pupils, was one I hadn't seen in a very long time. I opened my mouth and closed it, and, when no sound came out, looked away.

She seized my chin in her fingers. "Your eyes are empty, Avya."

I blinked. My voice came back. "I don't know what you're talking about! Everything is fine!"

She stared at me for a very long time, her eyes narrow and sharp as needles. "Don't tell me that bullshit. Did he hurt you?"

I froze again, my throat closed, and I couldn't speak. She drew me into her arms, stroked my hair. "Let me go to your parents," she implored. "Please. I can't watch you like this."

I blinked. She shook my shoulders. "What do you want from me?" she whispered. "I can't help you if you won't help yourself!" Tears trickled down her face, but her nose didn't run, and her gaze was steady.

All at once, before I understood what had happened, I was thrown back into my body. My throat tightened, my nose started to run, and I sobbed. I sobbed as I had never done, before or since then. Perhaps it was because I'd spent so much time out of my own skin, or the things Rodya had done, or seeing my parents as they really were; it had forced me so far from my own flesh that I circled back to myself like a boomerang.

I could *feel* things, now, and there was a gaping, searing pain from my belly to my collarbone. I felt like a gutted fish, I ached; I could barely walk. We heard the door open, and Natasha herded me into the wheelchair-accessible stall.

I sobbed with everything I had, the tears hot and burningly salty. Natasha held me close and, when I paused for air, wiped my face with her scarf.

"I tried to," I stuttered. "I told him I'd scream and then they'd know why I'd run away. And he wrapped his fingers around my throat and told me he didn't want to hurt me…"

I knelt on the tiled floor; she came with me, awkwardly supporting me as I fell. I let my face rest on her shoulder again, and she rocked me. I was still shaking, and panting, and my head felt like a crown-shaped vice was squeezing in on it. Misery was coursing through me, hot and wretched, and I was back to where I'd been, all those years ago: a frightened, frantic little girl, confused, aching.

Natasha understood, too, because she began to croon a lullaby in my ear, very softly. I closed my eyes and listened. I didn't mention this, but she has a pretty voice, a pellucid soprano you wouldn't expect, to look at her.

The song lulled me into a dose. I remember that she dragged me to a bench, I remember taking refuge in sleep, and I remember that she didn't wake me until we'd reached Calgary.

It was a late flight, and we didn't get back to Natasha's apartment until ten to midnight. Natasha had slept, too, but the airport and the emotions had taken their toll. We collapsed into our beds the moment we reached the apartment.

When I woke the next morning, I forgot, for several moments, that I'd had the worst holiday season of my life. As I lay there and stared at the ceiling, I had about half an hour of peace. I wondered whether the whole thing had been a wretched dream. Yesterday's clothes were still on me. I hadn't even had time to strip before falling asleep.

Lying there, so quietly, I could almost believe there was nothing wrong. Could there really be anything awful or terrible outside this room, this soft bed? I inhaled.

It was coming back, everything, the panic tightening in my chest and belly, wringing me like a dishcloth. Only one way to find out if it was real. I unzipped my jeans and touched myself. The ache between my legs confirmed it: it had all been real. Three days nights of unwilling sex had taken their toll. I was sore, and not just there, either; my legs and arms had been tense for days, and all at once I ached to the bone.

I thought, this is what you did to me, Rodya. A moment ago, before I remembered, there was peace and warmth and even the beginnings of hunger. I was thinking about the possibility of breakfast. Now, I've been hollowed out again, frozen, every vein as cold as a winter road. It feels like the blood cells are skidding around corners, not flowing smoothly, I'm full of ice, I'm aching, and I couldn't swallow anything if I wanted to. I want to shower to get your pollution off me—if I have to take a bath in rubbing alcohol, I'll do it.

THE LOVED, THE LOST, THE DREAMING

This is a young woman realising that something awful has happened to her; this is her, kneeling over a toilet, sick to her stomach. Me.

VIII: Interlude

Even now, my stomach twists when I write about this. The handwriting in the journals of the time is strained. Even now, there's the temptation to freeze up, refuse access to the feelings. That's too easy. To cease feeling is to remove myself from the story, and this isn't a matter of journalistic integrity, wherein self-removal is a kind of virtue. I'm thirty-nine, I've had enough of distance and self-restraint, I've had enough of the past tense. Our thoughts don't exist in a time or verb tense; feelings change over time, but they don't run by grammatical rules or calendar dates. Let life run by them; it gave me enough time to stabilise between visits and prepare myself for the inevitable torture.

IX

We returned the next year to find that Rodion had a girlfriend; the year after, they were married. Though there were chances, he never touched me again. When I had to hug him (only done when others were looking on) I felt his hands linger, his arms tighten, just subtly enough to escape notice. Even then, it never happened when his wife was looking. Sometimes, though, across the dinner table, he would glance at me and I would see the thin veil over the longing in his eyes.

Tear it aside, with the right remark, for instance, and he would have been utterly naked. I wanted to do that so many times, to ask him why he was looking at me like, that, did he have something to say to me? I could imagine his response, too, so precisely. The pupils narrowing, muscles in the face growing taught. He would blush. I would add something else—cat got your tongue? Come on, tell us what you really think. I'd provoke him until he cracked, until a little piece of truth fell out of his mouth. It would fall like a funerary urn, spilling the ashes, the secrets. There would be a Scene. Maria and Nicholas would be horrified.

Then what? Here, it became utterly vague. I wanted it so badly, and yet, I didn't have it in me. The only thing to do was to smile, and nod, and spend as little time alone with Rodya as possible. In the rare moments when we *were* together, we didn't speak to each other—he would try, that is, and I'd sit in stone silence.

Even now, I wince; the memories pull at the scar tissue and threaten to tear it away entirely. There are other balms—thinking of Mark, for instance, or Pyotr. I wouldn't have imagined that I could have such simple sweetness. I've relearned plain joys, and the strange backwards-delight of having ordinary stresses and strains to worry about. That seemed so impossible. Having times when pleasure and concerns of the moment could let me forget the abuse, could allow me to move on, was inconceivable, then...I digress and get ahead of myself.

So: back to 1992, then, in the month of November, when life changed again.

X

November, 1992. Queen Elizabeth II would later proclaim 1992 an 'Annus horribilis', owing to some particularly bad press for the royal family and a fire at the palace. Barcelona had hosted the Olympics. A car crash shattered my family. The Church of England decided women could be ordained. There were numerous plane crashes and a particularly destructive run of tornados.

All in all, excepting the Olympics and the Anglicans, it was another unpleasant year.

Natasha was the one who got to the receiver first. It was November 1st—I should have looked more closely at the calendar, because it would have given the warning.

And so it was that on *Dia de los Muertos*, the Day of the Dead, Nicholas phoned us at 2:16 in the morning—

his voice shaking badly—to say that Rodya had been killed.

I saw it on Natasha's face before I took the receiver. Cold plastic in my fingers, the speaker against my ear, none of it seemed real. The sound of my father, sobbing, seemed to come from a long way off. I froze again, and listened to the story.

Rodya's wife, Jenny, and their baby daughter, Rebecca Ekaterina, had been in the car. They'd been on their way home from a Hallowe'en party. It was midnight, and the baby, whose angelic head had been adorned with mouse ears, was asleep in the back of the car. Jenny was wearing a cat costume, modestly cut. Rod had refused to dress up, and had gone in a casual suit, all black, with a vivid orange tie.

When Rod realised he'd left his coat behind, he decided to leave his wife and baby at home and retrieve it. Jenny told him to come in, go to sleep, go back to the Jordans' the next day and get it then. Being stubborn, he insisted on returning.

"The last thing I said to him," Jenny sobbed, "was 'be careful, people drive stupidly at this time of night.'"

Then he'd kissed her goodbye and gotten into the car, and, not ten minutes later, was hit by a drunk driver.

Jenny told me this part of the story herself. She was at my parents' house; her parents were there, too, and the baby. Dad had to speak for Maria; my mother had been weeping continuously since that morning.

I could hear her crying, then, as they switched to speakerphone mode. Weeping, wailing, the rest of it: a world away. Owing to the hour, I thought I was still asleep. Outside, a night's fresh snowfall gleamed, white against a hundred shades of grey, of blue, of sodium-yellow streetlight. Everything was frozen and perfect. I didn't want to leave it. Natasha's mouth moved, I didn't hear her speak; the sounds coming from the phone made no sense. The language bleeding from the speakers was a mongrel mixture of Russian and English, but—no, it was the sounds, really, they wouldn't coalesce.

A few words slipped out of my mouth, but they were nonsense syllables. By the time it set in, we were in the airplane, packed and on our way to Winnpeg. Natasha looked at me as neutrally as possible; when she forgot, the anxiety was so naked I could only take her hand in mine.

"I'm in one piece," I said, each time she gave me that look.

Describing the chaos, the desolation, in my parents' house, can't be done in any language. The air was humid with tears. I let myself thaw just enough to weep; the tears were cold as glacier meltwater. There were so many things to feel, too many, anger and sorrow and relief, too, and beneath it all, an intense pain. Blood and biology bound us, and I loved him, just a little; so many emotions, and beneath it all, the clean, bitter sharpness of grief.

Natasha held her sister until they were both too exhausted to sit upright, and fell asleep in each other's arms. I, traitor as I was, couldn't bear their company. The vicelike feeling had returned to the top of my skull. Everyone else was lost, distracted, and I wanted a way *out*, a chance to breathe. And yet—there was something to attend to. For the first time in years, I walked down to the basement and returned to his old room.

Very little had changed since the last time I'd seen it, really. My parents hadn't moved much, and Rod had seen fit to clean up and remove some of the older posters, but that was all. There was dust on the shelves and on the covers of the bed. I looked around, taking it all in, and then, I broke the stillness and walked over.

I lay down without moving the covers, and stared at the ceiling. This is where it had all begun. Was this an ending, then? He was dead. Gone. I'd never have to suffer through another too-long embrace, a sorrowful look from across the table. Never had to worry that he'd come to my bed in the night and take what he wanted from my body. Oil-black eyes would never again stare beseechingly at me.

He had said he was sorry so many times. He had claimed to love me. The one thing he had been unable to ask for was forgiveness. He knew I wouldn't grant it. How could it be forgiven? The first time, when I'd wanted it, in spite of my fighting, that was one thing. The next times, when I'd returned, I hadn't wanted it. I'd said so. He hadn't gone, he'd hurt me. "I'm so sorry, I'm so sorry, I love you so much..." Never "what I did was wrong", though. He knew it was wrong, implied it, felt it, but he hadn't said it.

I turned it over, holding it in my hands. There was a stone-heavy lump of pain in my chest. He'd said "I'm sorry" so many times, said "I love you", but never "this is wrong" or "forgive me". Now I was lying in his bed and he was lying in a morgue. There would be no other chance to ask for forgiveness, even to offer it. And—what good could it done? It couldn't have healed the tear and couldn't undo the past.

I wept, wholeheartedly, until there was nothing left, and then I fell asleep.

The week was too long. People drifted in and out of the house, and when the family couldn't manage it, we locked the doors. I dealt with my own grief quietly. Better to counsel pleasant, pretty, heartbroken Jenny than to tell her what her husband had done to me. Natasha knew; that was enough. Still, that didn't stop me from seething, at times, watching them polish his halo to a firebright gleam. The dead are never more perfect than in the first moments of their loss.

I was getting cynical again, and cold. Worse to find, then, that in spite of it all, I still loved him. I couldn't help it. There was no lust left—no room for that. Even the thought brought hatred surging in. Not love alone, then, but lovehate, hatelove, the words melting into one another.

Over the past few years, I'd run into the occasional familiar face, but for the most part, people hadn't recognised me. That was a relief, really—dealing with them would have been too much. The explanations, the chattery coffee sessions, awkward 'catch up' family dinners—it would inevitably be used as gossip; that went without question. The family needed that even less than I did. Meanwhile, the only thing to do was to keep my head low when I made emergency runs to the grocery store. Natasha did a lot of that, too, and helped with the cooking—between the two of us, with a little help from Jenny's parents, we managed everything. I made sure we didn't serve any of Rodya's favourite foods. The portions were pretty small, though—no-one had an appetite for anything. Cleaning the house was easy; picking up the tissues was all that really had to be done. Nicholas and Maria took the week off from work, attended to the funeral preparations—when they weren't comforting Jenny.

Jenny spent a lot of time lying on the couch or in the guest bedroom. She would stare at the ceiling catatonically, or she wept. When she forced out a word or two, it almost always had to do with Rodya. Sometimes she'd sleep—eating was almost out of the question, though she'd drink, as long as it was water or milk.

Rebecca cried a lot, but three-month-old infants tend to. Jenny was too depressed to feed her, though, so I did that, as much as I could. I couldn't hate Rebecca. Ignoring the fact that Rodya was her father was easier than I thought. Then, too, she was a small baby—and half an orphan already. If you're a human being, hating a creature that small and defenceless is beyond the pale. She didn't need the burden of some mysteriously wrathful Baba Yaga of an aunt in addition to the rest of it. That, at least, was certain.

The week lasted for a century, and when the funeral finally arrived, I was anything but prepared.

XI

Rodion's funeral. That was the summit, really, the Moscow winter. I didn't do anything outlandish, like wearing red—I was in black, just like everyone else. I wore a hat with a low brim and tucked my hair under it. My eyes almost never left the ground. The priest droned on, but I didn't hear a word. I had an impression of a spray of roses and carnations on the casket (which was closed), of pretty windows in the church, and of a sea of coal-coloured clothing, but the rest of the funeral was a blur. A few of Rod's high-school and university friends had made it—there were a lot more people than I'd expected. They eulogized about the boy I thought I knew. The family was quiet, though; we were in no state to talk, and they didn't force us to. Jenny's family spoke. At some point, Rebecca began to cry and Jenny took her out for air. It went on forever, and then it was done, and then we were standing in the graveyard.

The pit was a rectangular window in the snow. As they lowered his body into the ground, I tried to fit my mind around it. I looked up—the sky was an overcast, blurred grey, almost the same colour as the ground. If you slitted your eyes, the two would blur—trying it left me with vertigo. Staring at the flowers was the only sane option left, so that's what I did. That only worked for so long—at the end of the final graveside readings, people came forward and plucked the arrangement to pieces, taking blossoms for remembrance' sake.

Natasha cut through the crowd and returned with a carnation and a rose, and handed the latter to me.

Purplish red, it seemed to throb against her light skin.

"It's kind of the colour of beet juice," I said. "Pretty, though." She embraced me.

"Are you sure you're going to be all right?"

"What about you? He was your nephew, too."

"And your brother..."

I shook my head. "Actually, that's not quite...true..."

Natasha's eyes opened wide, but just then, before she had a chance to say something—

"Avdotya? Is that really...is that really you?"

Nicole's lines were right out of the book. I looked up sharply, connecting the voice with the face. It was her, all right—she'd put on quite a bit of weight, but it was her. I froze immediately, resorting, as always, to un-Russian self-containment. The only thing to do was thicken my accent, look down, and hope for the best. She wouldn't know the difference; she hadn't heard my voice since high school.

"No—I am sorry. My family is from Moscow—we are visiting the funeral. Rodion vas my cousin."

The look of disappointment on her face almost broke me—almost. "I see. It's just...you remind me of his sister. She...went missing some years ago."

"Yeah. I remember—a tragedy."

She held a tissue up to her nose. To my surprise, I realised she was already developing the beginnings of fine lines at the corners of her mouth and nose. It might have had something to do with the wedding ring on her hand. A wedding ring and wrinkles already—I might as well have been dead, for everything I'd missed from her life.

"I'm so sorry to mention that," she said, sniffing. "It was so sad..." Bleary-eyed, she took a closer look at my expression. I made my face innocent. "Actually, I'm sorry, I don't know how I made the mistake—really, you look nothing like her."

I looked over my shoulder at Natasha—she was shaking with laughter and covering it with whimpering sounds.

"Don't worry about it," I said to Nicole. She nodded, and sniffed again.

"I'm sorry we met at a time like this—perhaps later. I have to go soon, actually..." She looked at her watch. Rolex—and not a knockoff, from the looks of it. She may have been stressed, but she wasn't starving to death.

"Yes, yes," I answered. "Thank you..."

She smiled, and a different face slipped over hers, a more controlled expression. "I'm so sorry about your losses," she said, and a few more things, and then, she made an exit.

I resisted the impulse to track her path through the crowd, but I did hear her parting remarks as she walked away.

"I just don't know, Parmi...I thought I saw Avya for a minute, but it was just her cousin—can you believe it?"

I let myself search the crowd, and not far behind the two, I thought I recognised brown hair, a certain gait—Nicole's sister. She was a taller, thinner ghost behind Parmi's sleekness and Nicole's pear shape. For a moment, I thought she glanced in my direction—I recognised her face, but our eyes didn't meet. That was probably for the best. She would have recognised me.

Natasha had managed to control her laughter in the meantime, and had, inexplicably, begun to cry again. I put my arm around her shoulders, feeling oddly protective.

"Strange," she said, clearing the tears from her eyes, "that *you're* the one comforting me." She shook her head. "You've done enough comforting this week." I nodded, my throat aching. She took my chin in her hand again. With that look focussed on me, hiding something was impossible. The ice around me began to crack.

She kept an arm around my shoulders as we headed towards the gates. Once we were outside them, and waiting for the cab, release came. I let the tears slide down, over my cheeks, my lips, wondered if it was cold enough for them to freeze immediately. Then again, I remembered, salt water freezes at a much lower temperature. There wasn't room for much emotion, not yet—thought was easier.

Natasha squeezed my shoulders. "I wanted to tell you—that was very Russian, what you did back there."

"Huh? What?"

"With that girl. Nicole."

"Ha! How's that? Deception? Downright fuckin' lying?"

"Well, that's how we won the Cold War..."

We managed to catch a flight out that evening. It was a silent return, too—but Natasha's silence reassured me. Each time our eyes met, she gave me a look that said: you have courage. Now, use it and tell me what you're thinking. That's not so much to ask, is it?

The sallow starlight of cities flickered up at us. The night had become surprisingly clear, and I could see everything below us. Maybe it was the altitude or the circumstances or the hour, but it all seemed so ridiculous. In all of those thousands of houses beneath us, similar dramas were undoubtedly playing out, sordid stories like mine. And yet—it all looked so utterly serene, from up here. You'd never know.

"What's on your mind?" Natasha asked. "You look...you have a funny expression on your face."

"I'm in one piece," I said. "I'm calm."

Still in shock, her expression said. I looked at her a little more closely, then. The lines around her eyes were deeper, and her light-coloured roots were showing through—she hadn't re-dyed her hair in a while. Her face had a certain kind of strength in it, beauty, but not the breakable kind, and she had—still has—the sort of mouth you'd call sensuous if not for the hardness it can hold. I don't mean that Natasha's a hardass or humourless, or that she was then, but her face does show that she's suffered through life.

I thought about this as I looked at her, and she knew what I was thinking, wondering about. "Stop analysing me," she said. "Stop thinking."

"What? But—"

"No, Avya." Her voice was so very quiet. "I am *not* picking up the pieces for you, just to let you turn yourself into the ice queen again."

It was like being shaken out of sleep by someone's hands on my shoulders. Natasha wasn't shaking gently, either.

"Fuck you," I whispered. The lady across the isle whipped her head around to look at me and I lowered my voice a little more. "Fuck you. What do you call everything I've been doing this week?"

She didn't even pause. "You're good at setting your own needs aside to help others, I have to admit."

"And you call me an ice queen? What the hell, Natasha?"

"I didn't say you were uncaring. I said you're thinking too much."

I switched over to Russian, just to show her how pissed off I was. "Thinking too much? What, this has been hard. Feeling it is..." I searched for the word, couldn't find it. Russian has too many words. "It's not impossible for me now, I..."

"...Didn't even get the chance to ask him the questions burning a hole in your tongue," she interrupted. That did it. I turned my head away from her. I felt the tears well up—they were hot and my eyes stung with the salt.

I was acutely aware of everything, of my body, in particular, and suddenly, that was the only thing I could experience. The lactic acid in my calves and lower back from all the tension. The numbness of my ass, my thighs, in the seat. The fabric of the blouse and bra against the skin of my arms and breasts. The tautness of my shoulders. The awareness of the hidden small white scar lines in unseen places on my skin. My body—shunned, betrayed, ignored, numbed, overused. It should have been worn out in every way.

THE LOVED, THE LOST, THE DREAMING

"Don't hide inside your skin," Natasha growled. I didn't care. My eyelids slammed shut. A sense of vertigo gripped me—I couldn't tell which way was up; it seemed as though I was slowly rotating on a wheel. St. Catherine bound to an invisible, gentler wheel.

I opened my eyes and looked at her. "Stop asking me questions," I said, in English. "Stop telling me what to do. You're my aunt, not my mother."

Her eyes widened with pain. "Avdotya..."

I shook my head resolutely and ignored her until the plane touched down, but I could see the tears rolling down her cheeks.

When we finally got back, it was nearly midnight. We collected our bags with a minimum of discussion, picked up the car, drove back without a word. I was feeling everything, and thinking at lightning speed— putting pieces together. The silence, for me, was no longer one of resentment, it was filled with intense thought.

Natasha didn't know that, of course. She was becoming more taut by the moment. As we reached the apartment, she finally broke the silence.

"Well?"

I looked at her. "What do you want me to say? I miss him? I wish he hadn't been my brother? I'm glad he's dead?" I spoke without thinking, and the mongrel mix of Russian and English came most readily. "There's nothing left to say. He's gone."

She gripped my shoulders. "You're still carrying him around."

I returned her gaze. "And what about you? You haven't said a thing about how you feel. Your blood nephew is gone. Your sister had to bury her own son." Natasha flinched. I went on, blood rushing to my head. Natasha didn't flinch, period. This was reaching home—there was something else going on in her mind.

"It gives me a sense of sorrow," she said, in English. "What else is there?"

"Well, you don't have any children yourself…"

That was one of the only topics Maria had told us never to ask Natasha about. As children, as teenagers, keeping the promise had been easy. We really didn't see her often at all. When I'd come running to her, I'd been wrapped up in myself. Now, grief and sorrow and anger were coursing through me, pounding through me. Every inch of my flesh was alive. I was hungry and thirsty, but catching the scent of something strange.

It was the right thing to say, or the wrong thing. She blew up. "How *dare* you needle me about that at a time like this! This is not about me!"

She threw her suitcases down, walked over to the sofa, and violently threw down her coat.

"Why don't you have children?" I repeated.

Natasha had never been like this. Until now, she'd been in the shadows, supporting me along the way, but never getting into the light herself. She was out of control of her emotions.

"Who ever said I didn't?"

Huh?" I hadn't seen it coming. Now we were both light-headed with anger and emotion.

"And here's another thing—have you even noticed that I look nothing like my sister?"

Somehow, we'd switched into Russian again. Everything is pronounced so clearly and carefully in that tongue that there's no room for mishearing someone, not really.

"What does that have to do with not having children or having them?"

We watched each other from across the room in silence for more than three quarters of a minute. When Natasha spoke, her voice was hoarse.

"Not tonight. Another night, I'll explain this. Let's go to sleep."

"Explain in the morning," I demanded. "Or now, so it doesn't keep me awake all night."

She wanted to tell me, I could see it. I was dying to know—and yet, all at once, I didn't want to know. There were too many questions. The adrenalin surged out of my system.

"Make it the morning," I amended. "Please? I just want to go to sleep. No more drama."

It was a bad word. The sparks kindled in her eyes. "Drama! Is that all it is?"

"Right now, yes," I interrupted. "Please?"

She threw her hands in the air. "Fine. Tomorrow, if you still want to know. Does it matter to you?" She paused, gathered her breath. "If you say no, I won't burden you with it. You don't have to care…"

"I do, though…"

A strange expression crossed her face. There was trepidation, relief, and fear there—and all at once, Natasha turned from me to return to the kitchen. She turned on the faucet, filled the teapot with water. Letting my eyes blur over the scene of the living room, I stared aimlessly out a window.

The snow outside had been shovelled away, and most of the remainder had been beaten into a taupe slush under the wheels of cars. There was still a bit of untouched snow here and there, and it was blue in the reflected light of the streetlamps. So much and so little had changed in the week.

Somewhere, a bell tolled out the hour. I settled into the folds of the couch and fell asleep before the tea was brewed.

XII: Interlude

Looking back at it now, I want to smack myself for failing to see what was right in front of my eyes. Then again, expecting a twenty-two-year old to decipher her own undisclosed family history—and before the current era of internet research, online family histories, and all the rest.

I suppose a long story ought to be kept short—that said, it's Natasha's story, not mine. There's no way to do justice to it when this manuscript has been selfishly set aside for my own narrative. Concentrating on her, on anyone, requires something selfless, something ferocious, something there's little room for here. It's an egocentric thing, to write out one's own tale, and even intoxicating. I don't want to share its space, in some perverse way, because the territory has been marked as my own.

And still—too many excuse. I'm thirty-nine; I have time enough for her story, or at least some of it.

XIII

Natasha was born about a hundred kilometres outside St. Petersburg on December 17, 1940, two years and nine months—to the day—before my mother was. Maria was born in 1943, so both of them were war babies. That meant poverty, for a while, and quotas, and a hundred darknesseses, great and small, that no-one ever seemed to get around to discussing.

"Times were hard, that's all. You might say—
'shitty' covers it well," Natasha said simply.
"Anyway—yes. I met Maria when we were teenagers."

Their families lived close by, in neighbouring
apartment buildings, so they'd known of each other
before. As Maria and Natasha sweated through the
same classes and whiled away hours at the same boring
communist youth clubs together, they became closely
bound, fast friends—more than comrades (and the
word is much warmer in Russian, more like 'friend').
Really, they were sisters: my mother, with her younger
siblings dead in infancy, and Natasha, an only child,
had always felt a sense of loneliness, a need for a sister.
In each other, the need was completed.

The only bit of trouble in the matter was the fact
that Natasha's father had had a few unpleasant run-ins
with the party members. He didn't hide his western
preferences well enough, and naturally, there was
friction. It wasn't quite enough for imprisonment—the
infractions were too small. At first. He had never been
a very useful sort of man, Natasha said, just mouthy
and inclined to small rebellions. "Something of an ass,
my father," she said, shaking her head. Not merely an
ass—a strike-anywhere match waiting for
circumstances to light him.

Her mother, on the other hand, believed in neither
the USSR nor the West. She wanted to keep her head

down and lead a life as pleasant as possible, within the confines of constant scarcity. An ordinary woman, with little colour in her life, as Natasha described her, who loved her husband and her daughter. That said, when the friction between Natasha's father and the party finally sparked into a fire, her mother had no qualms about marching down to Maria's and begging them to take Natasha.

Maria's parents had much better connections, were much quieter, and had enough money to shelter another teenage girl. Natasha was known for doing well in school, being clever, and generally, little trouble for figures of authority, so accepting her into their family was less of a risk than it might have been. Maria's (widowed) aunt had recently died, and with a great deal of bribery, risk, and recopying of red-ink documents, a newly orphaned niece was manufactured.

She took a new name, a new surname and patronymic—became more than a girl living in the shadow of a dissident father. Still—times were only getting more complicated. Slipping out of the country was the best option, and so it was—Maria's family brought Natasha with them when they fled to Canada.

The girls finished high school in Winnipeg and went off to university. Maria went into a quietly useful career—education—and Natasha fought her way through a journalism degree. One daughter married a nice second-generation Russian-Canadian, settled into a career and child-rearing. The other surfed the precarious tides of feminism and tried to make a living on writing what she saw.

It was the sixties, and even when times were lean, Natasha managed to do more than just get by. She became slightly notorious, modestly successful, and enjoyed life. She explored sex—and later still, fell in love a few times.

"Then I was pregnant, and the fun stopped."

"When was that?" I asked.

I will never forget the way she looked at me, then, squarely in the eye, with something almost like blankness, and said, "Oh, 1968, about nine months before your birthday."

Natasha couldn't raise me. However, Maria wanted a daughter, but Rodya's delivery had been difficult and conceiving again was contraindicated. If nothing else, at least my arrival was timely. Nicholas loved his wife enough to obey her decision, and had gotten the son he wanted. Soon enough, the papers were signed and it had quietly been arranged. Natasha changed her name one last time.

"I took this name because it's who I am, and I like it," she said. "My names before that, they don't matter, not now."

I blinked, thinking it over. Tried to get the word 'mom' to cross my lips. She seemed to read my thoughts.

"Just call me Natasha. Nothing else."

There was so much silence in the room. My tongue was dry—wrapping it around the next question was so hard.

"And what are you going to call me?"

"What I have always called you. It suits you, you know."

Natasha's expression had been shifting continuously. Now, a terribly gentle look had settled into the corners and creases in her face, the fine lines, and smoothed them. She didn't look any younger, though—older, in fact, but much lighter in spirit. I wanted to numb myself, but I was so raw, now, there was no hiding from it, from the facts. There was no room for comprehension, either, not really, even if it all made devastatingly good sense.

I couldn't think of a good question to ask her, not really. "Why does it suit me? It's from a book. She didn't even give me a name of my own."

Natasha inhaled slowly. "Avdotya comes from a Greek word meaning 'to seem well'."

To seem well, rather than being well. Yeah, that was about it. For the most part, I almost looked normal, looked like the girl who could handle anything. From within, gods only knew just how much of a trainwreck I really was. What could I say?

"One more question," I said. "Why didn't you tell us earlier? I don't even think it would have been so bad..." And yet, if the name on the adoption certificate had been recognisable, if only...I'd have known then, and so many questions would have been answered, so much earlier...

"That's why Maria and I barely spoke for years," she said. "I wanted to say something, she thought it would just hurt." She looked at me, blinked slowly. "If I had known what would happen, I would have kept you, damn the difficulties. But, a normal life for you...it seemed better."

"So much for that."

Natasha cleared her throat. I could tell it was a little sore from so much talking.

"Look...there's a lot...to think about...do you mind if I just...go for a walk, for a while?"

"That's...yes, that would be fine."

We didn't look at each other. Couldn't, in a way. I walked over to the door, pulled on my worn-out black parka, and prepared to face the cold.

The city offered the stony blankness of too much snow and concrete and glass. I stuck my hands in my pockets, fiddled with my keys. I couldn't register what

I saw, the sounds coming into my ears. I let my feet take me down the sidewalk, and eventually, across the road. A guy in a red sedan honked at me; I stumbled on a patch of ice and grinned feebly. Perversely, it felt good to make someone else come a sudden and unexpected stop.

I spent a lot of time wandering around that day. Nothing was really registering. It was as though the world was a film on mute, still going, images flickering, but there was no sound to connect the pictures and make sense of the shapes on the screen. I didn't want to go back to the apartment, because that meant seeing Natasha. I wasn't ready to face her yet.

Part of me wanted to scream at her until I went hoarse, myself. A very large part wanted to call up Maria and Nicholas and tell them what I'd just learned. It explained so much—why Natasha had been so willing to help me, the awkwardness in the family no-one would talk about. In some way, it even explained what had happened to Rodya—why he'd never quite seemed like a brother, why he'd never really seen me as a sister. Still—no—it didn't excuse what had happened, at the end of the day.

Eventually, emotions and thoughts were pounding away inside my skull and I had to go back to the apartment for painkillers. Natasha was still there, waiting for me, so I did what I'd never done before: yelled at her.

"Why didn't you tell me? I can't believe how much I've gone through just because I didn't know anything. How could you have done that to me? You're my mother!" And so on and so forth.

Something had finally snapped. Letting it out felt so damned good. There was no room to think. I can't even remember everything I said, in fact, just the release in the act of saying it. My head had stopped pounding, my mind was finally clear. I felt lighter.

It was the first time I'd let myself yell at someone, in fact, since I'd been a teenager. Maria and Nicholas didn't do that. We'd been a quiet family, things resolved peacefully and in a relatively orderly fashion, when necessary. (Apparently that's unusual for Russians, as I learned later. Gods, I would've given anything for a few good yelling matches. But, the grass is always greener.)

When I was finished, she blinked and went into the kitchen to make tea. I sat there, in the living room, and stared at the icons and photographs on the wall. Saints stared back, placid-eyed and pious, hands together and asking for mercy. Not this time, I thought. Mercy is a wonderful way to live until you don't have any left to give.

THE LOVED, THE LOST, THE DREAMING

Natasha stayed out of my way as the kettle boiled. Glancing over my shoulder, I could see that she was standing in front of the stove, bracing herself. The bracelets on her wrists glittered, and inexplicably, I thought of Christmas presents. She'd given me a lot of jewellery—I was wearing a bangle now, in fact. She'd always given the nicest presents, even when she and Maria weren't talking. Warm letters, too, in spite of everything. Funny how you can accept love so unconsciously and not even come to appreciate it until something drastic happens.

"Well," she said, as she set the teapot down in front of me, "at least you're not as fragile and repressed as your mother."

"You're not mad at me for yelling at you?"

She blinked again. "Why would I be? I'd have done some yelling myself, if I were you. It took you long enough."

I nodded and poured myself a scalding hot cup. Pitch-black, the way I liked it. "Can I have a biscuit? *Pojhaluista?*" (Please?)

"Of course." She pushed the bowl of cookies in my direction.

"*Spasibo.*" Thanks, and I meant it. I dipped it into my tea and bit gratefully. Comfort food.

We munched and sipped in silence for a while.

"So, are you going to call up and yell at your parents?" Natasha asked. I heard the timidity in her offhanded tone.

I swallowed and thought for a moment. "Nah. I have better things to do with my time. And, again, the timing would be horrible."

"Are you sure?"

"More tea?"

"Yes, but answer the question."

"Well…" I inhaled. "I had time to think, and you know, I realised something—if she doesn't want to tell me, she can't handle this. I can handle secrets, and I know that. So might as well not make her lose a daughter when she's just lost a son."

Natasha stared at me. "Are you feeling all right?" Traffic noise filled the space in a few beats' pause.

"Better than I have in a very long time," I said.

"Well, you don't yell at people, so I figured you'd either had a head injury or an epiphany."

"Mm-hmmm." There was another pause. "So, are you going to tell me any more about yourself?"

"Huh?" The cup nearly overflowed, she was so startled.

"Well, I have to go back to work soon, but in the meantime, I guess you might as well tell me about yourself. I mean, is there anything else I should have asked about, all this time?"

So she started to tell me. And, little by little, the weather lifted, and the sun came in.

XIV: Interlude

So, beginning abruptly and unceremoniously, I found myself liberated. Well, mostly. It always takes a good deal more time than you expect, the recovery process. Still, I was finally growing up enough to deal with my own shit—the time of stagnation, of freezing, was over at last. I'd still have cold spells, there was no denying that. I was learning to argue, learning to fight back against myself. It wasn't that I healed overnight, but the process did accelerate.

How else to describe it? It was about letting grief fade from daily memory. I went out more often. I started to speak to people more often rather than just getting by with the basics. I swallowed my fear. (And antidepressants—though they gave me nightmares, and insomnia for a much longer period than the usual couple of weeks. When it interfered with work I had to stop—by then I didn't need them as much anyway.)

Something about knowing that there never would be closure, while unsettling, gave me a reason to move on. It was a paradox worthy of a monk's contemplation—being inspired to do something by knowing you can't do the thing that matters most.

Confronting Maria and Nick was the worst. Telling them that I knew about the adoption was bad enough. I never could work my tongue around admitting the truth about Rod. Take that as you will; after the crash my mother was enough of a ghost. In my absence, Rod had become, if not the favourite, the only child. That was difficult enough—selfishness was a necessity, had been for a very long time, and I'm as inherently selfish as the next person. Realising what it was like to have the spectral daughter returned from the dead, only to lose the son who'd been there when I hadn't been…that made it even harder to tell them. Hatred for Rod—and I still harboured some—was inevitably tempered by that knowledge.

If he'd been a monster it would've been easier, but it wasn't, and I was suddenly enough of an adult to handle that. Maria is fragile even now—she never did move beyond it, and varied between long periods of not mentioning Rod at all to brief spasms in which she'd have a one-track mind related solely to things involving him.

Now, for the most part, things have been dealt with. Every Halloween and every end of November takes me a little farther away from that time, but in the last year, it's been haunting me more and more often. Pyotr makes coffee unasked, leaving it by my desk, and keeps a watchful eye—the minute a certain look passes over my eyes, he says, he knows what's on my mind. At times like that I'm likely to smell blinis cooking in the kitchen.

Why I've been thinking of the past so often, lately, I don't know. I suppose I could blame it on Maria's health, which is really shitty, or on the fact that Jenny's daughter has beautifully black hair and eyes just like her father. It could be any number of things. This time, I'm laying it to rest, writing the story out for the first time. Reputation be damned, the truth tends to out itself like a reluctant drag queen. And besides, who will believe a story like this?

XV

1995. The European Union gained three new members. The Oklahoma City Bombing happened and scared the shit out of everyone. Ebay and Yahoo were founded. Microsoft 95 was released. My life got back on track. Members of a Japanese cult released sarin gas in a subway. I fell in love.

It wasn't the best year for the world, but it was one of the best for me. It started, in fact, on July 22nd. It ought to have been an ordinary Saturday at the downtown Calgary public library. I had a pile of books sitting next to me on the desk, reference tomes, and magazines, and a number of windows open to websites on my laptop. I was pressed for time, owing to a looming deadline, and annoyed by the shitty quality of the muffin I was trying to eat. It was not an auspicious beginning to what would later become one of my favourite days of the year. I was more concerned about writer's block, dry muffins, and boring references. A stack of abandoned literary hardcovers on a desk nearby waited alluringly, and after a while, it was too much to take. I was hot, impatient, and tired of my own prose. I let the laptop snap shut with a satisfying click, and packed my things away.

As I was walking down the stairs, I noticed that someone had left a sandwich crust behind. Picking it up, examination revealed a small blodge of mustard near the edge of the rye. Scanning leftovers wasn't a particular habit, I just remember that sandwich because I was hungry. I picked it up and set about looking for a trashcan, and that's when it happened.

A guy was standing at the foot of the staircase ogling me. As always, dark hair and a similar build made me do a double take, but it wasn't a ghost. The guy didn't even look like Rodya, really. Part of a sandwich still remained in his hand, and when he saw me looking, he glanced away sheepishly. He couldn't be much older than I was, but there was already grey in his hair. He smiled shyly, hazel eyes tightening at the corners like a cat's.

He turned around and went back to his table. I was curious, so I crept down and spied on him. He had a briefcase pen on the desk—nice, calfskin, but it was open and messy. His clothes were nice, but seemed to be designed expressly to avoid drawing attention. He wanted to blend in. I felt a little guilty, clearing my throat, disturbing his peace.

"You dropped some of that sandwich back there," I said. I held it up awkwardly, and, noticing a trashcan, tossed it in.

Ah, right—thanks." His accent was pure Old Country. This was a nice Russian boy, all right, with those same sweet curling *r*s and smoky consonants.

"You might want to know that you left your crusts by the entrance to the literature deck. The librarian on the next shift is a clean freak, and you might want to keep an eye on it—she'll garrote you if she finds them."

"Thanks for the heads up," he said, and shot me an expression halfway between a grin and a smile. It was shy, sweet, and caught me off-guard: so open. That made me shy, so I nodded, and smiled in return, and left for quieter corners.

I saw him several times, in later weeks, and each time, we'd nod at each other, exchange small smiles. Finally, he broke from the usual routine to ask me my name.

"Avdotya Pulcheria Kalinnikov," I replied. His grin was less sheepish.

"Straight out of Dostoevsky? You don't have a brother called Raskolnikov, do you?"

He didn't even mean to say *his* name, but there it was. I blanched. "Are you all right?"

"Huh? Yeah, I'm fine. And, ah, I didn't catch your name."

"Pyotr Dimitrov."

It hit me so suddenly: I noticed that he had a really lovely face. Thick eyebrows, yes, a slightly-too-wide nose—those features recalled Rodya's, but Pyotr's cheekbones were higher. His jaw was softer, the hair a lighter colour, He looked nothing like him and still, the whisper of a resemblance was like steel blades against my skin.

"Are you sure you're all right?"

"Of course," I said, "just a bit of flu." I cleared my throat. "Actually, I want some coffee or something hot, so…yeah…would you…"

"I…I wouldn't mind a cup of coffee myself," he said. I managed to smile again. He stood, very cautiously, and lifted his briefcase. Then, all at once, we were descending the stairs and heading towards the café. He didn't lead, but he didn't follow, either—he walked at the periphery, as if distracted.

THE LOVED, THE LOST, THE DREAMING

Time passed, it always does. Saturdays began to acquire a familiar shape. Pyotr and I would have coffee, discuss books, and make small-talk. He was comfortable with silence, too, which I liked. I was instinctively comfortable with him, even his unRussian timidity. It took several months before we spoke of anything of real importance. I learned that he'd been through the circuit with women. He hadn't found anything he'd liked. I, myself, had not revealed the details of the brief, unhappy couplings I'd had.

There's really nothing like oblivion-sex. It's got to be one of man's most futile coping mechanisms. Sometimes, a human being who will look you in the eyes, with no idea about your past and share a bed with you, can become a saint. Then there's the next morning and the return to loneliness. When I'd talk with Pyotr, I didn't mention sex much. I was trying to leave behind those old attempts to try to induce amnesia about Rodya's hand on the hidden bridges and architecture of my spine. There were blueprints to redraw.

Natasha noticed my moods, and the gradual improvement, and couldn't help remarking on it. I admitted that I'd found a friend.

She raised her eyebrows and said, *"Friend?* And male?"

"Friend," I said.

She shrugged, but a grin played at her mouth. "As long as you're happy."

"Well, I am—he's a *friend*."

And it was true. I can't say I expected anything to happen, even though I knew he didn't have a girlfriend. He was handsome enough, in his own, very Russian, way, and he sometimes helped me stop thinking about the ghost in my closet. Ghosts. Every call from Winnipeg brought in trouble.

There was something familiar, too, about the look in Pyotr's eyes, which slipped through whenever he avoided referring to the past. He had his secrets, I had mine, and though we brushed against them every so often, it was better to speak briefly and move on. Still—for the most part, we could talk to each other, and daily troubles were easy enough to share. Then, too, thoughts of Pyotr relaxed me. When work was difficult, I could imagine his remarks, his grin, his habits of slurping coffee and slamming doors by accident, and get through it.

XVI

The first hint slipped out during coffee one day. *Anna Karenina* was sitting on the table, I was working my way through it for the second time, and Pyotr— who'd studied it in school, was explaining why he had a grudge against Tolstoy.

"He's a master of the human condition! How can you hate Tolstoy?"

He sipped his coffee—slurped it, rather, and hearing that noise, I hid a grin. "I don't *hate* him. I just think he's, you know, abstract. He chases after so many protagonists, so many stories at once."

"That's partly why I like him, though," I said. "He does it so well—and they all seem so real."

Pyotr shook his head. "Yeah, I know, but it seems to me that he's afraid of thinking about one person at a time. He gets so caught up in the grand scale of things that he doesn't concentrate enough on simple things. And he's not very nice to people."

"Life isn't nice to people."

"Well, *da*," (he pronounced it '*duh*', and made a face,) "but does it mean he has to be so cruel to his characters? A girl sleeps with the wrong man and she is condemned to ruin and being squashed under a train." He shook his head. "If I could write, it would've had a happy ending, or at least, she wouldn't have been splattered all over the tracks. Girls make mistakes like that, but if it was a man, he wouldn't have had to kill himself in the end, you know?"

I choked on my coffee. "Are you all right?"

"Yeah…" And then, as if a stage direction had been given, our eyes met. For about two seconds, I seriously considered explaining everything, all at once. Common sense got the better of me. "I suppose I can empathise with Anna, let's put it that way," I said, and left it at that. (In retrospect, I can give you some advice—tell common sense to fuck itself.)

XVII

I thought he considered me a friend, no more. I wouldn't have known otherwise if not for that night.

Jenny had become a friend, somehow. I hadn't told her about what had happened with Rod, of course, but liking her kid brought us together. She was a wreck for a long time, but I helped with that (making her less of one) and she turned out to be surprisingly strong. She, in turn, had become a surrogate daughter to Maria, and had kept an eye on things back home. Three years after the fact, after being completely broken down, she was like a reforged blade—stronger and cooler when it all went bad, but still capable of breaking down if the right point was touched. She needed all of it when she told me about the news.

It was a warm night, but not hot—pretty and breezy, almost September, softly autumnal. It was the night I heard about the accident. About another car crash, a mess, involving Maria. She was in the hospital with a few relatively minor injuries. She'd gone driving with cold medications on board. Stupid, stupid—but she'd collided with someone else. A lady driver was in critical condition. Jenny's voice shook when she told me the names and the information, and when I started to cry, she lost it too.

Oh, the irony, the cruel irony. Too neat to be real, I thought I was dreaming. It was the wife of the guy who'd hit Rodya all those years ago.

I couldn't process it all and decided to go down and get a couple of drinks. I know better, I knew better then, too, but it was beyond rational thought. When Natasha heard, she called me, and after we spent a couple of hours crying and worrying, I really needed an escape.

One of the least intelligent things I've ever done lead indirectly to one of the best things ever to happen to me. If I hadn't run into Pyotr as I was crossing the street, off-kilter after the vodka. If he hadn't asked, "Come on, your mascara's running, what's happened?" If I hadn't started crying again. If he hadn't said, "All right, fine, tell me your address and I'll get you home, because you're not in a condition to drive." If I hadn't gotten into a cab with him and felt the warmth of his legs through his khakis. And perhaps I wouldn't have brought him up. He wouldn't have made me coffee.

Most of all, I wouldn't have poured out the whole story about Rodya from so many years ago. He wouldn't have said, "Well, at least you weren't really siblings. Show me one person who'd never, ever had dreams about a hot cousin. And you weren't even cousins."

I wouldn't have started laughing.

If I hadn't been laughing and tipsy, but trying to sober up, I wouldn't have gotten coffee spilled all over myself. And then I wouldn't have had to excuse myself to get changed and put my clothes in the sink to soak out the stains. If I hadn't begin looking at myself, at my whole situation, and burst into hysterical laughter (again), he wouldn't have come into my bathroom.

He found me in my least-glamorous white underwear and brassiere. There, too, laid out for all to see, were the little white lines on the inside of my thighs and upper arms, only ten or fifteen of them, and small, but still there. Natasha had put a stop to the cutting, but pale skin keeps scars well. He looked, and the light dawned on him, and instead of turning away, he knelt before me.

"It's all right." And, if I hadn't begun to cry, telling him to go, he wouldn't have shaken his head and given me a look that said he knew sorrow inside out. He tucked me into my own head and fell asleep next to me, his body warm and soft like a dog's. In sleep, his arm twisted over me, and I settled into the curve of his side as if I'd been carved to fit it.

Then I woke the next morning, no hangover because I'd only had two shots of vodka, and Pyotr was there, kissing my forehead.

"I was hurt, too," he said, in Russian. "It's a long story."

"Tell me," I said. And he explained it all, slipping from English to Russian and back again.

Afghanistan had left its marks on him, he said, and showed me the white keloids from the shrapnel in his calf. He told me about "freedom fighters" and being cold and lonely and uncertain on the front. The sound of a rifle clicking and the explosion and the hollow, ugly feeling of knowing that a life was gone. His training kept him safe for a long time, kept the hollowness out. There was an old woman, one day, in a village, who screamed as soon as she saw his troop come to town, and wouldn't stop. His friend had shot her in the head, quickly, to make the screaming stop. Hours later, the old woman's son threw a lucky grenade.

Pyotr's friend hadn't stood a chance.

That was the end of the war for Pyotr. The hours after the grenade were a blur. The rest of the patrol squad had been killed. They found him in the morning, holding his friend's body, shaking and rocking. When it didn't go away, and when his screams kept the whole camp awake, he'd been sent back to civilization with a pall of dishonor and shame hanging over him. He told me about waking up in a cold sweat, screaming nightmares, and the hours spent talking to psychiatrists. Swallowing pills with unpronounceable names and getting every side-effect in the book. Feeling alone in spite of the knowledge that thousands of other soldiers were going through the same thing. Addictions on the horizon beckoning, the possibility of blurring and distancing himself in oblivion. He looked away when he described that part, trying to hide in drugs.

And, in spite of it, Pyotr had given the finger to all the possible fates. He'd held on to what he knew, which was not a hell of a lot but just enough. He held onto books and sex and Judo and sunsets. He lay there in my arms and told me everything he knew about himself. It was past noon when he'd finished, his throat scratching a little.

When he couldn't speak anymore, we lay there, listened to each other's breathing. When was the last time I'd just listened to a man's breathing, without fear or apprehension? The soft sigh of his lungs, knowing that he was resting, not on the hunt for me. A flutter of trust.

Sex had been a blur of liquor and mistrust and sharp cold distant things. It was Rodya's teeth in my neck. Pain. The walk of shame out of a chilly apartment. This was nothing like that. His warm skin, his scars, my scars. Pyotr's gentle mouth on my breasts, my shoulders, my hips. Tender need but no burning urgency, need but no painful desire to get to the orgasm and be done with it. No need to shut my eyes and clench my teeth. Our bodies melting together in the warm covers. His thrust and desire so, so gentle—and finally, wanted.

I would cry later, but then, I was too full of wonder and relief. A happiness so bright and good it hurt paralysed me. He urged me closer to him, and I let Pyotr draw me in. It took forever to break the silence.

I said, "Hey, it's Sunday, have breakfast with me."

Afterwards, after having eaten the greasy, delicious blini he somehow managed to make just about perfectly, I said, "Thank you for everything."

Pyotr looked up cautiously. "Are you sure?" I shook my head.

"Look, if you don't think I'm just a freak, call me some time." I took a piece of paper off my notepad and wrote my number on it in large, clear letters, and my email, as well, and slid it across the table. He looked down at it with something akin to sadness passing across his face.

"I will," he said. "Look, I *don't* think you're a freak. Not at all." Somehow, we rose at the same time. He cupped my face in his hands and kissed me. I kissed him back, didn't break it off for a long while.

"You have a normal life to get back to…"

"Normal?" He laughed. "With a side of fucking shrapnel? Believe me. I have an ordinary job and an ordinary house and ordinary stuff in my ordinary rooms, and I'm still not ordinary. Normal is fucking *out.*"

He was looking away. I reached for his hand. "We just need practice with normalcy…then again, it's fucking overrated…" I cleared my throat. "If you need someone around…I mean, I'm pretty screwed up, but…I can listen. If it's easier, though, you don't have to…come back…"

He looked up immediately, squeezed my fingers. "Thank you. But I want to see you again." His voice was plaintive. I smiled, and I knew it was too slow and sad to be a grin. "Come on, smile for me for real, Avdotya." And I did.

"I'll see you soon," he said, as he left. I didn't know whether he would or not. Happily, I didn't actually care. A small miracle had taken place, there was light in the sky. It seemed the chinooks were coming in at last.

A week later, I was at home. I'd been to the library, but I didn't see Pyotr there. I figured he'd taken my advice, but I hadn't given up on him yet. I'm a closet optimist. I had no plans that night, so I spent some time watching a movie, paying little attention. Humphrey Bogart was about to deliver a pithy reply when I heard the knock.

"Hello?"

"Avya? It's me."

I hung up and opened the door. There was Pyotr, grinning, looking a little self-conscious. I grabbed him by the lapels, grinning like a child, a fool, a saint. "Come in," I said, and he slammed the door behind him.

XVIII

In the middle of handling flights out to visit Maria and Nicholas, we got to know each other. It was a bit like scheduling dates between trench warfare shifts. Sex, soul-talk, and endless coffee made it all that much more bearable.

I had to tell him about the other things, too, the ugly details of my last few visits. He suggested I write them down. It was a shock to have someone really listen to me. Keeping all of it inside for years, numb and cold...I can't tell you what it's been like. Writing, in my chilly and uncertain style, has concealed a lot of it. The pain and the tears and the hot fury, those came along with things.

Pyotr. I expected him to run and leave me alone, grateful and wrapped in healed, numb skin. I expected a swift, gentle disappearance. He never did walk away. Perhaps it was because he needed me—I wasn't used to thinking of myself as the one to play the healer. It took so long to form my lips into the right shape.

I spent hours in bed with him, talking and exploring him over and over. My heart was a silent, desperate thing, beating with fear and love combined. Sunlight poured in and warmed us in his pale blue bed. His arm was flung back lazily, the other, wrapped around me. I knew what I wanted to say, and I let the words out in a sigh and a rush of breath.

"*Ya tibia lublu.*" I had to say it in Russian first.

"I love you too," answered Pyotr.

And—crack. I started to cry, he held me, and the future began.

When I told Natasha about him, she wept, and laughed. "Are you trying to give your poor old mother grey hairs, or have you really fallen in love?"

"*Mama,*" I said, relishing the word, "I think you should shut up and just meet him."

And now: the years slip past, I refuse to count them and take stock of the worldwide changes. I have a husband who loves me. I have a husband I love—me!

THE LOVED, THE LOST, THE DREAMING

Love! Even when the cold creeps into my bones, even when we've had a fight or the night has been long, the warmth is there. Love. It's a word that I can't stop running my tongue over, an endless sweetness. *We* have a healthy, smart son, a second miracle. I know my birth mother.

The tragedies that go by are someone else's—not mine. Not anymore. I have finally been strong enough to transcribe my tale. And still, it seems there is something missing.

A simple thing, then. I have enough love to share a little bit of it. Acknowledgement:

I still remember your black eyes and the taste of your mouth, Rodya Raskolnikov. I remember you and the boy I hated and loved—as a brother, but that's what you are: a memory. I don't keep your shadow trapped in my closet, and I don't glance over my shoulder to see if you'll be there every day. I don't know if your spectre paces the world, though I wonder sometimes. It would fit you, but I hope it doesn't. I hope you rest easily in death. I send flowers to your grave every year, and in spite of everything, I always will. Walk into the sun at last, brother. *Requiem in Pax.*

About the Author

Michelle Browne generally writes science fiction and cross-genre short works. She lives in Calgary, AB, Canada with her partner and their cat.

You can keep up with new releases or find out what else she thinks about the world at http://scifimagpie.blogspot.ca/ and on Twitter at https://twitter.com/SciFiMagpie/.
She is also on GoodReads, at http://www.goodreads.com/author/show/3301336.Michelle_Browne .

Other books by the author:

And the Stars Will Sing:
http://www.amazon.com/dp/B0075G7GEA
The Stolen: Two Short Stories:
http://www.amazon.com/The-Stolen-Short-Stories-ebook/dp/B0094B0WFY

Coming soon:

Synchronicity (Spring 2013)

The Underlighters
[stand-alone version] (Spring/Summer 2013)

After the Garden (Fall 2013)

The Meaning Wars (Winter 2014)

Printed in Great Britain
by Amazon.co.uk, Ltd.,
Marston Gate.